milly
johnson

White Wedding

**SIMON &
SCHUSTER**

London · New York · Sydney · Toronto · New Delhi

A CBS COMPANY

KT-436-893

First published by Simon & Schuster UK Ltd 2012
A CBS COMPANY

Copyright © Milly Johnson 2012

This book is copyright under the Berne Convention.
No reproduction without permission.
® and © 1997 Simon & Schuster Inc. All rights reserved.

The right of Milly Johnson to be identified as author of this work
has been asserted in accordance with sections 77 and 78
of the Copyright, Designs and Patents Act, 1988.

9 10 8

Simon & Schuster UK Ltd
1st Floor
222 Gray's Inn Road
London WC1X 8HB

www.simonandschuster.co.uk

Simon & Schuster Australia, Sydney
Simon & Schuster India, New Delhi

A CIP catalogue record for this book
is available from the British Library

PB ISBN: 978-0-85720-896-5
EBOOK ISBN: 978-0-85720-897-2

This book is a work of fiction. Names, characters, places
and incidents are either a product of the author's imagination or are
used fictitiously. Any resemblance to actual people living
or dead, events or locales is entirely coincidental.

Typeset in Bembo by M Rules
Printed and bound by CPI Group (UK) Ltd, Croydon, CR0 4YY

White Wedding

Prologue

'Oh hello again,' said Max McBride, looking across as the shop door opened with a tinkle and seeing an increasingly familiar face. 'Fancy meeting you here.'

'I think you're stalking me,' replied the tiny, spiky-haired Bel, coming inside quickly to escape the February chill. 'Either that or I'm stalking you.'

The two women smiled at each other. Five times they had visited this White Wedding bridal shop now and on every occasion it was to find the other one there. It was only a wonder that the third lady who also seemed to move in their orbit was absent – the pale woman with silver-blonde hair, whom Max was certain had gone to her school. She remembered a girl in the year below whom the other kids used to call 'Ghost' because of her unusual colouring.

'What are you looking for this time, then?' asked Bel.

'I'm only browsing really,' Max answered. 'We're having a small wedding, no fancy frills. But I just can't help myself looking.' That was the truth of it. Her fiancé, Stuart, wasn't a man for fuss. Plus, as he said, a wedding ceremony should be about two people and their vows, and though Max had nodded in agreement, her head had immediately started building up a list of embellishments; dress, cake, veil, flowers ...

'What about you?' Max asked.

'I haven't a clue,' smiled Bel. 'I was just passing and thought I'd call in and see if anything took my fancy.'

'Are you having a big wedding?'

'A hundred or so guests,' said Bel. 'Although it started off as fifty and will probably end up as two hundred.'

The more the merrier, she thought with a little kick in her heart. Her wedding day couldn't come quickly enough for her now and she wanted the whole world to hear her say the words 'I do' to Richard. She couldn't wait to be his other half, 'her indoors' – his wife. Recently, she thought she might burst open with joy at the thought of becoming Mrs Belinda Bishop.

'Are you both all right or do you need some help?' asked the shopkeeper as she approached them. She was a tall, elegant lady: grace personified. She exuded an air of calm that spread through the lovely shop and made it an almost magical place to mosey around. She wore a name badge – Freya – above her left breast. It seemed too modern for a lady of such advanced years, yet at the same time the delicate femininity of it fitted her exactly.

'I'm okay, thanks,' said Bel. 'I'm just looking. Again.'

'Me too,' added Max, with a little sigh in her voice. She could buy half of the stuff in this shop if she let herself off the leash. It was torture really, trying on tiaras and headdresses, knowing that she would end up wearing a plain beige functional two-piece suit for the registry office service that would bind her and her partner of seventeen years together. But ever since she discovered this shop quite by chance a few weeks ago, she hadn't been able to resist coming in. It was princess-heaven for Max to wander up and down the long, narrow shop that was packed to the gills with all manner of wedding paraphernalia. Her childhood bedroom had been filled with boxes of play jewellery, crowns and frilly dresses and when anyone asked her what she was going to be when she grew up, her answer was always 'a princess'.

Bel had just picked up a pair of tiny silk boots when the door-bell tinkled again and in walked a woman with long silver hair and deep-violet eyes.

'Well, blow me,' laughed Bel. 'How weird is this? We were just wondering if you'd turn up.'

'Fancy meeting you two here,' said the pale-skinned lady with a chuckle.

'We've done that line,' smiled Max. 'Anyone fancy a coffee across the road when we've finished shopping here?'

Belinda's Wedding

Chapter 1

Three months later

'Oh my GOD, look at that.'

'Yep, I've seen it.'

'And that. Oh look at that.'

'If she says "look at that" once more I think I just might murder her.'

'Look, LOOK at that.'

'Right that is *it*.' Bel picked up a small cushion and launched it at Max's head. Her mouth was so wide open she could have swallowed it whole had it landed on target.

But Max was too mesmerized by the world of the gypsy brides on the television screen to react when the cushion bumped into her shoulder. She had never seen anything like it. Those huge crinolines that the bride and her twenty-five brides-maids wore, the Cinderella coach, the cake – bigger than the house she was born in – it was all so over the top, unbeliev-able ... fabulous. It poked at the place inside her brain that still kept safe her latent fantasies about growing up and becoming a princess and dressing every day in a sparkling tiara and a swishy long frock. 'Look at that as well.'

'Can't you say anything else but "look at that"?' Bel pretended to be exasperated with her.

Violet half chuckled, half sighed. 'Do you know, Max, I've

known you for only a few weeks but I wouldn't have thought you'd ever be the type to be lost for words.'

But Max still wasn't listening. She sat entranced as a huge cloud of white net squeezed out of the Cinderella coach. The train went on for ever. The narrator was reporting that there was over a mile of material in the petticoats alone.

'Fill up, Lady V?' asked Bel, tipping the bottle neck towards Violet's glass.

'I shouldn't really,' Violet replied, not taking a breath before adding, 'Oh go on, then, if I must.'

'Good girl, and yes you must. This is my official hen night, after all. I'm not counting the family "ordeal" on Thursday.'

Bel lifted her lip in an Elvis sneer. She was looking forward to having a meal with her dad, and Richard would be there of course, and her cousin and bridesmaid, Shaden; but so would her Botox-frozen-faced step-aunt, Vanoushka, and her husband, slimy Martin, with his sausage fingers that were magnetically attracted to women's arses. Her stepmum, Faye, would be there too, naturally, making sure that the evening was as flawless as possible. The one thing Bel would wholeheartedly credit her for was her hosting skill.

'This must be a bit of a shit hen night for you,' said Max, giving her friends some attention while the adverts were on. 'I thought you might have wanted to go to a club with loads of your mates.' *Not spend it cooking chilli con carne in your apartment for two women you barely know.*

Bel shrugged her shoulders. The truth of it was that she didn't have any real friends. One by one, they had dropped away over the years; Sara had married a German, moved to Frankfurt, turned into an earth-mother and churned out five children, possibly more by now. Though they had been inseparable through their childhood and teenage years, they didn't even swap Christmas cards any more. Bel knew deep down that her inability to bear children and Sara's fecundity had sadly got in the way of their relationship. Amy had moved to London and got in with a weird bohemian crowd, and Shaden . . . well, suffice to say that she and her cousin had grown very far apart in adulthood.

'Couldn't be arsed going out. I just fancied a quiet night in with a bottle and a bit of light company,' sniffed Bel, knocking back half a glass of wine in one. Max and Violet exchanged a quick secret glance, both suspecting what the other was thinking: that this wedding-uninterested Bel was very different to the woman they had first met at the White Wedding shop, the one who walked on air, smiled a lot and said 'Richard' a damned sight more than she said it these days.

'Are you all right?' Violet asked, but tentatively, because she had picked up very early on that Bel was a woman who played her cards close to her chest.

'Yes, I'm perfectly fine,' said Bel with a firm nod.

'I expect you're knackered, aren't you?' asked Max. Maybe that would explain the tired circles under her new friend's eyes.

'Totally,' Bel affirmed and poured herself another wine.

'That's good, then. That you're all right, I mean. Not that you're totally knackered,' Violet said. Yes, that made sense. Bel had arranged her whole wedding alone, so she must have the energy levels of a dying sloth at the moment.

Bel smiled at their sweet concern. She had grown to like these two women enormously in the relatively short time she had known them. So much so that she wished she hadn't been so impulsive early on and invited them to her wedding. Still, she couldn't think about that now – what was done was done and she had to keep her head focused and her heart totally out of it.

'I thought we might meet your bridesmaid tonight,' said Max. It was a little odd that the maid of honour wasn't at the hen night while she and Violet were.

'She was supposed to be here but alas she's got a cold and didn't want to pass on her bugs.' The lie fell effortlessly from Bel's lips.

'Poor thing,' said Violet.

'Yes, she's so considerate of my feelings,' nodded Bel. *Dear*

Shaden. The thought of her cousin punctured a dangerous hole in Bel's composure.

'I hope you're having those nails done before next Saturday,' noted Max, nudging Bel.

Bel curled her bitten nails away from sight. She had gnawed them down to the quick and they throbbed.

'How's your new ice-cream parlour coming on?' asked Bel, batting attention away from herself before she said something she regretted, *before she let them in.* Violet was leasing a recently built small shop more or less across the road from White Wedding.

'Oh it's perfect,' sighed Violet with a beaming smile. 'I can't wait to open up. I'm just sad that Nan won't be able to work in it with me. She loved helping me in the old place that I ran.'

Violet had told them all about her beloved Nan, sadly in the early stages of Alzheimer's. Nan lived with Violet's mum, Susan, who was her widowed daughter-in-law. 'Mum found her slippers in the fridge the other day.'

Violet laughed a little, but there was a very sad quality to the sound. The old lady, once so sparky and fit, seemed to be getting frailer by the day – physically as well as mentally.

'Oh bless,' Bel wrinkled up her nose sympathetically.

'When's the grand opening?' asked Max. 'I love ice cream.'

'Well, the space is completely plastered and whitewashed now,' Violet bubbled with excited glee, 'so I put an advert in the *Chronicle* last week for an artist to paint a mural on the wall. I'm meeting one up at the shop tomorrow afternoon, actually. I reckon that I should be open for business by early August.'

'Who's going to work with you if your nan can't?' Bel muffled, through a mouthful of tortilla chips.

'Glyn?' Max suggested. 'Or is that a really bad idea?'

'That is a really bad idea,' said Violet, with quick protest. 'Could you honestly work with Stuart and Richard all day then go home and spend the night with them as well?'

Bel considered the question and wanted to laugh out loud. Maybe once upon a time she could have, but not now.

They didn't know that much information about each other's
fiancés yet, but what they had gleaned from their conversations
was that Richard was a drop-dead gorgeous high-flying banking
executive who had been in Bel's life for three years, and Stuart was
head warehouse storeman for a local supplier of nuts and bolts
who Max had been courting since they were sixteen. About
Glyn, the others knew least of all. Apparently he and Violet had
been together for just under a year and a half and he had been off
sick from work for most of that time – something to do with a
mental breakdown – so neither Bel nor Max thought it fair to
press her for details about him, however much they wanted to.

'Max, another wine?' asked Bel.

'Absolutely,' replied Max, holding out her glass. 'I might as
well take advantage seeing as I'm getting a taxi home. So, are you
going to keep hold of your mother's wedding dress for your own
daughter, then? That would be fabulous, wouldn't it? Three gen-
erations of women all wearing the same gown.'

Bel had told them ages ago in White Wedding that she didn't
need to buy a dress as she would be wearing her mum's gown
down the aisle. This was especially poignant as her mother had
died after complications in childbirth.

'I can't have kids,' Bel said as undramatically as possible to
spare Max's feelings. 'I have a rubbish womb. I won't bore you
with the tedious medical details, blah blah, but it will never
happen for me.' She watched that familiar mask of sympathy fall
on to the two female faces in front of her. 'It's okay. It's something I've known from having an operation as a kid. Ironically
my stepmother has the same condition. She can't conceive either.
"I can't have kids and neither can my mother" – ho ho.'

'Oh God, I'm sorry,' said Max. She herself had never wanted
children. Her healthy womb was going to be wasted and she suddenly felt really guilty about it.

'Oh come on, Max, how were you to know? Anyway, having
kids is a privilege, not a right,' said Bel kindly. 'There's always
adoption for people like me, so don't worry. It's just one of those

things that can't be helped.' She smiled and sounded a lot stronger than she felt; she always did when she was on that particular subject. She had honed the hiding of her true feelings about it to a fine art.

'Oh I see the adverts are over.' Bel alerted Max to the television in the corner as part three of the gypsy-bride programme started.

'How can she possibly wee in that frock?' asked Bel, spellbound by the antics on the screen as the bride's mother and three of the bridesmaids were lifting the big dress over the back of a chair so the bride was able to sit down at the top table. Those bridesmaids, with cleavages bigger than Pat Butcher's backside, were bursting out of their harlot-red corset tops. Bel imagined that shade of red against Shaden's golden hair. There was no doubt she'd be the true centre of attention in her strawberry-coloured dress. As she so deserved to be.

'Look at the bride's hair,' yelled Max. 'That wig is taller than the Empire State Building. I want one.' But it wasn't just the wig that Max wanted, it was the dress, the flowers, the cake – it was everything. There was a seismic rumble within Max. All those stored visions of her as a princess bride were shaking off their cobwebs and preparing to burst out of her head into the real world.

'You'd better tell Stuart to buy a defibrillator then because he's going to need one if he sees you coming towards him like that when he's expecting a woman in a beige suit,' chuckled Violet.

'Men are easy to get round,' said Bel, stuffing in more tortilla chips. 'Just give them a blow-job and they forget everything they've said before.' She laughed, and Violet noticed how strangely bitter she sounded.

Max sipped at her wine and thought that in seven weeks exactly this would be her last night as a single woman. That didn't give her a lot of time to change her plans – a thought that was both scary and exhilarating at the same time. Max was at her best whenever an improbable challenge lay ahead of her.

'Violet, are you still going up to White Wedding tomorrow?' asked Bel.

'Yep.'

'I'll come with you if that's okay.'

'Course you can.'

'Don't leave me out,' said Max. 'The beige suit is toast as from today.'

'I'll pick you up at half-past nine, shall I?' said Violet to Bel. 'Then we'll both come round for you, Max.'

'Don't be daft. That's too far out of your way,' Max protested.

But Violet insisted. 'No, really. I don't mind. It's a lovely drive up there.'

'I've nothing better to do either,' added Bel.

'Okay, then,' said Max. 'Bel, since this is your official hen night, totally shite as it is, I think we ought to have a toast.'

'Oh yes, we must toast you,' agreed Violet, raising her glass. 'To our lovely new friend Bel.'

'To Bel, may your wedding day be one to remember for ever.'

Bel raised her glass and chinked it against theirs. 'I think I can safely guarantee that it will be,' she nodded with a syrupy smile.

'What the heck is that mother of the bride wearing?' laughed Violet, catching sight of a huge woman on the television in a banana-yellow-and-white spotted dress that barely covered her knickers. The woman's spray-tanned skin was the colour of a teak sideboard. 'Do you think your mum would dress like that, Max, if you really do have a gypsy wedding?'

'There's no "if" about it,' Max said. And once Max had spoken, it would happen – and on no small scale. Max by name and max by nature. When Max put a plan into action, nothing stood in her way.

She sighed, drifting back into the fabulous world of the young traveller brides. All Stuart's plans for a small no-fuss registry-office wedding had been blasted into oblivion that evening. In place of the intended simple suit already hanging in her wardrobe, she was going to source a dress like no other. She saw acres of net and fairy lights that lit up as she glided down the aisle. She saw a sugar-iced palace cake, Kew Garden-sized flower displays. She imagined herself spray-tanned not so much to a sun-kissed mocha shade but to sun-shagged mahogany, and waving to passers-by in a carriage led by a team of white horses.

Bel watched the gypsy bride posing for photographs, her dress and flowers filling even a wide-angled lens. As mad as it appeared, it was still a real wedding, for a real bride in real love with her man.

As for Violet, she gulped at the emotion in young gypsy Margaret's face as she turned to kiss her handsome floppy-haired Joseph. They looked truly besotted with each other, which was just as well because they were expected to be together for the rest of their lives. Marriage was for good. *Till death us do part.* Or maybe even for eternity. An ice-cold shiver accompanied that thought.

Chapter 2

'Where have you been until this time?' Glyn called, leaning out of the open window.

'What are you doing, still up?' Violet raised her hand to wave a small goodbye to the taxi driver then she entered through the security door, taking the stairs at no rushed speed up to the first-floor flat. Glyn was waiting to greet her dressed in his faithful blue dressing gown, which had been voluminous on him when he bought it last year but now had barely an overlap of material at the front.

'You know I can't sleep until you're back home safely. There are so many nutters out there. Doesn't help that I've just been watching a *Crimewatch* special about a rapist on the loose in Sheffield.' He ushered her in through the door and helped her off with her coat.

'You worry too much, Glyn,' said Violet, as he leaned over and kissed her cheek, all smiles now that she was safely back in his world. Once upon a time she used to melt thinking about how much he cared and worried about her.

'I've just put the kettle on.'

Violet knew that kettle would have been on a constant boil for at least an hour in readiness for her return.

'Want some toast as well?'

'No, thanks. We had a Mexican at Bel's. I'm full to bursting.'

Glyn stuck his head near to her face and sniffed. 'I know, I can smell the garlic. Lucky for you I like it second-hand.' He grinned and tweaked her cheek, then went back to the job of brewing a fresh pot of tea. She noticed he had a huge plate of biscuits waiting on the coffee table as well. These days his life seemed so food-orientated. She often wondered if he was trying to fatten her up so much that she wouldn't be able to get out of the door.

'So tell me all the details,' Glyn said, taking the milk out of the fridge. 'I suppose it was all girly wedding talk.'

'More or less,' replied Violet. 'We watched that *My Big Fat Gypsy Wedding* programme on the television.'

'And?'

'And that was it really. Talked a bit.'

'What about?'

'Things.'

'What sort of things?'

Violet shrugged. 'Can't really remember, to be honest. All forgettable stuff.'

Glyn brought the tea into the lounge in his and hers mugs, a present from his mother. 'Want a biccy to dunk?'

She took the tea. She didn't want it but it was easier just to accept it and sip at it, otherwise there might have been an inquisition on the subject of why she didn't want a drink.

'Thanks, but I'll pass on the biscuit.'

'It's only one biscuit, Letty. You'll not get fat on a jam ring.'

'I said I'm stuffed, Glyn,' said Violet.

'Oh. I nipped to the shop and got them in especially,' said Glyn, his smile falling into a glum downward arc.

Violet watched his bottom lip start to curl over. She reached out and took a chocolate finger to pacify him. The sunshine flooded back into his expression again as he stared at her, relishing the sight of her eating one of the biscuits that he had so lovingly bought for her. When she was a little girl, Violet used to dream of being looked at so intently by a man.

'How tired are you?' he asked.

Oh God. 'Very,' Violet replied, forcing out a yawn. 'And I've got a full day ahead of me tomorrow.'

'Oh. Okay,' he sighed. Again that little cloud had floated over his head. 'I put the electric blanket on tonight as it's a bit chilly. It'll be lovely and extra-cosy in bed.'

Violet tried not to roll her eyes. She hated climbing into a bed that was already warm. She liked cool cotton sheets and sleeping with the window open so that a breeze could waft over her during the night. Glyn always had the heating turned up to full blast and all the windows closed. Violet found it hard to breathe in his flat sometimes.

She went through the pretence of drinking some more before taking her mug to the sink and pouring the tea down the drain. Then she sneaked her half-uneaten biscuit into the flip-top bin in the corner.

'I'll just have a quick shower,' she announced, heading for the bathroom.

'Want some company?' Glyn winked at her and snatched another biscuit.

'Not worth it, I'll only be in for two minutes. I'm too tired to stay in there for long. See you in bed,' she called briskly.

She would rather have had a long hot soak in the bath, but at least by saying that she was taking a quick shower she had more chance of some privacy. Still, she half expected to feel the water-proof curtain shift and then his naked body pressing into hers from behind. But, for once, that didn't happen. He was waiting for her in bed, though; ready to slip his arms round her and cuddle into her back until he fell asleep. Then she shifted ever so carefully away from his sweat-sticky fleshy stomach to the furthest edge of the bed.

Chapter 3

Max floated home on a vision of billowing net, silk, satin and white horses. She swaggered up the drive to the front door of her double-fronted detached house imagining that she was swathed in the world's biggest frock, the train stretching so far behind her that she needed binoculars to see the end of it. Hundreds of lights were sewn into the material, their glow soft and as fuzzily gorgeous as a soft-focus portrait. Gypsy Margaret had pink flashing flowers sewn on her dress. Max imagined butterflies for herself, with such vividly coloured wings that they showed up on Google Earth. At almost six foot tall, with curves that made the Alps look like a Dutch landscape, Maxine McBride was not built for subtle. And there was no place for anything discreet at a gypsy wedding.

Stuart was still up when she got home. He was watching a documentary about some old cricket player who had recently died. Max felt so happy about her newly revised plans for her wedding that she almost squashed her fiancé when she plonked herself on the sofa beside him and threw herself at him for a kiss.

'You've been on the vino, I see,' he laughed. 'How many glasses have you had, then?'

'Not that many,' she replied. 'I'm just high on life.'

'Have you eaten or shall we be really naughty and order a pizza?'

'Oh Stuart, I couldn't fit in so much as a Tic Tac,' said Max, puffing out her cheeks. 'Bel made a very large and garlicky chilli.' Then she breathed on him and he pretended to choke.

'Wonderful,' he said. 'I look forward to having relations with you tonight, then.'

'Ooh, are we doing it?' squealed Max. 'I'll go and eat a tube of toothpaste, shall I?'

She made to get up, but Stuart pulled her back.

'Don't you go anywhere,' he said. 'A mere smidgen of garlic won't put me off rogering my wife-to-be.'

'So what's put you in such a randy mood?' chuckled Max as Stuart moved in for a snog. 'You must watch programmes about dead cricketers more often. Can we buy some on Blu-Ray? Does that constitute cricket porn?'

'What's put me in a randy mood is actually seeing you for once. I've almost forgotten what you look like,' said Stuart, pushing his lips against Max's. 'If you aren't working you're talking weddings with your new mates.'

'I'll make it up to you,' said Max, thinking what Bel had said about blow-jobs being the way to a man's heart. Or at least, so she hoped, to the changing of it.

Chapter 4

Bel was unloading the dishwasher when her mobile went off. She picked it up and looked at the name on the screen: Richard.

She pressed the 'connect' button. 'Hi,' she said sweetly.

'So, had a nice time tonight?' he asked.

'Lovely, thank you. You can't go wrong with food, wine and girly gossip. What about you? What have you been doing?'

'I've been doing some very boring work. Friday night and I've been number-crunching. Can you believe?'

'Of course I believe you,' Bel's laugh tinkled down the receiver. 'Why wouldn't I?'

'Shall I come over and give you one?'

'Naughty, Richard,' purred Bel. 'You know perfectly well there is a bonk embargo on us until after the wedding.'

'But Bel, my knackers are the size of basketballs.'

'No buts. Think how good it will be on the wedding night. Think about me unbuttoning your shirt and kissing your chest.'

'I'd stop talking like that if I were you,' replied Richard breathlessly. 'It's cruel.'

Bel slipped into full seductive Fenella Fielding mode and lasciviously gave Richard a few more examples of how good their wedding night was going to be. She enjoyed teasing him. Boy, was she was going to blow his head off next week.

She put down the phone after working him up to such a pitch that his head — and other bodily parts — were in danger of exploding. She relished the thought of him wanting her and counting off the days until she did all the things she had just promised. Richard couldn't even imagine the half of what was waiting in store for him on their wedding day.

Chapter 5

Violet tried to sneak out of bed without waking Glyn, but failed, as usual.

'Come back to bed,' he yawned, attempting to pull her into his chest.

'I have to get up and go wedding-dress hunting.' She shrugged off his hold but he didn't seem to mind because the reason for her desertion pleased him.

'I can't wait to be married to you and for you to be Mrs Violet Leach,' he said as she gathered up her clothes. When she didn't say the same back to him, he sat up in bed and prompted her.

'Well? You're supposed to say, "I can't wait to be married to you either, Mr Leach."'

'Of course,' said Violet with a tut. 'You know that.'

'Men need to hear the words just as much as women do, you know.' He sank his head back on to the pillow. 'Sometimes . . .' he began, then stopped with a heavy sigh.

'Sometimes what, Glyn?'

'Nothing,' he said, in a sad low voice. The word trailed in the air like a hook in the water with a big fat worm on it waiting for the fish to bite. But Violet was in no mood for a 'why the dramatic pause' game and took herself into the bathroom to get washed and dressed.

When she returned to the bedroom for her shoes she found

Glyn still staring up at the ceiling with that glum expression on his face. She tried to ignore the accompanying small-but-meant-to-be-heard sighs and said breezily, 'Right, I'm off. I'll see you later.'

'What time?' His head turned slowly to her. She saw that his eyes looked a little watery.

'Oh it may take three hours, possibly four. I'll ring you if I'm going to be late.'

'You could be gone four hours?' Glyn's eyebrows knotted together.

'Yes. I've got to go to the shop after the dress hunt. I'm meeting a painter up there, remember? I'll be back for lunch.'

'Well, I'll cook us something really nice.' Glyn held out his arms for a hug. Violet leaned over him and turned her mouth away abruptly when he tried to kiss it.

'Watch out – I've just put my lipstick on,' she said.

'I'll kiss your cheek, then.' He studied her face as they drew apart. 'Is that a new shade of lipstick? It's very bright.'

'Yes, it's new. I wouldn't have said it was bright, though,' said Violet.

'What was wrong with the old colour?'

Violet tried not to react. It was hard sometimes not to scream at Glyn.

'Nothing was wrong with it. I wanted a change.'

As soon as she shut the flat door, Violet knew that Glyn's brain would be over-analysing why she had veered from the path of neutral colours and ventured into the realm of darker shades of lippy. She expected he would have devised a list of questions about it by the time she got home.

Glyn carried on staring up at the bedroom ceiling and listened to the sound of Violet's car driving off. The question whirling round in his head was: why was she wearing a different lipstick? What did it mean? He threw himself out of bed and dragged open the curtains to cast some light into the room while he searched through Violet's drawers to see what else she had bought recently that was different. He knew something was amiss. And he would find out what it was. It never crossed his mind that a new lipstick could be anything as simple as an act of rebellion against a corset-tight existence.

Chapter 6

'Your lift's here,' said Stuart, hearing a car horn beep outside. He pulled back the blind and waved at Violet and Bel. He saw two hands flapping back at him.

'Ooh lovely,' said Max. 'Quick, kiss me before I go.' She threw her arms round him. They were on eye level with each other when she was in her heels, although her darkest-red hair piled up in its customary bun gave her the final height advantage.

'Am I covered in lippy now, as usual?' Stuart asked, dabbing at his mouth.

'It's one of those ones that don't come off,' Max replied, her standard shade of tomato-red lipstick totally intact. You can scrub at it with a Brillo pad and it'll still be there.'

'So how do you get it off?'

'You scrub at it with two Brillo pads,' laughed Max.

Stuart shook his head. All that make-up lark was beyond him. He was glad he wasn't a woman. He couldn't think of anything worse than having to start off his day faffing about with eye colours and the like, as Max did every morning.

'Where are you all going, anyway?'

'Looking at wedding dresses.'

'Why are you going, then?'

'To give Violet the benefit of my expertise,' Max trilled casually.

But Stuart, who had known Max for seventeen years, could

smell a rat. He scratched his short mid-brown hair and narrowed his usually smiley brown eyes at her.

'What?' she said, such a picture of innocence that she made Anne of Green Gables look like a deranged Chucky doll.

'You do remember that we are having only a quiet registry-office do? A very, very low-key registry do?'

'Yes, of course I remember, Stuart. How could I forget?' Max's eyelashes were batting. He knew she was up to something when she blinked like that.

'We agreed to keep it simple. No fripperies,' he stressed. 'We don't need all those things after living together for so many years. It's just a formality.'

'I know what we agreed,' huffed Max, adding to herself: *but it ain't going to happen.*

'Good,' said Stuart with some relief, picking up his toast. He knew that Max being Max, she wouldn't be able to resist a few wedding extras, but as long as they only stretched their plans a little, he could live with that. He wouldn't begrudge her a bouquet or a hat to go with the smart beige suit she had bought.

Max decided to plant the first seed. 'Anyway,' she sniffed, 'I want to go with them to the wedding shop because I haven't one hundred per cent decided what I'm wearing yet.'

'I thought you had.' Stuart stopped mid-crunch on his toast. 'What's that suit hanging in the wardrobe for, then?'

'It's frumpy,' said Max, waving her hand as if the gesture would make it magically disappear. 'And it gets frumpier every time I look at it. Plus, you've seen it. And it's bad luck for the groom to see the bride's outfit before the wedding.'

She noticed the way he was studying her. 'Don't worry, blah blah, plain and simple.' Then she stuck out her tongue at him.

'Well, don't come in looking like a toilet-roll-cover doll if you buy another outfit, because I'll run off.' He laughed but there was a warning lacing his words.

'As if,' Max twinkled. 'Although I am planning to get married only the once so a white dress might be rather nice.'

'Maaax.'

Violet beeped her car horn again. Max jumped to order.

'Okay, I'm offski. Back later, darling. I won't be that long.'

'Good,' said Stuart, chewing on his toast again. 'It might be nice to spend some time with you at a weekend for once.'

'Let's do lunch,' suggested Max. She blew him a kiss as she opened the front door, then she trotted down the garden path in her tall pin heels.

'What have you been doing?' Bel shouted through the window of Violet's pink mini, adding, as a grinning Max opened the car door and got into the passenger seat, 'We've been waiting hours.'

'I have been busy making mischief,' said Max, patting her gravity-defying bun.

'What sort of mischief?' asked Violet, slipping into first gear.

'"My big fat gypsy wedding" Step One sort of mischief,' Max answered, clipping herself into her seat belt. 'I'm building Stuart up to it slowly. First, I've told him that I'm probably not going to be wearing the crappy wedding outfit that I bought. Then I'll add more details on a need-to-know basis. You wait, he'll be booking a 747 to arrive in before I've finished with him.'

Violet didn't know what sort of man Stuart was, but she had no doubt that if Max couldn't bring him round to her way of thinking, he must be made of stone.

As they pulled up at the side of White Wedding, the postman was just pushing open its door. It never failed to fascinate him how long the shop was inside. He had the feeling that if he went right to the back and pushed the last rail of dresses out of the way he'd end up in Narnia.

'Morning, ma'am. Parcel for you to sign for,' he said. He always called the tall, snow-haired lady who ran the shop 'ma'am'. She had a quiet elegance about her that would have made him want to tip his cap at her, if he'd worn one.

'Thank you,' she said, taking the pen he proffered. She was a beautiful woman; her skin was clear and youth-fresh, her cheekbones sharp and her eyes bright. She must have been a real stunner in her time, thought the postman. There was something regal about her, as if she was one of the Russian princesses who escaped from the revolution and had lost her fortune but never her dignity. He suspected she was a lot older than she looked.

She carried the parcel to the large counter halfway down the shop and looked at the label on the front. It was addressed simply to: Freya, White Wedding, Maltstone, Barnsley, South Yorkshire, England. It had come from Canada. She had an inkling of what was inside it – and she was right.

In the layers of white tissue paper was *the* dress, carefully folded. The long ivory-silk gown with the tiny peach roses at the neck looked as new as the day she had sewn it herself. As she lifted it up to shake out the creases, a small note fluttered to the floor and she bent to pick it up.

> Dear Freya,
> It was true. The dress was magic. It did show me happiness – and the way forward. It felt right to send it back to you.
> Thank you.
> D xx

Freya smiled. She remembered the girl with her lovely freckled face and sad, trembling bottom lip. Now she could supplant that memory with the picture of a smiling bride with sunshine in her eyes. In a different dress. This one was not meant for her, which is why she'd returned it.

All Freya's dresses were special to her, this one most of all: the first wedding gown she ever made, and it always came back to her. She had created it but never thought she would wear it herself. After all, she was married at the time. She shuddered at the thought of the cold, loveless life she once had. She had been determined that if she ever realized her dream to own a wedding-dress shop, she would ensure that any woman who crossed her threshold became a happy bride. Maybe not always in the straightforward way they imagined, though.

'I love coming here,' said Max, shivering with excitement.

'Me too,' echoed Violet, attempting to copy Max's enthusiasm. 'Did you buy your cousin's bridesmaid's dress from here, Bel?'

'No, Leeds,' replied Bel, remembering the day last month so well. She and Shaden had driven there and gone for a refined brunch in Harvey Nicks' first, where they ate grilled chicken salad and indulged in very small talk. The bridesmaid's dress had cost more than the whole of Violet's wedding probably would. However, nothing but the best for dear cousin Shaden. The dress was beautiful and her long bleached Californian-blonde hair looked stunning against it. *Strawberry-red silk.* A perfect fit as well. Not a stitch of alteration needed. Meant to be.

They all peered into the shop's bay window before entering. On display there was the prettiest selection of bridal accoutrements and all arranged perfectly. Confetti was scattered around the shoes and tiaras, veils and faux-fur stoles, and centre stage was claimed by an hourglass-figured mannequin wearing a plain white, but exquisite gown. Freya changed the window regularly and it always looked so beautiful.

Bel pushed open the door and the sound of the bell above it heralded their arrival.

'Good morning,' Freya smiled at them, nudging back a swoop of her hair with the heel of her hand. 'Back again, I see. En masse this time.'

'Morning,' they returned with a chuckle.

'Do feel free to wander as usual and if you want any help, just ask,' said Freya. Her attitude was so refreshing. In the shop where Max bought the beige suit, the assistant followed her around so closely that her CV should have read: 'Previous occupation:

shadow'. In retrospect Max wondered if she had bought the suit to get the hell out of there as quickly as possible.

'You're cutting it fine, aren't you? I can't believe you haven't found a dress you like yet,' said Bel to Violet.

Neither could Violet, if the truth be told. She had half-heartedly searched a few more bridal stores and tried on loads but still not settled on anything. Maybe she was subconsciously putting off buying a dress; that was the only possible explanation. She knew she would have to pick one soon, and something kept pulling her back to White Wedding.

'This is nice, but it's more bridesmaidy than bride, don't you think?' said Bel, holding up a cream ballerina-length dress with puffy sleeves.

'Talking of which, how do you fancy being my bridesmaids?' asked Max suddenly.

'Max – I thought you weren't having any.' Bel thought that Max would have forgotten all about her new daft gypsy wedding plans after a good sleep. It wasn't as if she had time to arrange something of that magnitude anyway.

Max raised her eyebrows innocently. 'Bel, if I have a gypsy wedding I can't possibly go down the aisle with no bridesmaids behind me, can I? And who else can I ask? I don't know any women except the ones that work for me and the ones I sell things to. Or my cousin, Alison, who would scare the living shit out of Jeremy Kyle,' she said with a shudder. That was the trouble with workaholics – they too lost their friends along the way.

Bel looked around idly. There were some gorgeous dresses in her sight but none as beautiful as her late mother's gown. She was surprised her stepmother, Faibiana, hadn't got rid of it; in fact she had done the opposite, placing it in a suit cover to preserve it for the day when Bel might need it. Not that Bel ever thanked 'Faye', as she preferred to be called, for that. Faye Bosomworth had breezed into Bel's widowed father's life twenty-eight years ago on a hearty gust of floral perfume and totally and immedi-ately enchanted him. To her stepdaughter she was nothing but kindness and patience, yet Bel had never quite lost the feeling that the new queen of her father's heart had unlawfully usurped the old one, who should have reigned for ever. Bel had never called Faye 'mother' and Faye had never pressed her to. Luckily her stepmum was nothing like her cow of a sister Vanoushka – Shaden's mother. Or her sow of the other sister, Lydiana, who, thankfully, now lived in Melbourne, Australia, and visited only once yearly. And that was once yearly too much.

Max carried on hunting along the rails, but there was nothing remotely like gypsy Margaret's dress. Freya directed Violet to her new stock but she still couldn't see a dress she liked enough to consider buying. The only one she tried on had a neckline that was far too low and didn't flatter her almost non-existent cleavage at all.

'O. M. G.' Max's scream was so high-pitched that dogs started barking outside. Violet jumped.

'What's up?' she said, rushing over, closely followed by Bel.

'Look. At. That.'

'Here we go again,' smiled Bel, following the track of Max's pointing finger. At the very back of the shop, and taking up a lot of its width, was a headless mannequin wearing a gargantuan white dress. It made gypsy Margaret's look like a shift.

'That's it.' Max was so emotionally overcome that she addressed the gown directly. 'You're the one I want.'

'Ooh ooh ooh, honey,' trilled Bel behind her, but Max wasn't listening. She was cocooned in a world where only she and this big white cloud of dress belonged.

'I'm making this for display,' said Freya, appearing at her shoulder.

'Is it for sale?' Max asked breathlessly.

'Well, yes, if I found a buyer, I suppose,' Freya answered.

'I think you've found one,' said Bel.

'Can you customize it?' Max asked Freya. 'Can you add bits? Flowers? Lights?'

'Caravans,' put in Bel.

'Of course,' nodded Freya, as if she were asked every day to sew weird things onto dresses.

'Your fiancé is going to kill you, I think,' Violet warned her in a sing-songy voice.

'Oh I'll work on Stuart, don't you worry,' Max flapped her hand at her friend. 'I've got a few weeks to bring him round to my way of thinking. It's never been that hard before.' She clapped her hands together and turned back to Freya. 'Is there any chance I could try it on?'

'I'll have to pin it round you,' said Freya.

'I don't mind,' said Max, whisking off her jacket and throwing it at Bel as if she were a stripper.

Freya slipped the gown off the mannequin before following Max into the changing room. As soon as Max stepped into the dress she *knew* this was the one she had to have. There was absolutely no way on this planet or any other that she was going to wear that beige suit, which was becoming fouler in her mind with every passing minute. She would be married in this dress or die. And if she had this dress, she needed the setting of a church in which to wear it, not a room in the town hall. And a host of people to show it off to. And bridesmaids, photographers – and a cake the size of Kuala Lumpur. How could she have a dress this size and not have a cake? And flowers. Balloons. Fireworks. And sod having an intimate lunch for two after the ceremony – now she foresaw a banqueting hall, caviar starter, fillet of beef main, trios of chocolate desserts – nay, quartets of cheesecakes, quintets of meringues, sextets of cheeses ...

'Jesus Christ.' Bel's blasphemy broke into her reverie as she and Violet sneaked a peak behind the changing-room curtain. 'That is one seriously massive frock.'

At nearly six foot tall, her head inches away from the low cottage roof of the shop, Max looked like Alice in Wonderland after she'd done the 'drink me' thing and grown out of the room. The corset top made the best of her full bust and nipped-in waist and Marilyn Monroe hips. She looked gobsmackingly stunning. And that smile spreading across her lips was as mischievous as an imp's on April Fools' Day.

'Uh-ho,' said Bel and Violet together as they saw her expression. They suspected that a giant can of worms had just been opened. But even they could never have suspected how many worms would spring out and how much damage the little buggers would do.

Chapter 7

Violet walked straight into the end house on the row of terraced villas on Spring Lane, then down the long hallway and into the kitchen where, more often than not, she would find her mother. The back door was ajar and her mum, Susan, was in the garden.

'Hello,' she called.

'I'm bringing in the washing,' said Susan. 'Nan's in the front room. I'll be with you in a minute, love.'

Violet doubled back and went into the lounge. Her nan jerked awake as the door creaked open.

'Oh sorry, Nan. Didn't realize you were asleep.'

'No worries,' said the old lady, stretching her thin limbs. 'Did you find a frock at last, then?'

'Ah you remembered I was going shopping.'

'Course I did. I don't forget everything, you know. Not yet, at least. And I remember that you were going with two other ladies that you've become friends with lately. Maxine and . . . Melinda?'

'Nearly,' Violet smiled. 'Belinda.'

'See? I reckon that merits a score of nine out of ten,' twinkled the old lady.

Nanette Flockton was as sharp as a knife when she was compos mentis. Alas, the days when she was mentally alert were becoming less frequent. She forgot the simplest of things and sometimes had moments when she talked distressing gibberish, although she couldn't remember doing so. Violet relished the coherent times, for she knew there would be fewer and fewer of them as the months went on. Nan was her paternal grandmother. She moved in to help nurse Violet's dad, Jeff, when he fell victim to a stroke ten years ago. He died two months later but Nan stayed put and her old cottage was rented out. Violet's mother had always viewed her as more of a mum than the one she already had; Violet's maternal grandmother, Pat Ferrell, was a creature with a soul of ice. Nan often said that the woman should never be visited without the escort of an exorcist.

'I didn't find one, no,' sighed Violet. 'I'm still on the lookout.'

'I saw an angel last night. Lovely red hair she had,' said Nan. 'Don't look at me like that, Violet. It was only in a dream. I don't mean she was in the room with me. She was humming.'

Violet laughed with relief that this wasn't one of her 'episodes'.

'What was she humming, Nan?'

'The theme tune to *Coronation Street*.'

Violet chuckled. 'Fancy a cuppa? I'm gagging for some tea.'

'Not for me. I want one of those little lagers in the fridge. Ask your mum if she wants a drink, will you, love? She could do with a sit-down. She's been washing bedding all morning. She never stops.'

Violet went into the kitchen and as the kettle boiled she watched her mum through the window unpegging sheets from the line. She changed the beds every weekend, she always had. Violet used to love her 'clean sheet night' every Saturday: white cotton in summer, flannelette in winter. Violet knocked on the glass and did a drinking mime at her mum. Her mother stuck a thumb up before dipping into the peg basket again. Violet brewed the tea and got out the cups. Her mum and Nan always drank out of delicate bone china. Nan's cup had a big black cat on it, Susan's featured butterflies.

'Fetch the Jaffa Cakes in as well, will you, love?' called Nan. 'Apparently I've to have more fruit in my diet. I'm counting those as a couple of my five-a-days.'

Violet smiled and went to the cupboard where the biscuit tin was kept. Her phone went off in her pocket just as she was tipping the Jaffa Cakes on to a plate. Glyn. Violet felt herself stiffening at the sight of his name on the screen. She knew exactly why he was ringing. *Where are you? How long will you be?* She was tempted to press 'ignore' but knew he wouldn't let up if she did that.

'Hi,' she said, lifting the phone to her ear.

'Hi, hon, where are you?'

'I called in to see Mum and Nan before I meet the painter.'

'How long will you be?'

'Three-quarters of an hour, maybe.'

'Don't be too long, will you?'

'No, I won't be,' said Violet, grappling with the annoyance that she felt.

'Can you pick up a bottle of white non-alcoholic wine for lunch tomorrow? That one Dad really likes. I think it's an Eisberg Riesling.'

Violet winced. She had forgotten she was going to the Leachs Senior tomorrow.

'Yes, of course.'

'I'm making a meat and potato pie.'

'Okay,' replied Violet.

'Do you want peas or beans with it? I don't mind, I'll have whichever one you decide.'

Violet rolled her eyes. If she told Glyn she wanted to eat her pie with Italian smoked oysters, he would get them for her. So many women would envy her his concern for her needs.

'I don't know, I'll decide later.'

'Okay. See you soon, then. Love you.'

'See you soon.' She pressed the call end button and shoved the phone back in her pocket. She turned round to find Nan in the kitchen doorway.

'So, how long to the wedding now?'

'About two and a half months.'

'About?' replied Nan. 'When I was getting married to your grandfather and anyone asked me that question, I knew the time down to the exact minute.'

Violet opened her mouth to speak, but she feared that if she did she might never shut it again.

'You all right, my little Violet?' asked Nan. As her sharp grey eyes locked on to her granddaughter's, Violet felt as if Nan could see right through to the workings of her brain and make sense of them – which she couldn't.

'Course I am,' said Violet, pinning on a smile. 'What makes you ask?'

'Oh nothing,' said Nan after a pause. 'I just sometimes feel that you're not as happy inside as you try to pretend you are on the outside.' She opened the fridge and took out a tiny bottle of Belgian lager and then went to the drawer for the bottle opener. It took Violet a few seconds to work out what her nan was trying to prise the top off with.

'Nan. Where on earth did you get that?' Violet pointed to the large carved-wood bottle opener.

'Edith brought it back for me from Corfu,' said Nan. 'Why, what's up with it?'

'Have you seen what it is?'

Nan turned it round in her hand. 'It's made out of an olive tree,' she said, unable to add anything else to the description.

'Nan, it's an enormous willy.'

Nan looked at it again in the light of this new information and then burst into a peal of laughter. 'Well, I never noticed. And I'll bet you Edith didn't either. She does all the sandwiches for the church meetings. I hope she hasn't bought the vicar one. Oh my, how funny is that.'

Still giggling, she held out a hand for the plate of Jaffa Cakes, just as Susan came in through the back door, pushing it fully open with her ample bottom as her arms were full of dried washing.

'Susan, look at this. It's a penis,' said Nan.

'Good grief, so it is,' said Susan. 'How come we never noticed? Oy, you, no chocolate,' she said, seeing Nan's fingers reach for a biscuit.

'Oh, one won't do me any harm, Susan.'

'You've just had tests for diabetes,' snapped Susan sternly. 'They told you no sweet stuff. I don't know what to do if you fall into a coma.'

'You'll be glad to get rid,' winked Nan. 'You'll be planning the funeral song as soon as my eyes close.'

'I've picked it already,' said Susan. '"Ding Dong! The Witch is Dead".'

Nan squawked with laughter. 'I thought you'd be saving that for your mother.'

'No rules saying I can't have it for you both,' replied Susan, picking up a cup of newly poured tea. She sighed with pleasure when it hit the back of her throat. 'How did the dress hunting go?' she asked.

'Rubbish,' huffed Violet. 'I couldn't find a thing.'

'There's always my dress if you're desperate,' suggested Susan.

Nan and Violet exchanged horrified glances that made them both blurt out a big fat giggle.

'It's not that bad,' said Susan, affronted.

'It is,' put in Nan.

'It can be altered, Nan,' countered Susan.

'I'm sorry for laughing, Mum, but no way will a dress that's made for you fit me,' said Violet.

'And aren't you the lucky one, where that frock's concerned,' said Nan.

Susan and Violet were as unlike physically as a mother and daughter could be. Violet had a slight five-foot-five build with the very pale skin and straight white-blonde hair of her father, whereas Susan was dark and curly haired, slim-waisted but full-busted, and five inches taller than her daughter.

'Look, I'll go and get it and show you what I mean,' said

Susan, putting down her cup. She trotted up the stairs and Violet slapped Nan's leg gently.

'Don't be naughty, you.'

'Pat designed that dress. You could tell she didn't like your father. She was hoping he'd be so horrified he'd run off.'

'Shhh,' said Violet as her mum's quick footsteps sounded on the stairs on the way back down.

Susan appeared with the long white dress in a polythene cover. The dress really was an amalgam of all the worst bits of the early seventies. It had a high lacy neck and huge puffball sleeves. There was no definition to the waist and it had a strangely placed bow high up on the back. There was no volume to the skirt, but at the bottom of the dress was a deep and disturbingly horrific lace flounce.

'I thought,' began Susan, 'that if you got someone to take off that frill and drop the neckline a bit . . .'

'And cut off the sleeves and that bow that looks as if it's trying to escape upwards,' added Nan, still chuckling.

Susan ignored her. 'It's lovely material.'

'Apart from the net-curtain bits,' Nan batted back.

'Which I'm suggesting you take off,' Susan volleyed.

'I think I'll pass, Mum,' said Violet decisively.

Susan took a long hard look at her dress and then pulled the plastic cover back over it. 'No, you're right. It's bloody awful. You never wanted to play with it even when you were a little girl, Violet. I should give it away.'

'Obviously you can't give it to charity,' chirped Nan. 'You'd traumatize the people who opened up the bag.'

'I kept it because it had such happy memories for me,' said Susan. 'I *had* to wear it, because Auntie May made it and she wasn't well at the time. She died not long after the wedding.'

'Too bad she didn't die before it was finished and give you the chance to get a proper dress,' said Nan, as Violet gave her a gentle but firm nudge.

'God forgive you, Nan,' said Susan, trying hard to stifle a laugh.

'You should have seen the bridesmaids' dresses she made as well,' said Nan to Violet. 'I hope I never seen that shade of green again outside a sewer.'

'Oy, my mother designed all the dresses,' tutted Susan.

'I know. Coco Chanel must have been terrified of losing her crown.'

'It was a lovely day, though, wasn't it, Nan?' said Susan, slipping back into a cosy spring-scented memory. 'And it was the seventies, so the dresses didn't look as out of place as they would today.'

'Aye, it was a lovely day,' said Nan, thinking of her son, full of life then, a young man with his future stretching out before him. 'The sun was shining and you were smiling like lunatics – you and our Jeff.'

Susan's eyes bloomed with water.

'Right, best get cracking,' she said, rising quickly to her feet. 'I want to Vax the upstairs carpets before I go out to the book club.' She turned to Nan. 'I'll leave you two alone. I assume you haven't got round to telling her yet.'

'Not yet,' said Nan.

'Telling me what?' asked Violet. Her phone was rumbling in her pocket again. She didn't need to look at it to see who it was.

Susan smiled enigmatically then disappeared up the stairs.

'What's going on?' pressed Violet as Nan took some little shuffling mouse steps over to the sideboard. She opened a drawer, took something out and sat down again. She pressed a set of keys into Violet's hand. Then she answered the questions in Violet's eyes.

'They're for Postbox Cottage. The tenants have left and I'm not renting it out any more. I'm giving it to you.'

'What?'

'You heard. Unless you're getting as daft as me.'

'Nan—' Violet began to protest but Nan held up her hand.

'I know you've never liked Glyn's flat and, well, I shan't ever be living there again in my state. I'll only be getting worse and

I want to know that you have it before anything happens to me. I want to enjoy giving it to you.' Violet gripped Nan's hand and felt very close to tears thinking about life without this lovely old lady in it.

'I'm sorry, love. I've made you cry.' Nan pulled out a tissue from her sleeve and dabbed at Violet's eyes. 'That's the last thing I want to see you do. When you're happy, I'm happy. I want to think about you having your turn at life and being settled with a nice man who thinks the world of you.'

Violet's tears flowed faster. Tears about being happy, which she could use to disguise her tears of sadness about her nan.

Nan had been terrified about this illness, terrified that her brain would be dead far in advance of her body, meaning that Susan would have even more to do. She knew that for all her brusque manner, Susan would never let her go into a home. Soon Susan would stop going to her book club meetings. She'd say that she was getting bored by them, but Nan would know that it was because she no longer felt she could leave her mother-in-law alone for an hour and a half.

Nan presumed it was a dream last night when she was talking to the angel about her fears, but it felt too real to be that. The angel said that it was such a good idea to give the cottage to Violet. And she also said that Nan wasn't to worry about Susan because she wasn't destined to be lonely and unloved. Nan didn't disclose that, though, because talk like that would have worried her family. Or had them ringing for the men in white coats.

'Your mother doesn't half get dressed up to go to her book club,' said Nan playfully. 'I reckon there's a fella there she fancies.'

'Mum? Give over.'

'I bet you anything there is,' said Nan.

'That would be nice, wouldn't it?' said Violet. 'I wish Mum would meet someone.'

'Yes, I do.' Nan sighed. She worried that if there was someone on the scene, Susan would feel too disloyal to the memory of Jeff to let it develop, and that would be such a shame. Susan deserved to be loved and looked after, so Nan really hoped the angel was right. She studied the key sitting in Violet's hand.

'That cottage is yours whatever,' she said.

'What do you mean, "whatever"?' asked Violet.

'It's not a wedding present. It's for you because I want to give it to you. *YOU*. It's yours and you can do whatever you want with it. You can move into it, rent it out or sell it and buy somewhere else. It's legally yours to do with as you will. I did all the signing and sealing with the solicitor when I was "of sound mind", as they say.'

'Oh don't joke,' said Violet. Her world felt as if it was turning on its head. Her mum and Nan were constants and she never wanted them to change or grow old or ill, but she knew she was helpless to stop that. 'And of course I wouldn't sell it. I'll live in it.'

'Well, you might for a bit, but it won't be big enough if you have children.'

A picture of Glyn and her living in the cottage with children flashed across her mind. Except they weren't really children; they were mini versions of him with his head on their flabby little bodies.

'Just you remember something for me,' said Nan. 'If you're unhappy, you'll kill me quicker than anything happening in my brain.'

Violet fell against her nan's fragile shoulder and the old lady put her arm round her. She smelled of a lovely old nameless scent with a hint of face powder: warm and safe.

'There's nothing better than a good marriage,' said Nan. The warmth of the memory with her life's love was suddenly chilled by the thought of her first husband, whom she married at seventeen and divorced aged twenty-one. No one in the family knew about him. No one need know how many cuts and bruises she sustained at his hands, and the baby he made her miscarry. 'And there's nothing worse than a bad marriage,' Nan went on. She looked hard at her granddaughter. 'If you have any doubts in your head at all, don't put that ring on your finger.' She touched her own wedding ring. It had worn thin over the years but still she could recall the feeling when Grandad Jack slid it on to her finger and whispered to her, 'You're mine now and you'll stay mine.' It brought a delicious thrill to her heart.

'Your grandad used to drive me insane burning holes in everything with his bloody pipe, but it'll be nice to see him again,' smiled Nan.

'Do you really believe in heaven, Nan?' asked Violet, gulping down the tears that were rising to her eyes.

'Course I do,' said Nan with a wink. 'Where do you think that angel came from last night?'

Chapter 8

Bel had just unlocked her front door when the phone rang.

'Er, Miss Candy, this is Pip from For Goodness Cake.' Bel raised her eyebrows at the ridiculous name of the shop every time she heard it. 'Er,' carried on the terribly puzzled female voice on the end of the line, 'I've received your email about the alteration to your wedding cake design. And I just wanted to check that I've got this right.' Then she read out word for word what Bel's email had said.

'That's it. That's exactly what I want,' said Bel.

'Oh. Right.' Bel heard Pip's pronounced gulp.

'Can it be done?'

'Yes . . . yes, of course. If that's what you want.'

'It's what I want,' said Bel.

'Definitely?'

'Oh absolutely,' said Bel. 'You'll do it?'

'I will if that's really really what you want.'

'Oh yes.'

'Well, then, I'll do it,' agreed Pip, still not sounding convinced. She had done cakes for some wild and wacky occasions but this one would take the biscuit.

After Bel ended the call, she scratched hard at the skin on her arms where it had grown increasingly flaky over the past few weeks, like a nervous-eczema flare-up. She'd be a pile of powder by the time she got married at this rate. They might as well cut to the chase and do the 'ashes to ashes, dust to dust' service.

The house phone rang again, just as she turned away from it.

'Hello, darling,' trilled the merry voice of her stepmother.

'Hi, Faye,' returned Bel.

'I thought I'd let you know, I've just picked up my outfit for the wedding. It had to be taken in a bit at the waist – I must have lost weight.'

'That's nice,' said Bel, wishing she could get off the line to open a very early bottle of red wine.

'And Aunt Vanoushka will be in Dior.'

Step-Aunt Vanoushka. Owner of a barn conversion with five bedrooms, each with an en-suite (which she pronounced enn-suit), as she told everyone, and a hot tub in her Swedish garden summer house. Every pretension that it was possible to have, Aunt Vanoushka had it, from her Louis Vuitton set of luggage to her garden 'moat', which encircled a small island where she'd had a dovecote erected. She had a Lhasa Apso stud dog called Arctic Master of the Polar Hunt for the Sun – which made as much sense to Bel as the lyrics to 'Whiter Shade of Pale'. Thanks to the three tons of Botox she'd had injected into her head, Vanoushka's expression would remain the same if she lost all her shares in a market crash or won the Euromillions lottery. And recently she'd had her lips so inflated that she could have rented them out as a bouncy castle. It wasn't hard to see what Shaden was going to turn out like in twenty-five years' time.

There was no doubt that Vanoushka would have another expensive top-up of rubber-face before the wedding. Something Bel was trying hard not to think about: how much time and money were being spent on her behalf for this wedding. But if she didn't push such thoughts to the back of her mind, she would never be able to do what she had to do.

'Dior? Oh will she?' Bel attempted to sound impressed.

'Are you sure there's nothing I can do to help you arrange things?'

'No, it's all done, thank you,' said Bel, wishing she had a pound for every time Faye had asked her that question. She knew how much Faye would have loved to help her; but Bel was independence personified and had insisted on doing everything herself. Plus, Faye wasn't the real mother of the bride. That woman had been snatched away from her baby daughter and it would have been the ultimate betrayal to her mother to have another woman step in and help with table plans and menu choices. If her real mother wasn't around to help, no one else would do.

'Okay, darling,' said Faye, managing to cover ninety-five per cent of her disappointment. 'We'll see you for the family dinner on Thursday, then. Just call me if you need anything.' She emphasized the last word and she meant it.

Bel knew she had been unfair to Faye over the years. Her stepmother had done nothing other than be a secretary who had fallen in love with her widowed boss, then married him after a whirlwind romance and been kind to his daughter.

Bel went upstairs and opened her large French wardrobe door to look at her mother's beautiful dress hanging there, freshly dry-cleaned for her by Faye, altered to fit her small waist and waiting for her to wear. It was so beautiful: a dress for the elegant woman her mother must have been, although the details Bel had of her were sketchy. There were only a couple of grainy photographs and her father didn't talk much about his first wife. Bel knew it upset him to think about her or talk about the loss of her, so she had built up the picture of her mother in her imagination instead. There she could clearly see the statuesque beauty of Helen Candy, her long raven-black hair and red lips as she walked towards her husband-to-be in this dress, ready to say her sadly prophetic vows. *Till death us do part.*

Then Bel moved the dress to the side and took out the other one on the rail behind it, the one she had bought online. It was a gown so plain and boring the coathanger holding it was yawning. Round neck, straight sleeves, no detail on the bodice, no bow on the back – even a puritan bride would have expected more. It was cheap, dull and exactly fitting for the occasion to come.

'I'm sorry, Mum,' Bel said, turning her head upwards. 'I can't wear your dress. I have to wear this one. Stay with me. Keep me strong, Mum. I love you.'

Chapter 9

While Max was stuck on the internet that afternoon, gorging herself on pictures of gypsy brides and hunting for ideas, Violet was on her way to the new ice-cream parlour to meet with the painter. She loved it so much and couldn't wait to start up business again. Previously she'd leased a shop near the park, but it was dropping to pieces inside and the landlord was a nightmare. When her lease was up, she hadn't renewed it. It meant that there would be a few months of not trading, but she was sure it would be worth it. As soon as Violet had viewed the lovely new conical building in the Maltstone Garden Centre, she knew she had to have it. The rent was considerably higher than her last place, but her new – and much more amenable – landlord said that he would let her have one month rent-free and two months at half price if she decorated it after the builders had finished with it. Plus, the footfall would be high all year round as the garden centre also had a flower shop, a furniture shop, a nursery, a coffee shop – which, by agreement, wouldn't sell ice creams – and a beautiful gift shop too.

She'd had an instant vision of the shop as soon as she walked in. Carousel. Golden poles, pictures of carousel horses around the walls, even fairground music. The only trouble was that she couldn't paint for toffee.

Violet unlocked the door and walked into her new kingdom. She might have to abandon her vision of the horses if this painter couldn't give her what she wanted. So far no one else who had rung and offered their services painted murals. And there had been no take-up when she'd asked at the local art college.

She was just trying to imagine how the place would look with plain walls when there was a knock at the door. Through the glass Violet could see a dark-haired young man standing there, carrying what looked to be a huge board.

Violet sprang to open the door for him and knew that the pupils in her eyes must have widened to the size of crop circles. The man who stood there was like the sexy brother of Christ. Tall, wide-shouldered, heavy black stubble the same colour as his loose-curled hair and eyes like blue lagoons *à la* Robert Powell in *Jesus of Nazareth*.

'Miss Flockton,' he said in an accent that she couldn't place, but it wasn't British. Heaven, possibly. 'I am Pawel Nowak, here about the painting of the horses.'

'Come in,' said Violet, standing aside to let him in, hoping that her legs wouldn't wobble so much that she fell over in front of him.

'Thank you,' he said, striding past her into the shop.

He had a long, powerful-looking body and the muscles on his thighs pushed at the material of his jeans. Athletic and strong. Not what Violet had imagined the artist to be like, from reading his email. Actually she'd envisaged someone with Elton John glasses and a mincing walk, who spoke like Alan Carr. This man – Pawel – looked more like a builder who had worked the hod since he was old enough to lift it. Admittedly that couldn't have been very long ago, though; he must have been only in his early twenties.

He put what was not a board but a huge art folder down on the counter and then held out his hand for Violet to shake. He had a strong handshake to say the least. Violet felt the crush on her fingers long after he had released them.

'I have brought my portfolio to show you what I can do,' he said.

'Would you like a coffee or a cup of tea, Mr Nowak?' asked Violet.

He paused for a moment, then shook his head. 'Thank you, but it's fine. I'm okay.' She felt he wanted one but was being polite.

'I'm having one,' she smiled, going into the kitchen to put on the kettle. 'I'm thirsty.'

He relented. 'Yes, please. Coffee, please. Black no sugar, thank you. And please, call me Pav. Everyone does.'

While Violet busied herself making two coffees, Pav prepared to impress her, spreading out his portfolio on one of the tables. Violet's phone rang in her pocket. Glyn again. She pulled it out and switched it impatiently to silent. She noticed she'd apparently missed another call from him ten minutes ago.

She carried over the coffees, placing Pav's well away from his artwork. She looked down at the first picture and her eyebrows raised.

'Wow,' she said at the floor-to-ceiling artist's impression of carousel horses: nose to tail, brightly coloured, golden spikes rising from their backs.

'Now I can see the walls, I have a better vision of what you want,' he said.

'This is just what I want,' said Violet breathlessly. In fact she lied, because this was much much better than she wanted. 'You can paint these horses? On my walls?' His artwork was on par with that in the Sistine Chapel.

'Yes, of course,' said Pav, as if it would be the easiest thing in the world to do that.

'How much do you charge, though?' asked Violet, getting ready to cringe.

'Ten pounds an hour.'

'Ten pounds?' Blimey, thought Violet – he's giving it away.

'Is too much?' Pav sounded concerned.

'No, no,' said Violet, suddenly thinking that it might not be such a bargain if it took him all day to paint one horse's eyeball. 'How long do you think it would take you?'

'It's hard to say,' he said. 'I will have to work after I finish my day job. I am a builder. Maybe some full days at the weekend. When are you planning to open?'

'First week in August,' said Violet.

'Yes, it will be ready for then,' said Pav.

'How would I pay you?'

'Cheque or cash is fine for me,' said Pav, taking a long sip at his coffee. 'I have a legitimate business. Everything goes into my books.'

'When can you start?' asked Violet, trying to appear businesslike and not as if she was fantasizing about what his arms would feel like round her.

Pav smiled and Violet noticed that he had the beginnings of crinkles at the corners of his eyes. He must laugh a lot to have got those so young.

'I can make poles for you too,' said Pav. 'A pole from the ceiling to the floor through the tables and painted gold like the carnival horses have. I can make them on a router – you know a router?'

'Yes, I know what a router is,' said Violet. 'My dad was a joiner.' Had he still been alive today, he would have been in this shop kitting it all out for her and loving every minute.

'And that would be fantastic,' said Violet. She could see the poles now. The excitement levels inside her for her new venture ratcheted up another couple of notches.

Pav studied the walls hard then announced with contagious enthusiasm: 'The horses will look as if they leaping out when I paint them.' His hand made a flourish in the air. He had large square hands, long clean fingers.

Violet's heart was racing like a carousel at full pelt, just imagining it. She had dreamed of having her own ice-cream parlour since she was a little girl, but it was only three years ago that she had taken the bull by the horns, left the head-pastry-chef job she had in a Sheffield hotel and ventured out on her own. She had made her last place into a really successful little business, but the building didn't have a fraction of the charisma of Carousel.

'I'll probably be here a lot of the time when you work. In the kitchen. Making stocks of ice cream and getting things ready, or doing my books in the room upstairs,' said Violet. 'I won't be in your way, will I?'

'No, no,' said Pav. He took a tape measure out of his pocket and a notepad. 'Excuse, please.' He began to take the measurements of the walls and write them down with a pencil so small it was lost in his hand.

Violet drank her coffee and realized she wasn't just watching him, she was appraising him. He had such a calm air about him, so different from the hyper-ness that surrounded Glyn. Pav's eyes were darting around the space as he planned his masterpiece and scribbled down notes and ideas. She recognized the passion he had for his work because that's what she felt about her ice cream, wanting to make the best in the world and then market it across the globe – although it sounded a little silly to admit that to anyone so she never had. Well, she had once – to the careers officer at school, who had laughed and told her to get her head out of the clouds and stop deluding herself. The echo of his words had rung loud and long in her head and served to hold her back from her true potential. It had far outweighed any encouragement her family and friends had given her, even though she knew it shouldn't be that way.

Violet snatched her attention away from Pav's big frame and back to her coffee. She shouldn't be eyeing up young men like that. He must be about ten years her junior. Cougar. Or, worse: cradle-snatcher. She would be married in eleven weeks and the part of her heart that might thud for another was destined to die.

Chapter 10

Glyn's parents, Joy and Norman Leach, were the sort of couple who finished off each other's sentences and wore matching home-knits with native American grey wolf heads on the front. They were joined at the hip, had the same dislikes and likes, and everything in their house, where possible, was labelled 'his' and 'hers'. In a previous life they would have been a Twix. Norman painted small models of soldiers when he wasn't gardening and Joy did cross-stitch pictures, usually of owls, which Norman then framed and hung on the walls for her. Joy thought she was being wanton if she had a glass of sherry at any time other than Christmas – and always Croft Original, never Harveys Bristol Cream. Norman reached the heights of ecstasy looking through *Caravan Monthly* magazine or buying seeds. They were kind and gentle people, if incredibly dull. They made a wet weekend in Grimsby look like a fortnight's luxury cruise in the Bahamas.

They'd had Glyn – their only child – considerably late in life. Joy was forty-two and they had both given up hope of ever conceiving. As such, he was their precious jewel and they worried about him constantly and still treated him as if he was five. When she was in town Joy was always buying him pants and socks.

Their house was a remarkably neat and twee bungalow in Pogley, backing onto a dribble of a stream known as the Stripe. Their garden was immaculate and would have made Alan Titchmarsh's head nod in approval. Everything about the Leachs was immaculate. Even Misty, their immaculately Persil-clean West Highland white terrier, always shat in the same spot in the garden – out of sight behind the aloe vera plant.

They gushed out of the door when they saw Violet's car draw up, waving and fussing. They were so pleased to see her that Violet felt more than a stab of guilt that they annoyed her so much with their over-the-top gratefulness to her for marrying their son. There was no harm in either of them, quite the opposite – they would help anyone with anything within their capabilities. They were wonderfully agile for a couple in their mid-seventies. The ill-health fairy had stayed away from their door, except for a heart scare for Norman last year, and the odd cold. Mental illness was something they couldn't understand – and wouldn't ever be able to – so they overcompensated and padded around Glyn on eggshells, not wanting to risk upset and send him back to the dark places he had visited during his breakdown.

Norman rushed Glyn inside to show him the new TV they'd just bought for their caravan. Joy followed behind with Violet, taking slow pin steps and hoping for her usual 'quiet word'.

'How's he been?' she asked, her smile sad but hopeful of good news.

'Fine,' nodded Violet. 'In good spirits.' She didn't add that his paranoia seemed to be getting worse. That if she was out of the house for longer than an hour without reporting in, he would get in a flap. Some things were best left unsaid. The Leachs were Olympic champions at worrying.

'You are making sure he takes his anti-depressants regularly, aren't you?'

'Yes, Joy,' said Violet, psyching herself to ask what had been on her mind to say for weeks now. 'It might . . . it might help if you encouraged him to go out and get some fresh air and stretch his legs. Occasionally.'

Glyn's diet wasn't the healthiest and the fact that he got absolutely no exercise bothered Violet. Especially because her concern seemed to gratify Glyn and made him doubly reluctant to do anything about his increasing waist measurement. 'It's not good for him to be so inactive, Joy. I wish you'd say something to him about it. He won't listen to me.'

Joy's eyes nearly sprang out of their sockets in horror. 'He needs to rest, surely. At least for the time being. It's early days, Violet. A breakdown can take years to get over. I got a book from the library about mental health. He goes out in the garden, doesn't he? He tells us he's planted all sorts of flowers. Daddy's given him all manner of seeds.'

'He has, yes,' conceded Violet. The flats all had individual patches of garden at the back. Patch being the operative word.

'And he's growing some violets for you, I hear.' Joy grinned at the romance of it all.

'Yes, he's growing some violets,' echoed Violet, knowing now that she was on the highway to nowhere by asking Joy to help her gee up her son.

'Violet, dear, I know Glyn feels bad about not being strong enough yet to get another job, because he's always had such a professional work ethic. But, for the moment, he's enjoying being at home and looking after you. And that can only be a good thing – if he's happy.'

'Yes, yes, I know,' said Violet. 'I wasn't implying he was lazy, it's just that . . .'

'These modern marriages have a lot to be said for them when the wife is happy working out and the husband is happy working in.'

Violet didn't say it but she felt that wouldn't have been the natural way round of things for Joy. She couldn't imagine either Joy mowing the lawn or Norman ironing. But Joy had obviously tried hard to rationalize the situation so that it made sense to her tradition-loving brain.

Glyn wasn't idle, but he was doing himself no favours 'institutionalizing' himself in his flat. His therapist had said the same, until he stopped going to see her. Violet was now totally on her own trying to get him back to being part of the bigger world again.

She followed Joy into the chintzy roast-pork-scented kitchen, where a warmed teapot was waiting under a crocheted cosy. Pans of vegetables were bubbling away on her old electric hob.

'Can I do anything?' asked Violet as Joy slipped her apron back on. She always felt duty-bound to ask though she knew that Joy would sooner gouge out her own eyeballs than have anyone help her in her kingdom. Unless it was after the meal when Norman had the customary duty of drying the washed plates.

'No, dear, it's all under control.'

Joy stirred the gravy with one hand and tipped the teapot over her china cups with the other. It looked a struggle and Violet watched her awkwardly. It was uncomfortable to be so redundant. Both here and at home.

'We've brought you some of that non-alcoholic wine,' said Glyn.

'Oh lovely. We'll have that with pudding,' replied Norman.

'It's ready,' trilled Joy as a choir of buzzers all went off at the same time. 'Daddy, would you carve?'

'Certainly, Mum,' saluted Norman, and he picked up the meat and the electric knife and then carried them into the dining room.

'Go and sit down, dear,' Joy instructed, juggling pans with the panache of a top-of-the-bill circus act.

Violet followed Norman and Glyn into the wood-panelled dining room. The decor of the house was immaculate but dreadfully dated. She was sure the Leachs had injected all the furniture with formaldehyde because it was all so fabulously preserved.

The table was set with frilly doily place mats and beige cloth napkins and an ancient silver cruet stood in the middle of the table, sharing space on a wooden trivet with a milk jug and sugar bowl. In one corner of the room was the old hostess trolley that Joy still occasionally used when they had visitors; in another corner stood an upright piano polished to a dazzling shine.

Neither of them could play it. It was a relic from the music lessons Glyn had taken between the ages of seven and fifteen.

'Dad has asked us if we want to borrow the caravan for our honeymoon,' said Glyn, with the excitement of someone who had just found a Rolex in the street.

Violet gulped. 'Oh. A honeymoon? I didn't even think about that. I presumed you wouldn't be able to manage one.'

'We should at least consider it. And quickly,' said Glyn. 'The wedding will be here before we know it.'

'Seventy-six days and counting,' chuckled Joy, ferrying in dishes of vegetables. 'You might as well have a nice holiday, just the pair of you, before the babies come along.'

'Babies?' Violet nearly choked.

'You don't want to be hanging about at your age,' said Joy. 'The younger you are when you have children, the more energy you have – trust me on that one. If you're thirty-three now, even if you caught on straight away, you're going to be halfway to thirty-five by the time the first one comes along. Then you'll need a rest before number two . . .'

Violet didn't say anything; she just let Joy prattle on about grandchildren and kept schtum. She and Glyn had talked about having children in the heady rush of feelings at the beginning, but it hadn't been mentioned since. He wasn't in any fit state to be a father with his agoraphobia and anxieties. And it wasn't on Violet's agenda any more.

'I need to get my new business up and running,' Violet excused.

'And I'm quite happy for you to do that,' smiled Glyn. 'I'm looking forward to being a house-daddy as well as a house-husband.'

Blimey, he'd got all this worked out in advance, thought Violet. It was like watching John Noakes on *Blue Peter* saying, 'Here's one I made earlier.' She had an awful feeling that if she looked in Joy's knitting bag she would find a stockpile of little blue and pink cardigans.

'Glyn says you haven't got your wedding dress yet,' said Joy, passing the sprouts.

'Not yet,' said Violet as she speared some pork. It was cooked to perfection, as always.

'You're leaving it a bit late, aren't you?' Norman put in.

'Well, it's not a big wedding, is it? I'm sure I'll find something in time.'

'I don't mind coming shopping with you, if you want,' Joy volunteered.

'No, it's fine,' said Violet. 'I'm more of a lone shopper.'

'But you went dress hunting with friends yesterday, didn't you?' said Glyn. Violet could have kicked him. Luckily she thought of something off the cuff that sounded perfectly acceptable.

'Yes, and that's most probably why I didn't find anything, because I'm better off shopping by myself. Other people put me off.'

'Come on, Violet. That wouldn't fill a bird,' urged Joy, gesturing towards her plate. She said the same every time they dined there, though Violet wasn't a huge eater.

She glanced over at Glyn's plate, which had an Alp of food on it. He was tucking in as if he hadn't eaten for days. His chin was glossy with dribbled gravy and Violet flicked her eyes away because these days the sight of him eating made her feel slightly queasy. He hadn't been overweight when they met; in fact at a distance, with bad glasses on, he could have passed for a Phillip Schofield look-alike. Now he had a big wobbly belly and more than a hint of moobs. Glyn didn't see a problem in his meteoric weight-gain – he just said that there was 'more of him to love'.

'I can't wait to get married. I don't know how I'd live without you, Violet,' Glyn reached over the table and squeezed her hand.

'Aw,' chorused Joy and Norman.

Chapter 11

Monday morning was the first chance Violet had to visit Postbox Cottage. For once, Glyn remained asleep when she stole out of bed. She tiptoed around getting dressed and didn't use the loo in case the flush woke him. At every second she was convinced his eyes would flick open and there would begin the inquisition about where she was going and when she would be back and what did she want to eat for lunch/tea and what should he buy from the shop. Glyn had a strange kind of agoraphobia, Violet decided. It would allow him to visit the row of shops round the corner and his parents' house, but nowhere else. Although she could add a caravan at the seaside to the list as well now, apparently. As guilty as it made her feel, Violet was only glad that his complex neurosis didn't permit him to venture to her workplace. Going out to create her dishes was her freedom, her oxygen. Without it, she didn't know how she would stand her life. And now she had another place – a secret place – to hide.

Miraculously she made it outside into the fresh air and couldn't help but breathe a massive sigh of relief after starting up the car. She knew that she shouldn't feel so 'free' at being away from the man she was going to marry in seventy-five days. But, for now, there was nothing she could do about it but enjoy the periods of parole away from the prison of his flat.

Postbox Cottage was on the other side of Maltstone, in a

nuclear hamlet called Little Kipping. The last in a row of three double-fronted – but tiny – properties, the cottage resembled a doll's house with its lozenge-paned windows. Violet sat behind the steering wheel staring at the facade of her grand-parents' cottage and she sighed. She couldn't believe it was all hers.

She eventually got out of the car, pushed open the creaky wooden front door and lifted up all the junk mail that had collected behind it. She walked from room to room, seeing it through new eyes: the eyes of an owner. It sent a delicious thrill tripping across her heart. The last tenants had left it in a reasonable state inside but not clean enough by Violet's standards. The bathroom, especially, needed an extra scrub, and a lot of food had been left in the cupboards and needed to be thrown out.

It was a dear little place. The front windows were small and leaded and didn't let in a great deal of light so Nan and Grandad Jack had knocked down the wall between the lounge and kitchen to 'borrow' light from the south-facing back windows. A heavily shelved cellar housed a box freezer and was dry enough to be used for storage. Upstairs there was a large bed-room, a much smaller bedroom and the sweetest square bathroom ever; on the second floor was a long attic room with a large dormer window affording views of the Pennines and beyond. Outside at the back was a cottage garden, once Jack's pride and joy but now an overgrown mess. Violet had spent many happy hours trailing after him, helping him plant seeds and taking the fat white rose heads that he cut off for her so she could make some rose-water perfume with Nan. But now the rosebushes and flower beds had been swamped by virulent chok-ing weeds rampaging over everything they could grab at and cling to.

Violet's eyes filled with a blind of tears. She loved this cottage; it was so full of warm memories for her. She wished she could lock the door and stay there.

So why can't you? asked a tempting voice inside her. *It would be the simplest thing.*

She opened the bag of cleaning products she had bought en route and began to scrub at everything in sight, as if she were scrubbing at her own life, trying to take the grunge from it and make it clean.

Chapter 12

Bel's father's house was a beautiful new build, constructed to make it look old and as if it had been there for ever. An architectural triumph, it was built five years ago on the site of his previous house – the much smaller, but still sizeable, nineteen thirties dwelling in which Bel grew up. Faye was naturally gifted at interior design and had done a fabulous job of making the huge new home feel like an old lived-in and loved one. While Vanoushka and Martin's house was magazine perfect, it wasn't cosy at all. But the Nookery was a place where comfort came before the need to impress. It was a welcoming house, and even though Bel had long since left home, the Nookery had a bedroom for her use only. Not that she had ever used it.

It was a source of annoyance to Vanoushka Bosomworth-Proud that her sister's house had more rooms than hers. And an orangery. Vanoushka would have sold her liver for that orangery, but her husband's financial advisory business wasn't nearly as profitable as her brother-in-law's confectionery factory. Treffé Chocolates had started life as Trevelen Chocolates – a two-man business consisting of Trevor and Helen Candy. It didn't do that well, though, and was wound up. Helen died within the year and Trevor went back into business management, only to marry his secretary – Faye – who reignited all his dreams of being a chocolate magnate, and thus Treffé

Chocolates was born. They worked well, and hard, together and Trevor had learned a lot from mistakes made the first time round. Now Treffé had stretched over the sea, first to Germany then to France and Belgium, giving the experts there a run for their money. Their products had won many awards and the company was defying the recession and rising from strength to strength. Bel only wished the success story had been her mother's and not Faye's.

'Hello, darling,' said Trevor, coming to the door to greet the daughter who always rang the bell to gain entry rather than just walk in, even if both Trevor and Faye told her that the Nookery was as good as her home too. He had a pipe lodged between his lips and he removed it in order to give Bel a peck on the cheek. With his large ears, thinning grey hair and easy way, he had more than a passing resemblance to Bing Crosby. 'Come in, come in. And by the way, I have a bone to pick with you. Why haven't you banked that cheque I gave you for the wedding yet?'

He smacked his daughter's bottom lightly as she walked into the house.

'No rush, Dad. Too busy at the moment,' said Bel.

'Hello, darling,' chirped Faye. She'd appeared at the lounge door wearing some sort of pale blue kaftan that would have looked ridiculous on anyone else. But on tall, slim Faye it looked like something a top model would have worn, and the shade was stunning against her expertly dyed caramel-blonde hair, which was piled into a messily perfect bun.

'Hi, Faye,' called Bel. As in recent days, more so than ever before, the smile on her lips didn't quite reach her eyes. Because Faye was one of them – a Bosomworth – even if she was the only one of the three sisters who didn't still cling to their maiden name to force a double-barrel. But blood was thicker than water, after all.

'Glass of champagne?' asked Faye. 'Come and try this new fizz from France.'

'Thanks, but I'm driving.'

'Driving? You can't drive tonight; it's the family equivalent of a hen night. Leave your car here and pick it up tomorrow,' Trevor nudged her. 'We've got this champagne in especially for you. It's called Belle de la Nuit. Come on, Bel, let your hair down. This is the last time you'll be with us as our "Miss Candy girl".'

'I'll be okay with just the one glass, Dad. I've got to keep a clear head – I have so much to do in the next couple of days,' she said, more than half wishing she could lift a bottle of Belle de la Nuit to her lips and drink it in one.

'All right, then, if you're sure,' sighed Trevor, handing her a glass of bubbly. 'It's so nice to see you here. You don't come often enough, you know. And we'll probably see even less of you when you're married.'

'You're welcome any time, you know that,' said Faye, nodding heartily as she moved towards Trevor. He slipped his hand round her and something flicked at Bel's heart. Even now, after all these years, she wanted to rush between them and say, 'He's mine, not yours. Mine and Mum's.' Trevor and Faye had always been affectionate with each other, hand holding, darling this, sweetheart that. Even after twenty-eight years of marriage.

'Have you changed your mind about the house?' asked Faye. 'I notice it's still for sale.'

'Nope,' said Bel. 'I told you, I've gone off it.'

This was another lie that hurt to tell. She had fallen in love with Bell House when she and Richard had found it three months ago – even the name made it sound like it was meant to belong to her. So everyone was stunned when she announced the following month that she was no longer interested in it.

In the same week she told Richard that she wouldn't be staying at his flat any more until after the wedding. And he wasn't to stay at her apartment either. She said she wanted her wedding night to be special – unforgettable. Something worth waiting for. Explosive.

Richard was next to arrive, just as Bel took a huge gulp of the zesty fizz. She felt it trace a cool path down to her stomach. Then she pulled in a deep breath as her gorgeous, suave and sophisticated fiancé made a perfect-white-toothed smiling beeline for her.

'Hello, stranger,' he said, draping his arms round her shoulders and kissing her firmly on the lips. 'This separation is killing me, you know.' He leaned in close to her ear. 'I have a constant hard-on like you wouldn't believe.'

She gave his crotch a surreptitious single stroke. 'Don't worry,' she whispered, licking her lips. 'It's really only hours away to our wedding night.'

'Hello, Richard,' Faye interrupted, handing him a glass of champagne and clinking hers against it. 'What a happy evening we're going to have with you both here together.'

A car pulled up harshly in the drive, spraying gravel everywhere. Martin's Aston Martin. Like everything else he had, it was being paid off monthly. He was obsessed by the need to keep up with the Joneses – the Joneses in his case being his sister-in-law and her husband, who, it grieved him to think, could have paid for his car and his house with change from their arse pocket.

'Vanoushka's here,' Faye trilled, running to the champagne bottle to pour out three more glasses, for her elder sister, brother-in-law and niece.

'Whoopee,' said Bel drily to Richard. 'At least it will be nice to see Shaden. You haven't seen her for ages, have you?'

Richard didn't appear to have heard the question. Instead he whispered in Bel's ear, 'So how many times do you think Martin will say the word "investment" tonight, then?'

'Oh at least forty-five,' smiled Bel, enjoying the sensation of his arm round her, squeezing her into his side. It felt so nice she wanted to cry. Her bottom lip began to tremble. She hadn't figured tonight would be so hard.

Vanoushka was first through the door, with her perfect

bottle-blonde hair, Botox-frozen head and Goodyear-tyre lips. She made Jackie Stallone look like Shirley Temple. She kissed the air at either side of her younger sister's ear as she breezed in on a perfume cloud of something as heavy and spicy as a Moroccan market. They could probably smell it in Morocco, as well – she'd put enough of it on for that to be possible.

Behind her came the heavily jowled Martin, who'd also had a bit of work done recently. His eyebrows were virtually lodged in his crown. There was nothing frozen about his eyes, though, as the little beady blue circles roved around the hallway, taking in everything, checking for things that were different from his last visit.

His greasy lips spread into a smile as he air-kissed Faye too and shook Trevor's hand. Bel prepared herself for ordeal by air-kissing, although 'Uncle Martin' didn't air-kiss her – he laid his big slobbery lips on her cheek and his hand was more on her bum than her back, as usual. Then he grabbed Richard's hand, nearly breaking it off with the shake he gave it.

Then in came Shaden, looking more like a clone of Vanoushka every time Bel saw her, which was rarely these days. Gone was the mousy-haired, lumpy, quiet thing who had been like a little sister to Bel as they were growing up. They'd found common ground in jumping on the trampoline in the garden, playing hide and seek among the many trees behind the Candys' old house and a desire to snog Simon le Bon. They'd been close, until Shaden's twenty-first birthday, when she – totally out of the blue – announced that her mother was giving her a boob job as a coming-of-age present. Bel had laughed, presuming she was joking. Shaden didn't even wear foundation and skipped past the make-up pages in girls' mags.

Ten years after her pneumatic breast implants, Shaden was unrecognizable as the girl Bel knew. Waxed and preened, teeth straightened and whitened, lips inflated to pout-perfect standards, weekly spray-tanned, hair bleached to Californian blonde – much to her mother's delight, Shaden Bosomworth-Proud had become a miniature Barbie whose knockers arrived in a room five minutes before she did. Only her nose remained the same: long with a small bump near the top. Bel didn't doubt that her conk would be the next thing on the plastic-surgery list and probably would have been done already if Martin hadn't been struggling financially for a few years, although no one would believe that from the family face they showed to the world.

Shaden had acquired a glam set of her own friends who swarmed around her as if she were a queen bee, and she no longer had use for the cousin who used to outshine her at every turn. In fact Bel hadn't seen her – or heard from her – since choosing the bridesmaid's dress in Leeds.

'Hi, coz,' Shaden smiled at Bel, and whereas years ago she would have bounced over and thrown herself on Bel, now she teetered over on her huge spiked heels and kissed the air inches away from her cheek. Bel watched as she greeted Richard the same way: brief, perfunctory, polite.

'I can't believe the wedding is only two days away,' smiled Faye. She was getting some really heavy creases round her eyes when she laughed, thought Bel. She obviously hadn't had any of the work done that her two older sisters favoured.

'Is everything arranged, then?' Vanoushka asked her.

'I . . . I . . . think so,' began Faye, looking to Bel for comment.

'I've done everything myself. I didn't want any help,' explained Bel.

'Oh? Why not?' asked Vanoushka in her plummy tones. She always spoke very slowly, feeling that added an extra notch of class to her voice. 'It's quite an undertaking to arrange a marriage by yourself, Belinda.'

'I knew what I wanted so it wasn't necessary to involve anyone else.'

Vanoushka would have raised her eyebrows if she could. Bel knew that when Shaden got married, Vanoushka's nose would be well and truly stuck into the business of organizing the wedding. Although Shaden was quite happy playing the field for now. She was holding out for a multimillionaire with a dicky ticker and no concept of the phrase 'pre-nup'.

'I don't know yet what we're going to be eating at the reception,' laughed Richard.

'Even you haven't had any involvement? In your own wedding?' Vanoushka looked horrified – at least as much as she was able to.

'Well, Liam and I have picked our suits. That's about it,' he replied. 'And I've arranged the honeymoon in Las Vegas. The Bellagio.'

'Very nice,' sniffed Martin. 'Although I'd have gone for the Venetian myself.'

Like he would know, thought Bel, pressing down on the snarl her lip wanted to make. He was only saying that to intimate that he was a savvy world traveller. Bel bet that he wouldn't know a Ritz hotel from a Ritz cracker.

'Still, in our circles it's a bit odd, surely, for the bride to arrange everything herself,' said Vanoushka, sounding exactly like the snob she was.

'I want everything to be a surprise,' Bel smiled sweetly. If only they knew how much scheming this wedding had taken. It was hard enough work organizing the original one, but when all the plans had to be changed . . .

'Are we allowed to know what we're having to eat, then?' asked Martin, holding out his glass for a refill. Food was constantly on his mind. 'Lobster? Beef?'

'That's another surprise,' Bel carried on smiling, as beatifically as Mother Teresa.

'I love lobster,' announced Martin, his pronounced paunch grumbling.

'That's lucky,' beamed Faye. 'Because that's what we're having today. Come to the table, everyone. The caterers are ready to serve us.'

Vanoushka's face nearly turned the lime-green shade of instant jealousy. Lobsters and caterers and champagne. And a wedding in a couple of days that would have cost a small fortune, most likely.

'Don't forget to put that cheque in the bank,' Trevor reminded his daughter yet again as they walked arm in arm into the dining room. 'I haven't strictly paid for your wedding until you do, you know. And that's not right.'

'I know, Dad,' said Bel, adding to herself: *But that's the idea.*

Bel noticed that Shaden sat as far away from Richard as she possibly could at the table. Faye relinquished her seat so that Bel could sit next to her father. That was sweet of her, Bel conceded grudgingly. Mind you, she had him 24/7 so she could afford to let him go for an hour or so.

At the other side of her Bel felt Richard squeeze her leg and her heart beat against her chest wall. He really was so handsome. She'd thought that from the first day she met him in her office three years ago. The new business contact at the bank, he'd breezed in exactly on time for their appointment, tall and cocky in a black Armani suit . From the moment his soft and sexy iceblue eyes locked on to hers, she'd almost dissolved into a pool of drool.

'When are your parents arriving from France, Richard?' asked Trevor, as a waiter served him with a pot of buttery shrimps.

'They'll be flying over as we speak, with my brother who's been out there for two weeks.'

'Such a shame they couldn't have got an earlier flight and joined us,' said Faye.

Bel rather thought that Madeleine and Monty Bishop had timed their flights from an early summer stay in their crumbling residence in the Dordogne deliberately. They came from oldmoney and didn't like to think that their precious elder son was marrying into the common nouveau riche. They were the coldest people Bel had ever met. 'Oh no, I don't do demonstrations of affection,' Madeleine had said, twisting away from Bel when she had first met her and bent to kiss the shrewish little woman with the bright beady eyes of a seriously pissed-off hawk. Madeleine was so brittle that Bel hadn't a clue how she could have survived the impregnation shag without shattering into a million pieces. Monty was a snob of the highest order too. They made a wonderfully suited couple.

'How long are they home for?'

'Two days,' said Richard. 'Then they're flying back again until September.'

Just enough time to witness their son make the biggest mistake of his life, thought Bel wryly.

'What are they giving you for a wedding present?' asked Martin, reaching over for his fourth bread roll.

'They've given us a cheque,' replied Richard.

'Don't you think it was rather off to ask for no presents and just cheques,' said Vanoushka, glad that she'd been given the opportunity to voice her opinion on that. She'd been intending to give them a rose bowl, which she'd had in a cupboard for years, until the invitation addendum came out a couple of months ago and with it the gentle guide on present-buying.

'I think it's a great idea,' said Faye, bouncing in with a firm defence. 'Who wants duplicate presents? This way Bel and Richard can buy what they need.'

'There is such a thing as a wedding list,' said Martin, in support of his wife.

'Actually, I thought a cheque would be easier for everyone,' said Bel, as the waiter removed her starter plate. She was as calm as a cucumber on the surface, but underneath she was a boiling torrent. Vanoushka was probably kicking up because she had some old vase stored away that she wanted to palm off on to a 'not real relative'. Still, she needn't worry about her wedding present, Bel nearly said to her. Her money was quite safe.

'You're quiet, Shaden,' called Bel. 'Everything all right with you?'

'Yes, I'm fine,' nodded Shaden. She looked anything but fine.

She looked as stiff as a board and as if she wanted to be anywhere in the world but here.

'Dress hanging up and ready?' asked Bel.

'Of course it is, yes.'

'Lovely shade of tomato,' said Vanoushka. 'It'll look beautiful against Shaden's hair.' She leaned over and stroked her darling daughter's head.

'It's not tomato, it's strawberry,' stated Shaden. 'The shade is strawberry.'

'Who's doing your hair and make-up?' asked Faye. 'I wish you'd let me book Anita for—'

'Don't worry, Faye, it's all under control,' said Bel.

'I'll come to your apartment as soon as my stylist has been,' said Shaden, tossing her long golden hair over her shoulder.

'The Rolls will be taking you at one forty-five,' said Bel. 'Make sure you're early so we can have a glass of champagne before.'

'Sounds lovely,' said Faye. 'Are you sure you don't need any help getting ready? That dress has a lot of buttons.'

'I won't . . .' Oops, nearly. 'I . . . er . . . will be fine. I'm perfectly capable of putting on a wedding dress.'

'You're a very controlling person, aren't you?' said Vanoushka, dressing her annoyance with a laugh that was both tinkly and as hard as crystal.

'Vanoushka, Belinda is not controlling, she just knows what she wants,' said Faye in a firm voice, much to Bel's annoyance. She didn't need her dad's former secretary fighting her corner. She was quite able to do it for herself. More than able.

'No, Vanoushka is right, Faye,' said Bel, trying not to say it through gritted teeth. 'In the plans for my wedding, I've been psychotically controlling. I'll be honest; I wanted a day like you've never seen before. And, when I need to be focused, I work best alone.'

Bel turned her full gaze on Shaden. 'Are you bringing a plus one with you? You haven't said. I never hear about your conquests these days.'

'I'm happily single at the moment.'

'Richard's brother is free,' Bel winked at Shaden.

Shaden rolled her eyes but said nothing. Liam was the slimiest little toad in the world; they were both agreed on that. A smaller stouter version of Monty Bishop. Bel suddenly found herself wanting to giggle.

'So where are you both going to live?' asked Vanoushka, as soup was served and a waiter handed her a bread basket. She waved it away impatiently, as if she expected him to know that carbs were fat from the devil's arse.

'Well, the plan is that I move in full-time with Richard for now,' Bel answered. She and her fiancé had more or less lived together anyway until a couple of months ago, when she decided to move back into her apartment, saying she wanted their cohabiting after the wedding to feel fresh.

'All packed for the honeymoon, then?' said Martin, dribbly butter shiny on his chin. He addressed Richard, who seemed not to hear, so Bel answered for him.

'Suitcases packed and ready, don't you worry,' said Bel. 'I can't wait to get away from it all.'

She almost said 'you all' then. With the exception of one person at the table.

There followed a period of silence until they'd finished the soup. Then Martin let loose a huge burp and Vanoushka nudged him hard with her bony elbow, wearing a look of abject disgust on her face. Bel rather thought that if Vanoushka had money of her own she would have left him. He'd settled happily into fat and too much of the good life, which gave him many episodes of gout. She had a sudden horrible picture of Martin above her, grinding into her, his stomach hanging down, his chin wobbling.

'Lovely starters,' agreed Trevor.

Vanoushka dabbed delicately at her mouth but didn't comment.

'Can't wait for the lobster, though,' said Martin, rubbing his hands together.

'Well, tuck in, Martin, because there will be plenty.'

Bel looked sideways at her dad. He was such a diamond, always saw the best in people, was generous-spirited and calm-tempered. She wished she could have been as gentle. She must have got her feistiness from her mother's side. As well as her mother's black hair and mint-green eyes, which were again prickling painfully with tears.

Shaden remained very quiet at the end of the table through-out the meal, as if she were undertaking a great chore by being there. She didn't eat much either. She was terrified of ingesting a potato or anything with starch in it, in case it upset her Atkins-friendly eating regime, so the peanut-butter cheesecake – Bel's favourite – was a definite no-no.

The Bosomworth-Prouds left soon after coffee, hurried along by Shaden, who was driving. This was much to Martin's annoy-ance as he had set his mind on making a hole in Trevor's supply of brandy. As Faye and Trevor waved them off, Richard grabbed Bel and pulled her into the snooker room.

'Sleep with me tonight,' he said, leaning over and nibbling her neck. He knew she wouldn't be able to resist that. But she did and pulled away from his hold.

'Nope. This is about as near to a virgin bride as I can possibly get. In forty-eight hours, it will be our wedding night with fire-works, lover boy.'

'You're so mean,' said Richard, tweaking her nose. Such an intimate, loving gesture. Bel found herself wilting inside, as if the snap had gone out of her spine.

'Go and get your coat and leave me. The sooner you do that, the sooner I can start the countdown to seeing you again,' she said, rallying herself, straightening her back, galvanizing her resolve.

'If I must,' he replied with a resigned sigh.

'Do you think Shaden has a bloke?' tested Bel. 'She used to tell me about everyone she had her eye on.'

'I'm not interested in anyone else's business,' said Richard, moving in again, hoping to change her mind. 'Bel, I'm so hard. You can't send me home like this.'

'Coat. Go. Now,' ordered Bel.

Richard raised his palms to her in a gesture of surrender.

'Okay, but you'd better promise me that Saturday is going to be dynamite.'

'I can do that with all my heart,' said Bel, her cat-green eyes glittering.

Chapter 13

'Hello, what are you doing here?' said Bel, opening the door to Violet.

'It's the night before your wedding and you aren't spending it alone,' insisted Violet, pushing Bel out of the way and striding into the flat holding a bottle of chilled sparkling Pinot Grigio.

'Are you by yourself?' said Bel, half expecting Max to trot in behind her.

'I am,' said Violet. 'I wanted to talk to you.'

'Oh okay,' said Bel. 'I'll get a couple of glasses, shall I?'

She returned seconds later just as Violet was pushing the cork out of the bottle.

'So, what do you want to talk to me about?' asked Bel.

'You tell me,' said Violet, plonking herself down on Bel's big red-leather sofa.

'What do you mean?' said Bel.

'Well, this is the night before your wedding and you're sitting in alone watching *EastEnders*.'

Bel shrugged. 'I want a calm and peaceful night, that's all.' *Before the storm.*

'Really?' Violet raised her eyebrows and crossed her arms over her chest. 'Look, Bel, tell me to go away and bugger off—'

'Violet, go away and bugger off.'

'I'm being serious, Bel,' Violet's soft voice was cranked up to its full firmness. 'As I was saying, tell me to go away and bugger off, but I can't help thinking that something isn't right with you.'

Bel tried not to react. 'In what way?'

'Because, when we met, you were as giddy as a kipper about your wedding. Then you . . . you changed. It was like . . . like you suddenly went flat. As if something had switched off inside you.'

'Don't be ridiculous,' said Bel, taking a sip of fizz.

'Well, whatever, call it intuition. I just had to call in and see if you were okay. I was worried. I'm glad I got it all wrong, then.'

Bel laughed but, as usual when she laughed these days, she felt the ache of sadness behind the sound.

'Violet, you are very sweet,' she said, 'but trust me, I'm on top of my game. I'm perfectly fine.'

'I wanted to double-check. I know you said you were tired out from all the wedding arrangements, but I felt there was something else bothering you.'

Bel pulled out all the stops to hold her composure.

'When you get to know me better, Violet, you'll realize that I'm not very good at talking things over with people. When I feel any pressure I disappear into myself. I always have. Maybe I'm secretly a man. Just because I'm not having a typical mad last night of freedom, please don't worry.'

A typical mad last night of freedom. Violet hadn't even thought about what she'd be doing on the night before her own wedding. Glyn wouldn't be having a stag night, that was for sure. He didn't have any friends. Anyway, there was time to think about that later; for now there was Bel to consider.

'I hope you'll forgive me for coming round,' said Violet. 'I feel a bit daft now.' She noticed that Bel had had her nails French manicured for the wedding, and her eyebrows shaped and waxed. That gave her some comfort.

'There's nothing to forgive,' replied Bel, swallowing down the tears that *must not* seep out and weaken her.

'So you really do want to be by yourself tonight, then?' Violet asked.

No, I want you to stay with me while I get totally hammered and dance on tables.

'Yes, Violet, that's exactly what I want. I'm tired.'

Violet drained her glass and stood up. 'Well, I'll be off, then.' She stood and gave Bel a big squashy hug.

'I'll see you tomorrow. I'll be the one in white,' Bel smiled, while thinking, *Is there anyone I haven't lied to recently?* She let her weary head fall on Violet's shoulder and breathed in her friend's lovely flowery perfume. It would have been so easy to stay there and let her tears fall. Bel had to call on all her reserves of strength to step away from her friend.

As Bel waved her off she wished that Violet would come down with a slight mystery illness overnight that would prevent her from attending the wedding tomorrow. Bel didn't want her there. She opened her mouth to call out to Violet as she reached her car door, then slammed it shut again. It was all too late. Damage was inevitable and would have to be borne. She could only go forwards now; there was no way back.

As Violet drove off, though, she still couldn't shake off the feeling of dread. And noticing that she had three missed calls from Glyn on her phone didn't exactly lift her mood either.

Chapter 14

When Bel pulled back her curtains the next morning, the sky was as blue as could be, without a single cloud blighting it. The sun was round and yellow and full of warm promise; perfect white-wedding weather. How ironic was that, thought Bel.

Shaden still hadn't arrived by 1.20 p.m., which was no surprise to Bel. She would have put a substantial bet on her cousin not wanting to share celebratory champagne with her. Her taxi eventually arrived ten minutes later, just as Bel was polishing off a single neat brandy – a Dutch-courage lunch.

Bel had slept surprisingly well considering this was her big day. She hadn't even dreamed anything during the night, which was odd as her head hadn't stopped whirring like a nuclear concrete mixer for weeks. When Shaden's taxi arrived she took a deep breath. She heard the snap of a clapperboard in her head announcing another scene to be acted.

'Sorry I'm late, Belinda. Francine couldn't get my eyes right so I made her start again.'

Unlike herself, Shaden was freshly spray-tanned and coiffured. Red – *strawberry* – flowers were expertly woven into her golden ringlets of hair. Shaden's eyes pulled into focus on her whey-faced cousin and her obviously home-done hair and make-up, and wrinkled her bumpy nose.

'Where's your stylist?'

Annnd action.

'Oh I thought I'd do it myself,' said Bel. 'I always hate how they make me up.'

Shaden's eyes swept over her gown next.

'That isn't your mother's dress.'

'I ripped it. I had to go out and buy another off the peg.'

'You're not serious. It's a bit plain.' Shaden looked as if she had just walked into a joke.

'I know. But it fits. It'll do.'

Shaden shook her head in disbelief. 'How come you're so bloody calm about such a disaster?'

'Calm?' said Bel smoothly. 'What else can I be? It's only a dress, anyway. I'll get the other one mended. Maybe I'll wear it to renew my vows one day, if I feel that Richard is slipping off the straight and narrow and needs a gentle reminder that he has promises to stick to.'

Shaden didn't react – or maybe she didn't hear what Bel had said because she was busy primping herself in Bel's huge wall mirror. She adjusted her neckline to make sure her red bra didn't show. Then she adjusted it again to make sure it did. Bel knew that the cogs were turning in her brain and any moment now her lovely cousin would realize that there would be lots more attention on her if the bride looked such a dog.

'Would you like some champagne?' asked Bel.

'Oh yes, just a glass,' said Shaden.

Bel popped the cork out of the bottle of waiting Cristal and filled up two long flutes. Just as Shaden was about to take a sip, Bel stopped her.

'Before you taste, you have to toast,' she smiled. 'Now what are you going to say?'

Shaden thought for a moment, then her scarlet lips curved upwards and a light bloomed in her big brown eyes. 'To Richard's fabulous wife. May every good thing in life land in her lap.' She chinked her glass against Bel's and drank. That knocked Bel a little because Shaden's toast had sounded very heartfelt and genuine. She took a long drink of champagne herself and shivered as it slipped, cold and fizzy, down her throat.

They both heard the sound of a car pull up outside. Shaden went over to the window and saw the white Rolls-Royce.

'The car's here,' she said, returning to the mirror to check her make-up. Once upon a time she didn't know what a mirror was, thought Bel, harking back to the days when they were both in dungarees and sliding down the long polished banister in her dad's old house. But those days were so long gone they might as well be wrapped in dinosaurs' bog roll.

Trevor pushed open the door, full of smiles.

'Hello, love, you look beautiful. That dress doesn't half look different on you to how it looks on the hanger.'

'It's not the same dress, Uncle Trevor,' tutted Shaden with a tone in her voice that intimated her uncle must be simple. Bel felt herself rearing in daughterly defence, then she took in a very big breath and counted to ten.

'Right, I'll be off, then,' Shaden said, putting down the unfinished glass of champers. 'See you in church, coz. Break a leg.' She blew a kiss in Bel's direction, then she was off out of the door, her high heels clicking on the ground, and into the Rolls en route to the church.

'Where's your mother's dress, then?' asked Trevor, giving her a kiss.

'I can't wear it, Dad,' said Bel, pushing down the tears that were getting harder and harder to stem. 'I ripped it ...' She couldn't elaborate on the lie. Not to her dad. Especially as he put his arm round her and gave her a squeeze.

'You look lovely, anyway,' he said. 'And it's not the end of the world.'

Oh Dad, it is, she wanted to say. I don't know where I am.

Trevor pulled her at arm's length and looked down into her face. He was a foot taller than her, groomed and still so very attractive despite the advance of the years. She knew how lucky her mum had been to marry him.

'I need to have an eleventh-hour talk to you, my darling,' he said. 'You are absolutely sure you want to marry Richard? Because if you aren't, you must not be afraid to say it. No one will judge you. And if they do, they'll have me to answer to.'

Bel formed her next words very carefully. She had been prepared for this question and she knew how to answer it and look someone straight in the eyes while she was doing so.

'Dad, I want to walk down that aisle today more than I want anything else.'

But Trevor wasn't having any elusiveness. 'I didn't ask that. I asked if you want *to marry Richard*.'

He was looking at her with such tenderness that she wanted to crumble against him. But she had come this far. Her blinkers were on. She knew what she had to do and she had to stick to it because it was the only path she knew now.

'Yes, Dad. I love Richard.' And boy, was that true. That's why she was a jelly inside her iron-like exterior. She would have made a great Dalek.

'Oh my love,' sighed Trevor, cupping her face with his hands. 'I hope you're as happy as Faye and I are.'

Faye. Bel didn't want to hear her name today. Why couldn't he have said 'as happy as your mum and I were'? That was her signal to leave his embrace and pull the veil over her face. The Rolls would be coming back in five minutes. Richard would be waiting for her at the altar with his seedy brother, their sour-faced parents sitting behind them. And at the other side of the church were the Bosomworth lot and a load of people she neither knew nor cared about. And very shortly all of them were going to see a wedding as they'd never seen one before.

Chapter 15

Max sat in church between Stuart and Violet. Glyn hadn't come, which was a shame because Max was dying to see what he was like in person. From what she knew about him already, she didn't think she'd have a lot of patience with him; he sounded a bit wimpy for her tastes.

'You really should get out more,' Violet had told him as she was pinning up her long hair. 'It isn't doing you any good being inside all the time. You should try and come with me today.'

'Why would I want to go and make small talk with people I don't know? Do you have to go?' Glyn whined.

Violet was horrified he even had to ask that. The look on her face made him retract it immediately.

'Sorry, of course you do. Oh forgive me, Violet.' He reached for her hand and kissed it. 'I get myself in such a stew sometimes. I know you won't be long.'

'Well, I'll be back tonight,' corrected Violet. 'I'm not missing the reception.'

'No, no, of course. Not too late, though? I'll wait up.'

Violet didn't say that he didn't have to; she knew he would, anyway.

'Isn't this a gorgeous church?' Max said to Stuart as her opening gambit. Her eyes roved over the stained-glass windows and the long, long aisle. She imagined her gypsy train trailing down it, her bridesmaids behind, their dresses trailing too.

'It's all right,' sniffed Stuart. 'If you like churches.'

'I do like them, very much,' said Max. She knew that with her big fat gypsy frock on she would have to be married with some pomp and ceremony and church music and an aisle to walk up.

The bells started another ringing session.

'Ah would you listen to that,' sighed Max, when they'd finished pealing. She sounded like gypsy Margaret's Irish mother. 'Wedding bells. A wedding just isn't a wedding without that sound, is it?'

Stuart didn't react, but Max knew he had heard her. She was just hoping one of these seeds she was planting would start to germinate. She didn't have a lot of time to play with. Forty-two days, to be precise.

Violet twisted round in the pew to see if there was any activity at the door. She could see flashes of Shaden's red dress as she walked up and down impatiently outside.

'There's a real wedding feel in the air in this church, isn't there?' Max asked Stuart, as they listened to the organist begin to play. He laughed. He wasn't daft; he knew what she was up to.

'More than there would be in a registry office, you mean?' he answered.

'I can't imagine a registry office would have any sort of atmosphere. It's just an office really,' said Max. 'It won't have that slightly damp churchy smell and the flowers . . . hang on, where are the flowers?'

She had known there was something missing as soon as she walked into the church, but only now had her finger fallen on what that was. There were no displays of flowers on the end of the pews or by the altar. Not so much as a leaf. That was weird because she was certain that in one of the first conversations they all had, it was evident how much Bel loved flowers and that she intended to festoon the church with them for the ceremony.

It was something Vanoushka had noticed too. She had been smirking to herself about that.

'This is what happens when you don't take control,' she had told her sister. 'No flowers at a wedding, how preposterous. And did Belinda book a photographer? I haven't seen one.' Then she tutted for so long that she sounded like a morse-code message coming through.

The organist stopped playing the church musak and the opening bars of 'Here Comes the Bride' speared the air.

'She's here,' said Max, flapping her hands. She turned round to see a small woman in white in the doorway. 'Hang on, what's she got on?' It certainly wasn't her mother's beautiful silk and lace dress, which she had been led to believe Bel would be wearing. For a moment Max thought another bride had turned up at the wrong church.

Violet had also noticed the dress; it was nothing like the description Bel had given of it. Her feelings that something wasn't quite right about this wedding were prickled awake again. She hoped she was wrong. And when Bel swept past them, eyes intently forward, Violet could have sworn there were nettles sitting among the spray of red roses.

Whereas Trevor walked slowly and proudly down the aisle, grinning, Max and Violet saw that underneath her veil Bel's face was expressionless – as though carved of stone.

Big nerves, thought Max.

What's going on, Bel? thought Violet.

Max and Violet were particularly keen to see Shaden. She was every bit as golden and glossy as Bel had reported her to be. Oooh but she looked a madam, they both decided. They watched her swagger down the aisle with her Pippa Middleton bum. She totally outshone the bride – and she knew it.

Bel's eyes were fixed on Richard at the head of the aisle. He was looking impossibly handsome in a black morning suit, a red rose in his lapel, and beside him his brother, who carried a chip the size of Wales on his shoulder because he hadn't got his brother's height, looks or charm. Bel despised Liam. Strangely enough her hatred of him restored her strength, which seemed to have been seeping from her legs with every passing second.

The vicar welcomed everyone to the church, then announced the number of the first hymn.

'"Fight the Good Fight"?' Max whispered to Stuart. Considering the number of heads that were turning towards each other and the ripple of comment from many of the guests, she wasn't the only one who found that odd.

Violet couldn't relax. There really was something not right here. She could hear her heart thumping in her chest while the couple took their vows. Richard was respectfully serious but Bel was delivering her lines like a constipated robot, staring up at Richard intently, repeating everything the vicar said in a flat, but firm, tone. Violet was dreading the bit about 'just impediments', because that was the moment she *knew* something pivotal was going to happen.

It didn't.

The moment passed. The guests turned to the next hymn – 'Oh God of Truth'. Only the die-hard churchgoers seemed to know it; the rest just mimed, moving their mouths over the words like marionettes being worked by a crap puppeteer.

'Bit of a boring wedding, isn't it?' whispered Stuart, playing right into Max's hands.

'And a wedding shouldn't be boring, should it, Stuart? It should be memorable. I would never have thought that Bel was the type of person so have such a dull wedding as this.'

'But, you don't know her all that well really, do you?' he answered.

'I wouldn't feel properly married if I had a boring wedding,' said Max, forcing a tremble into her voice.

'Hmm . . .' said Stuart. Max sat back in her pew so he wouldn't see her smiling. It was the sound he made when he was deep in thought and it usually preceded the words: 'Okay, Max, maybe you're right.'

The organist began to play again as the happy couple emerged from the vestry arm in arm and walked back down the aisle, although 'happy' didn't really cover it. Bel had a fixed smile on her face that was as fake as Jordan's boobs. Behind them Shaden sashayed in her gorgeous *strawberry* dress, pouting as if she had graduated with honours from a Victoria Beckham mouth-arranging institute.

Outside, people loitered and waited to have their photographs taken, until Trevor regretfully announced that the photographer hadn't arrived. Vanoushka flashed a superior look at her sister again. One thing was for sure: Shaden's wedding – when it happened – wouldn't have much to beat.

To further the disappointment, Bel got straight in the Rolls rather than pose for guests to snap shots with their personal cameras, dragging Richard behind her. Some people hadn't even left the church when they realized that the bride had gone ahead to the reception. There were a few murmurings about this being a very odd and cold wedding, and not at all what was expected of people with such wealth to their name.

The Bishop elders kept a quiet dignity about the proceedings, but it was quite obvious from Madeleine's face that she was furious. Her scowl was even more pronounced than usual – and that was saying something. She had spent a fortune on her navy outfit and was wearing a hat the size of a spaceship. She made Vanoushka in her Dior look like Bob Geldof climbing backwards out of a hedge. For all the expense she had gone to, she wanted to be immortalized in her son's album and be the talk of the neighbourhood. She was also absolutely disgusted about the non-presence of any press. Typical of commoners, she adjudged. Still, there was always the hope that this farce might be the first step towards a divorce.

'Well, if this is what a "plain" marriage is like, I'd rather not have one,' said Max outside the church. 'That has to be the most miserable ceremony I've ever been to.'

'Hmm,' said Stuart again, climbing into Violet's car.

It was a short drive to Maltstone Lodge, where the reception

was to be held. Dark-pink cocktails with sugared rims were waiting for the guests.

'Bloody hell, that's strong,' said Stuart, coughing as the alcohol
hit the back of his throat. He made Violet laugh. She had liked
his smiley, warm self on sight.

'What is it?' She took a sip and nearly choked. Blimey, more
than one of these and she wouldn't be able to drive anywhere for
a fortnight.

'It tastes of vodka and some more vodka,' said Max, licking her
lips.

'And there's deffo a big splash of vodka in there too.'

'It's called a "Viva Las Vegas",' said the waitress, overhearing
them.

'Ah, that'll be because they're going to honeymoon in Vegas,'
said someone behind Max, picking up what the waitress said.
'How very sweet.'

Violet caught Bel's eye across the room and waved, but Bel
didn't wave back. Her face was like granite.

Bel saw lovely Violet wave to her and she turned away, pretending she hadn't seen her. She had to keep away from nice
people and carry on mixing with the odious Liam and her step-
family and all the Bishop side of the clan that she didn't know all
that well and wanted to know even less. Only that way would she
stay true to her convictions.

'Where's the cake?' asked Vanoushka, looking around. 'Surely
she hasn't cocked that up as well.'

'I'm sure she hasn't,' said Faye, feeling terribly guilty now that
she hadn't insisted on helping. Bel must have been under such
pressure to arrange everything, and had so obviously failed.

'I'm starving,' said Martin. 'When's the lobster happening?'

Bel was posing for snaps for those guests who had brought
their own cameras. Unlike Shaden, she wasn't relishing any attention from the lenses, merely enduring it. Then she excused
herself and slipped away to the ladies' toilet, picking the furthest
away of the ten cubicles. She sat on the seat, letting her head drop

into her hands. It seemed to weigh a ton, as if all the hurt and anger in there were solid rocks jarring against each other. She felt the jabbing of her fifth stress-headache in two months.

The pain in her temple momentarily weakened her. She wasn't sure she could do this any more. *This is recoverable, if you want to back out,* said a soft, seductive voice inside her. *No one need ever know if you change paths now.* She was married. Her name was officially Belinda Bishop – even though anyone looking closely enough to decipher her scrawl would see she had signed the register *Bellend Bastard* . . . The voice continued: *This could all be over now.*

Then she heard Vanoushka enter the toilet.

'I just hope the meal makes up for it.' She thought she was whispering, but the acoustics of the toilet carried the sound down to Bel. 'If I'd known it was going to be so hideous, I wouldn't have bought something new. What a waste of Dior.'

'Awful, isn't it?' giggled the second voice, instantly recognizable by the put-on rounded vowels: Shaden. 'And what *is* that dress she's got on?'

'Christ knows. It looks like a sack. You are the belle of the ball today, my darling. I bet Richard wishes he was marrying you. Hold my handbag while I have a pee.'

Bel's resolve recovered instantly on hearing that. She waited until she heard a flush, the taps turn on and off, the hand-dryer finish blowing and the door close. Then she stood, ready for the final act: *Fight the Good Fight. She'd show them how un-fucking-sweetly a Candy girl fought back, all right.*

Let battle commence.

Chapter 16

Much to Martin's delight, people were starting to filter into the dining room. His stomach was groaning so loudly it sounded like a one-man brass band. The sight of the waitresses bringing the starter was the gastric equivalent of music to his ears. Mysteriously the cake was covered with a fine white cloth on a separate table in the corner of the room.

The first course was a hearty soup with thin slices of toasted baguette floating in it, topped with melted cheese.

'This is lovely,' said Richard, sinking his teeth into the bread. Then the full force of the cheese hit his taste buds and he wheezed as if he'd just been punched in the gut by Muhammad Ali. 'Goodness, that cheese is strong. What is it?'

'It's called Stinking Bishop,' beamed Bel. 'Isn't it the best find?'

Judging from all the coughing going on around the room, others were finding it equally as brutal on their internal workings.

Vanoushka was less than impressed.

'Soup? Could there be a more ordinary starter?' she moaned to Martin, who nodded in agreement, although he collared the waitress for a second helping of it. She hoped Belinda was never going to take up wedding planning as a career. Especially as the main course was nothing out of the ordinary either. Coq au vin.

'I always think that coq au vin sounds like someone's had sex in a van,' laughed Bel to Richard. She was staring at him, unblinking. 'Don't you?'

Inside him something stirred and he felt a pang of alarm. Why would she say that? Did he detect a hint of knowledge in her words? Then again, coq au vin *did* sound like someone having sex in van. He was being paranoid and as such he gave himself a mental slap.

'Yes, it does,' and he laughed heartily. 'I'd never thought of it before.'

'I know it's a bit naff, but it is the chef's speciality here,' Bel went on. Not that she could eat much of it as her insides were churning.

Then the main-course plates were taken away and strawberry tarts were served. Richard had just stuck his fork into the pastry when Bel asked him, 'What do you think of the strawberry tart, darling?'

'It's really lovely,' and he winked. 'I like a bit of tart. I hope you've got something very tarty on under that gown.'

Bel placed her hand on her dress, where her heart was. 'Under here,' she said with her sexiest lopsided grin, 'is something very wild and wicked especially for you.'

As the dessert plates were being collected, Bel stole a look across at her friends. She noticed that there was an empty space next to Violet; Glyn hadn't come. Well, at least that was one less witness. Poor bloke, though. He obviously couldn't face a crowd of strangers. Depression was a terrible thing. She had felt herself standing at the edge of a very deep, dark chasm recently and the only way she could pull herself back from it was to plan, scheme, hate.

The waitresses were gearing up to serve coffees, which meant the speeches were minutes away from starting. Bel's heart was like a battering ram against her chest wall. She felt light-headed, slightly sick. She was seeing the world in slow motion: Liam standing, people starting to applaud as he called for order.

It was a typical Liam speech. As shiny and slimy as a snail trail. With a big beaming smile he talked about his sister-in-law being a beautiful bride, even though Bel knew that he must have been crying inside to have to adhere to that rule of protocol. He relished telling how she had tamed his wild brother. Bel wasn't fooled. She was waiting for Liam to stick a big infected needle in her day.

'So please raise your glasses to the bride and groom. Richard and Sh— Bel.'

He turned to Bel and the superior look on his face told her that he *knew* too. That split-second shushing sound wasn't a mistake. She didn't hear the toast. Her ears were full of her own heartbeat; it was the sound of an iron ball thundering down the barrel of a cannon, dangerous and unstoppable. Again in slow motion she watched her dad begin to stand, and she shot to her feet first. She waved at him to take his seat again.

It's still not too late, Bel. Say 'thank you for coming' and sit down.

'Bel, what are you doing?' This from Richard, tugging at her hand. She ignored him.

'Ladies and gentlemen. Just before you hear any more, I'd like to say thank you all for coming.'

There's still time, Bel. Sit down and this will all be over. No one need ever know.

But a stronger, harder, nastier voice inside answered.

Fuck off, sensible thought. This day has been too long in coming. You *sit down.*

'And thank you to Liam for a wonderful speech.' She flashed a smile of such sweetness at Liam she hoped it would give him instant diabetes. 'You truly are a master of the spoken turd, sorry, I mean "word".'

A titter of unsure laughter rippled around the room in the pause that Bel then left.

'I just want to tell you all how much I love Richard,' said Bel. The room was filled with 'aws'. 'And even though we aren't strictly related, how much I adored my cousin Shaden, my lovely bridesmaid.'

She raised her glass in Shaden's direction and then drank from it.

Violet didn't like this at all. Vibes were missiling from Bel and none of them were good ones.

'I say "adore-*d*" because it's past tense. I adore-*d* her until I found out that she was shagging my fiancé.'

Oh God.

Bel didn't hear the gasps. She didn't even notice Richard stand in front of her and try to reason with her, persuade her to leave the table and come outside to calm down – or sober up. But Bel was stone-cold sober and he couldn't have budged her with Semtex. She was anchored to the spot with the three tons of hurt that had been stored inside her for two months, fermenting until they were rotten and stinking and toxic.

'And according to the texts and emails I found, shagging, amongst other places, in the back of one of my dad's vans, which she borrowed from him apparently to move some furniture. So here for your amusement is one of those many emails that passed between them.'

As she fumbled to pull out a folded sheet of paper from up her sleeve, Richard again tried to pull her to her seat but she pushed him off. Bel's voice was strong as she began to read, but the hands holding the sheet of paper were shaking. Some of her fingers had long false French-manicured nails on them; she had bitten the others off in the last half-hour, ripping them from the nail bed. They thrummed but she was glad of the pain because it was another factor which helped to drive her on.

'"Dear Big Dicky".' No one even tittered. '"It's done, thank God, so you don't have to worry any more – and neither do I. The B-word will never know. Had a few cramps and unpleasantness, but it was a small price to pay. Silly us, getting that carried away. Good job I did an early test and we didn't leave it any later. Can't wait to see you tonight. I'm going to eat you for supper – and breakfast."' Long-stored-up fat salt-filled tears started to plop down Bel's cheeks on to the snow-white tablecloth.

'Oh God,' said Violet. 'Max, should we go to her?' They stood up.

'No one move, please,' said Bel with the aggression of a severely hacked-off headmistress heading up an assembly full of coughing children. The room was locked in an excruciatingly uncomfortable vacuum of silence. Everyone and everything with a mouth held it agape.

Bel picked up her champagne glass.

'"The B-word" would like to raise a toast: to the Stinking Bishop and the Strawberry Tart,' she said and sank the contents in one. 'May you both rot in hell.' With one fluid movement that a bullfighter would have been proud of, Bel reached over and whisked the cloth off the cake. A beautiful three-tiered pure-white confection was revealed and on the very top layer were three figures – a golden-haired bridesmaid in red with her knickers down, leaning over a table, a groom with his trousers to the floor behind her – and a short spiky-haired bride walking off with her fingers raised behind her in a large V.

Richard reached for her hand. Bel removed it with a mighty jerk. Then she marched out of the reception at the speed of Usain Bolt approaching the finishing line.

There was stunned silence for a few seconds before a low hiss of gossip broke and people sprang into action. Faye ran out first, followed by Violet and Max, then Trevor, who would have been in the lead had his knee not been playing up. They were all just in time to see the waiting taxi zoom off.

'Jesus,' whistled Max.

'I knew something wasn't right,' said Violet, on the edge of tears.

'Excuse me,' called a young man coming from behind the reception desk. 'I've been asked to give out these envelopes. The bride . . .'

Max leaped over. There were two – one for Max and Violet, one for her dad.

Max ripped open the envelope and held it out so Violet could read it too.

Dear M & V,
Despite what you've just seen, I'm okay. I wish I
hadn't invited you to the wedding. I wouldn't have,
had we met a month later. I need to be by myself for
a bit so don't worry. Don't try to ring me; the
mobile will be switched off. I'll be in touch with you
about your wedding, Max. I won't let you down. I'll
be there for the dress fitting (if you decide to have
me).
I'm so so sorry for putting you to any expense or
trouble. I just had to do this.
Bel xx

A devastated Trevor read his out so Faye could share the
words. There were a lot of apologies in the first paragraph.
Then:

Dad, tell everyone I've ripped up their cheques. I
shan't be cashing them. I'm sorry they've all
splashed out on outfits, but no doubt the gossip
value will be worth it. I'll be in touch. Don't worry
about me. Sorry to leave you to sort this out but,
rather selfishly, I hate Richard and Shaden far
more than I love anyone else at the moment.

Chapter 17

Bel climbed out of the taxi and headed straight for the car waiting outside her apartment with her suitcase already packed in the boot. Also in the car was a box of food that she had hastily collected in the last few days, although she had no appetite for any of it. It contained stuff that didn't take much thought to eat: Pot Noodles, tins of soup and rice pudding, coffee, tea, some powdered milk, a family pack of KitKats. There was no time to go into the flat and change her dress; it was the first place they would all come looking for her. At least, she knew her dad would. Richard – she wasn't sure about. She couldn't face any of them yet. She couldn't even face herself in the mirror. She bunched herself and her dress into the front seat of her Merc, let out two huge lungfuls of air and then stuck the key in the ignition.

She wanted to be alone with her brain, a few boxes of Kleenex and a big fat bottle of red wine for a couple of days. And that is why she set off for Emily, the larger of the two adjoined Bronte Cottages that her dad owned out on the edge of the West Yorkshire moors. She had always had a set of keys for them, although she hoped her dad didn't remember that.

Emily was a substantially sized open-plan snug-as-a-bug cottage, with oak panelling on the walls, an inglenook fireplace and a darling bedroom upstairs with white-painted eaves. Next door, Charlotte was a tiny doll's house of a place. And next to that was

Anne, an old stable that her dad had always meant to convert, but never had. Some moody, rainy moors were just what she needed. Total bitter isolation.

Damn, she suddenly realized that she'd left the wine on the worktop in the kitchen. She squealed up beside a shop called I Guess That's Why They Call it the Booze and ignored all the sideways looks she received as an angry bride buying two bottles of Koonunga Hill on a £9 special deal.

The light was falling early when she arrived at Bronte Cottages. Grumpy, dark clouds were gathering in the skies. She twisted the car up the hill and parked, then slid the key into Emily's slatted wooden door. She planned to throw herself on to the big squashy sofa there and crack open one of the bottles of red wine. She wouldn't even care if it spilled over the cheap frock because before she went to bed that night she intended to rip it off and incinerate it in the wood-burning stove. She grabbed her suitcase in one hand and expertly carried the two bottles of wine by their necks in the other.

The cottage felt incredibly warm when she entered, which was strange because it was so old that it took a few hours to lose the chill after it had been standing empty for longer than a day. More unusually, the kitchen light was on. And whoever had been here last hadn't done a good job of tidying up because there were newspapers spread on the table.

She put the bottles of wine down and gathered up the papers. As she glanced at the front page she saw it had a picture of the prime minister getting an egg thrown at his back. Hang on, she thought. That happened yesterday.

She checked the date on the newspaper. She barely had time to absorb that it really was today's paper when a boom of a man's voice behind her made her jump.

'Who the bloody hell are you?'

She turned to see a tall bare-chested man with wet darkest-brown hair and a towel wrapped round his waist. Had she not been in a man-hating mood her pupils would have dilated and danced all over that chest. As it was, she just saw a man. A bastard with a penis.

'Who the bloody hell are you?' the bride threw back.

The man scratched his head. 'Am I dreaming this? Are you real? Or am I the victim of some voodoo spell?'

'If you don't get out of this cottage in five minutes, I'll ring the police. They don't take kindly to squatters in this neck of the woods,' said Bel indignantly.

'I'm not a squatter. I've rented this cottage. So I'll be obliged if you carried on your fancy-dress party in another house.'

'You're renting it? From whom?' cried Bel. Could this day get any worse? 'For how long?'

'Just hang on a moment,' said the man, dripping water all over the wooden floorboards. 'I don't have to answer questions from you. And how did you get in, anyway?'

'And I don't have to answer questions from you,' snarled Bel, grabbing her bottles of wine and clutching them to her chest.

'No, all you have to do is turn round and go out of the door before I ring the police to come and take you to a nice cosy cell.' He took a step forwards and Bel took one backwards.

'Don't you dare lay a finger on me,' she warned. 'This is my family's cottage and you are trespassing.'

'I've told you,' the man's eyes narrowed in anger. 'I am renting this from a friend of a friend.'

'Called?'

'Trevor Candy, if you must know. And I'm renting it for as long as I want – it's an open agreement. Satisfied?'

'Oh,' said Bel. She didn't know her dad ever rented out the cottage. As far as she knew, it had been standing empty for over a year, which is why it seemed the perfect place to escape to.

'Oh indeed.' The man had his arms crossed now and was tapping his foot, waiting for her to go.

'Well, I'm sorry for interrupting you.' Bel sounded anything but sorry. Her mouth might have said 'sorry' but the tone said 'bollocks to you'.

He nodded as if accepting the apology that both of them knew wasn't an apology at all.

'I'll go, then, Mr . . .' She left a space for him to supply his name. He didn't. When she looked at his eyes they were travelling up and down her wedding dress as if trying to work out what her story was.

'Yes, it's a wedding dress,' snapped Bel. 'A real one, not a fancy dress one. Okay?' She turned on her heel and, carrying wine bottles and suitcase, had to struggle alone with the front door because he didn't come to her assistance.

Shit and double shit. That wasn't in the plan at all. She could stay in tiny, freezing, uncomfortable Charlotte or – better still – get a hotel for the night and assess the situation again in the morning. Then she noticed the front passenger tyre on her car. Flat. Treble shit. She'd thought she could 'feel the road' for the last few miles. Well, wasn't that just the bloody icing on the cake? She thought disasters like this happened only in rubbish 'B' horror films.

'What next?' she screamed at the sky. 'What bloody buggering bastard next?'

There was a grumble above and a big spot of rain landed slap bang in her eye. A rainstorm had broken. That's what was next. Seconds later the heavens opened.

There was nothing for it but to take the second key and open up Charlotte. Bel scurried towards it as a spear of lightning shot through the sky. Charlotte was totally freezing when she opened the door. She could feel the cold air rush past her to go outside to warm up. At least it was clean – because her dad employed a woman in the nearby village to come in every so often and keep on top of the dust. Not that there was that much to clean in Charlotte.

The ground floor of the cottage consisted of one room only. There was a two-seater battered leather sofa and an extendable coffee table – which doubled up as a dining table – in the front half; a small run of cupboards and worktop, a two-ring hob and a tiny round sink constituted a kitchen at the back. There was a store cupboard under the stairs, which rose to a bedroom big enough for a single bed, a wardrobe and a bedside table, and a bathroom so compact that even an estate agent would have trouble describing it as anything other than a shoebox. This was bijou living to an nth degree, although apparently it once housed a family of eight. They must have had to sit on each other constantly, thought Bel. And they certainly wouldn't have been able to do any hokey-cokeys at Christmas.

The trouble was that all the sheets and towels, pillows, quilts and pans were in Emily – stuff that she hadn't brought with her because she hadn't even considered she'd be staying in this mouse hole. And there wasn't even a damned television in Charlotte either, only a small radio next to a kettle so old it boiled in Latin.

As she stepped over the threshold, she heard a tear. The bottom of her dress had caught on a splinter on the door. It appeared the dress-tearing ritual had begun itself.

Chapter 18

'Well,' said Stuart, and he said all that needed to be said in that one word. His eyebrows were stuck up in the ceiling fans. They had good company because a lot of others were lodged up there too.

There was a variety of activity going on. Richard had made a hasty exit with the seedy Liam, and a tearful Shaden was led out sandwiched protectively between her mother and father. Vanoushka's free arm was primed in position to give a Bruce Lee chop to move anyone out of the way who invaded their personal space. Richard's enormous-hatted mother had a 'told you so' smirk on her face as she conversed animatedly with her sandy-moustached husband.

Trevor seemed in shock and wet-eyed. He walked back into the reception with Faye trotting at his side.

'Erm, ladies and gentlemen, I don't know what to say,' he said, his voice trembling. 'I think I can safely say that the celebrations are at an end. Er . . .' He looked round him at the sea of faces and froze. Faye stepped forward and took over.

'Please, everyone, feel free to stay and collect yourself, and if you want a cup of tea or a brandy or anything, please order it at the bar and we will pay for it, of course. Trevor and I are so sorry you've been inconvenienced. We can't say any more than that at the present time. Thank you for coming and please bear with us.'

'It's gone straight through to Bel's voicemail,' said Violet, clicking off her phone.

'Did you expect anything else?' said Max.

'No, but I thought I'd give it a go.'

'Do you want to drive over to her flat?' asked Stuart.

'She won't be there,' said Max. 'Bel has obviously had all this arranged for a long time. I expect that's why she didn't wear her mother's dress.'

'Or spend money on a photographer and flowers. Poor Bel,' sighed Violet.

The betrayal must have crippled her. And to find out that Shaden had had an abortion too, casually flushing away something that Bel would never have. Not to mention the disrespect that Richard had shown her by not using protection while having sex with Shaden. And fancy allowing lovely Bel to be referred to merely as 'the B-word'. On so many fronts he had crushed the woman he purported to love. Violet despaired of how cruel people could be to each other. She knew only too well that feeling of utter desolation. The last boyfriend she had before Glyn had dragged her heart through the mud and stamped on it. She wished Bel had felt able to confide in her. Then again, Violet knew that some things were just too painful to share with anyone; they were burdens to be carried alone.

'I'm glad we're having a less complicated wedding,' said Stuart.

Max bit down on her lip. Bel hadn't really done Max's cause any favours here. Not that Max could blame her for that.

'Well, it hasn't exactly been a typical church wedding,' snapped Max, becoming a little shiny-eyed with frustration. 'Everything was lovely until . . . until . . .'

'Until the bride revealed her husband was shagging her cousin?' Stuart supplied, pulling at his shirt collar. These designer clothes that Max bought him always seemed on the tight side. They didn't fit his body shape half as well as a shirt he would have picked from the rail in Burtons. He figured it would be okay now to loosen his tie and the top button.

'So what do we do now?'

'I don't know,' said Violet. 'Go home. I feel so helpless. I want to do something, but I don't know what.'

'I notice the groom ran off as if his arse was on fire,' tutted Max.

'Be fair, Max. He probably went to see if he could find Belinda,' said Stuart.

'Convenient way to exit quickly, I suppose. Under the guise of concern,' put in Violet. Poor, poor Bel. She hoped she didn't leave it too long to get in contact.

'I just want to get hold of that bloody Shaden and kick her teeth in,' growled Max. 'What a complete cow. Her own cousin too.'

It must be the worst feeling in the world to find out how little you know about someone you loved and trusted; to realize that you didn't really know them that well, after all.

Violet drove Max and Stuart home. They lived out in a hamlet off the Manchester Road, with views of the moody Pennines.

Stuart hated living out here in the sticks. He was a town-boy, always had been. He loathed living on such a new poncy estate miles from his mates and his parents. It didn't matter to him that they had his and hers nice cars to drive anywhere they wanted with ease and comfort. He would rather have lived closer to town and caught the bus to where he needed to go.

'You have such a lovely house,' sighed Violet, pulling up beside it. She would have loved a house like that. Even though, as Bel had just proved, money did not necessarily make you happy.

'Well, when you make your millions from Carousel, you'll be able to buy one that makes mine look like a shoebox,' said Max, giving Violet a kiss on the cheek.

'Drive carefully,' Stuart warned, leaning over to kiss her also. 'You get some right nutters on that top road.'

He liked Violet on sight. Fancied her a teeny bit too, if he was honest. She was fragile and vulnerable and she appealed to the macho protective part inside him that Max had rendered redundant because she never needed to be protected from anything; she was Boudicca incarnate. Capable of fighting all her own battles with no need to call on the testosterone-filled for aid.

Max opened the door and picked up the single piece of mail. An official white envelope. She slit it open with her fingernail, read it and then promptly burst into tears.

'They've got to do essential maintenance work on the town hall for a month,' she said. 'Our wedding's been moved to the building on Fieldgate. That's all I bloody need.'

It was the cherry on the sad day's cake. The town hall had a beautiful facade with the high clock tower and the run of stone steps rising between beautifully kept flower beds. As civil weddings go, it was a lovely place to have one, but the horrible Fieldgate building looked like an old loony bin. 'What a horrible day,' she sobbed.

Stuart stepped towards her and gathered her into his arms. Max wasn't easily moved to tears and a big part of him was pleased that he was needed to comfort her.

'Look—' oh God he couldn't believe he was about to say this, but he was softened by her sudden and rare vulnerability – 'if we can find a church that's free and will have us at such short notice, we'll book it. Will that make you feel better?' He didn't fancy getting married in Fieldgate either. It was once an old hospital where he'd had his tonsils out when he was six. A totally depressing place that he couldn't think of without evoking the smell of strong chemicals and an underlying hint of wee. It didn't have the best memories for him.

Max brightened instantly as if a big cloud had been booted out of the way.

'I'm warning you, Max. That's as big as this wedding gets. Just us, parents and Luke. Nothing's changed but the venue.'

'Can Violet and Bel come too? ' asked Max, dabbing her eyes.

She had quickly cottoned on to the fact that if she sniffed pathetically, Stuart lowered his guard.

'I suppose. But that really is as far as we go. I mean it.'

'Of course,' said Max, careful not to add, 'I promise'. There would be a church free because she'd find one. Max would have one built if she had to.

Chapter 19

Violet drove the long way home, via Maltstone. Glyn wasn't expecting her for hours and she felt as if she'd been let off a leash. There weren't even any missed calls from him. She decided to take herself off to the Maltstone Garden Centre coffee shop and delay going home until she really had to.

There were temporary roadworks on the main road and she had to pull up and wait at the side of the White Wedding bridal shop. Freya was in the window adjusting a dress on a mannequin. Violet did a double-take and knew she'd have to go in and take a closer look.

When the lights turned green, she turned right and parked at the side of the shop.

She pushed open the door to White Wedding and the bell tinkled above her head. Freya had a large pin cushion on her arm as she arranged the dress.

'Hello, again,' she smiled. 'I'm glad you came back. I have some new stock.'

'That dress in the window,' said Violet quite breathlessly. 'It's beautiful.'

'Yes, isn't it?' said Freya. 'It's no trouble to take it out, if you want to try it on.'

'Could I?' asked Violet.

Freya leaned into the window and undressed the mannequin.

The dress was ivory silk with three-quarter sleeves and tiny peach rosebuds decorating the scooped neck.

'It's a vintage dress,' she said. 'It's just been dry-cleaned.'

'It's beautiful,' gasped Violet. 'Is it terribly expensive?'

'Fifteen hundred pounds,' replied Freya.

Violet's balloon of hope popped. There was no way she could afford half of that, so it wasn't any good even trying to bargain.

'Try it on,' said Freya, holding it out.

'There's no point really,' said Violet.

'Indulge me,' Freya urged.

'I shouldn't,' said Violet, but her hands were reaching out for it.

'Try it on.'

Violet took the gown. It felt much heavier than it looked. She pulled back the curtain to the changing room and slipped out of her blue suit, which she had bought especially for Bel's wedding. She stepped into the dress and Freya called her, asking if she needed any help fastening it up. She did.

As Freya zipped up the back, Violet stared in the mirror and saw how beautiful the dress looked on her.

'Stunning,' said Freya, clasping her hands together in delight.

'I wish I hadn't put it on now,' sighed Violet. She knew this was *the* dress. It wasn't like anything she had fantasized about, but it warmed up the tones of her skin and made the best of her slender figure.

'I can hire it to you for the day if you really want to wear it,' offered Freya, watching as a smile took over Violet's lips.

'Would you? Would you really?'

'One hundred and fifty pounds,' said Freya.

'I can afford that,' said Violet excitedly. 'Can I book it?'

'Consider it yours,' said Freya.

Glyn was on the laptop when she got back to the flat. He bounced to his feet and came over for a hug.

'You're back early,' he said, delighted.

'Well, the wedding was ... cut short,' she said, for want of a better expression. She recounted the story in a factual ungossipy way, while he listened intently.

'Blimey,' he said eventually. 'What can one say to that?' But he looked more pleased to have Violet home than concerned and ready to commiserate with her about her friend's misfortune.

'Poor Bel,' she said wearily. 'She must have been going through hell. Having to arrange a wedding with so much hurt burning inside her.'

Glyn squeezed Violet's arm. 'It hasn't put you off, has it?'

'No, no,' said Violet. 'Of course not.'

'Our wedding won't be a disaster like that,' he smiled. 'Because I would never be unfaithful to you.' His hand threaded into her hair and drew her face towards him. She felt his tongue push between her lips and she pulled away, laughing.

'Give up, you softie,' she said. 'I'm going to open a bottle of wine. I need a drink. Shall I get out a glass for you too?'

'Why did you pull away, Letty?' he asked. 'You do that a lot.'

'I do not,' replied Violet vehemently. But she knew she did. She didn't like kissing him any more. She didn't like the taste of him. She could manage this relationship when it was on a platonic footing and she tried her hardest to keep it there, but invariably it veered on to a more physical plane.

'Prove it, then. Give me a snog. Now.'

Violet leaned towards him and kissed him. She closed her eyes, aware that his were open and searching her face for evidence that she didn't enjoy kissing him. Had her eyes been open too, he would have found it.

Chapter 20

Max was ringing her ninth vicar, the Reverend James Joseph Folly. Now Stuart had agreed to a church wedding there was no time to waste. She was going to secure a booking before he changed his mind. She had left messages on the answerphones of six. Two had been very sorry but they were booked solid until November. Nine was her lucky number, she told herself. She was born on the ninth of September, weighed 9 lbs 9 oz when she was born and her first address was number nine, Fraser Street. She willed the vicar on the other end of the line to somehow respond to that coincidence at a crucial point in the cosmos.

'Good afternoon,' she said, in her best no-brooking sales voice when he answered. 'Please can you help me? We were due to get married on the second of July in the town hall but they've moved the venue to the old hospital, which has bad memories for us. Everything was arranged for that day and I don't know what to do. Could you marry us? Please? I don't care if it's midnight. Could you do it?'

There was no answer at the end of the line. Max wondered if he'd hung up, until she heard him pottering about in the background.

'Sorry about that,' came a slightly shushing voice eventually. He sounded like the bloke from the Mr Kipling advert. 'I was just reaching for my diary. Now when did you say?'

'Saturday the second of July.'

'Next year?'

'This year.'

'Oh dear.'

'Please don't say no. I'm desperate.'

There was a pause at the end of the phone.

'What time where you thinking of,' said the vicar.

'Anytime at all.'

'Eleven o'clock in the morning?'

Max gasped. Even with all her uber confidence that was a bit of a shocker.

'Really?'

'I have had so many of these emergencies over the years that I leave a slot each week in June and July for such eventualities. You're my first taker.'

'Oh Reverend, that's amazing,' said Max. She was in such rapture that she felt light-headed and had to sit down on a nearby chair before she fell.

'I'll need to see you and your fiancé at your earliest convenience,' he said.

'Name the time and the date and we'll be there.'

Max could not keep the excitement out of her voice. She'd done it. That was surely a sign that her big fat gypsy wedding plans were fated to be the right ones.

Chapter 21

Bel was freezing. The portable electric fire gave out as much heat as a tub of Haagen Daaz. She had even put on the two-ringed electric hob to add some heat to the place. The only option was to warm herself from the inside; soup was as good a method as any. The trouble was that the tin opener was in Emily.

Luckily the wine had a screw-top. After a very long glug from the neck, she found enough inner bravado to knock loudly on Emily's door and alert the 'tenant' there to answer it.

'Who is it?' said the voice within.

'Angelina Jolie,' said Bel.

The door swung open. 'You've shrunk, Angie,' said the occupant, now wearing a black marl sweatshirt and dark-grey Nike bottoms.

Bel felt extremely short gazing up at him. Not that it fazed her.

'Could I trouble you for a quilt and a pan and a tin opener?' said Bel, trying to do a pleasant smile, although it wasn't happening very well. The rain was drenching her as she stood on the doorstep and rather ungallantly he wasn't inviting her even as far as the inside doormat. 'Charlotte isn't really equipped for anyone staying there for any length of time. Well, any longer than five minutes, if I'm honest.'

She looked beyond him and saw the log-burning stove crackling and the TV on. And there was a smell of beef stew snaking around him.

He stood there for too long deciding whether to assist this suspicious and half-tiddly rain-soaked woman in a torn wedding dress, so her arm came out to shove him out of the way.

'Whoa, there,' said the man. 'How do I know *you're* not some squatter? Or a mad woman from the village. I've paid a bond on this place. I do not want to be fined for missing implements.'

'I've told you, this is my father's house.'

'So you said. I think I ought to ring him first, to check,' said the man, taking his phone out of his pocket.

'No,' yelled Bel. 'Don't do that. I don't want anyone to know I'm here. Plus, you can't, anyway. The nearest place you'll get any mobile reception is at the bottom of the hill. And the house phone only takes incoming calls.'

'Well, until I get confirmation of who you are, you aren't having anything out of here,' said the man, crossing his arms and assuming such a stance that he filled the doorway.

'I am who I say I am,' puffed up Bel. 'I just don't want anyone to know I'm here, so if anyone happens to ring you, I'd be obliged if you say you haven't seen me.'

'I really don't want to get involved in whatever your business is.' The rude stubbly man then tried to close the door, but Bel's hand came straight out to stop that happening.

'Who's involving you? Just say you haven't seen me, if anyone asks. End of. It's not that complicated.'

'Sounds very complicated to me,' said the man, and his eyes, so dark they were almost black, swept over her. 'Jilt someone, did you?'

'None of your sodding business,' said Bel through gritted teeth. 'Now – please – a pan, a quilt and a tin opener and I'll be out of your hair. In case you haven't noticed, it's absolutely pissing down with rain and I'm soaked standing here.'

'Ask nicely.'

'What?' Bel reared.

'I said "ask nicely". Without talking to me as if I'm some sort of pleb.'

'Just give me the bloody . . .'

The door slammed in Bel's face. She growled like an angry wolf and jumped up and down in frustration.

'Doing a war dance outside my front door won't get you what you want,' she heard the man say from inside the cottage. 'Or is it a rain dance? If so, that's working.'

Bel took a slow deep breath and counted to ten. Then another ten because the first ten didn't do much good. She rapped lightly on the door and waited.

'Who is it?' came the voice from within.

'It's me. From next door,' said Bel with faux sweetness.

The black-eyed man appeared again at the door.

'What do you want?' he asked, with a raise of two innocently arched eyebrows.

'I wonder if you'd be so kind as to lend me a pan, a quilt and a tin opener. Thank you,' said Bel, with a very wet smile. She could only imagine what she looked like by now. Rivers of black mascara had left black dots on her dress and her hair would be as flat as a fart.

'Certainly,' he replied, with the same painful rictus smile. 'Where are they kept? Do come in and tell me.'

Bel stepped across the threshold and wiped her feet on the coconut mat. Then she crossed to the far corner of the room, where there was a large chest dressed as an occasional table with a cover on it and a lamp. She took them off, opened the chest and helped herself to a spare quilt, pillow and sheet. Meanwhile, he had located the tin opener in the drawer and taken a pan from the cupboard.

'Here you go,' he said.

'Thank you,' said Bel, not sounding the slightest bit grateful.

'You've ripped your dress,' he said.

'I know and – guess what? – I couldn't give a bugger,' said Bel, striding out and shutting the door hard behind her.

Bel locked herself in Charlotte and took a tin of vegetable soup out of her box of supplies. She wasn't hungry in the slightest, though, as she turned the tin opener round the rim and poured the contents into the pan and heated it. In the small cupboard she found a huge bowl and a pint glass. She half-filled the latter with wine and necked it in one. It didn't make her feel any better. She turned the soup off when it started bubbling and transferred it to the bowl.

By the time she had finished it, the mascara blobs had been joined by splashes of orange soup and Australian red wine. Bel sat on the sofa and picked up the skirt to examine the tear. She slipped her hands inside it then pulled them apart, and the material split with a satisfying rip. Five seconds later she was locked in a dress-destroying frenzy, shredding the material between her bare hands, yanking wildly on the sleeves until they were dragged away from the rest of the gown and thrown across the room. She tugged at the neck and felt the zip at the back split. The tattered dress fell to the floor and she picked it up and wildly tore where she could at the net underskirt, swearing as she kicked it around the room. Then she slumped to the sofa in her underwear, the fight in her spent. All the strength that had carried her through the past two months was now depleted and the walls holding back all her hurt and pain crumbled in on themselves. Bel's body curled into a ball and she dragged the quilt over her. In the sanctuary of her fifteen-tog nest, she cried and cried and cried.

Chapter 22

Glyn was humming in the kitchen as he cooked breakfast for them the next morning. His fry-ups were getting bigger, and if she didn't finish off her plate his lip curled like a disappointed child's.

'Didn't you like it?' he would say if she left more than a mushroom. He wouldn't mention the fact that he'd put enough on her plate to feed a small emergent nation for a week. She wouldn't have been so cruel as to mention that he had outgrown all the trousers in his wardrobe and so slopped around in baggy lounge pants that made him look enormous. Instead she just hinted that so much fried food really wasn't good for anyone. Violet wasn't a food fascist – how could she be when she made ice cream for a living? – but Glyn grazed constantly on crisps and biscuits and sweets. They weren't treats; they constituted most of his staple diet.

'Breakfast is ready,' he trilled.

'Coming.' Violet sprayed on her perfume and went into the kitchen. This morning's effort was a belt-buster.

'I can't eat all this, Glyn,' she tried to say kindly. He'd doubled up on everything. 'I won't fit into the shop if I finish that lot off.'

His cheery little smile faded.

'I'm not saying it doesn't look delicious,' said Violet. 'I'm just saying there's a bit too much for me on the plate. You know I'm trying to keep in shape for the wedding.'

He brightened at the thought of the wedding. Behind him the kettle whistled and he leaped up to brew some tea.

Violet sat at the table and tucked into one of the four rashers of bacon. That satiated her appetite but to appease him she ate a little of the black pudding, half the egg, the end of a sausage and a couple of mushrooms. She pushed the remainder around on her plate, trying to make it look as if she hadn't left as much as she had. As she used to do with school dinners.

'Which one do you want?' asked Glyn, holding up the Sunday newspapers that the paper boy had delivered to their mail slot downstairs.

'You have first choice,' said Violet, picking up her plate and going over to the bin in the corner. 'I'm having a couple of hours in the shop.'

'But it's Sunday, Letty.'

'Just an hour or two,' said Violet. 'The decorator is arriving tomorrow and I want to tidy up before he comes.'

'Oh.' Glyn's face made Eeyore's look like Frank Carson's.

'It's only a couple of hours.'

'What does he look like?' Glyn asked the question casually enough, but Violet knew that his insecurities had been cranked up by mention of the painter.

'He's just a young gangly kid,' she mirrored the casualness. 'Student-type. Arty-farty.'

'Right.'

'The sooner I get everything done, the sooner I can move in and start making some money.'

'If you say so.'

He had resorted to sulky monosyllables now, which Violet had no patience for. She grabbed her handbag, breezed out of the flat and said that she'd see him later.

She knew he would be waving her off through the window, but she kept her eyes firmly on the road as she drove off.

'Oh God, help me,' she said as she rounded the corner. Because He was the only one who could.

*

There was a bride special in the *Sunday World* supplement. Max almost dropped her yoghurt with glee when she saw it.

Stuart looked over her shoulder and virtually heard the cogs turning in Max's head.

'Max McBride, I know you. Don't you dare be getting any daft ideas about turning up to church in a crinoline,' and he kissed her cheek. Max chuckled along with Stuart but gulped inside.

It was a good job he hadn't seen the list in her diary of all the things she had to get him to change his mind about. First, she needed him to upgrade his suit and for that she would enlist the help of his best man and oldest friend, Luke. Then there was the matter of a slight tweak on the number of guests they would invite; after all, it would be daft to have the whole church to themselves. Then a reception, because it was only right and proper to feed all those guests. And you couldn't have a church without flowers either – Bel's wedding proved that one. The church was naked without them, totally without atmosphere. And bridesmaids, and a palatial cake. And she couldn't arrive at church in an enormous frock in just an ordinary 'Barry's Taxi'. It would have to be a stretch limousine or – even better – a coach and horses. Max was gripped by a momentary panic at such an impossible task, but then again, Max had always been known as 'Max'll fix it' – they'd even made her a fake Jim'll Fix It badge once at a conference – because if Max couldn't bend a will and get her own way, no one could. Looking at Stuart, now sitting across the kitchen table, still with that rare defiant look in his eyes, even Max knew she had her work cut out.

Chapter 23

Bel woke up with the hangover from hell and found she was cuddling an empty bottle of wine. She opened her eyelids and the thick belt of pain in the front of her head thrummed even more, then she closed them again and nestled back into the quilt.

Someone knocked on the door with a big fist.

'Bugger off,' said Bel from her cocoon. But the knocking didn't stop.

'Hang on,' she said, pulling herself up to a sitting position. There was a big iron weight in her head that prevented her from doing that quickly. 'I said "hang on",' she shouted at the door when it rattled again in its casing.

She was wearing only her knickers as sometime during the night she had unhooked her bra and placed it on the coffee table. She pulled the quilt around her and waddled to the door. She didn't even think, or care, to check what she looked like in the mirror. What opened the door to her renting neighbour wasn't a pretty sight.

His fist was raised to knock once again as she threw open the door. He really wasn't the most patient of fellows.

'Yes. Can I help you, Mr . . .'

Again he didn't supply his name. She'd just have to call him knobhead, then.

'The tin opener. Could I have it back, please?' She saw his eyes drift to the ball of shredded dress on the floor. But she didn't give a damn what conclusions he might draw from it.

'Yes, I suppose,' she said and pin-stepped to the sink. When she returned with the tin opener, she held it out as far as she could without letting go of the quilt and giving him an impromptu floorshow.

'Thank you,' he said, and he turned away.

'Absolute pleasure,' she said.

'Oh and your father called me on the house phone,' he said, just before the door fully closed. 'He said it was a long shot but had I seen a "lady" of your description. I told him I hadn't seen anyone.'

'Most kind,' she said, ignoring the sarcasm he attached to the word 'lady'.

'By the way, I'd appreciate it if that's the last of my involvement in your family squabbles,' he said. 'I came here for isolation, not to practise any skills of duplicity . . .'

'Yeah, join the club,' said Bel, slamming the door. The cheek of the man. She'd only asked him for a quilt, a pan and a tin opener, which happened to be her family's quilt, pan and tin opener, actually. And not to mention to anyone that he'd seen her. It was hardly asking him to forge a passport for her and smuggle her over to Cuba.

She wondered what his story was and why he wanted to be here in the middle of nowhere. Then again, it was quite obvious he didn't have many social skills. Living a hermit existence was probably better for both him and the world.

She listened to some music on the rubbish radio while she made herself a coffee and hunted for her charger. Even though her phone was switched off, the light was flashing to say it was running out of juice. She couldn't find it anywhere. She couldn't actually remember packing it. And there she was, thinking she'd been well organized.

There was a universal phone charger upstairs in Emily, if Bel could but get to it. She wasn't going to knock on the door and ask Mr Stroppy Git for it. She would sneak in and steal it at the first opportunity – he'd be none the wiser.

She took some Nurofen and sat in the silence waiting for them to kick in. The only sound was the rhythmic tick of the old clock on the wall, which began to lull her back to sleep. Then the sound of a car revving up jerked her rudely awake. She sprang to the window just in time to see her miserable sod of a neighbour's Range Rover driving out of sight. The nearest shop was a ten-minute drive away, which would give her ample time to get into Emily and take what she needed.

Quickly, she grabbed her jeans, bra and a top, threw her feet into some shoes and slipped out of the back door, taking the bunch of keys with her. She opened up the rear door of Emily and stole in. She nearly tripped over a briefcase, which had gold initials under the handle: DR DR. Bel wondered if he was a doctor, or had a stutter where lettering was concerned. Anyway, she'd muse about that later as she currently had a job to do. She went straight up into the larger of the two bedrooms and into the corner where there was a narrow 'glory hole' cupboard. There on the top shelf was a shoebox full of bits and bobs such as fuses and the charger she needed. She took it out, put the box back and made sure the cupboard door was fully shut so as not to arouse suspicion. He couldn't possibly have told that she had been in his bedroom. Mission complete.

She was safely back in Charlotte a good fifteen minutes before he returned. By which time Bel had charged up the phone sufficiently to write a text to her dad to reassure him that she was fine and staying in a hotel down south, then one each to Violet and Max.

Just to let you know that I'm really okay. I still need some time out. No one can find me where I am. I know you'll both feel helpless but don't let this spoil your own wedding arrangements. Sorry again. Will be in touch very soon, B x

Bel walked to the bottom of the hill where the small curling private road met the main road to the moors. It was the nearest point where there was any phone reception. When she saw that her outbox was now empty, she quickly turned off her phone because it had already started buzzing with messages received and she really didn't want to read any of them at the moment.

It was raining yet again. Fat drops that were so big they were hitting the ground and splashing back up. She was soggy by the time she had walked up the hill. She sneered at her perfidious car with its flat tyre, then noticed that the man in Emily was looking smugly through the window at her, dry and cosy in the cottage that she should have been in. She curled her lip at him and narrowed her eyes, and only just stopped herself from giving him the Vs. Then Bel unlocked Charlotte's door and slammed it so hard she hoped the reverberations would knock something heavy off a shelf next door that would land on his head.

Her duty to her friends and dad performed, she could go back to being Greta Garbo 'vonting to be alone' for a while. Until her brain had a clue what it had done and what it was going to do now.

Violet smiled sadly when the text came through while she was sitting at the Leach family dinner table again. She would have given anything to be having a coffee with Bel and Max in the Maltstone Garden Centre coffee shop, having a laugh. Their friendship was already precious to her. Apart from them she had only one other friend in life – her cousin, Eve, and they didn't see enough of each other. Eve was probably the only person to whom Violet could have poured out her heart about the mess she was in, but the lovely Eve was grieving for her soldier fiancé, killed in Afghanistan. She had enough sorrow in her world. So going out for a gossip and a meal and wandering around White Wedding these past few weeks with Bel and Max had been so lovely, *so needed*.

Sitting here now with her future father-in-law doing a running commentary on his beef-slicing and having Joy give her disapproving looks for checking her phone at the table, Violet wished she could take a giant leap back into her past and start her adult life again. No men, more ice cream. When she had finished her course at catering college, the world really did feel like her oyster. Dreams were within her grasp but mortgages and pension-planning and dull stuff like that were miles off. And marriage was something that would happen one wonderful day when she was madly in love with a man, and he with her. Life was sweet, uncomplicated and *light*. Now she felt weighed down by chains – like a living Jacob Marley.

Chapter 24

A wave of tiredness washed over Bel as soon as the door slammed behind her. She slumped on the sofa and wrapped the quilt around her again to extract some warmth from it because she was shaking with damp cold. Even her bones felt wet. It wasn't a healthy tiredness that was pulling her down; it was a fatigue born of depression and exhaustion. Her body wanted oblivion, and she felt sniffly too. She knew that adrenaline had kept her back stiff, her body in perfect working order, her head like a polished computer ready for her big moment, and now it was no longer pumping through her, her body was seizing the opportunity to break down.

She switched on the radio just in time to hear the news on the hour – none of it good. A teenager stabbed in London, a soldier killed by a roadside bomb, someone shot dead outside a nightclub. The same old usual depressing crap. Her thoughts were grabbed by the final news item, though.

'Police in West Yorkshire are still on the alert for an escaped convict. Dr Donald Reynolds absconded from a secure hospital unit in Wakefield last Thursday afternoon. Reynolds was found guilty of stabbing six of his patients in a killing spree last January and of garrotting his wife. Fifty-six-year-old Reynolds is six foot three, with greying black hair, and has an athletic build. Members of the public are advised that Reynolds is extremely dangerous and must not be approached under any circumstances.'

Dr Donald Reynolds. *DR DR?* The initials on the briefcase? And the height and build fitted – and the hair colour, give or take a rinse with Just for Men. But no way was he fifty-six. Unless he used a super moisturizer that made him look a lot younger than his age. Or he'd had a bit of plastic surgery done. It explained why he wanted isolation. He may have lied about renting the house from her father and just broken in. He could have easily found out who owned that cottage from a casual question or two in the village. Jeez, as if life couldn't get any worse.

Of course the stroppy man next door isn't a serial killer. Get a grip, Belinda, said a stern voice in her head. But still, she got up to wedge a chair behind both doors. Just in case.

Chapter 25

Max looked at her legs before slipping on her tights for work. Not only could they do with a shave, they were also the colour of a snowman's arse. She needed to start building up that tan. No self-respecting gypsy bride would turn up looking whiter than her own frock.

Max had her own company: San Maurice. She had started it up five years ago after seeing a gap in the market for quality fake-tanning products at much lower prices than the then market leaders. She took a leap of faith, leaving a very well paid marketing job to set up by herself, and it had paid off dividends. Since then the company had branched out into bubble baths and body creams, scented sachets, drawer liners, soaps. The firm was whipping the backsides of its competitors at award ceremonies, thanks to a mix of fabulous creations and brilliant teamwork.

As soon as she got into work that morning, she asked her PA, Jess, to bring her a box of fake-tan bottles from the mezzanine. Then she put Operation Stuart's Suit into action.

Max rang Stuart's best buddy on her mobile and he picked up straight away.

'Hello, Max,' came his cheery voice down the phone. 'How's the bride-to-be doing, then?'

'Fine and dandy, Luke. Can you talk?'

'Yes, I can talk.'

'Sure? You're not in a board meeting or anything important, are you?'

'Just let me check. Nope, only me in my office. Unless you count the rubber plant.'

'I need a favour. A huge secret-squirrel favour.'

'That sounds ominous.' Luke drew in his breath but Max could detect a smile in his voice.

Luke was the MD of a huge firm dealing in property. He and Stuart had started together in the warehouse of Crabbe's Nuts and Bolts, doing Saturday jobs at fourteen, but whereas Luke's ambition had taken him to university to read business studies then on a steeply rising career path, Stuart's total non-ambition had kept him where he was, give or take the recent promotion he had earned. Not that Max cared about that. Stuart was happy doing what he was doing and she earned enough for both of them and more. But she really did admire Luke's work ethic, partly because it closely mirrored hers. He loved work. He loved to earn money and then spend it on good clothes and fast cars. But for Luke, as for Max, it wasn't the money that was the real thrill, it was sealing the chased deal; the money was just a welcome by-product of the success. How Luke Appleby remained single was anyone's guess because he was a six-foot-five hunk with very short grey-white hair (it had turned that colour in his twenties) and smiling grey eyes. He'd had many girlfriends over the years so Max knew he wasn't gay, but they never seemed to last very long.

To be honest, she'd really fancied Luke when they were all at sixth-form college together, but it was Stuart who pushed himself forward and asked her out. They'd been joined at the hip ever since. Luke had been part of her life all this time, because he and Stuart remained close, but only as a sort of honorary brother. Still, he was someone she always had a lot of time for and couldn't ever imagine not being around.

'Darling Luke, what is the likelihood of persuading Stuart to wear a morning suit at the wedding?'

Silence reigned at the other end of the phone for a few moments.

'Max, you said you wanted a favour, not a miracle.'

'Well, at the weekend Stuart agreed that we could get married in church.'

'Oh, er, did he?' Luke replied awkwardly. He didn't add that Stuart had already told him that in a phone call; nor did he add that Stuart had also said, 'But that makes no difference to any of the other plans. Still ultra casual, still just a skeleton group of guests. Still no party, no cake, no official photographer, no arty-farty wedding bollocks.'

'Please, Luke. Please try for me. I'll love you for ever.'

'I'll do my best,' smiled Luke, trying to sound more positive than he felt. He couldn't say no to Max; no one could. And he felt for her, to be honest. Why shouldn't a woman have the wedding of her dreams? Someone like Max wasn't born to be married on the quiet, with no frills.

He had even said that to Stuart, but for once Stuart was digging his heels in. 'I'm making a long overdue stand,' Stuart had explained to him. 'It's always been Max's way or no way, but not this time. This is the start of a new chapter – and I'm going to start as I mean to go on.'

On this issue Luke knew that Stuart wasn't going to be his usual walk-over self.

Chapter 26

Bel knew she ought to try to rouse herself. It was now Wednesday lunchtime and she had done nothing but sleep since Sunday, give or take making herself the odd cup of Oxo mixed with hot water when she got really thirsty. She knew she was in the tightening grip of something dark; she was staggering at the lip of a great black abyss of depression that was calling to her to jump in. She hadn't even had a shower, or changed her clothes. She had no appetite but knew she should eat something. Anything but a Pot Noodle, though; she'd throw up if she had one of those.

It took her a lot of self-encouragement to stand up, and her legs felt weak when she did, but she needed the loo pretty badly. She caught sight of herself in the mirror and it was Medusa crossed with a zombie; not a look that would ever catch on, even in the most bizarre of fashion circles. Considering her hair was so short, it was quite an achievement to get it so messy. She looked paler than Violet and her eyes were puffy with too much heavy sleep. Her lips were cracked and sore-looking too.

When she stripped off for the shower there was no doubt about it: she had a less than fragrant aroma about her. The trickle of water from the rubbish shower was, nevertheless, warm and soothing and the lemon shower gel helped to drag her a few steps away from throwing herself into the abyss. In fact, as she towelled herself dry, for the first time in days she felt a craving for something tasty. She had a tin of Ambrosia creamed rice pudding in her supply box. But – aarrgh – no tin opener. She needed that sodding tin opener.

But what if he's DR DR, the escaped serial killer?

Bel was craving that rice pudding so much she would have taken on Jack the Ripper to get it. There was nothing for it but to go around to Emily and ask nicely.

She knocked on the door. There was no answer, so she knocked again. And again. She knew he was in there because a) his car was parked outside, and b) through the window she could see his outline as he sat at the table.

This man was standing between her and the tin of creamed rice. She knocked with her fist now and kicked at the door at the same time. Her persistence paid off. The door was snatched open and Mr Sociable stood there with a boiling expression on his face.

'Could I please borrow the tin opener again?'

'No,' came the answer and the door was shut rudely.

Bel stood there for a few moments in shock, feeling as if he had just thrown a bucket of cold water over her. How bloody dare he, she thought. She stomped back inside Charlotte muttering to herself what a hideous man he was. She *needed* that rice pudding badly. She had just about gee-ed herself up to storm into Emily and demand that he hand over the family tin opener when she heard his car door slam shut, and seconds later, through Charlotte's small front window, she saw him drive off. The tin opener was in her grasp.

If she acted fast, she could take it and return it without him noticing she'd been in Emily. She'd easily managed to sneak in for the phone charger. She knew he hadn't suspected a thing or he would have been round to Charlotte, being caveman-like and rude and belligerent and obnoxious.

She grabbed the keys from the hook and hurried out of the back door of Charlotte and in through the back door of Emily, again nearly falling over that damned briefcase.

As luck would have it, the tin opener was on the draining

board, so she seized it quickly, then stopped suddenly, noticing the words on a notepad at the side of it.

> *Bride arrives at a house. Dress torn. Obvious runaway. Preferred method of murder – strangulation? Stabbing?*

A cold feeling slithered down her back and the words 'serial killer' side-winded across her brain. She looked around her for evidence of the man – the mad garrotting doctor – who the police were looking for. On the dining table was a book by an author called John North, *The Strangling Man*. Bel gulped. Somehow it wasn't that ridiculous any more that she might be staying next to someone very dangerous. There was a long narrow scarf draped over the chair – innocent enough under other circumstances, but in this scenario it added to the suspicion, to the mounting list of clues.

There was also an open laptop on the table. The screensaver showed various book covers by the same John North. Obviously a fan, then. The name was familiar. It must have been her dad who read books by him because Richard never read books, only pink newspapers. He thought reading was 'a waste of time'. Especially women's fiction.

'Why would you want to read a book when you know what the ending is likely to be?' he'd scoff, picking up one of her lovely Midnight Moon romances and throwing it back down with a disdainful laugh.

'Because it's escapism.'

'What do *you* need to escape from?'

It's a good job he wasn't here to ask the same question now. She wanted to escape from everything. If she could have crawled into a book and lived out a happy ending, she would have.

She picked up the John North and read the blurb: *When a woman is found garrotted in a busy restaurant, how is it possible that no one saw who did it?*

She stopped reading. Not the sort of escapism she fancied today.

Then she froze. There was a car coming up the lane and it could only be his because the postman had been already. She'd dawdled and left it too late to use the tin opener and then return it again. She should put it back and leave it, but the thought of a bowl of creamy rice pudding made her stomach growl and her grip tighten on the precious implement.

She quickly slipped out of Emily's back door and crossed her fingers that he'd go out again soon so she could return it. Annoying man. How dare he come back early and stop her snooping?

Chapter 27

Violet couldn't help staring at Pav as he worked. He had finished the brief outline of the horses and had just put the first loaded paintbrush of light grey paint on the wall. The first horse was going to be dapple, it seemed.

He turned, as if sensing her eyes on him.

'I'm sorry,' Violet immediately apologized. 'I'm just fascinated. I can't draw anything.'

Pav grinned. 'I can't cook ice cream,' he said.

'Oh, anyone can make ice cream,' smiled Violet. She knew she should go back to the kitchen but she was mesmerized by how he smoothed the paint on to the wall.

'I'm used to people watching me work,' said Pav. 'I don't mind.'

'Can I get you a coffee or a tea?'

'A coffee would be really nice,' he replied.

'No probs,' said Violet, taking herself off to the kitchen before he noticed she was flustered.

She stood waiting for the kettle to boil and tried to imagine what Carousel would look like when it was finished. It was such a pretty conical building made from old refurbished stone, with a lounge and private shower room upstairs under the pitched roof. In the past couple of months, she'd had a sofa put up there and a table, a couple of chairs, a thick rug, and an old portable TV. It was somewhere to come and do her books and get away from Glyn's poky depressing flat. She spent more time than she needed to in that room above her ice-cream parlour, just to be on her own and away from looming wedding plans. And now she had Postbox Cottage too.

She took the coffee to Pav and as his long fingers closed around the mug, she imagined them weaving in her hair, pulling back her head to allow those soft generous lips, which were now smiling a thank you to her, to have access to her throat. She imagined he would be a very nice kisser. The thought of kissing Pawel Nowak brought a warmth to her cheeks and her whole insides and she retreated into the kitchen to work before she grew a blush that could be seen from Mars.

In her office, Max studied the box of San Maurice products. She hadn't ever used any of the fake tans herself but she knew that Jess really liked them and used them regularly.

'This is the one you want,' said Jess, pulling out a bronzing mist. 'It's a new one. Look, I've been sampling it. Juanita sprayed me. This is the result of three coats.' She pulled down her skirt at the waistband so that Max could see the slight difference where Juanita, the product development manager, had been testing it on her skin. 'You can see where I had the paper knickers on, and yet I look nice and naturally sun-kissed, don't I? Not orange, like some of these women go.'

Jess did look a very healthy shade. It was too subtle for a gypsy bride, though. Currently, San Maurice did Sun Mist in light/medium only so Max reckoned she'd need at least ten coats. But she might as well use her own products and advertise them. The press were bound to be interested in how to prepare for a local big fat gypsy Yorkshire wedding.

'And the best thing is that it doesn't come off on white clothes,' added Jess.

'Are we paying you for sampling it?' asked Max, spraying a little of the Sun Mist on her hand and waving it dry.

'Yep,' nodded Jess. 'I'd have done it for free because it's fab stuff, but I'm not turning down the cash. By the way, the medium/dark is coming in soon. I'm sampling that as well, but I think it might be a bit extreme for me.'

'Make sure I get to see it as soon as it arrives, Jess,' asked Max, ticking another box on her wedding chart. She liked that word 'extreme' very much.

Chapter 28

There was a knock so forceful it was a wonder the door didn't come off its hinges. Bel stayed silent but he wasn't fooled.

'I know you're in there. Will you please give me back what you took from me before I come in and get it.'

'I haven't got anything of yours,' replied Bel, trying to sound cocky and super-confident. She didn't want him to smell the fear. Psychos got off on that – she'd seen a programme on the Crime Channel on the telly about some nasty American nutter who kept his victims alive so he could torture them and keep himself on the edge of ecstasy for hours as he listened to their screams. She batted that thought away quickly because it was scaring the living daylights out of her, not that she wanted him to know that.

'I need that tin opener. And will you please stop snooping around my house?'

'It isn't your house, it's my dad's,' snarled Bel, half shaking, half unable to stem her annoyance, despite the fact that it might inflame him further and result in her imminent death.

There was a sinister silence, which totally freaked Bel out. She had visions of him looking around for a big rock to throw through her window. Or an axe.

'I'll do a slow count to ten, then I'm going to kick the door in.'

Bel's head began to whirr. If she slipped out of the back door, she could sneak to her car and drive off. It would totally ruin her flat-tyred wheel, but a knackered wheel was better than a crushed throat.

'Ooone . . . twooo . . .'

She unlocked the back door, wincing as it opened with an agonized creak. She could hear Psycho-man counting, but only just, because her heart was thumping so loudly it was as if Keith Moon was pounding on her chest with his drumsticks.

She dropped her keys and swore under her breath. She couldn't hear any more counting. As she straightened up, she found out why that was. Because Psycho-man was standing in front of her. And then he ran towards her and pushed her hard against the outside wall, crying out something unintelligible, like Braveheart did while charging the English.

Chapter 29

Bel didn't pass out, but she was a) winded by having been rugby-tackled by Mr Psycho-killer, and b) seeing stars because she had been hit over the head. Her eyebrow was wet, and when her fingers travelled to it she smelled the iron tang of blood before she felt it drip on to her cheek, warm and sticky-wet.

It wasn't much good shouting for help, seeing as the only people around were her and Peter bloody Sutcliffe. Plus, her vocal cords had all fused together.

Strangely, Mr Psycho wasn't finishing off the job; he was holding her up and asking if she was okay.

Yes, she was fine. Her fiancé had been shagging her cousin, she had just wasted twelve squillion quid on a sham of a wedding, run away to a cottage so well equipped that she'd had to resort to stealing a tin opener from the maniac next door, and now that man had her at his mercy after bashing her over the head. Oh yes, she was bloody marvellous.

'We need to get you to hospital,' he was saying to her.

Bel was lucid enough to think that he must be one of those nutters who suffered from Munchausen's. He had battered her over the head and now got off on rescuing her with a mercy mission. He was pressing something against her scalp and then lifting up her hand so that she kept the pressure on it as he straightened her up.

She was distinctly woozy as he half carried her into his car and strapped her into the passenger seat. Blood was still dripping from her head and she had the foresight to make sure some of the drops landed on the car upholstery for evidence.

'The nearest hospital is the Bronte, isn't it?' Harold Shipman next to her was saying as he started up the car. 'I vaguely remember how to get there.'

Bel stayed silent. She was trying to think of the best way to play this. Should she initiate conversation to form a social connection between them and address him by his name – even though she hadn't got a buggering clue what it was? He obviously enjoyed being in a medical role so referring to him as 'Doctor' might be a wise idea. Or would that infuriate him – make him realize that he wasn't really a doctor even though at school he aspired to be one, but managed only a GSCE in woodwork? Should she just stay meek and mild? But then, sadists loved that too. She'd always imagined that people in this situation would try to jump out of the car or leap on the driver and force him to crash, but she was frozen to the seat. Watching out of the window as the car drove at speed down a dual carriageway, she had a real fear that, at any moment, he might take the slip road which led up on to the moors.

Instead he stuck to the busy main roads, eventually taking a left into the Bronte Hospital car park. He swerved the car expertly into a parking space a few steps from the Accident and Emergency entrance, then he snapped off his seat belt and threw himself out of the car to come round to the passenger side and pull open the door. Gently he reached over and unfastened Bel's seat belt for her and helped her out of the car and into the building.

There was a tired-looking receptionist manning the desk as they approached it.

'Name?' she asked curtly.

'Belinda Candy,' said Bel, although really she was Belinda Bishop, she supposed. Not that she would ever call herself that. The receptionist seemed to be taking an age to stab the letters into the computer. Bel's head was still bleeding and blood was dribbling down her face.

'And what seems to be the trouble?' said the receptionist.

'I've stubbed my big toe,' Bel said impatiently while thinking: how thick can a person be?

Psycho-killer followed up with a more sensible answer.

'She needs an X-ray and stitches. And immediately.'

'Well, we'll see what the doctor has to say about that,' said the receptionist.

'I am a doctor,' Psycho-killer said in the same impatient and ever-so-slightly belligerent tone which the desk Hitler was using towards him. 'Dr Dan Regent. And this lady needs to be assessed *now*. Can you get someone quickly, please?'

The receptionist's whole demeanour changed then. Her regard for the general public, who gave her so much daily hassle, was inversely proportionate to the esteem in which she held anyone with a medical degree. She jumped to her feet and scuttled off.

Bel slumped on to a chair.

'Are you really a doctor?' she asked. 'Or did you just say that?'

'Yes, I'm really a doctor,' came the reply. 'I'm on a sabbatical. I'd hoped I wouldn't see the inside of a hospital again until at least Christmas.'

On the wall facing them was a television on which the jingle for the news was playing. The lead story was that the psychotic killer, Dr Donald Reynolds, had been apprehended in the Lake District. Despite the pain she was in, Bel couldn't suppress a little giggle leaking out.

'What's the matter?' said Dr Dan Regent.

'Nothing,' said Bel, pressing her head even harder in the hope of stopping the sickening throb.

'You ought to ask your father to get the roof fixed,' he said. 'There were a few tiles loosened during the night. That one that fell off was so sharp that it could have killed you.'

'A tile?' said Bel. 'A tile fell on my head?'

'It just clipped you. I saw it falling but I wasn't in time to push you out of the way entirely.'

'Oh you were *saving* me.' Bel laughed through the pain.

'What on earth did you think I was trying to do – kill you?'

'Of course not.'

Bel's eyes drifted back to the TV screen as the image of the recaptured real psycho appeared. He looked much older than his purported fifty-six. And if he had an athletic build, she was Keira Knightly.

A soft-voiced doctor in scrubs called her name and Dan helped Bel to her feet and took her through to a cubicle.

She needed five dissolving stitches in her head. She felt like Frankenstein afterwards as she walked back to the car, holding on to Dan's arm. Her head felt as big as a watermelon inside the bandage. In her free hand she was gripping a leaflet about head injuries.

'Would you like me to ring anyone for you?' Dan asked, surprisingly gently for a once-suspected serial killer, as he pulled the seat belt from her hands to fasten it for her.

'No, I'm okay,' she said. 'Thank you.'

'Quite the independent, aren't you?' he levelled at her.

'Yes,' was all Bel said by way of return.

She sat in silence as he drove down the bypass and headed out to the edge of the moors. Thoughts of her dad and Max and Violet pushed through to the front of her brain. Despite the notes she had left them and the texts she'd sent, they'd be worried sick, she knew. It made it all the harder to go home. She hadn't given much thought to their distress levels in the run-up to the wedding; instead she had concentrated on imagining the shame she hoped Shaden and Richard would be feeling. She had prioritized the ones she hated above the ones she loved.

Her eyes began to drip tears and she attempted to wipe them away, cursing herself for the involuntary sniffing.

She saw Dr Dan glance over.

'You all right?' he said.

'Never better,' she said, keeping her eyes facing forward; yet out of the corner of her right one she sensed him smiling.

'You know, you really oughtn't to be by yourself for a few hours.'

'There's a pet shop in Keighley. If you pull in, I'll buy myself a goldfish,' Bel replied, squaring up to the momentary weakness she felt. There were unpleasant thoughts coming at her now from all angles, and she didn't want them bombarding her and battering holes in her self-protective armour.

Dan indicated right and started up the twisty lane that led to the cottages. As he pulled on the handbrake outside the front door to Emily he sighed heavily.

'Annoying as this is for us both, I think you'd better come into *my* cottage,' he said, stressing the possessive. 'As a doctor, I am duty-bound to insist.'

Like hell, her thoughts said. 'If I must,' her voice said. She supposed it made sense. Plus, she knew that he really would insist and she felt too weak to win the argument, so it was best to simply agree.

It was raining yet again. A typical British weather day: dark, wet, depressing. It was as if the inside of Bel's head was projected on to the sky.

Inside Emily, she sank onto the huge comfy sofa and put her feet up on the equally fat footstool. Dan went straight to the kettle and clicked it on. He stacked up the litter of A4 sheets on the coffee table to make some space.

'Tea or coffee?' he asked her.

'Brandy,' said Bel.

'Not wise,' Dan replied. 'You have three options: tea or coffee or nothing.'

'I'll have a coffee, then, thank you. Strong, milk, a quarter teaspoon of sugar.'

'A quarter?' mocked Dan. 'Is that worth putting in?'

'It's just for a hint of sweetness,' replied Bel. 'So, yes, it is worth it to me. It doesn't have to be an exact quarter.'

'Okay,' Dan said, resigned. 'But I'll try to get it as near as dammit to the requested fraction.'

She rested her head against the back of the sofa and closed her eyes; it really was the most comfortable seat in the world and the one she had imagined curling up on after fleeing the wedding reception, instead of the poky lumpy thing in the cottage next door.

Dan coughed to alert her to the fact that he was standing next to her holding out a drink. She took the mug from his hand. A big solid left hand, she noticed. No ring on the third finger, but a large gold signet ring on the middle one.

'Thank you,' said Bel.

He sat down in the armchair – her dad's old chair. She used to snuggle up on his knee on that chair and he'd read her a story. *Beauty and the Beast* was always her favourite. She'd always dreamed of marrying someone like the nice beast with the big heart. Well, she'd married a beast all right, but the reverse kind – one with the beauty on the outside and the ugliness within. *Bloody tears. Bugger off back to where you came from, will you?*

'So,' said Dan, cradling the mug in his hand. 'This is all a bit surreal, isn't it?'

'You're telling me,' said Bel. She wondered how long it would take him to start asking questions. Not long, apparently.

'Can I just ask—'

'Please,' she held up her hand. 'No questions. I shan't ask any or answer any.'

'I was only going to ask you if you wanted a bowl of soup,' said Dan with the hint of an impatient grumble in his voice.

'Oh.'

'Heinz Tomato. Nothing fancy.' Then he slapped the heel of his hand to his head.

'Of course a tin opener would be handy at this point.'

Bel cringed. 'Can't remember what I did with it.'

Their eyes locked and then simultaneously, and without

planning to, their faces broke into wide smiles. 'I'll find it and get it back, I promise,' said Bel.

'I could make us a sandwich,' Dan suggested. 'I don't need the can opener for a cheese toastie.'

'I'm fine, thank you. I'm not hungry.'

'I am,' said Dan, and he switched on the grill. Soon the smell of toast and cheese was filling the room and Bel's stomach growled like a wolf in pain. She wished she had said yes to the offer now.

Dan switched off the grill. Bel almost started to salivate as she heard a knife crunch through the toastie. Then Dan put a plate down in front of her.

'Just in case you've changed your mind,' he said.

'It's rather possible that I might have,' said Bel with a sniff.

Chapter 30

Bel awoke to the sound of a boiled kettle clicking off and the chink of a metal spoon against a china mug.

'What the—' she exclaimed, pulling herself up to a sitting position.

'Morning.'

She was huddled in a quilt on the large squashy sofa and Dan Regent was stirring coffee into a cup. He had bed-hair. Dark and messy, his look was something top male models in magazines probably took hours to acquire.

'It's the morning?' Bel foraged in her mind for the point when she'd felt too tired to say: 'I feel tired and I need to go back to Charlotte.'

'Let me save you the bother,' said Dan, as if he could see the whirrings in her mind. 'You drifted off to sleep and I didn't wake you. I thought it was best if I kept my eye on you.'

'Thank you,' said Bel, not quite sure if that was the right thing to say, but saying it anyway.

'I'm going to the village shop later, if you should need anything.'

Bel stretched under the duvet. He must have put it over her. Oh God, she hoped she hadn't been snoring. Richard used to say that she made little snuffly noises during the ni—

She cut off the thought of him because it hurt. As her anger was dissipating the pain was getting through.

'I'd better go next door,' said Bel as she stood up, then fell backwards again. If only Dan wasn't here, she could quite happily have stayed snuggled in that quilt on the sofa and watched *Antique Aunties*, the show where two funny old ladies went around people's houses snuffling out their treasures like truffles.

Her wound throbbed under the bandage wrapped around her head. She made a note not to look in a mirror as she was sure a very pale and tatty Björn Borg might stare back at her. Her bladder had woken up as well now and was screaming for the loo. Bel started to fold up the quilt.

'Just leave it, it's fine. I'll do it,' said Dan. 'But I would appreciate the tin opener if you can find it.'

'I'll find it,' said Bel, pulling herself to her feet – successfully this time. She opened the creaky cottage door. 'Thank you for er . . . babysitting me.' That sounded ridiculous.

'It wasn't as if I had a choice,' replied Dan.

'Well, you did,' said Bel, rearing a little. 'It's not as if you haven't denied me entry to my own family's property before.'

'I didn't mean . . .'

'Please don't explain. I get your drift. I'll be off now. To hunt for the tin opener you are so desperate to retrieve, despite my escape from death's clutches yesterday.' And she exited Emily with a haughty flourish.

Normal relations were resumed, it seemed.

In the tiny bathroom in Charlotte, Bel braved a full-on study of herself in the mirror and jumped back in horror. She looked terrible; whey-faced and gaunt. Like something out of a *Living Dead* film. A zombie who played tennis in its spare time. She dampened a flannel and pressed it against her face.

She suddenly wondered what Shaden was doing now. Perfect, glossy Shaden with her eyes perfectly made up and lipstick perfectly applied. Was Richard with her?

A harsh series of raps on her outside door snapped Bel away from thinking about them. She dabbed her face dry and didn't hurry down the stairs. It was obviously Dan who would be standing there when she opened up.

'Erm ... did you want me to bring you anything back from the shop? And did you find the tin opener?'

'I haven't looked yet,' Bel bristled. As she moved to the kitchen drawer she felt Dan enter the cottage behind her.

'Bit small in here, isn't it?' he asked, squeezing past the sofa.

'Apparently a family of eight once lived here.'

'Eight what? Mice?' grunted Dan. 'That's the tin opener, isn't it?' He pointed to the said article, sitting like an egg in a nest of screwed-up veil.

As she lifted it up, it caught on the material, and as she jerked it free, the veil snagged.

'It's torn,' commented Dan, taking the tin opener from her.

'I don't give a flying fart, actually,' said Bel, slipping into cross mode as she felt tears rising up to her eyes again. 'And I'm okay for groceries, thanks.'

Dan gave a less than subtle glance towards the short run of kitchen worktop, where the cans and Pot Noodles were standing.

'As you wish,' he said, banging his head on the low hanging lightshade on the way out. 'Don't say I didn't ask.'

At the door he turned round. 'I trust you won't be snooping inside the cottage again while I'm out, will you?'

'You have my word,' said Bel.

'Hmm,' he replied. He looked unconvinced by her honour as he shut the door behind him.

Chapter 31

'Hello, there,' greeted Freya, as Violet pushed open the door to White Wedding.

'Hi,' Violet waved at her. 'I was passing. I came in to have another look at the dress, if I could. Just to make sure that I still like it.'

'Of course,' Freya smiled. She walked down to her workroom at the far end of the shop. Like so many people, Violet wouldn't have been surprised to find that as a younger woman Freya had been a ballerina. She had the poise and elegance of a dancer. They would have been gobsmacked to discover that in fact she had been a farmer's wife. Once upon a time she had lived a cold, hard existence with only her dreams to keep her warm and give meaning to her days.

Freya returned with the beautiful ivory silk dress draped over her arm and Violet nodded as the older lady handed it to her.

'Oh it's so beautiful,' said Violet. If she had to get married, there could be no sweeter dress to wear than this one. She had dreamed about it last night, which was what had inspired her to come here today. In the dream she hadn't married Glyn, but someone in a uniform – a soldier. And her heart had been flooded with happy feelings as he kissed her at the altar.

Then she had slid into consciousness to find that it was Glyn who was kissing her and ready to make love to her. And she had tried to think of someone else so she could endure it, but her brain wouldn't quite let her because it felt like a betrayal.

Violet shrugged off the uncomfortable memory and put on the dress. Freya zipped her up and looked over her shoulder into the mirror.

'When I made this dress, it had buttons up the back,' she said.

'You made it?' asked Violet with a little gasp of delight.

'Yes, it was the very first wedding dress I ever made. I got a bolt of silk from the black market and stitched it by hand. But over the years it has been altered so much, to fit all shapes and sizes.'

'Did you make it for yourself?' asked Violet, smoothing the silk over her hips. As perfect as it looked in the mirror, there was something wrong with how it felt on her – she couldn't put her finger on what the problem was. It was almost as if it was twisted round her body.

'No,' said Freya, examining the fit. 'I had always wanted to make wedding dresses, from being a small child. But my family were farmers and we moved in small circles and so I ended up marrying a farmer too. A career in dressmaking was just a pipe dream then.'

'Wow,' Violet blew the air out of her cheeks. 'I can't imagine you milking cows and feeding pigs. Were you happy, though? All that country air and apple picking?' Say you were, thought Violet. She wanted to picture Freya in sunshine and jolly harvest times.

'No, I was desperately unhappy,' said Freya, her eyes dull with the pain of the memories. *Leonard – my husband – was a cruel and brutal man.* 'I didn't live, I existed.'

'What happened?' asked Violet softly.

'Into my life came a young man, a German. Vincent.' *A prisoner of war who worked on the farm.* 'I fell in love with him on sight. But I was married, of course. Trapped, incarcerated, imprisoned. As much as I wanted to leave my husband, there was nowhere for me to go. Especially not in those days.'

Violet studied Freya and noticed that, whatever she was thinking, there was a light growing brighter in her eyes.

Freya could feel *his* hands deliciously weaving themselves into the long, flame-red hair she had back then, smell him, see him in that ridiculous POW brown suit with the bright orange patch on the back. And his voice was still a clear and perfect sound in her head.

'*When I can go back to Berlin, Herzchen, I am going to take you with me.*'

As if a champagne cork had been pulled from a bottle in her brain, a fizz of memories foamed up behind it. The Italian POWs, so much fun to be around; Leonard, jealous of Vincent's popularity with everyone, having the camp transfer him to another farm miles away; the end of the war; the slow repatriation of the German and Italian POWs.

When the last of the prisoners left the farm, Freya knew she would never hear laughter there again.

She pulled herself into the here-and-now and smiled at Violet.

'I will never know how I found the strength to leave, but one day I just picked up my bag and my sketchbook and I walked out of the front door and never went back. I think the last remaining self-protective part of me finally realized that a life without hope is a living death.'

Violet wanted to cheer. But what about Vincent?

'I caught a bus into town, then another and another until I ended up in Derbyshire. The last bus dropped me outside an inn where they were advertising in the window for someone to help run the bar and clean. It was like a gift from God that I could walk straight into that job, and the people who owned the place were so kind to me. In the evenings, I would sit with the family and talk, and I would embroider as I was doing so. And one day the son of the family brought me a bolt of silk and I sat and stitched this dress with all the care I could take, a dress fit for the bride of a beautiful man like Vincent.'

Violet felt her spirits sinking. Other brides had worn this dress, but Freya never had. It felt all wrong on her today, but maybe that was because there was so much sadness caught up in the threads.

'And one day Vincent walked into the bar. He'd been home to Berlin then he came back for me, but he was unable to find me. It took him months, but he didn't give up.'

'Oh my.' Violet's eyes filled up. 'Tell me that you left with him.'

'I left with him.'

'And you married him and wore this dress?'

'I married him and wore this dress.'

'Thank God,' said Violet, patting her beating heart. 'Did you ever see your husband again? Your first one, I mean?'

'Only once,' said Freya. 'And he looked like a stranger. Even now I have nightmares that I could have wasted my life staying with a man I didn't love, a man I had married for all the wrong reasons.'

Violet swallowed. 'Freya, why did you marry him in the first place?' She listened to the answer carefully.

'He swept me off my feet with a charm offensive. I didn't have time to breathe, or to think. I was flattered. I didn't see the rot beneath the gleaming veneer,' she said. 'The only reason anyone should marry is for love, but you'd be surprised how many don't. Now, let's get you out of this dress. It's such a perfect fit now, but brides do tend to change shape in the weeks leading up to their wedding.'

As Violet let Freya assist her, Freya's words played on a recurring loop in her brain.

The only reason anyone should marry is for love, but you'd be surprised how many don't.

No, Violet wouldn't be surprised at all.

Chapter 32

After a snooze and flicking through the pictures in a very old *Hello!* magazine retrieved from the rack in the corner, Bel heard Dan's car trundle out of sight and she huffed. She was bored rigid, but she couldn't go back home yet even if she wanted to. No way was it safe to drive with her injury, not for a couple of days; plus, her car still had a flat tyre. She needed something to do that didn't take up a lot of effort but would pass the time, and she wasn't in the mood for reading.

She remembered that there was a box of games from her childhood in the cupboard upstairs in Emily. Buckaroo and Ker-Plunk and some packs of cards: Old Maid and Donkey and – ho ho – Happy Families. Faye used to play them with her when they visited but she always let Bel win, which was boring because, even when she was little, Bel was militantly independent. There was no fun in being handed victory on a plate; she wanted to win it for herself. But it wasn't just that; every time Bel was in danger of enjoying Faye's company, she felt an overwhelming betrayal to her mother's memory. It had kept her from ever loving her kind stepmother, and it always would.

But hopefully the big jigsaw was still there too. She smiled at the recollection of her dad hunting for the flat-sided border pieces and passing them to her, while Faye tried to cobble together the hard and boring featureless bits in the middle. The thought of those days was flavoured with toasted buttered muffins and hot chocolate with crushed Flake sprinkled on the top. Such happy times. As a child in that cottage, she never knew that one day she would be an embittered old bag freezing her tits off next door after marrying a bastard with a roving dick. Her eyes prickled with painful tears and she blinked them down again. She needed diversion. She needed that jigsaw.

She could sneak back into the cottage and get it without Dan knowing. Then again, she had given her word. *Well, you only promised not to snoop, didn't you? And you wouldn't be noseying around, just going in, getting the jigsaw and coming back out again,* countered her brain. *I think you should go for it. Get the jigsaw, Belinda. It is essential for your mental health.*

So, once again she unhooked the keys and sneaked into next door. The quilt she had slept in had been put away and the cushions plumped up on the sofa. She honoured her promise to him and went straight up to the cupboard and got out the jigsaw. The room carried a faint air of his aftershave. It wasn't as spicy as the one Richard wore, and which she secretly didn't like all that much.

She looked around at the bedroom. She couldn't help herself. Another book by John North was splayed open, pages down, on the bedside cabinet. It said along the bottom 'Proof Copy, Not For Resale'. There was a set of keys next to it. She picked them up to see the large square keyring more closely because there was a picture of a couple inside it: a younger Dan, clean-shaven and thinner and a tall and willowy woman with long blonde hair. They were both smiling for the camera and he had his arm round her slim waist. The woman wasn't unlike Shaden in her looks, which sent a pain tearing through Bel. She wondered if she would ever again think of her cousin without a wave of hurt engulfing her.

She went downstairs and saw his laptop open on the kitchen table again and there was a stack of books to the side of it. Biographies of Peter Sutcliffe, Fred West, Ed Gein, John Wayne Gacy and Harold Shipman – obviously he liked a light witty read. His notepad was closed underneath them. She slid it out and poked her nose inside. It was half full of scribbles now, most of it undecipherable to her because it was written in infamous doctor's handwriting. The bits she could work out made grim reading:

buried where? ~~strangulation.~~ Bride the
murderer, masquerading as the victim?

She slipped it back under the pile of books, but it didn't quite look the same as before. She chided herself for not remembering to check which way the notebook was facing.

She thought it best to leave sooner rather than later, feeling a tad bad that she had totally reneged on her promise not to snoop. Safely back in Charlotte, she cleared the table and tipped out the jigsaw pieces on to it. They smelled slightly musty, the scent of happy old memories. Then she wondered what exciting concoction she could make for lunch out of Pot Noodle and a ring-pull can of beans.

She heard Dan's tyres roll up just after she had put the unopened beans back on the worktop. She wasn't that hungry at the prospect of them. Through the window she saw him ferrying stuffed carrier bags into the house. She poured some hot water over an Oxo cube and took it to the table to hunt out the corner jigsaw pieces first. Her eyes zoomed in on the picture on the box. How could she not have remembered what it was – a wedding scene. The bride was shapely and blonde with an arrogant pout to her lips. The groom was brown-haired and handsome, like Richard. *Richard Richard Richard*. She remembered how tender and sexy he had been at the family dinner before her wedding. Maybe it had just been a panicky fling between himself and Shaden that he regretted. Maybe he had truly realized what he wanted and ended the affair, hoping she would never find out. Maybe she had missed out on being showered with his love after he realized his mistake. Maybe she had been a total and utter cow and everyone hated her and had made voodoo effigies of her out of wax and were repeatedly stabbing pins into the dolls' hearts. She shifted her attention back to finding the four corners but her eyes blurred over and then salty tears started dropping on to the table and the jigsaw pieces.

Then Dan Regent stormed in through her unlocked door, without the courtesy of knocking, and started ranting.

'What is it with you and that tin opener?' he boomed. 'I go out for half an hour and you break in and ... If I don't get it back, I'll let the air out of your other front tyre. See how you feel to be stolen from.'

'I don't have it,' Bel replied, weakened, her words scraping on her throat. 'I never touched the tin opener.'

He saw her face as she lifted it up. The tears twinkling on her lashes. He extinguished the fire inside him immediately.

'I don't believe you. Please return it within half an hour or I'll be back. Thank you.'

And he was gone.

A spiral of anger suddenly pulsed through Bel, flattening her momentary depression. At least the man was good for something – making her rage instead of cry. She looked at the clock. Well, let him come back in half an hour, then; she'd be ready for him. Because she really didn't have his bloody tin opener. *Her* bloody tin opener.

The clock hands moved round. After twenty-five minutes she heard the door to Emily open, and after a pause there was a surprisingly gentle knock on her door.

Bel crossed her arms. All she needed was a headful of curlers and a rolling pin to complete the picture of 'northern woman doing business'.

'Come in,' she said, back to being 'in-control Bel'.

He opened the door slowly, as if he expected a cartoon boxing glove on a cantilever to spring out at him. He smiled, contritely, and held up the tin opener.

'I am so sorry,' he said. 'I really am. I thought you'd been in the cottage while I was out.'

'Yeah, well, you shouldn't go around accusing people.' Then her cockiness level dropped quickly because the moral high ground wasn't hers. She had been in the cottage – and she had been snooping.

'Look,' awkwardly, he raked a hand through the messy waves of his hair. 'Peace offering. I'm just cooking a casserole. Nothing fancy. There's plenty for two. There's actually plenty for six, portion control was never my strongest point.'

'Good for you,' sniffed Bel. 'Did you come here just to show off your big quantity?'

It came out unintentionally smutty. Her fiercely sparking eyes locked with his and, once again, they both broke into involuntary smiles.

'I'm asking you to break the bread of peace. Unless you've got a date with your Pot Noodle,' he nodded to one of the plastic cartons on the worktop.

'I haven't got a bottle to bring,' said Bel.

'I'll throw one in as part of the peace deal,' replied Dan with a sloppy grin.

Bel pretended to think it over but her stomach crackled like a wave of thunder across the sky. Dan heard it.

'I'll take that as a yes, then, shall I?'

Chapter 33

Stuart felt quite smiley inside as they left the vicarage after being interrogated by the Reverend Folly, even if in a past life the old clergyman must have been a member of the Gestapo. For all his grandfatherly exterior, he subjected them to an interrogation that made Stuart feel soul-ravaged. However, by the end, the old vicar seemed satisfied that Stuart and Max were getting married for all the right reasons.

He and Max had courted for seventeen years and cohabited for ten of those without complication. He blamed his mother for upsetting their happy apple cart and starting off all this wedding bollocks. Well, his mother's home-made cherry brandy, anyway. Most of a bottle of that while watching the Boxing Day *Bridget Jones* film and it had seemed like a good idea to propose just after Mark Darcy had. What followed was a few gasps and an 'Are you serious?' And though Stuart hadn't planned to say it or thought it out beforehand, in his inebriated state he thought: why not? He and Max had stayed the course. And the thought of her being Mrs Taylor – of bearing his name – suddenly very much appealed to him.

But, and he spelled this out from the very beginning, this was to be *their* wedding, not *Max's* lone project. For once, he was in charge. He and Max were to be the central players; they weren't going to get swallowed up and lost in a sea of expensive and unnecessary wedding paraphernalia. Their day would be about sealing their relationship and formalizing their commitment to each other. And for that, they didn't need flowers or cakes or fancy flouncy clothes.

And as they were leaving, when Max told the vicar that a wedding rehearsal wouldn't be necessary, he was touched by that rather than suspicious. He really believed that she had accepted his plain and simple plan for their day.

Chapter 34

In the five minutes that elapsed between Dan leaving the cottage and Bel following him, after a quick brush of teeth and checking that her eyes weren't bloodshot with crying, the sky darkened from light grey to sodding-angry black. Then the rain really started. Again. This had to be the crappiest start to summer on record, on so many levels. Bel was soggy by the time she knocked on the door, although that was partly because she had taken a few steps' detour to the side of the house to pull off one of the pink roses that grew up the wall. She put it into the empty tonic-water bottle that had been standing on the windowsill.

'Wow, where did the rain come from?' said Dan, standing aside to let her into the warmth of the cottage, rich with the smells of chicken and red wine.

'My guess is up there,' said Bel, pointing skyward. 'I brought a bottle – of sorts. It's rude not to.'

'Thank you,' said Dan, taking the impromptu vase from her and setting it in the middle of the kitchen table. 'A very good year.'

'Oh yes, the best,' said Bel, with a lot more bitterness than she intended. Embarrassed, she slapped on a smile and asked if there was anything she could do.

'Nope,' said Dan, stirring something that was bubbling away on the stove. 'I think I have it all under control. It's nothing fancy.'

'When you've been living on what I've been living on recently, trust me – it's a feast.'

She studied the back of Dan as he tipped the rice into a colander and jiggled it around. He had very broad shoulders and a fabulous bum. She bet that under that blue shirt and jeans he was the right side of muscular. He was taller and chunkier than Richard. *Richard*. The name needled at something raw and sore inside her and she quickly dabbed at her eyes before Dan turned round and saw her.

'I don't even know what's been going on in the world. I don't suppose you have a newspaper I could look at, do you?' she said.

'No,' said Dan quickly. 'I didn't . . . buy one today. The headlines were all doom and gloom.' He placed a glass of dark-red wine into her hand. 'Here you go.'

'Thank you.' Bel sipped at it and it slid a warm trail down her throat. It was amazing how good things tasted after a few days' starvation.

The window rattled with the force of the rain lashing at it.

'Wouldn't think it was late May, would you?' Dan commented, looking out of the back window; it afforded a long view over the moors. 'It's more like November.'

Bel didn't reply. Being cocooned in Emily like this felt as delicious as the wine tasted and the food smelled. Even if it was with a belligerent stranger. At least this stranger knew nothing about her circumstances, why she was here, and felt obliged to pad around her for fear of upsetting her. His grumpiness was quite refreshing, really; it gave her something to kick against.

Dr Dan put two plates on the table. 'Feel free to admire the fancy presentation.'

'Aw lovely,' said Bel, sitting at the table and looking at the plate of chicken, shallots and mushrooms in a thick red-wine sauce, with an accompaniment of mangetout peas, and, at the side, spring onions chopped and tossed in with white and wild rice. There was a sprinkle of paprika over the whole lot – presumably the 'fancy presentation' to be admired. Bel stuck in her fork and lifted a big chunk of chicken to her lips; it was hot and delicious. She tried to throttle back on the pace at which she was attacking it. She was scoffing at the speed of a starving shark.

'This is lovely,' said Bel. 'Thank you for inviting me. Sorry I won't be able to reciprocate. Not unless you want beans on toast. Without the toast.'

'I didn't invite you for you to reciprocate,' said Dan, spearing a clutch of mange tout.

'Do you know, when I was little, I saw "mange tout" on a label and thought it said "man get out",' chuckled Bel.

Dan grinned. His eyes crinkle up when he laughs, thought Bel. Richard didn't have any crinkles around . . . *man get out*. Tears blindsided her and spurted out of her eyes. She tried to wipe them away surreptitiously but it wasn't happening. Aware that Dan was looking at her, she apologized.

'Sorry,' she said, trying very unsuccessfully to laugh off her embarrassment. She wafted her hands at her eyes and addressed them, like a mad woman: 'Stop it. Dry up, you pair of bastards.'

Dan reached behind him, tore off a strip of kitchen roll and handed it to her without saying a word. It felt too strange to be sitting there unquestioned, trying to eat chicken and dabbing at leaking eyes. Bel felt she should offer some sort of explanation before the tension in the room popped like a massive balloon full of carbon monoxide and killed them both.

'I jilted my fiancé,' Bel blurted out. 'Well, technically he's my husband because we married before I walked off.'

'Ah,' said Dan, keeping his eyes on his dinner.

'Just in case you were wondering why I turned up as a bride in your house. Would you pass the salt, please?'

Dan passed the salt. 'You're licking your wounds, then.'

'I don't know what I'm doing,' said Bel, spearing a mushroom.

Silence reigned for a few moments as they both sipped their wine.

'If it makes you feel any better, I'm kind of doing the same,' said Dan at last. 'Licking my wounds.'

'The woman on the keyring?' said Bel without thinking. She clamped her hand over her mouth.

Dan's head slowly twisted round to her.

'I knew it. I was right. You *were* snooping in here earlier.'

'I saw it the other day,' said Bel.

'Liar.' Dan wagged his finger at her. 'I found those keys under my seat in the car last night, so you couldn't have.'

Bel held up her hands. 'I'm sorry,' she said. 'I sneaked in to get a jigsaw from the cupboard upstairs.'

'The cupboard that is nowhere near where I left my keys.'

'Okay, okay, I admit it. Shall I leave?' Bel growled, cross at her own big-mouthed stupidity. Dan shook his head and Bel noticed he was grinning. The only way out of this really was to make him smile some more, she decided.

'You might laugh, but the other day when I came round I saw your notes about strangling a bride and I thought you were that escaped serial killer.'

'You looked at my laptop?'

'No, I just saw your notes.' Bel smiled nervously, unsure now if she should have said anything. 'I didn't take anything of yours.'

'You took my tin opener.'

'It's not technically *your* tin opener,' said Bel firmly.

'I refuse to have another argument about my tin opener,' said Dan. 'Now shut up and eat your meal.'

'It's really my tin opener.'

Dan harpooned a chunk of chicken while making a growling noise in his throat. The rest of the meal-eating was conducted in a strained silence. When she was finished – and she didn't leave so much as a mushroom stalk – Dan whipped the plates from the table and transferred them to the sink.

Bel sipped at her newly replenished glass of wine.

'What's for pudding?' she asked. Dan whirled round with a dish brush in his hand. Then he burst out laughing, shaking his head slowly from side to side.

'This has to be the most bizarre week of my life,' he whispered to himself. 'Being mistaken for a serial killer by a jilting bride who is haunting my house and stealing my implements.'

'You have to tell me why you were writing notes about strangling brides.'

'What happened to "no questions"?'

'Sod "no questions",' said Bel. 'I'm too nosey.'

Dan brought over a plate full of various cheeses.

'Bronte farm shop,' he began to explain. 'Alas they were a bit short of desserts so I got this cheese with apricots in, and this one – with raspberries – tastes like cheesecake if you spread it on a digestive biscuit, so the woman in the shop told me. Great selection considering the shop was about as big as my thumb.'

He has huge thumbs, thought Bel as he put the plate down between them. Richard had long, slim, soft fingers.

As if Dan had plucked the name from her head he said, 'I'll do you a deal. I'll answer your questions about bride-strangling, and you tell me the full story about you and Richard.'

Richard?

Hearing his name said aloud stung Bel but she swallowed the pain and nodded. 'You first, though.' She sliced off some of the soft cheese with raspberries and spread it on a digestive. It did indeed taste quite cheesecakey.

'I'm a doctor – a GP. Dr Dan Regent. But I'm also John North, crime writer.'

He spread some of the cheesecake cheese on to a biscuit too. They were shortly going to end up fighting over the last of it.

Richard?

'That doesn't explain why you're shut up on the moors wanting isolation,' pressed Bel. 'I'm guessing it's something to do with the blonde.'

Dan took a long swig of wine.

'I've taken a holiday from the medical profession because I wanted to write the mythical "breakthrough book". I was a lucky man: two dream professions and I had the choice of which one to pursue, healthy three-book deal, gorgeous house, gorgeous fiancée, great car – I thought I had it all. Then, eight months ago, I came home from the surgery to find the house half empty and a note from Cathy on the table saying that she'd left me for a guy she worked with. I didn't have a single clue she was having an affair.'

'Ouch,' said Bel.

Richard?

'The long and the short of it was that as well as losing my fiancée, I lost my writing mojo. I was looking for somewhere to hole myself up, concentrate on trying to get myself back on track, and a friend knew a friend who had a cottage in the middle of nowhere and asked him if he would rent it to me. It sounded ideal. No distractions. Just me and the wild, windy moors.'

'Oh,' said Bel nodding. 'The healing powers of the Bronte sisters.'

'Well, I'd been here for weeks and my brain was still dead. Then –' Dan's mouth stretched into a wide smile – 'the sight of a mad bride bursting into my house gave me the perfect idea for a plot.'

'So I wasn't all bad news, then,' said Bel, trying the apricot cheese, leaving the rest of the raspberry for Dan.

Richard?

Dan had said, 'Richard.'

Bel's brain suddenly tracked back. No, she was sure she hadn't mentioned her bumhole of a husband's name.

'You said "Richard". How did you know he was called Richard? I never mentioned it.'

'You must have,' nodded Dan.

'No, I know I didn't,' said Bel, her eyes narrowing suspiciously. Dan opened his mouth to say again that she had but he could see he'd slipped up too.

'Oh hell,' he stroked his forehead with his big doctor's hand. 'Okay, I read about you,' he said.

Bel swallowed. 'Read? What do you mean, "read"? Where?'

'In today's newspaper.'

Bel paled before his eyes.

Ah. So he did buy a newspaper. And she was in it. That's why he didn't let her look at it when she asked him earlier if he had one.

'Can I see?' she said in a distinctly wavering voice.

Dan stood and walked to the sofa. He lifted up the base cushion and retrieved the newspaper that he had hidden there. He turned to the relevant page and handed it to Bel.

'Oh GOD, it's a national paper,' was her first cry. Her second: 'I take up the whole of page five.'

The heading read: *White Wedding Day Blues*. There was an old picture of her looking frumpy, with long hair and much plumper cheeks, which some press agency must have had in stock for years because it had appeared in old Treffé press releases. Underneath was the wording: *Bride Heiress*. Jeez, it was equating her with Paris Hilton and spoiled-brat rich girls. Then there was a recent picture of Richard, the caption reading: *Man in the middle, Richard Bishop*. And, underneath, the largest picture of all of a heavily pouting and scantily clad Shaden. Or, as the wording announced: *Blonde Beauty, Shaden Bosomworth-Proud*.

Bel's mouth moved silently over the words as her eyes tracked them across the page. There was a completely over-the-top multimillion-pound turnover figure for the Treffé company. Then followed an account of the events of the reception: the speeches, the cake. The black and white newspaper account masked any sympathy for the wronged woman. Instead Bel was portrayed as a deranged, mad, vengeful, nasty, jealous, calculating bitch. Oh her old cow of a mother-in-law, Madeleine Bishop, was going to love this, if she ever deigned to sully her hands picking up a tabloid. All her suspicions about the nouveau-riche family her precious son was marrying into would be confirmed and double-confirmed. She would ignore, of course, the part about her son's wayward willy. That would be excused as the mere lustiness of a red-blooded male of their class – after all, royalty didn't keep it in their trousers, did they?

The paragraph about the baby that Shaden had accidentally conceived and 'heartbreakingly had to lose' included a comment from 'a friend', who apparently told the newspaper that Bel had a defective womb and would never be able to have a child of her own. It intimated that if Shaden had carried on with the pregnancy, Bel would have killed and eaten all the rabbits living within a ten-mile range of her cousin's house.

Bel's eyes misted up and she blinked furiously to clear them. She hadn't cried for years and now she couldn't sodding stop. She wondered which 'friend' had blabbed something like that to the newspaper. The only real friends she had were Violet and Max and she knew without any doubt in her heart that it wouldn't have been them. They weren't the sort of women to splash her personal sorrow across the pages of a tabloid. It had to have come from Shaden. The mercenary cow had obviously sold her story for the money to buy some liposuction. Bel felt sick.

The article ended with the words: 'The whereabouts of Mr and Mrs Bishop are currently unknown.'

At first Bel thought they were talking about Richard's parents, then she realized they were referring to her and her new husband. She had rolled the name Belinda Bishop round in her mouth like a delicious sweet since her engagement a year ago. Now it tasted sour as her lips closed and parted over the Bs. It also made her sound not unlike a porn star.

The whole of the UK had today witnessed her shame. She tried to imagine what anyone reading it would think about her: plain-looking spoiled-brat 'heiress' used to her own way and driving her man into the arms of a beautiful fecund woman with her obvious mental hang-ups. Her embarrassment was further compounded by the fact that Dr Dan had probably invited her round for a meal only because he felt sorry for her.

Bel folded up the newspaper. A glass of brandy had miraculously appeared at her side, poured by Dan while she was reading. Her hand was shaking as she reached out for it. She glugged a mouthful and it was like liquid fire on the back of her throat.

'If it's any consolation,' said Dan gently, 'I think it was a very brave thing to do.'

Bel pressed her fingers into the daft bandage on her head. The wound pulsed as if her humiliation had kicked it. 'It all looks very stupid now. Vindictive, evil, self-centered and unhinged. I'm not sure I dare walk out in public and face anyone ever again.'

Dan put his brandy glass down and asked, 'Are you all right? Is your head hurting?'

'I'm okay. Apart from feeling like a nutter.'

'People do crazy things when they're hurt,' nodded Dan.

'Yeah, well, I bet you didn't go through with a sham wedding and organize a cake featuring a model of the bridegroom shagging the bridesmaid.'

Dan laughed, then apologized for it. 'No, not quite.'

There was a few seconds' silence before he braved the question: 'Is it true about your infertility?'

'Yes,' nodded Bel.

'It was cruel to print that in a newspaper.' Dan shook his head with heavy disgust.

Bel shrugged. 'I've known since I was thirteen that I'd never be able to have children. I've had plenty of time to accept that. And Richard was always so understanding about it. Now, I just wonder if that wasn't part of my attraction: that there was never any need for contraception and I wouldn't litter up his life with brats. He and Shaden joked in their emails about how easy it was to flush away that little life they'd started. Oh God. I'm going to the loo.'

She flung herself out of the seat knowing that she was about to make even more of a fool of herself by sobbing in front of Dr Dan. She went upstairs, dried her eyes, gave herself a pep talk in the mirror and walked back downstairs again to find Dan twisting up the pages of the newspaper and burning them in the wood-burning stove.

'What do blokes do when they're heartbroken?' asked Bel in all seriousness. 'I'm presuming you don't get the lads round and sing "I Will Survive" on a karaoke.'

Dan chuckled softly. 'I think you girls have a much healthier way of dealing with it. Seeking out friends and driving out the pain.'

'Except I didn't,' replied Bel. 'I felt ashamed that he could do that to me and I wanted to hurt him, and I knew that if I told my friends I'd never have the strength to go through with my plan. I was thick. Because now everyone will hate me. My step-aunt bought a Dior dress especially for the occasion. She hated me before; she'll really really hate me now.'

'Men test-drive fast cars, drink too much and treat women like objects when they're hurt,' said Dan, cringing as he delivered the words. 'I expect there are a couple of women out there that hate me far more than your step-aunt could ever hate you.'

'I bet she'd give them a run for their money,' said Bel.

'Did you get loads of wedding presents?'

'I asked everyone for cheques,' said Bel. 'Then I could rip them up. A couple of people bought presents, but I'll return them. I paid for the wedding myself, so I wouldn't waste Dad's money.'

'So you weren't entirely selfish, then,' Dan gave her a lopsided grin. 'It must have cost you a fortune.'

'I thought it would be worth it. Not so sure now. I could have given that money to charity and done some good with it rather than all that bad. Something else I'll go to hell for.' She felt more foolish and ridiculous by the second. How would she ever sort out all this mess? She felt suddenly very embarrassed in front of him. 'I should go,' she said.

'What and cry into your pillow?' scoffed Dan. 'In ten minutes there's a film on. *Ghost Town* – Ricky Gervais. Have you ever seen it?'

'No,' said Bel.

'Neither have I. Let's cheer ourselves up and watch it. Sorry, no popcorn. But I have more cheese.'

'Cheese it is, then.' Bel popped a chunk of Cheddar into her mouth. It was very strong, delicious and moreish. Nothing at all like Stinking Bishop.

Chapter 35

The editor of the *Melbourne Star* was an ex-pat Brit who knew that there were quite a few fellow 'Poms' amongst his newspaper's readership. Consequently, it always carried a few quirky stories from back home. He particularly liked this recent one about the Yorkshire bride, heiress to a chocolate factory, who had engineered a huge wedding only to dump her philandering husband at the reception. It would make a great feature for the Sunday edition in the glossy mag supplement.

Chapter 36

Bel couldn't remember laughing as much in ages. Half the time she was giggling more at Dan's reaction to some of the one-liners than at the one-liners themselves. He had a boom of a laugh, with a deliciously infectious quality to it. Three-quarters of the way through the film, Bel thought he was going to have an aneurysm. Tears were dropping out of his eyes and he was holding his aching stomach. Bel's cheek muscles were sore by the end; she felt exhausted – and a little bit drunk from all the top-ups of brandy they'd had.

Dan clicked off the TV with the remote and they both sat slumped against the fat feathery sofa cushions, sleepy and smiling. Bel realized she ought to make a move before she drifted off again and spent another night asleep in the cottage, even if the prospect of that was a nice one.

'I'd better get to bed,' she said. Her bandage had slipped over one eye.

She got halfway to her feet before falling backwards with a giggle. Dan stood and held out his hand.

'Let me help you,' he offered. His hand was warm, his fingers strong as they closed round her own. 'And let me take that bandage off.'

'I look ridiculous in it, don't I?'

'Yes,' said Dan, gently unwinding it from around her head.

Then he inspected the wound. 'That's healing well, but don't wash your hair for another two days.'

'Yes, Doctor sir.' Bel gave him a comic salute.

'Two days at least. Promise?'

'Promise. Right, I'm away. Charlotte will be wondering where I am.'

'You know, I haven't been to the Bronte parsonage yet. I really must make the effort to go,' mused Dan.

'I'll take you tomorrow, if you like,' Bel said. 'It'll be my thank you for making me a meal and introducing me to Ricky Gervais films.' She added quickly – and slurringly, 'Not that I'm trying to hit on you or anything.'

'Good. It's a date,' said Dan, holding out his hand to shake on the deal. 'Although not a "date" date, obviously.'

'Obviously,' nodded Bel.

Dan walked her to the door, still holding her hand. He let it go when she needed to put it into her pocket to get out her key.

'Eleven o'clock in the morning okay with you? Bronte parsonage, here we come,' said Dan.

'Be there or be square, Mr Doctor,' replied Bel.

'Goodnight, Miss Bel,' smiled Dan, standing at the door to make sure she managed to find the keyhole.

'Goodnight, Dr Bride-murderer.'

The doors to Charlotte and Emily closed simultaneously. Bel found herself smiling at full lip-stretch without actually knowing why as she walked up the wooden hill to bed.

Chapter 37

Bel was slightly hungover the next morning, but it was nothing that a coffee and a couple of Nurofen couldn't overcome. She was a good hour into the morning before she realized the word 'Richard' hadn't entered her head.

She so wanted to wash her hair but remembered her promise to Dan that she wouldn't. She dabbed at the wound with damp loo roll and arranged her hair so the raw red line wasn't visible. At least she looked better without her Rab C. Nesbitt bandage on, she decided as she studied herself in the mirror and smoothed some foundation on her face for the first time since her wedding day.

She wondered if Dan would remember their plan to visit the parsonage. She wouldn't have reminded him if he had forgotten because they were both a bit plastered when they made their arrangements. However, she didn't need to worry. At eleven o'clock precisely, he rapped on Charlotte's door.

'Good morning,' he said with a bright smile. 'What a gorgeous one it is too. Look – we have sunshine.'

Bel poked her head out of the door. It was a very promising start to the day – blue skies whipped through with just a few wisps of mares' tails clouds. A day that proclaimed that summer might finally be on its way.

They drove in Dan's Range Rover, which easily took the dips and bends of the roads traversing the moors.

'There's a car park at the side of the parsonage,' Bel pointed to the right to indicate he take the turning. 'I'll even pay for that.'

'I fully expect you to,' said Dan. 'It's my time to freeload today.'

His black-brown eyes were twinkling with amusement. A bus load of Japanese tourists were just alighting from a parked bus. They were strung with cameras like parodies of themselves. A stern-voiced guide was trying to herd them towards the church that stood at the other side of the graveyard from the parsonage. He had a task and a half on as his group seemed intent on photographing everything, even a woman walking a sable collie. 'Lassie!' they nodded with excitement as they clicked, upsetting the dog, who just wanted to poo in peace on the grassy verge.

'Quick, let's go in before it gets overrun,' said Bel, pulling at Dan's sleeve. He had on a thick oatmeal-coloured jumper; it gave him the look of a renowned explorer.

There were only two other couples in the parsonage, both heading upstairs when Bel and Dan walked inside and turned left into the dining room.

'I've always thought that Branwell sounded like a healthy breakfast cereal,' mused Dan as he studied the artefacts on the table.

'Behave,' chuckled Bel, looking up at the portraits on the walls.

'No, really, I have,' Dan continued. 'Mind you, how old was he when he died? Twelve? Maybe not such a good product name, after all. Not much of an advertisement.'

'I don't think his death had anything to do with breakfast cereal,' Bel returned, putting on a very mock-serious voice.

'I hope not,' Dan whistled relief. 'Imagine the outcry there would be if it was discovered that bran was the devil incarnate and in fact "Golden Nuggets" were really the key to immortal life.'

'You're insane,' Bel remarked, following him across the hallway into Mr Bronte's study. 'You'll be telling me next that the sisters all died young because they overdosed on high fibre.'

'A little-known fact of history,' sniffed Dan, faux-imperiously, sweeping his hand out to the scene beyond the window. 'They don't call these the windy moors for nothing.'

Bel laughed then clamped her hand over her mouth. The parsonage had a church-like quiet about it mixed with a little sadness and it felt wrong to be so jocular in it.

'I'd love an office like this,' said Dan. 'I might convert a room and buy a quill and some ink.'

'Where do you live now?' asked Bel, picturing Dan in a swanky converted loft. Something very modern with a lot of chrome and glass.

'Sheffield,' replied Dan. 'Large Victorian villa, currently up for sale if you're on the lookout for something. Bargain-basement price for a quick sale.'

Bel presumed the house now had unhappy memories for him. There must have been some connection with it being for sale and his ex-fiancée because his next words were: 'Cathy used to remind me of Catherine Earnshaw.'

Bel almost said, 'Was she was a totally selfish bleeder, then?' before she bit it back. Her Bronte book of choice was *Jane Eyre*, though Richard had never reminded her of Rochester. He had been more of a St John Rivers type: impossibly handsome, arrogant, serious, intense. Shaden had recently fitted into the story as Blanche Ingram: haughty, beautiful and self-obsessed. Not dissimilar to Catherine Earnshaw – the flighty cow.

'Anyway, that's a closed chapter, if you'll excuse the pun,' smiled Dan, pulling himself away from those thoughts. 'Where's the kitchen? And do you think they'll let us put on the kettle?'

Bel followed him out of the room and down the hallway. They passed an old couple just entering arm in arm and they exchanged smiles.

People must suppose we are a couple too, thought Bel. She

had a sudden moment of disorientation about being paired with a man she had known for no length of time, and yet strangely, too, she felt as if he had been in her life for much longer than he had. Today they had butted together like a couple of old-standing, joking, totally at ease with each other. As if to demonstrate the point, Dan turned round as they were about to enter the kitchen and said, at Brian Blessed volume, 'Hurry up, woman. It's nearly lunchtime.'

They walked up the staircase where Branwell's portrait of his three sisters hung. There was a ghost of his own figure between them, washed out. Bel felt a sudden wave of sadness overcome her.

'All that passion inside them, gone to waste,' she sighed. 'Do you pour your heart out on to the page, Dan?'

'Oh yes,' he replied, scratching his head. 'My writing has taken a very dark turn in the past months.' They walked into Charlotte's room, where lots of her work was displayed in cabinets. 'What do you do to exorcize your demons, Bel?'

'I write poetry,' she replied, and saw that she had shocked him. He probably expected her to say that she shopped. 'I've never told anyone that. It's private stuff, not for publication.'

'Recite some to me,' Dan said.

'Bugger off,' Bel replied.

'I didn't have you down as a secret writer,' he said, grinning a very lopsided grin.

'Yeah, well, the feeling's mutual,' Bel smiled back because that grin was contagious. 'Remember, I thought you were a homicidal maniac. Didn't have you down as a doctor either, for the record. But I bet you thought I was a rich bitch from the off.'

'Well,' began Dan, 'I must confess that our introduction gave me the impression you were a –' he searched for a diplomatic description – 'a lady of means.'

'Oh yeah,' sniffed Bel. 'I might have a rich daddy and my own Mercedes-Benz but I'm currently living off Pot Noodles in a freezing cupboard and daren't go home because I dumped the groom who was knobbing my cousin. I'm living the dream, I am.'

She felt tears rising up inside her and turned away just as another couple came into the room. Bel concentrated on viewing the tiny-waisted dress in a cabinet. It looked more like the dress for a doll than a full-grown woman.

'I can see you in that dress,' that Dan. 'You're as petite as a Bronte.'

'I'm as petite as a Bronte-saurus, you mean,' tutted Bel, batting away the compliment because she wasn't sure if he was being serious or not. Richard wasn't hot on giving out compliments; she'd forgotten the art of accepting them from a man other than her dad.

The woman behind them smiled at their exchange and glanced wistfully at the serious-faced man she was with.

'I mean it,' said Dan, looking as if he did too.

'Yeah, right,' said Bel, still not quite trusting him. 'Not even before all that cheese we had last night could I fit into that frock.'

'Okay, you've said a food word.' Dan clapped his hands together. 'I can't wait any longer. I need lunch. I'm a growing boy.'

'Which part of you is growing, then?' said Bel, without thinking how that might sound.

Dan raised his eyebrows and again the woman behind them silently chuckled as Bel playfully slapped him on his arm.

The woman continued to watch them as they walked out of the room and down the stairs, and wondered why she had settled for a man who never made her smile and had never been playful with her. It had been a huge mistake. She made up her mind at that moment, watching the younger couple together and the warmth that was so evident between them, that she would leave Gerald when they got home that evening and go to her sister's house. Life could not be colder without him than it was with him. They had given her the final push she had needed for so long.

'What time is it?' asked Bel.

'Don't know. I forgot my watch and didn't bring my mobile phone out with me,' replied Dan. 'I know that as soon as I'm in an area where there is any reception, the damned thing won't stop ringing.'

'Ditto,' Bel agreed. If the truth be known, she was enjoying this little bubble in which the world she didn't want to know about was kept at bay.

'It's time for some nosebag, that's all we need to know,' said Dan.

'I hope no one recognizes me as that sad cow in the newspaper,' said Bel, feeling a sneeze coming on and pulling a tissue out of her pocket. She wished she had brought some sunglasses and a hat.

'That picture looked nothing like you,' Dan whispered into her ear. 'You're much better-looking in real life. I'd put my life savings, all fifty pence of them, on a bet that you are safe from any lurking paparazzi.'

'Excuse me,' said a woman from behind them, touching Bel's arm. Bel stiffened. 'You dropped this.' The woman handed over a receipt that had fallen from Bel's pocket when she took out the hankie.

'Thank you,' said Bel. Then she and Dan looked at each other and laughed, he out of amusement, she out of relief.

Her kitten-heeled boots weren't conducive to walking on the streets of Haworth, but they were the most suitable she had brought with her. Another cock-up on the packing front. She stumbled on a cobble and Dan gallantly held out his arm, which she took gratefully. Richard never offered his arm. To Bel, it was a small intimacy that made her feel quite mushy. Men, she thought to herself with a sigh, didn't really have to perform grand expansive gestures to have a woman melt inside. A simple arm crooked for their use was the equivalent of at least a dozen bouquets. Dan's arm felt firm and solid and he didn't seem unduly worried that he was linking arms with a midget.

At the top of Main Street was a pretty café tucked next to the Apothecary. Cathy's Café.

'This looks okay,' said Dan, studying the menu in a glass case outside it. 'We could explore further down the hill but I might die of hunger if we did. And you might break your neck.'

'Let's go in here, then,' said Bel, pushing opening the café door. She didn't much care for the name of it, but it was marginally better than going arse over tit on the steeply graded cobbles in front of the crowded Shirley's Cake Shop.

They both chose Isabella's Chilli con Carne. They chose this above Agnes Lasagne and Branwell Beef and Ale Pie.

'This is a really clever menu,' whispered Dan with such seriousness that Bel got an extreme fit of the giggles. 'I think I went to school with Agnes Lasagne.'

Bel wiped the tears from her eyes with a serviette. 'Stop it, you're so mean.'

'Have you seen the desserts?' Dan leaned in close to her. 'Wuthering Heights Bakewell Tart. How can you have that? It's like saying you've got a Lancashire Yorkshire Pudding?'

Bel pulled herself together. 'I hope I have room for the Linton Trifle afterwards,' she said, perusing the menu.

'Oh Lordy, watch out: it's Mrs Rochester,' said Dan, as the waitress wended her way towards them. She happened to be an extremely white-complexioned woman with a hedge of long greying hair. She was carrying a box of matches and struck one to light the tiny candle on the table. Bel thought she was going to burst from keeping her fit of giggles under control.

'Tell me about chocolate,' said Dan, after Bertha Rochester had taken their order.

'Brown stuff. Comes in bars,' said Bel, deadpan.

Dan tutted. 'Cheeky. What do you do in the company?'

'PR Director is my official title,' Bel began to explain seriously, 'but I end up doing a bit of everything because we are a "family firm" and all of us muck in when needed. I often handle big sales because people like to deal directly with the family, but then sometimes I end up driving some chocolates over in Dad's van if a client wants them, like, NOW.'

'Do you get a lot of freebies?'

'Loads.'

'Yowzah. Will you marry me?'

Under normal circumstances Bel would have laughed at that, but the words just didn't tickle her funny bone because these were far from normal circumstances. Dan noticed her non-reaction.

'I'm sorry,' he said, cringing visibly. 'Bad joke.'

'It's not your fault. It was funny. My sense of humour has a cog missing at the moment,' said Bel, smiling kindly at him.

The chilli arrived. It was garnished with a swirl of sour cream and a couple of sliced jalapenos on top.

'So, you like chocolate?' asked Bel, reaching quickly for her glass of water as a jalapeno stung the back of her throat.

'I love it,' said Dan. 'I think you really would have to go far to beat a huge bar of Cadbury's Fruit and Nut.'

'Washed down with lots of coffee,' smiled Bel.

'Sitting in front of a roaring fire.'

'Watching a Ricky Gervais film.'

'Cathy wouldn't eat choc—' said Dan, without thinking. He bit off the word and shook his head. 'Sorry.'

Bel recognized that dark, haunted look in his eyes.

'Richard didn't either, for the record,' she said, pushing the rest of the jalapenos to the side of the plate. They tasted like they'd been marinated in nitroglycerin. 'He was a bit of a food fascist, to be honest. He never got excited about meals out – food was fuel for him, not an indulgence.'

Dan nodded as if he understood. Bel had a picture of Cathy in a crop top pushing weights in the gym and eating whites-of-an-egg omelette. She could feel the cold vibes coming off the image in her head to such an extent they were giving her brain-freeze.

'In case you were wondering, I eat lots of chocolate,' said Bel, taking the last forkful of rice. She picked up the dessert menu.

'So, forget the Linton Trifle, I'm going to have a piece of Brocklehurst Chocolate Fudge Pie instead.'

'Oh sod it. I'll join you,' said Dan, visibly cheering. He waved over to Mrs Rochester. 'Could we have Brocklehurst Chocolate Fudge Pies for two,' he asked. 'And two large cups of Grace Pool Coffee.'

Bel snorted back her laughter at the waitress, who was clearly wondering what the customer was talking about. Grace Pool Coffee? What a ridiculous concept.

They called in at the farm shop on the way back to the cottages to stock up on supplies. Bel nibbled on all the free samples of bread and cheese on the counter while she waited for Dan to pay for his goods.

'I don't think I have met anyone who eats as much as you,' he marvelled. 'How do you stay so thin? If you turned sideways, you'd disappear.'

'I'm not usually *this* thin. I've lost a lot of weight recently through . . . circumstances. But I am lucky with my metabolism,' said Bel, mid-munch. 'I'm making the best of it because I know that one day I'll wake up, eat a cornflake and put on twelve stone.'

'I like a woman with some meat on her bones myself,' winked Dan.

'I'll give you a call when I'm forty,' Bel said through a mouthful of Hawes Wensleydale. 'The years will have caught up with me then.'

'It's a deal. But only if you bring mucho chocolate with you,' said Dan, opening the shop door for her.

Chapter 38

Max nibbled on her lunchtime sandwich and flicked through the glossy magazine. There was a feature about women's lips. The main picture was of a mouth that made Mick Jagger's look like a pencil line. It was painted sex-red and sparkled like a disco ball. It was a mouth that a gypsy bride would be proud of.

'Wow,' gasped Max and she whistled, imagining her own lips twinkling in the church like twin rubies. She was in the grip of a wedding-obsession vice now and her inner radar was constantly on the lookout for embellishments for her big day. She knew she shouldn't, she knew that Stuart had forbidden it, but she simply couldn't help herself. Her insides were rebelling against all the spartan plans – like a woman on a diet stuffing herself full of Star Bars. She had to add those lips to her ever-growing list of must-haves.

Jess entered with a coffee and a plate of biscuits.

'Hi, boss,' she said in her usual cheery way, then she looked over Max's shoulder to see what she was reading. 'Wow' was her verdict also.

'Look at that lippy. Isn't it fabulous?' Max held up the page for her to see it more closely.

'That is major,' Jess said.

'How do they get that effect?'

'It's glitter that you paint on to your lipstick. Barry M do it. I think it's really meant for your eyes but you can put it on your mouth as well. Comes with a sort of top coat, as far as I know.'

'Well, that's me heading to Boots right now,' said Max. 'Sorry to waste that coffee, Jess, but I don't think I can wait.'

'Oh it's fine,' said Jess, flapping her hand. She was used to Max's inability to ignore an impulse. 'I'll make you a fresh one when you get back.'

Max grabbed her coat and an updated vision of herself drifted into her brain as she stood in the lift: a gypsy bride with sparkling lips. She wondered if she should paint her toenails to match.

Chapter 39

They left each other at their respective doors with a mutual 'see you later'. Dan was burning to write, which he welcomed because after Cathy's betrayal he'd wondered if he would ever feel passion for anything ever again. Bel was bored within three minutes of the door shutting behind her. She killed time by reading her book and doing a bit more of the jigsaw. Then, at seven o'clock, Dan Regent knocked on her door.

'I seem to have bought too much cheese. Would you care to let me repay you for lunch by sharing cheese toasties and tomato soup with me and indulging in another Ricky Gervais film?'

Bel found she really had to throttle back on sounding too keen as she said yes, she would like that very much.

'I thought you were going to work,' said Bel, dipping the edge of her toastie into her mug of accompanying Heinz tomato soup.

'I did. A full day's word count in a few hours. I think I've been bitten by a Bronte muse,' said Dan, swigging down a large mouthful of red wine.

He was burning logs in the stove. They were glowing gently with the odd lick of flame and adding a warm glow to the room. An unbidden memory blindsided her of being little, in a cosy pink dressing gown, and sitting on a sofa with Faye eating buttered toast. It must have been her birthday because she always had new pyjamas, a new dressing gown and new slippers for her birthday. There was soot on Faye's face because she had just

stoked up the fire and Bel remembered giggling at it and prefer-
ring not to tell Faye that she looked silly. Bel felt a wave of guilt
at her meanness – twenty-plus years too late.

'Penny for them?' Dan asked.

'They're not worth that much,' said Bel.

'Try me,' Dan crunched down on his second toastie.

'I was thinking about my stepmother,' Bel confessed. 'The fire
jolted a memory.'

'Was she an evil stepmother? Beat you senseless and forbade
you from going to the ball?'

'Actually, no, she was always very kind to me. Always.'

'I sense a "but",' Dan topped up Bel's wine. It was called Old
Vine and tasted like its name – rich and mature and fruity.

'But I never managed to love her.' Bel felt another wave of
guilt at saying the words aloud, as if Faye might hear them too.

'Why was that?'

'I always felt that Faye had supplanted my mum,' nodded Bel.
'But mum died when I was a baby. Faye came along five years
later. She never . . .'

'Never?' prompted Dan eventually.

'She never forced a mother status on me. She always told me
that Mum was a star in heaven and was the one that twinkled the
most when I looked up at the sky, as if she was winking at me.'

'That's cute,' said Dan.

'But if I ever felt that I wanted to call her "Mum", then she
would be so happy.'

'But you never did.'

'No.'

'She sounds a nice lady,' said Dan gently, hearing a wobble
appear in Bel's voice.

'She's a really lovely person. Dad adores her.'

Suddenly, the way she had treated Faye over the years, freezing
her out, resenting her, was too uncomfortable to think about. She
reached over to her wine and glugged a throatful.

'What did your family think of your fiancé?'

'They liked him. At least, I think they did. They welcomed him into the family, anyway. Then again, Dad and Faye are so bloody nice I think they'd have welcomed Fred West into the family if I loved him and he made me happy. What did your family think of Cathy?'

'Everyone loved Cathy,' said Dan, blowing the air out of his cheeks. 'She had a fantastic ability to charm the birds out of the trees.'

Bel felt her nose wrinking up. She didn't like the sound of Cathy at all. She couldn't imagine her now without thinking of her in a billowing white nightshirt, flying over the moors and smashing up nice men's hearts. Bel wondered what she found in the other man that she didn't find in Dan. He was great fun, good-looking, courteous. Even if she had once thought he was a psychopath.

'What was the other guy like?'

'Ex-model, lantern jaw, Porsche-driver, gym-fanatic, fellow non-chocolate eater. They make a very beautiful couple. What was the other woman like?'

'A swan,' said Bel. 'Spoiled, golden, leggy, sexually alluring, non-chocolate eater also. Although when we were kids, she used to mainline Mars bars.'

'I think we possibly both had a lucky escape,' said Dan, reaching down behind the sofa arm and pulling up the biggest bar of chocolate Bel had ever seen. 'Care for some Mrs Fairfax Fruit and Nut?'

After three glasses of wine, Bel had an unexpected moment of clarity, noticing how much closer Dan was sitting to her since the film had begun. His arm was touching hers, the hairs on his tickled slightly when he shifted. She loved the cinema, but there was never anyone to accompany her and she didn't like the idea of going there alone for fear of looking as if she'd been stood up. Richard didn't like films. If they ever went out it was to serious networking dinners or for showy, expensive meals. Thinking about it, it was one of the many points on which they differed. But that hadn't really mattered because she had always believed

the adage 'opposites attract'. He wouldn't have dreamed of looking round the Bronte parsonage or even stepping foot in a café
that sold Isabella's Chilli Con Carne.

Actually, Richard was a bit of a boring bastard, thinking about it.

For all their reserves of money, the Candy family had always
enjoyed simple pleasures: fish and chip suppers, looking through
Argos catalogues, hot buttered toast for tea and fresh, new night-
clothes . . .

'I can't believe that two gorgeous people like us are cuckolds,
can you?' said Dan, turning to Bel and disgruntledly placing two
hands on his hips as the film credits rolled.

'I'm not gorgeous,' said Bel. 'I'm far too short to be gorgeous.'

'Fair point,' Dan conceded. Bel chuckled, picked up a cushion
and smacked him around the head with it.

Then Dan picked up a cushion from his side and hit Bel on
the arm with it.

'Ouch,' she said.

'I barely touched you,' Dan returned. 'I think you've been
injured enough recently.'

'Liar. You hit me like this,' said Bel, and she belted him hard
with the cushion.

'No, I did not. I hit you like this,' Dan's cushion swung round
again. Bel yelped dramatically and hit him back.

'This means war,' said Dan.

Bel lifted her arm to swing the cushion and Dan tickled her
underneath it. Then they were rolling around on the sofa. And
then Dan was holding her face in his hands and his lips were
brushing against hers.

Then they both sprang apart.

'Oh no, rebound alert,' gasped Bel.

'You're telling me. Most obvious fall in the book.' Dan
launched himself into a standing position and started pacing up
and down in front of the fire. 'That was so close.'

'I'd definitely better go back to Charlotte,' laughed Bel. 'That's
my cue. Nearly snogging an ex-serial killer. Ugh.'

'Yeah, ugh,' shuddered Dan with the affected playground disgust of an eight-year-old boy.

'I'm saving you from a fate worse than death. I'm far too hard to love.'

'I think you'd be very easy to love, Miss Bel,' said Dan Regent with too much tenderness in his voice for comfort. Bel felt alarm bells go off deep inside her. She was too vulnerable for this and had to leave – quickly.

'Dream on, Doctor. I have a heart of stone,' she sneered, injecting some attitude into her voice to mask the fact that her heart felt about as rock-like as an Angel Delight.

'Yeah, go before we both do something we really regret. We would only have ended up in bed,' said Dan with forced casualness. 'You'd obviously scream out my name fifteen times and then be unable to look at me in the morning.'

'You wish,' smiled Bel, pulling her keys out of her jeans pocket. She lifted her eyes to his and saw the very wounded man behind the jokey exterior. Spending the night with him was something she would imagine in bed, alone, in safety. 'Thank you for another lovely evening, Dan.'

'Don't forget to thank Ricky too,' Dan reminded her, gesturing towards the TV.

'Thanks, Ricky,' said Bel.

She looked up at the nice kind face of Dr Dan and thought that Cathy must be a fool. She didn't move away as his hand came out and gently tweaked the tip of her nose.

'Goodnight, Miss Bel. Thanks for sharing my cheese. Oh God, that sounds so wrong.'

Bel chuckled. 'Goodnight, Dr Dan.' She held up her fingers in a two:two formation. 'Live long and prosper.'

Charlotte was very very cold when Bel walked in and switched on the light. She touched her nose where Dr Dan's fingers had landed and felt more alone than she could ever remember feeling before in her whole life.

Chapter 40

Nan had a good talk to the lovely angel with flame-red hair in the middle of the night. She had tried to whisper so Susan wouldn't hear. Susan would only have said the angel didn't exist, but Nan knew without any doubt that she did. The angel didn't talk back to her physically, but Nan *felt* her answers.

She and the angel had a lot in common. They'd both known what it was like to be locked into an unhappy marriage and also the joy of finding their one true love. The angel said that Nan wasn't to worry about her family when she was gone, and she knew what Nan was especially concerned about. Nan wanted to see her granddaughter happily married before she went; she needed to know that she had found her soulmate, her *Jack*. She hadn't seen that much of Glyn but it was obvious that he adored Violet, worshipped the ground she walked on, even; but he wasn't someone that Nan would have picked for her lovely girl. She wanted Violet to be looked after, not *do* the looking after.

The angel had smiled at her and said something quite odd: 'You will send him back to her.' When Nan asked what that meant, the angel just repeated the words: 'You will send him back to her.' And though Nan hadn't a clue what she was on about, she trusted the angel enough to know that she was telling her that everything would be all right.

Chapter 41

Bel woke up suddenly just as Dan was leaning over her and about to kiss her. She sat up in bed and patted her racing heart because that dream had felt so real she could almost taste his lips as they touched hers. She had gone to bed thinking about him, and he had been in her thoughts all night. Now she had woken up annoyed that her dream had ended. She was heading for trouble because she was wise enough to recognize how her poor battered heart was reaching out to the warmth and kindness within its immediate radius – Dan Regent – as he was reaching out to her. They were two crazy mixed-up people incapable of making sensible decisions. It was time for her to rejoin the real world before she made any more mistakes – or got hurt again.

She washed and dressed and gathered all her stuff together, packing it into her case. Hearing a clang she looked out of the bedroom window to see that Dan was bending down by her car and taking off her tyre. As if he sensed he was being watched, he turned his head upwards and waved. He had such a kind face when he smiled, even if it was a bit on the saturnine Heathcliff side when he didn't. She laughed to herself thinking about the concept of a 'nice Heathcliff'. That was the trouble with *Wuthering Heights*, in her opinion: all the characters were too polarized. Edgar was so caring he was wimpy, Heathcliff was a total bastard and Cathy was a cow. Give her *Jane Eyre* any time, with her perfectly imperfect characters: the feisty, lovely heroine and the manly, passionate – but ultimately decent – Rochester. Yes, Dan was definitely more Rochester than Heathcliff. He had gentler, warmer eyes than Heathcliff could ever possess, even if they were almost black. They were eyes that could make a woman melt seeing them first thing in the morning, turning to hers on the pillow. Bel blew out two large cheekfuls of air and shook her head. The sooner she left the better. She was, after all, a married woman.

He gestured to her that she open the window.

'Morning,' she called.

'What light through yonder window breaks,' grinned Dan, opening his arms in an expansive gesture. 'It is the east, I think, and . . . what's your name again?'

'It's west, by the way.'

'I need your keys so I can put your spare tyre on.'

'Are you fixing my car so I'll offer to cook lunch?' she said, oh so aware that she was flirting – not that she even attempted to stop herself.

'Actually, I have to go to Skipton to get some printer ink. Want to come with me for the ride? And cake? After I've sorted out your car.'

You really must not go, said her brain. You need to return home to Barnsley and face the music. You have to say no.

'Yep,' she said. 'I'll get you my keys.'

Then she closed the window and skipped downstairs like a five-year-old child on her birthday.

Dan's car had just gone down the hill when Bel's phone started playing out a series of chimes. Then, in his pocket, Dan's phone started to play the theme tune to *Doctor Who*.

'We both brought our phones,' said Dan with a resigned nod.

'I figured it was time I needed to face up to things,' said Bel, sighing as she pulled her phone out of her bag and looked at the list of emails from Amazon, clients, spam. Texts from Max and Violet, Faye, her dad, none from Shaden – surprise, surprise. She scrolled past them all looking for ones from Richard ... and found them, loads of them. They all said more or less the same thing:

Bel, darling, we need to talk. Please ring me.

She had a lot of missed calls from him too and her voicemail was full of messages that she couldn't bring herself to listen to yet.

Her heart seemed to twist inside her. She hadn't reckoned on feeling so confused when she saw his name on her phone screen. She had envisaged raising two fingers to it but instead there was a great big fat ache inside her, as if she had just been kicked all over again.

When they pulled up in the car park in Skipton town centre, Dan pulled out his phone and looked through the mails and texts received.

'Well, well, Cathy wants to talk to me,' was all he said, before he put the phone back in his pocket. He wasn't smiling as he said it.

He was silent as he bought his printer cartridges. Even though Bel had met Dan Regent only a week ago, she knew what was going through his mind. She wanted to pull his head down on to her shoulder and stroke his hair. She wanted to hold his face and kiss his lips. Oh yes, it was definitely time to go home and get off the rebound bus.

'Right, I promised you cake and cake we shall have,' Dan said, clapping his hands and trying to inject a bit of jollity into proceedings.

'I seem to remember there is a tea shop to die for at the back of the castle,' Bel replied.

'Bit extreme,' said Dan, still not quite out of the grim-faced woods but his voice was warming to playful. 'I'd rather live to enjoy more cake. But lead the way. I'm in your hands.'

An image flashed through Bel's mind of Dan Regent in her hands, in bed, naked. She bet he was lovely in bed ... tender. The sort of man who got up and brought you a cup of tea in the morning. Richard never did that. He was full of great big expansive gestures like booking weekends to Rome and buying jewellery and bouquets of roses, but he never brought her morning cups of tea or held out his arm for her to take.

Bel led the way to the tea shop, hoping it was still there. It was, and just as teeny and pretty as Bel remembered. She and Faye and Dad had eaten the biggest pieces of Death by Chocolate here once after staying for a weekend in Emily. She remembered them all moaning about how sick they felt afterwards.

The Pudding House had very low ceilings and Dan tutted as his head crashed into a hanging lampshade.

'You didn't tell me it was suitable only for Borrowers,' said Dan, feigning pain while rubbing his head.

'Sit down, you wuss. Anyway, if you've injured yourself, you can sort it.'

'Physician, heal thyself,' boomed Dan so loudly that the woman at the next table jerked and a profiterole dropped off her fork.

Dan slipped into gentleman mode, apologized quietly and went scrabbling around on the floor for the fallen profiterole, while Bel turned away to disguise her laughter.

Profiterole retrieved, Dan sat down and studied the menu, then he cast it back on to the table.

'It just feels wrong without all the Bronte names,' he said. 'Which sounds better: "Carrot Cake" or "St John Rivers Carrot Cake"?'

'Do you really want me to answer that?' asked Bel, raising her left eyebrow.

'I'll order, but it's not the same.' Dan shrugged his shoulders and pretended to be disappointed.

What a lovely, fun man, thought Bel. She never had any of this silliness from Richard. He was – she searched inside her for a description of him – *so adult*.

They ordered two slices of coffee and walnut cake and a huge cafetière of coffee. Not even Bel could finish the giant wedge that was delivered to her. Under the table Dan's leg was touching hers. It felt lovely and she didn't move away.

'So, which Bronte character do you think I most resemble?' asked Dan, picking up the last nub of walnut and placing it between his lips.

'Nelly Dean,' said Bel with a straight face.

Dan chuckled. 'No, really. Am I a Heathcliff, a Hindley, an Edgar?'

'What am I?' asked Bel.

'No question about it. Jane Eyre,' said Dan with conviction.

'Ah, so I'm small and plain. Cheers,' huffed Bel.

'You're small,' Dan nodded. 'Not in the slightest bit plain, though. Jane Eyre was a force to be reckoned with. A formidable woman. Now, me?'

Bel tried not to make eye contact with Dan. Because to say that of all the Bronte characters he most resembled Rochester would have been dangerously flirty.

'Heathcliff,' she said. 'Moody, particularly where kitchen implements are concerned.'

'You're lying,' said Dan, his eyes twinkling so much that Bel felt a rare blush sweep across her cheeks. And she hardly ever blushed.

'How long will you stay in the cottage?' Bel changed the subject before her cheeks got any hotter.

'I don't know. I need to do some serious writing,' said Dan. 'Especially now that you've given me my mojo back.'

'How does your bride get murdered?'

'You'll have to wait for the book,' grinned Dan.

'And what about Cathy?'

'Ah, that's a plot I'm not sure how to write,' said Dan, his grin shrinking. 'What about Richard?'

'I don't know,' said Bel. 'I'm going to have to talk to him at some stage. We're married, after all.'

Dan put his hand over Bel's and made it feel as warm and safe as she wished the rest of her felt. His touch was almost painful in its tenderness.

'I can't believe I'm saying this but I'm actually going to miss you,' he said, mirroring her own thoughts exactly. 'Who will I blame when the tin opener goes missing?'

Bel shrugged silently and dropped her head. Dan realized that she was close to tears and kindly took the opportunity to go to the loo so that she might compose herself. The waitress brought over the bill and Bel paid it immediately, before Dan came back.

'Do you and your husband want a doggy bag of the cake you left?' the waitress asked.

'Thank you, but no,' said Bel, suddenly wishing that she was married to someone like Dan Regent. Someone who took her out for afternoon tea and got dirty kneeling on the ground to change her tyre. Someone who liked to walk arm in arm with her and didn't fuck her cousin. She pulled a deep calming breath inside her and managed a smile as Dan returned.

'Tell me you didn't pay the bill,' he said.

'I did, as thank you for changing my tyre.'

'Now I owe you,' he said. 'This could go on for ever.'

She wished she could stay. She wished he would insist on paying her back for the coffee cake by making her cheese toasties again. Then she could pay him back with a tin of soup, if he would lend her the tin opener.

They walked back to the car slowly, in genial silence. Then Dan slipped the car into gear and left Skipton behind them.

'When are you going home?' asked Dan, as he pulled on his handbrake outside the cottages.

'Now,' replied Bel. 'You'll be able to get some work done in peace.'

'About time too,' said Dan drily. 'And I can stop fixating about missing tin openers.'

They both climbed out of the car and turned awkwardly to face each other because there was a heavy goodbye hanging in the air.

'So,' said Dan.

'So,' echoed Bel.

'Good luck,' he said. 'I hope things turn out okay for you.'

'And for you,' replied Bel, defying her eyes to leak. 'And good luck with the bride-murdering book.'

'Thanks,' said Dan. Then he bent to kiss her cheek. One single soft kiss that she felt all the way down to her toes. Then he was gone.

Bel picked up her case from Charlotte, locked the door behind her and drove down the lane to the main road without a single glance in the rear-view mirror. She didn't want to risk seeing Dan Regent standing there and waving to her, because she knew she would have gone back to him.

Max's
Wedding

Chapter 42

'Can I help you?' Max turned round from looking at a wall full of wigs to find a petite woman with eyelashes the length of daddy-long-legs' legs and backcombed hair. The waist-length ash-blonde ponytail of hair that draped over her shoulder was obviously false but was a fabulous colour match to the rest of her barnet. This was Angelique, the owner of Angel Hair – wig heaven – a tiny and exclusive shop on the Penistone–Holmfirth Road. Despite its remote location, apparently it had no shortage of clientele, including a few celebrity clients if the *Chronicle* was to be believed. Male and female. She did a cracking line in toupées as well as beehives.

'I'm getting married soon,' said Max. 'And I want . . . need a hairpiece.'

'Then you have come to the right place,' said Angelique, sweeping her hand around her shop, which was floor to ceiling full of hair. Angelique had tiger-striped false talons and a gorgeous spray-painted mocha tan that made her blue eyes pop out. Max couldn't wait to begin her transformation. She hoped her cocoa-coloured eyes shone as brightly against a backdrop of San Maurice spray tan.

'What were you thinking?' asked Angelique. 'Something like this, maybe?'

She picked up a small round of hair and clipped it expertly on to Max's head.

Max shook her head. 'Too small,' she said, while lasciviously eyeing up the long Rapunzel-like locks to her immediate left.

'O-kay,' said Angelique, taking down a tumble of dark hair and pinning it with expert ease on to the crown of Max's head. It weighed a ton. Angelique reached for some big pins and began to pile up the hair into a huge tower. Then she reached for a sparkly tiara and slotted it into her hair creation.

'You see, hair like this and you'll look like a princess on your big day.'

Princess – magic word. It was as if Angelique could see right into Max's head and tailor her sales banter accordingly.

Max stared back at the beginnings of a gypsy bride in the mirror. The glittery embellishment was far too small, though. It wouldn't even show up on a gypsy girl's radar. A wig of this magnitude needed a full Russian tsarina's Swarovski-encrusted shebang. In her head Max added that tiara, glittery lips and massive eyelashes to her image in the mirror. She batted away the vision of Stuart wagging a warning finger at her.

Her hair was a gorgeous spire of fabulousness. The wig was taken off, bagged up and bought. Of course now she needed to go hunting for that blingy tiara. And she had allowed herself the full Saturday to go wedding shopping. Yet another item was added to her list of 'boughts' and another to the 'to buys'.

Chapter 43

While Max was in Angel Hair, and from the sanctity of their study Stuart heard the key in the outside door, bang on time. If he was in, he always kept out of the way when Sheila came on Saturdays and Tuesdays because he felt guilty that they had a cleaner. He couldn't lounge about while she busied around him; he would have felt uncomfortably indulgent. Instead he would bob his head out of the door to say a quick courteous hello and then pretend he was busy.

Although this time when he emerged to say his hello it wasn't Sheila who was standing with her bucket full of cleaning items but a much younger woman.

'Oh hello,' he said, thrown a little. One, because it wasn't Sheila, and two, because the short, slender woman with the swingy brown ponytail was vaguely familiar.

'Hi,' said the woman. 'I'm Sheila's daughter, Jenny. I'm covering for her as she's pulled her back and can't walk . . . Stuart?'

Then she smiled and he realized exactly who she was. 'Jenny? Jenny Thompson?' *Smiling Jenny*.

'Stuart Taylor. Oh my God, how lovely to see you again. How many years has it been?'

Stuart smiled. 'Oh too flaming many,' he said. 'Seventeen?'

'It's never that long since we left school, is it?' Jenny started to tot up in her head and gasped. 'My goodness, so it is. How scary is that!'

'I didn't know that Sheila was your mum. All the time she's been working here, and I never knew.'

'Well, Thompson's a common name,' said Jenny beaming that same smile she did at school. 'Smiling Jenny' she used to be called, and she was always wearing bright colours. The clothes had changed, seeing as she was in jeans and a black T-shirt with a cleaning tabard over it, but her smile was the same.

'So, what's happened to you since I saw you last?' said Stuart, realizing that he was grinning as widely as Jenny was. 'Are you still with Gav? Surely not, after all these years.'

Jenny and Gav were glued at the hip and had been since primary school.

'Sadly not,' said Jenny. 'He was killed in a bike smash ten years ago.'

Stuart was genuinely shocked. 'Oh Jenny, that's awful. I'm sorry, I didn't know. '

'It didn't make the newspaper at the time,' said Jenny. 'And his parents didn't want any obituaries written. You're not the first to say you never heard about it.'

Stuart was really cut up by the news. When they were kids, they all thought they were immortal.

'That must have been terrible for you. And his family, of course.'

'Yes, yes, it was,' she replied quietly. 'I thought we'd be together for ever. But . . . not to be.' She raised her shoulders and dropped them. 'Anyway, never mind about that, I hear you're getting married soon. At least, Mum said that the people she worked for here were, so I'm presuming that's you.'

'Yep,' nodded Stuart, but he didn't want to talk about that. He wanted to find out about Jenny. The years between now and their schooldays melted away in an instant.

'Did you and Gav get married, then? Before . . .' He tailed off, not really knowing how to put it sensitively.

'Naw,' Jenny answered. 'We were happy as we were, really. We lived together and probably would have got married one day, if we'd been lucky enough to have kids.'

'Where are you living?'

'Same street I grew up on,' said Jenny. 'Farthing Street. Although the kids are always painting out the "h" and the "s" – little buggers.'

They both chuckled then Jenny said, 'Maybe if I'd been cleverer at school I could have had a posh job and bought a big house like this.'

'Don't be fooled,' said Stuart. 'All this comes from my partner.'

As soon as he said it, he felt embarrassed. As if he was poncing off Maxine.

But Jenny didn't seem to notice. 'I wish I'd been blessed in the brains department like Gillian Stephenson and Luke Appleby. Wonder what they're up to these days. Running ICI, most like.'

'I'm still best mates with Luke,' said Stuart. 'And he's doing very well for himself.'

'Oh that's good,' Jenny replied with a genuine smile. 'He was a nice lad.'

'He doesn't know about Gavin either or he would have told me. He'll be shocked as well.'

Jenny nodded. 'Ah well, best get on.' She picked up her cleaning stuff. 'I've got to shoot off home quickly after this so I can let the neighbour's dog out before I do my afternoon shift.'

'Yes, of course, don't let me get in your way. I'll be in the study if you want me for anything.'

It didn't sit easy with Stuart that he was flicking through eBay pages while Jenny was cleaning their three toilets. He could think of better ways for her to spend a Saturday morning. She probably thought he was doing executive things like stock-moving and share-dealing. If only she knew.

He was glad when she knocked on his door and said she had finished and was going home. He offered to give her a lift. She turned him down and he insisted. It wasn't as if he had anything else to do. Maxine was out shopping and as usual he was waiting around for her to come home.

Stuart pulled into the huge estate, known locally as the Money

Box because most of the streets were named after coins – Penny Road, Guinea Terrace, Tanner Lane, Farthing Street, among others. Jenny's was the middle one in a row of five terraced houses. The windows were sparkling clean and white lacy curtains hung at the windows, swooped up with ties at the sides.

'Looks a nice house,' said Stuart, meaning it.

'Next to yours? You're kidding,' laughed Jenny. 'Although mine is plenty big enough for me and Alan.'

'Alan?' asked Stuart. So she had found someone else after Gav, then.

'Do you want to see him?' said Jenny. 'I love showing him off.'

Stuart followed her in through her front door. The whole downstairs was open-plan: a small square front room then a breakfast bar and beyond that a kitchen. It was fresh and light – and had such a cosy feeling he found himself sighing with delight. The sofa that sat in front of the fire was full of cushions and he just wanted to relax into it. It looked a hundred times more comfortable than the 'stylish' black-leather ones with the low backs that they had at home.

One of the furry grey cushions had ears. At first Stuart thought it was a toy, but then Jenny picked it up and placed it on his shoulder.

'He's housetrained so don't worry,' she said. 'This is Alan. He's a British Giant Rabbit.'

'Oh my,' chuckled Stuart. 'He weighs a ton.'

'Scratch his ears, he likes that,' said Jenny proudly. 'He's such a tart. He'll go to anyone who'll give him some attention.'

Stuart gave a mock-scream as he felt the rabbit prodding his ear with his twitching nose.

'He likes to smell ears,' laughed Jenny. 'He's a bit weird.' She took the weighty Alan from Stuart and put him back on his cushion. 'He watches *Emmerdale*, can you believe? Wherever he is when the music comes on, he runs to sit on the sofa and take his place next to me. I bet he thinks it's about carrot farms.'

Stuart smiled. 'He's great. I can see your tap is on, by the way.'

'Oh it's always on the dribble. I can't turn it off properly,' said Jenny. 'I should really get a plumber in to sort it.'

'Here, let me have a look at it,' said Stuart.

'No, don't worry . . .' Jenny protested but Stuart was already walking over to check it out.

'Have you got an adjustable wrench, by any chance?'

Jenny reached under the sink and pulled out a tin of tools. 'Is there one in there?' she asked.

'Perfect,' said Stuart, picking out what he needed. He had the dripping tap mended in a jiffy.

'Aw, thanks ever so much for that. It was driving me mad,' said Jenny, foraging in her handbag. 'What do I owe you?'

'Jenny Thompson, don't you insult me,' returned Stuart fiercely.

'Okay,' said Jenny, snapping shut her purse. 'Thank you.'

If she'd offered him a cup of tea, he knew he wouldn't have refused it. He didn't put her on the spot, though, and wait to be asked, but he thought he could have stayed in that little house all afternoon catching up with Jenny Thompson. As he walked back to his car, Stuart felt his chest puff up with the pride of being needed. Yes, that was it. For a few minutes he was needed. He had forgotten what that felt like living with the super-competent Max.

Chapter 44

Later that day, as they leaned on the bar in the Lamp, Luke picked his moment.

'What are you going to be wearing – to get married in?'

Stuart spluttered into his pint. 'What sort of a question is that for a red-blooded male to ask? Man-up, you big girl.'

'I'm asking because I want to know what I need to wear,' replied Luke. 'I'm going to look a bit stupid wearing a Hugo Boss suit if you're wearing jeans.'

'I can't wear jeans now we're getting married in church, can I?' said Stuart. He didn't want to talk weddings – especially not tonight.

'Well? Are you wearing a suit or what?'

'I'll have to, won't I?' huffed Stuart.

'Buy a new suit for your wedding,' pressed Luke.

'I don't want to buy a new one. I've got a couple of work suits and a black one for funerals. One of those will have to do.'

'You can't wear a funeral suit for your wedding,' Luke scoffed.

'It's just a black suit. It doesn't have "For Funerals" embroidered on it.'

'You can afford a new one,' said Luke, wishing that Max had never asked him to interfere. Stuart could be really hard work when he dug his heels in.

'It's a waste of money for one day.'

'I would have lent you one of mine but that wouldn't really be much help.'

'If you'd had the decency to stop growing when you were seventeen it might have,' said Stuart.

As boys they had been of a very similar build, if not colouring. Stuart had brown eyes and mid-brown hair; Luke's hair was very dark but his eyes were light grey – the exact same colour his hair would turn in his early twenties, in fact. By seventeen they were both six foot tall; by twenty-one Luke had added another five inches to that and bulked up in the gym. They now had very different physiques.

'Well, let's hire some suits, instead,' Luke suggested.

Stuart stared into his pint. 'Whatever. What-fucking-ever.'

'What's up with you?' said Luke, raising his eyebrows at Stuart's rare profanity.

'Sorry, mate,' said Stuart, puffing the air out of his cheeks. He took another sip of beer. 'I saw Jenny Thompson today. Do you remember her?'

'Course I remember her,' said Luke. 'Smiling Jenny? That's a blast from the past. Where did you meet her?'

'She was cleaning our three bogs.'

'Eh?'

'Our cleaner is off with a poorly back. So her daughter turned up to cover her shift and that daughter happened to be Jenny.'

'Small world,' whistled Luke. 'How's she doing?'

'Did you know Gav White was killed on his bike ten years ago?'

'Bloody hell, no, I didn't.' Luke was rocked by that news. Gav was always so full of beans. Solid as a barn door and bike-crazy. 'Were he and Jenny still courting when it happened?'

'Yes, living together. No kids, though. Shame, isn't it?'

'God, yeah,' said Luke, shaking his head. Twenty-three was no age to die. 'You've got to enjoy it while you can is the lesson there, I think.'

'Yeah,' said Stuart. 'Isn't it just?'

'Next Saturday, we'll check out some hire suits. Oh hang on, that's your birthday.'

'It's fine. I won't be doing anything special. Max will probably be working,' Stuart grumbled.

'Okay. Next Saturday afternoon it is, then.'

'If I must,' said Stu, though suits were way down on the list of things agitating his brain. He didn't admit to his oldest friend that Jenny Thompson was top.

Chapter 45

'Oh my GOD, you're back!' Faye shrieked at the door when she opened it to find Bel on the step. 'Come in, come in.' Her arms were flapping like windmills because her immediate instinct was to throw them round her stepdaughter, but she didn't because Bel didn't do hugs with her. Only at birthdays and Christmas.

Trevor appeared from behind her and Bel walked straight into his outstretched arms.

'Oh love, we were so worried. Are you all right?'

'Yes, I'm fine,' said Bel, savouring the warmth of her dad. 'I'm so sorry.'

'It's okay, don't you worry,' said Faye, speaking for Trevor. 'We're both just glad you're home and safe.'

'Have you heard from Richard?' asked Trevor.

'Yes. He texted and left a lot of messages. He wants to talk to me.'

'I'll bet he bloody does,' growled Trevor. 'No one knows where he's hiding. Or Shaden. I wouldn't be surprised if—'

'Trevor,' warned Faye. She knew him well enough to know how all his sentences ended. Implying that Shaden and Richard were together wasn't what Bel needed to hear.

'Sorry, love. No doubt they'll both crawl out from under their stones soon enough,' huffed Trevor, giving his daughter another squeeze.

'Would you like some tea?' asked Faye. 'Shall I make us all a big pot of tea? The kettle's just boiled.'

'Please,' said Bel. Faye strutted off in her feathery heeled mules. Bel didn't think anyone but the Bosomworth sisters wore those any more.

'Come and sit down,' said Trevor, pulling her by the hand into the lounge. 'Where have you been?'

'I went up to Haworth.'

'Where did you stay?'

'The cottages,' said Bel.

'The Bronte cottages?' asked Trevor.

'Yes, Dad. The Bronte cottages.'

'How did you get in?'

'I've had a set of keys for them for ages. I hoped you wouldn't remember that.'

'I didn't remember,' said Trevor. 'But I rang Emily just in case. It's being rented out to a man—'

'I know. I told him not to tell you where I was.'

'Oh you silly girl,' said Trevor. He was wearing a woolly cardigan, a real Dad knit. Bel suddenly felt like a little girl again. She plonked herself down on their lovely big sofa and nestled into the cushions.

'What you have to remember, Trevor, is that Bel had to deal with things in her own way,' said Faye, returning with the pot of tea on a tray and a plate of biscuits. Then she added hurriedly, 'At least I hope I'm right in that.'

Bel spotted the worry in Faye's voice that she had said the wrong thing. Bel knew she made Faye feel on edge, even after all these years. How awful was that really?

'Yep, in a nutshell, Faye. You know what I'm like. Headstrong to the last,' said Bel to her and Faye smiled. Bel noticed, probably for the first time, how much her small kindnesses meant to her stepmother.

'Have you seen your friends yet?' asked Trevor as Faye poured tea, tipping the pot gracefully over the cups, like a lady of the manor.

'No, that's my next job.'

'Hang on,' said Trevor, suddenly recapping. 'If Emily was rented out, where did you stay? Surely not Charlotte?'

'Yes,' nodded Bel. 'It was okay. Functional. Needs a tin opener in the drawer, though.' She smiled at her private joke and felt a strange pang inside her that she couldn't explain.

'I'm selling the cottages,' said Trevor. 'Just to let you know. I've been thinking of doing it for some time, to be honest.'

'Selling them?' Bel was horrified.

'Oh Bel, we don't go up there any more; they're sitting empty and it's a shame. They're a developer's dream. But I haven't got the energy to oversee another project – not with the business expanding into the continent – so I'm letting them go.'

Her dad was right. He and Faye never went there these days and it would make a beautiful retreat for whoever bought it. Still, the sale of Bronte Cottages would mark the end of an era. There had been so many lovely weekends spent there with her dad: the wind howling outside while they were cosy within, logs burning in the stove, warming their hands on giant mugs of hot chocolate . . . She had taken Richard up there once for a cosy weekend, but he had turned up his nose at the basic accommodation and booked them into the nearest swanky hotel instead. He had never known the deprivation that a missing tin opener could cause. A ghost of a smile visited Bel's lips at the thought of her spats with Dan Regent.

'What's tickled you?' Trevor nudged her.

'I was just thinking about the guy who was renting Emily. He's a doctor – and a writer.'

'I know,' said Trevor. 'John North. I've read all his books. I heard he'd lost the plot, if you'll excuse the pun. Woman trouble. Had a bit of a breakdown.'

'Really?' said Bel.

'Oh yes. His fiancée ran off with—' Trevor stopped, realizing that maybe he shouldn't talk about unfaithful partners.

'It's okay, Dad. Go on,' Bel was thirsty for more details.

'Well,' began Trevor cautiously, in case he upset his daughter, 'she ran off with his best friend. He's a friend of Bob Rogers, from the packaging company we use. Well, Bob's stayed at Emily before and asked me if I'd rent it to John North for a couple of months because he wanted to hole himself up in the country. He was absolutely heartbroken apparently.'

'Poor man,' said Faye, handing over a plate of biscuits. 'Did you see much of him, Bel?'

'A little,' said Bel, trying not to let thoughts of Dan Regent into her head. He was a closed chapter now. Cathy had wanted to talk to him and that could only mean that she had realized her mistake and wanted him back. Just as Richard had realized his.

'You should eat something, Bel. You're so thin. Can I make you some pasta?'

Faye's cooking was lovely. She always took such care over it, but Bel wasn't hungry. She wanted to go and see the friendly faces of Violet and Max. Then she needed to go home and think about what she was going to do about Richard.

Chapter 46

Lydiana Bosomworth-Greaves was slightly tiddly. She'd had far too much wine at the ladies' luncheon, and when that happened her voice lost all control over its volume button.

Talk had bent round to the big story in the *Melbourne Star* that day: the Barnsley bride who ran away after dumping her new husband so spectacularly at their reception. Someone had mentioned that Lydiana came from the same Yorkshire town of Barnsley, didn't she? One of the lead *dramatis personae* was called Bosomworth too. The story was deliciously tacky.

'Are you related to the "Blonde Beauty", Lydiana – or is Bosomworth a very common name in Yorkshire?' asked Carolyn Huggins with a snigger.

'It certainly is not common,' bristled Lydiana. 'It's very rare. As far as I know there is only the one family called Bosomworth in the whole county.'

'Oh so are you related to the people in the story?' said ex-Leeds lady Mary Philipson, who was delighted that the stuck-up Lydiana had links to a sex scandal. From what she could see the 'Blonde Beauty' looked more like a little scrubber to her. The story had obviously been sold by her to throw the poor bride into a very dark light.

Out of the corner of her eye Lydiana could see that Elle White, Fiona McCarrick and Ruthie Hunnerton were equally enjoying watching her squirm.

'My sister married the father of the bride, Trevor Candy.' Lydiana decided to deflect attention away from her errant niece and on to something that would make them all shut right up. 'They have a multimillion-pound fortune in chocolate. More than multi. The newspaper has grossly underestimated the worth of the company. And I do believe that Trevor is up for a knighthood. My sister is actually in negotiations to move the whole operation to the States,' she lied, enjoying the sight of Mary Philipson's smirk drying up. 'Or Switzerland. Possibly both.'

Interesting, thought one of the group. *What a very small world it really was.* And one which would soon be traversed with a flight, if what she had just heard was true.

Chapter 47

Max didn't say a word when she opened the door to Bel. She just threw her arms round her friend and squashed her.

'You silly cow,' she said, pulling Bel to arm's length. 'We've been worried sick about you.'

Violet gave her a gentler hug, which was good as Bel's ribs were now bruised.

'I've opened a bottle of wine,' said Max. 'And got some nibbles in. Sit – and talk. We've got the house to ourselves because Stuart is out with his best mate, Luke, who should be, as we speak, trying to persuade my stubborn fiancé into a top hat and tails for the wedding. Oh Bel, I am so glad you rang.'

Violet was glad too. It gave her a perfect excuse to get out of the house. Glyn was in one of his planning moods, talking about futures and children and how he planned to convert the spare room in the flat to a nursery. And though she wanted to scream at him that he couldn't even make it as far as bloody B&Q to pick up some wood, it was easier just to let him ramble on. Getting a text from Max, asking her if could drive up to hers because Bel was coming round, was a blessed relief and worth all the sulking she would have to endure when she got home.

Bel sat down on Max's black-leather sofa next to Violet while Max poured her a drink. She recognized it as a very pricey wine.

'That stuff is twenty quid a bottle; put the cork back in immediately.'

'I will not,' said Max. 'You deserve it.'

'Oh heck, I wish you hadn't told me that. I'll go and spill it now,' said Violet in a panicky voice. 'I'm starting to shake with fear already.'

'Get it down your neck, then, and steady your nerves,' said Max, raising her glass. 'A toast. To Bel. For being the bravest woman I know.'

Bel huffed. 'I'm not brave. I was vengeful. What drove me to do what I did was hate, not bravery.'

'Or hurt,' put in Violet. 'It must have hurt a lot what Richard did behind your back.'

'When did you find out?' asked Max, savouring a mouthful of wine. It was lovely. She was glad she wasn't driving, as the other two were.

'Two months ago. I swear I have never looked at Richard's phone messages before, ever, but that day his phone was charging in the kitchen and I can't explain it – I just felt that I *had* to look at it, as if I was drawn there by some force or intuition . . . I don't know what it was. And I found loads of messages from "S": "S" couldn't wait to see him again, "S" had had such a good time with him, stuff like that.' Bel didn't tell them about the seedier messages: that "S" was wearing crotchless knickers while waiting for him and how "S" really enjoyed their weekend in Las Vegas together. She knew that if she ever did get back with Richard again, that would only give everyone more to forgive him for – and they had too much already, thanks to her. 'I could have put Miss Marple to shame with all the detective work I did after that little discovery,' she went on.

'Like what?'

'Going through his pockets, hacking into his email.'

'I can't believe he saved stuff on his computer without deleting it,' said Violet. 'At least that shows he's too thick to have had an affair before.'

'Or that he's totally cocksure,' said Max with a huff.

'He'd saved all her emails in a file,' said Bel, coughing away some rising emotion. 'I mean, you save things you want to look at over and over again, don't you? '

'If you're a girl, you do,' said Violet. 'Maybe he put them in a file so he could delete them all at once.' It was a lame counter-argument; she knew that as soon as she had said it and so moved on quickly to another question. 'Have you heard from him?'

'Oh yes. He's left lots of texts and messages. He wants to talk. I haven't replied yet but I'm going to have to meet with him, seeing as I married him.'

'Are you married? Is it legally binding?' asked Violet. 'I mean, you haven't consummated it, have you?'

'I'm guessing it's all legal,' said Bel.

'Maybe you can have it annulled.'

'Why didn't you walk out before the bloody vows? I hope he's not entitled to half your money now,' snapped Max.

'I don't know if he is or not. I obviously wasn't thinking that straight when I planned all this,' said Bel, taking a throatful of wine. 'I thought I was but, as I now find, I was totally blinkered, with no real sense of my true course.'

'Anyone would have been, in your shoes,' said Violet in a soft, kind voice.

'What happened after I left? At the reception?' asked Bel.

'Carnage,' replied Max, through a mouthful of stuffed olive. 'Richard followed you out and didn't come back; your aunt wrapped herself round your slaggy cousin like a human shield and they disappeared. Your dad and stepmum gave an announcement that the day was probably over but the drinks were on the house if anyone needed a brandy for the shock—'

'Your stepmum was brilliant,' Violet butted in. 'She bustled around everyone and calmed everything down. She got rid of the cake and spoke to the hotel staff. I think your dad was a bit too overcome to do much.'

Bel dropped her head into her hands. When she concocted her plan, she hadn't thought about the fallout left in her wake.

The fantasy in her head had ended with her flouncing magnificently out of the reception, leaving a sea full of agape gobs.

'I wish we could have helped you through it,' said Max, proffering a bowl of Japanese crackers. 'I wish you'd felt able to talk to us.'

'Yes, I should have. But I didn't,' said Bel. 'Alas, I've always been the same. I always think I know better than anyone else how to deal with things. I bury myself away and then emerge to find out that, actually, I don't know that much after all.'

'Where did you go?' asked Violet, reaching for a Parmesan twist.

'My dad has some cottages on the edge of the Haworth moors,' said Bel. 'I stayed in one of those.'

Next door to a doctor with an equally smashed-up heart. A doctor who imploded instead of exploding, like me. A doctor whom I'll never see again so I really ought to stop thinking about him.

'Anyway, cheer me up,' said Bel, turning to Max. 'What's happening with your wedding plans?' If anything could chase Dan Regent out of her head for an hour or so, it would be Max's plotting.

'Ooh yes, do tell,' added Violet.

'Well,' began Max with a smile as wide as the River Nile – and soon Bel and Violet wished they'd never asked.

Chapter 48

Violet pushed open the door quietly, hoping that Glyn was in bed and fast asleep. She should have known better.

'Where've you been? I've rung you loads of times,' he said, coming from the kitchen holding a mug of tea and a half-eaten cream doughnut.

'You know where I've been – at Max's house,' she said. 'Bel's come back home.'

'I was getting worried. Why didn't you answer the phone?'

'Because I was talking to my friends,' snapped Violet. 'And my phone going off every two minutes is really annoying, Glyn.'

'I only wanted to check you were okay,' said Glyn in a hurt tone. 'Pardon me for caring. It's dark and drivers on the roads up there are mad. There are always accidents happening and being reported in the *Chronicle*. There was a fatality not that long ago.'

Violet bit her lip. It was too late for an argument and if she started shouting she might not be able to stop.

'I made you four teas that went cold,' said Glyn.

'Well, why did you do that?' Violet said with a dry laugh that was empty of humour but full of exasperation. Who in their right mind did that?

'Because I thought you'd be home earlier than this,' was his answer. 'You know I had a headache earlier.'

Violet growled inside. 'I'm going straight to bed,' she said.

Glyn was at her heels a minute later, after turning off the lights and abandoning the tea but finishing off the bun.

In bed he snuggled up to her back and she totally shrugged him off for once. Her phone had shown there were twenty-three missed calls from him during the two hours she was at Max's and she was really annoyed with him.

'I'm too warm when you hold on to me,' she said.

She felt him slink over to the far side of the bed then heard his head fall heavily on to the pillow with a barely stifled sigh.

She closed her eyes and tried not to scream. She felt totally wound up and knew she wouldn't get to sleep for ages. But if she got up now and made herself a drink, he would trail after her like a hopeful puppy wanting a stroke. She lay still and hoped he would drift off soon.

When they first got together – sixteen months ago – his attentions to her welfare had been like a cold drink on a thirsty throat. She had just been dumped by her boyfriend of six months, Greg, who went back to his ex and ripped her ego to shreds in the process. She had been sitting alone in a coffee shop in Meadowhall and Glyn asked if he could share her table as there were no other places spare. He was smiley and attentive and ended up buying her another coffee and taking her number. Her savaged heart enjoyed the male attention; for a while it drove away painful thoughts of Greg.

Glyn took her to a restaurant for their first date. He opened the door for her, pulled out the chair for her, seemed engrossed in everything she said. And he paid at the end. He made her feel like a lady and it was intoxicating.

By date three she was hooked. She had never had so much attention from a man. Over cocktails that night he told her that he had just left work and was suing his ex-boss for constructive dismissal. On the day when they had met in Meadowhall, he had just been to see a therapist for the first time because he was steps away from a full nervous breakdown. He said that meeting Violet had pulled him back from the brink and he loved her for it.

Violet felt so sorry for the vulnerable man, even if she did think it was a little early to be talking about love. He told her that without her in his life he knew he would slip back further than ever. Violet was a naturally caring person and she felt that she wanted to help Glyn recover from his depression; plus, she felt slightly obliged to him after entering his life and letting him consider her as 'his rock'. But his panic attacks started getting worse not better and going outside the house was increasingly a chore for him, so they stopped going out and they spent all of their time together at his flat.

She moved in fully with him within three months of their initial meeting and at first it was sweet how he always had her dinner ready for her when she came in from work. But within a very short time the relationship started to feel cloying rather than loving. What had been sweet attention at the beginning had become a constant demand for her attention, her approval. He was always pawing her, trying to hold her hand, touching her, needing to have sex as proof that she wasn't going off him. And the more she pulled back, the more he swamped her. She was rooted in his life by then; she had made herself indispensable. To extricate herself would rip him apart. He told her that if she left he would be in a worse state than when she found him.

She heard him snore gently beside her and she tentatively slunk out of bed and padded out of the bedroom and into the kitchen. There she made herself a hot chocolate and sat at the table wondering how she could stop the conveyor belt that she felt strapped to as it hurtled towards her wedding day, because Freya's cautionary tale had been circling in her head ever since she heard it.

Chapter 49

It took until Tuesday for Bel to ring Richard's number. She put it back down again the first time it started ringing; her hands were shaking.

'Come on, you silly cow,' she gee-ed herself up. Again she pressed in the number and waited. He picked up on the fifth ring.

'Bel,' he said in a voice flooded with warmth and relief. 'Are you all right?'

All the words Bel had prepared crumbled into bits like flaky pastry in her mouth. How did one answer that after all that had happened?

'Well,' was all she managed before her throat clogged with tears.

'I haven't known whether to ring you or leave you to think things through. I am so glad you rang, honey. I can't tell you how much.'

His voice was so soft and tender and full of concern. She tried to speak but nothing came out.

'Bel, I don't want to rush you. You take all the time in the world. You call me all the names under the sun if it helps. But I want to make this up to you. I don't know how, but I'm going to try and I promise you I *will* succeed.'

The part of Bel's heart labelled 'Richard' began to thaw. He was saying everything she wanted to hear.

'I know you're upset and you probably can't talk . . .'

He was so on her wavelength. He was being strong for her.

'Bel, I'm not going to harass you. I want to see you but only when you're ready to see me. I must have been mad to risk losing you. I wish I could tell you why I did it.'

Bel sniffed.

'There I go upsetting you again. Bel, we're going to be fine. In your own time. Take as much of it as you need.'

Bel pulled in a huge breath to ask the big question, which came out of a very croaky throat.

'What about Shaden?'

'What about Shaden?' Richard growled with passion and just the right amount of venom. 'I never want to hear that name again. I could vomit when I think about her. And, trust me, I don't think about her one bit.'

'So, after the wedding, you didn't go off together?'

'NO, I DID NOT,' he yelled, as if that was the most ridiculous thing in the world. 'I don't know where she is, nor do I want to.'

'Okay,' said Bel, hating herself for being so floppy and full of tears. She had wanted to conduct their first conversation with the stance and attitude of a world-famous boxer.

'Honey, I love you so much. I'm going to prove that to you. Call me any time, day or night. I want to see you so much. When you're ready. But soon, I hope.'

Bel put down the phone, unable to reply. She was a wreck. He had smashed her with his nice warm voice. She just wished time would rewind to the day when she picked up his phone in the kitchen and checked it. She should have confronted him and worked this out then, when there was merely water under the bridge, and not left it until now, when there was a tsunami's-worth of ocean thundering under it and threatening its total collapse.

Chapter 50

Stuart came home from work an hour early with a headache. He was prone to migraines, always had been. Luckily, though, the Nurofen he took before setting off had done the trick and by the time he reached home the headache had almost dissipated. For once he wouldn't need to go to bed with the lights off, avoiding even the slightest of sounds.

As he unlocked the door, he heard the sound of vacuuming coming from down the hallway and he felt his heart give an excited little jump in his chest. Of course, the cleaner came on Tuesday. He knew he would be disappointed if he found Sheila there and not Jenny and – God forgive him – he hoped Sheila wasn't well enough to come back and resume her twice-weekly duties.

Jenny jumped when he pushed open the lounge door.

'Blimey O'Riley, I thought you were a burglar,' she said.

'Sorry, Jen,' he laughed. 'I was actually trying not to scare you.'

'You did a rotten job of it,' she smiled, palm flat on her panting chest. 'You okay? You look as if you've been whitewashed.'

'I'm just at the tail-end of a migraine,' said Stuart.

'I've got some paracetamol in my handbag in the kitchen. Shall I fetch them for you?'

'It's fine, I've taken something,' said Stuart, touched at her concern.

'Mum gets those. Do you get the flashing lights ones or the sicky ones?'

'The sicky ones,' replied Stuart.

'Sit down and I'll make you a cuppa,' said Jenny, clicking the Dyson to an upright position.

'I'm fine, Jen. I don't want to disturb you.'

'It's no trouble, honest. I've just this one corner to vacuum then I'm done, anyway.'

'Tell you what, I'll go and put the kettle on,' said Stuart. 'I'll make you a cuppa instead while you finish off.'

Jenny smiled her Jenny Thompson smile and conceded defeat.

Stuart walked into the kitchen to find it gleaming, even more than it did when Sheila tackled it, if that was possible. The kettle had just boiled when Jenny joined him. She flicked her hand towards his nice suit.

'It's all that executive stress bringing on these headaches,' she said.

'I'm hardly an executive, Jen,' Stuart laughed a little at the thought. He'd worn a suit to work for the third time ever because he had been recently promoted and would be called on to go to meetings round a table periodically. Max had seen the position advertised in his company newsletter and nagged him to apply for it. Why shouldn't he have a better pension and more work benefits when he deserved them after seventeen years of loyal service, was her argument. His boss was pushing him too from the other side, telling him that the new job was in the bag and there would be a significant pay increase that came with it. It wasn't a fraction of what Max brought home, of course, but he felt increasingly under self-pressure to contribute more to the household pot. He hated meetings, though. He was out of his comfort zone in a suit and making small talk. Thank goodness it wouldn't happen all that often, but still he wished he'd stayed in his old position where he was happy and unstressed and relatively migraine-free.

Stuart poured boiling water over the instant coffee in the

mugs. Max had bought a huge fancy Krups machine but he had never mastered how to use it. Not that it mattered, because he didn't want a throat-punching espresso or a fluffy cappuccino, anyway – a bog-standard cup of instant Douwe Egberts had always been good enough for him.

'I thought you weren't supposed to drink coffee when you had migraines,' said Jenny.

'Mine aren't triggered off by food,' Stuart replied, tipping milk into the mugs. 'I get stress-heads.'

'The smell of oranges can set Mum off,' said Jenny. 'And cheese. Shame, really, as she loves cheese but she just can't have it.'

'How's your mum's back?' Stuart handed the coffee over to Jenny.

'She's doing okay. She'll be up on her feet again soon. It's killing her lying down and having to rest.'

'I would have thought it would be killing you, doing her jobs for her as well as your own.'

'We're a team,' Jen said. 'She'd do the same for me. Look.' She reached into her coat pocket. 'We've just had these printed.' She handed over a pretty pink business card with the company name: Two Women and Their Mops.

'We've even got an accountant now,' beamed Jenny. 'We're doing really well. We've got lots of customers.' The pride was bursting out of her.

'That's brilliant, Jen,' said Stuart, impressed. 'Don't overwork yourself, though.'

'No, I won't do that. A two-woman cleaning business is about as ambitious as I'm ever likely to get. I like being at home with Alan in the evenings too much. I don't want to be one of those people that never has any free time.' Jenny looked up at him with her pretty hazel eyes. 'I bet that sounds really sad to someone like you.'

'No, no, it doesn't at all,' said Stuart, and he meant it. 'Lucky Alan.'

'Why don't you have any pets? You've got enough room for a herd of Great Danes in this place. Or is it a flock?'

Stuart smiled at the thought of a flock of Great Danes. Jenny really was sweet and funny.

'Max doesn't want any pets,' he replied. Something else Max had got her own way on. But change was afoot, thank goodness – better late than never.

'Mind you, your lovely white rugs wouldn't stand a dog or a cat trailing in muck from the garden. Even Alan's hairs stick on the cushions,' chuckled Jen. 'Listen to me talking like a nutter about a rabbit. Anyone would think we sat down at the end of the day and had a discussion about politics.'

'Don't be daft,' grinned Stuart. 'I know what you mean. It's just nice to have another living breathing presence in the house.'

'If you haven't got the alternative of a living breathing partner,' added Jen.

'Yeah,' said Stuart, thinking that he might as well classify himself as living alone for all he saw of Max these days. Right on cue the phone went off in his pocket. A text from her.

Won't be home until late. Eat without me.

'I'd best get off,' said Jen, draining her mug.

'Got another job?'

'No, I want to get to a shop before it shuts,' said Jen.

'Come on, I'll give you a lift,' said Stuart.

'No, you've got a headache. I'll get the bus . . .'

But Stu wasn't going to take no for an answer. It was going to be another long lonely night. Taking Jenny home would at least drag it out a little less for him.

'Four six five.'

Sitting at her desk, Max dictated the security number of her Visa card down the phone. She had just bought a honeymoon – a weekend in a gorgeous country spa hotel in Stow-on-the-Wold.

Personally she would have liked to have gone somewhere hot and sunny, but Stuart hated going abroad. He burned so easily and got bored, whereas Max could have vegged out all day by a pool doing nothing but reading and sipping cocktails. He was probably going to be a bit cross that she had booked a honeymoon behind his back, seeing as they had planned to spend the weekend quietly at home – but after seeing her swaggering down the aisle in her lovely gypsy wedding dress he would figure she had more surprises in store. She knew him inside out after many years of courting, and was confident he'd ride with it and grudgingly enjoy it all. Nothing surer.

Once the booking had been confirmed, Max started googling the finest country house in the area for their reception.

Chapter 51

'Just drop me off here, will you, please?' asked Jen, pointing to the chip shop on the edge of the Money Box estate.

'Wonder what you're having for your tea, then?' smiled Stuart.

'I'm going to get fish and chips and peas on a tray and eat them as I walk home.'

'And how are you going to manage that and your mop and bucket?'

'Ah,' Jen clicked her fingers. 'That's why I was never in the top class at school.'

'Tell you what,' Stuart suggested. 'How about we get two trays and sit and eat them in the car? I haven't had fish and chips for ages.' He was salivating at the thought.

There was a fancy baguette waiting for him in the fridge at home. French cheese and salad and bollocks. He could eat that alone in the cavernous kitchen or have fish and chips and a chat with Jenny.

'Your lovely car will stink of vinegar,' warned Jen.

'Sod the car,' said Stuart, clipping off his seat belt. 'Scraps as well?'

After he had dropped Jenny off, he drove over to call in on his mum and dad, who still lived in the small house in Rose Lane they had bought when they were first married. He didn't want to go straight home and rattle around in Max's big house by himself. He was a people person and always had been. He liked living on an estate and seeing things happen outside the window. And he was an animal person too. After the wedding he was definitely going to get a cat or a dog or something. Or a rabbit – like Alan.

He sat in the fish-and-chip-scented car for a few minutes after pulling up outside his parents' house. He caught sight of his face in the rear-view mirror and saw that he was smiling. And he knew that smile was a direct result of thinking about Jenny Thompson and Alan. He had no right storing them both in the part of his brain where his best thoughts were kept, not when he was getting married in just over a month's time. And so he was here at his mum's house to try to herd himself back on course.

'Hello, love,' said Sandra Taylor, as her son came in through the door. A homely smell of beef hash cooking on the hob greeted him. 'Cuppa?'

'Go on, then,' said Stuart. The kettle was always on at his mam's house. He threw himself on the sofa next to his dad, who was reading the racing results.

'I wish I'd bet on that bugger Big Fat White Wedding,' said David Taylor. 'It came in at twenty to one.'

'Tea, David?' called Sandra.

'Aye, go on, then,' replied David, still shaking his head slowly from side to side.

'Why didn't you bet on it?'

'Because it's his first race and the stupid bloody racing pundit said it had no chance.'

Funny that his dad should be talking about weddings, thought Stuart. Was it a sign that what he was about to ask was the right way forward, after all?

'Mum, can I ask you a favour?' he said, when Sandra delivered two cups of milky tea to him and his dad.

'Course you can, love.'

'Any chance of you making me a small wedding cake?'

'For you and Maxine? I thought you weren't having any trim-mings. When I asked you before if you wanted me to make you one you said no—'

'I've changed my mind,' he cut in. 'Nothing too fancy. And I think I might book a meal after the ceremony at the Lamp for us all. As a surprise. I was in there the other day with Luke and they've redecorated it. Looks nice.' *Not to Max's standards, but okay to mine.*

'Of course I'll bake you a cake,' said Sandra, clapping her hands together with delight. 'You know I've wanted to do that from the off.'

'Good,' said Stu. 'Don't say anything to Max.'

'Well, we hardly see anything of her, really,' said Sandra, unable to keep the disappointment entirely out of her voice.

If Jenny were going to be her daughter-in-law, she'd always be round here, Stuart said to himself, before he reprimanded himself for thinking that. He did wish his fiancée and his mum were closer, though. Considering how many years he and Max had been in a relationship, she and Sandra hadn't met as often as they should have. It wasn't as if they didn't get on, but he knew his mum felt awkward in the posh surroundings of Max's big house, so she visited them less than ever these days. And Max never had any time to go visiting because she was always working. A wed-ding reception would be a nice place to do a bit of bonding, Stuart thought.

'I'm glad you're having a bit of a do,' said David, folding up the newspaper.

'It's not that much of a do, really,' Stuart clarified the point.

'Is it the cost that put you off having a big wedding, because we've got savings—'

Stuart raised a big arresting hand. 'No, Dad, it's nothing to do with money.'

God knows they had enough of it coming into the house to easily pay for one of those big fat gypsy weddings that were all the rage and that every girl at work seemed to be talking about, but Stuart saw all that as Max's money. He wanted a wedding *he* could pay for, not her, and he was determined to get his own way on this. He could afford a meal for a few friends and family, and a cake was a nice touch that would just set the day off right. He wasn't a man for fuss, anyway, but he certainly wasn't going to start off his married life poncing off his wife. And that was a non-negotiable point in Stuart's head.

Chapter 52

In his lunch hour the next day, Stuart nipped up to the Lamp to book the very small wedding reception. The menu looked lovely: ham salad, roast beef and then sweets from the trolley. Simple but perfect in his book, especially as the new chef at the Lamp had a very good reputation. It wouldn't be good enough for Max, of course, but it was better than the nothing she was expecting, so he thought.

As Stuart was handing over the deposit, Max, in her extended lunch hour, was just being shown round the hospitality suite in Higher Hoppleton Hall by the events coordinator, Nina.

'We have two dining rooms,' explained Nina. 'This is the smaller of them.'

Max looked at the ornate ceiling and the many mirrors on the walls. Nine guests would rattle around in here. An extra twenty guests would make all the difference. Thirty – even better.

The second dining room was as big as a ballroom. Max would need a minimum of two hundred guests for that one, and she knew she wouldn't get away with that.

'I think the first room would be more suitable for us,' Max decided, despite secretly wishing for the second.

'Excellent,' said Nina. 'Then let's peruse some menus.'

Coffee and petits fours were waiting in her office.

The first menu was a no-no. It wasn't the exorbitant cost that was the guiding factor on that decision, but the food itself. Stuart was a man of plain tastes and the menu choices were heavy in all the things he didn't like – foie gras, chicken-liver pâté, Stilton – and fish, which he hated unless it was battered cod. Max moved on to the second, but she didn't like lamb and the puddings were too stodgy and ordinary for her tastes: spotted dick or apple pie and custard. School-dinner puddings had moved back into vogue apparently, but not on her planet, so she rejected it.

'Now this one, I like,' Max declared, seeing the third. For starter: a choice of scallops in pea froth, an Italian antipasti platter or soup. For main: Beef Wellington, Chicken Forestière or Mediterranean tarte for the veggies. For dessert: a trio of cheesecakes, a quartet of chocolate desserts or summer-fruit pudding with clotted cream. Port and a cheeseboard to follow, then home-made truffles and coffee. That menu had plenty of choice for the unfussy Taylors as well as her scallop-loving self.

Did she want flowers on the table, asked Nina. Did bears shit in the woods, she almost answered.

'Oh yes, shocking-pink flowers,' smiled Max, thinking of gypsy Margaret's wedding. 'And lots of them.'

The rein inside her that would have pulled on her and urged her to be careful had long since snapped. From now on she was booking everything she had dreamed of, everything that little princess-loving girl that still remained inside her wanted on her wedding day. By the time Max left the building, she had ordered pink champagne, pink balloons, and pink-boxed favours of pink chocolates. She had a sudden moment of panic when she started her car and thought of everything she had just committed to. Stuart was going to be really cross, she knew. But she also knew that nothing – including the whole British army, navy and air force combined – would stop the speeding snowball of her wedding arrangements.

Chapter 53

Once again Violet had lied to Glyn and said that she had a meeting with a supplier, but instead she had gone to Postbox Cottage, picking up a bilberry tart from Potts Bakery on the way.

She sat on the sofa with her legs up on the pouffe, a pot of tea and the fruit-filled pastry on the table at her side, while she dreamed up some new flavours that she intended to trial in Carousel.

In summer there would be Nan's Sherry Trifle, and Cream Tea. In autumn: Pumpkin Pie, and Cinnamon Apple. For winter she would make Mince Pie with Brandy Butter, and Snow-cream – a smooth white vanilla with tiny dots of white chocolate and edible glitter. And then for next spring, Crystallized Rose Petal, and Carrot Cake. That would do for starters, but there were so many flavours she was desperate to make. And sitting in Postbox planning it all was a little piece of heaven.

She called in at Carousel on the way home. When she opened the door Pav came out from the kitchen and startled her.

'Sorry,' he said.

'I didn't expect you to be here today,' she said, half laughing, half panting.

'I am not needed on the building site. So I come here. That's okay, isn't it? I rang your mobile an hour ago to tell you.'

'I forgot to bring it,' said Violet. It wasn't that big a deal, though. At least she was spared taking it out of her pocket and seeing that Glyn had rung her loads of times. 'And yes, of course,' said Violet. 'That's why I gave you a key, so you could come and go as you pleased. No need to ring.'

The second horse was painted and Pav had started on the third. The attention to detail was incredible. She hadn't expected that standard when she took him on.

'You like?' he asked, noticing her studying his artwork.

'Oh I like very much, Pav,' said Violet. 'You're just so ... so talented.'

Pav smiled and rubbed his knuckles against his shirt. 'Yes, I know this,' he said haughtily, then he chuckled and Violet's laughter joined with his. She couldn't remember the last time she had laughed with Glyn.

'Coffee?' she asked. 'I just came to —' *avoid going home for a little longer* — 'check on some stocks.'

'Thank you,' said Pav. 'I will take a break.'

As she passed him, she noticed the smell of him — something foresty and masculine — and her lungs breathed him in with a sigh. She wondered how old he really was. He was younger than her for sure, but by how many years? He wasn't perfect-looking — his nose wasn't perfectly straight and there was a rough scar, faded to silver, under his left eye — but he wouldn't have looked as striking without them; the imperfections only added to his manly attractiveness. But it wasn't just the physical appearance of him that Violet found so powerfully alluring; when he painted, his calm manner seemed to radiate out vibes that soothed her frazzled nerves like lavender oil.

'Did you go to art college, Pav?' Violet asked, as she stood waiting for the kettle to boil.

'No, I have no formal training,' he replied.

'You left school at sixteen?'

'I was eighteen.'

'Ah.' Violet got ready for the big question and tried to deliver it as casually as possible. 'How long ago was that, then?'

'Five years.'

So there were nine years between them. That wouldn't have been so much had they both been in their eighties, but when she was twenty, he had been only eleven. Not that it mattered, she reprimanded herself. It wasn't as if there would – *could* – be any romance between them, anyway. He was far too young for that. And she was engaged. Plus, he was bound to have a girlfriend, being so beautiful and talented and gentle.

'I can't believe you do what you do without formal training,' marvelled Violet, bringing two coffees out of the kitchen.

'Did you go to ice-cream school?' asked Pav, grinning at her.

'Yes, I did,' said Violet with a totally straight face. 'I am actually a doctor of ice cream.'

'I will have to try some of your ice cream one day to see if you are telling me the truth,' smiled Pav, his ocean-blue eyes fully trained on hers. Violet looked away, as if burned by their attention.

'I see you are engaged,' said Pav, patting his own bare ring finger.

'Yes,' said Violet, sipping her coffee. She was aware that her hand had curled in on itself as if trying to hide the evidence. Glyn had chosen the heart-shaped diamond ring himself. The first time he presented it to her, it had galvanized her into telling him that they should split up. The second time, she had accepted it and put it on.

'When is your wedding?'

'The thirtieth of July.'

'Not long,' he mused. Then, 'You will work with your husband here?'

'Oh God, no,' said Violet, her dismissal of the idea firmer than intended. She saw Pav's eyebrows rise. 'We wouldn't work well together,' she added.

'What does he do?' asked Pav.

'Nothing at the moment. He ... erm ... he's been poorly.'

Pav shook his head, not understanding what she meant.

'Poorly – ill,' clarified Violet. 'He's been ill. He used to be a salesman for computer software. But then he ... he had a ... he became ill and couldn't work. What about you, Pav? Are you married?' Violet quickly moved the subject away from Glyn. She didn't want to talk about him here. Carousel was a Glyn-free zone.

'I am single,' Pav said, to her utter surprise.

In fact she was so shocked that she couldn't speak.

'Violet? Are you all right?' Pav asked, seeing her mouth frozen in a perfect O.

'Yes, yes, of course,' she said, feeling a treacherous blush rush to her pale cheeks. 'I'm just ... just ... wow.' She coughed and laughed nervously and knew she must look like an idiot. Especially because he seemed to be amused by her dumbfoundedness.

'I am –' Pav cast around for the word he was looking for – 'fussy. What is your man like?'

Oh God. 'He's quiet, homely. I've got some biscuits in the cupboard, I think.' She turned and went into the kitchen, knowing that she had no biscuits but making a pretence of looking for them all the same by loudly opening and closing cupboard doors and muttering to herself, 'Damn, I was sure I had some.' She returned to him empty-handed.

'It's okay,' said Pav. 'I am watching my figure.' He rubbed his flat stomach. Violet bet there would be a rippling six-pack of muscles under his shirt. She didn't want to even think about comparing it to Glyn's belly, which was getting bigger and wobblier by the month. 'I think perhaps that you need to buy some biscuits for yourself, though,' said Pav. 'You are so small.' He held his hands as if he were encircling a tiny waist. 'And pale.'

'I've always been like this,' said Violet. 'They used to call me "Ghost" when I was younger. But trust me, I eat well. I just don't have much colour.'

'Your eyes have colour,' said Pav, in such a warm gentle way that she gulped. 'They are violet like your name.'

Violet laughed bashfully. 'Thanks,' she said, not knowing

where to look. 'Ooh well, I'd better get off home now.' *Before I turn deep purple and my head blows up.*

Pav grinned. 'Thank you for the coffee,' he said. 'And the company.'

'Pleasure,' said Violet breathlessly, grabbing her handbag and trying to look composed despite bumping into a stack of boxes on her way out. Once behind the steering wheel, she looked at herself in the rear-view mirror and wondered how she was still whole and hadn't melted into a liquid. And thought how much easier life would be if hearts took the simpler, sensible paths.

Glyn had left eight increasingly frustrated voicemail messages on Violet's mobile before finding it in her underwear drawer, switched to silent.

Violet never knew that he occasionally looked through her drawers and her handbag or looked at her emails and the list of callers on her mobile phone. To be fair, he had never found anything to be suspicious about until recently, when a new name had appeared in the address book of her mobile: P. Nowak. And P. Nowak had rung her today and left a message.

Glyn rang her voicemail and deleted the first four of the messages he had left, then he heard the voice of P. Nowak.

'Hello, Violet. Just to let you know that I will be painting at Carousel today as I have no other work to do. Thank you. It's Pav, by the way.'

Glyn listened to the next message – one of his own. His voice sounded thin and reedy in comparison to the low, foreign voice of 'Pav'. Glyn felt a paranoid anger surge through him. He wanted to smash the phone against the wall but he forced himself to calm down and delete the other messages that he had left for Violet.

Then he went to the bathroom, brushing furious tears from his cheeks, and emptied the laundry basket to check for any evidence that Violet might have been unfaithful to him.

Chapter 54

'Hello, Shelleybrations. Shelley speaking. How may I be of assistance?'

'Oh good afternoon,' said Max, delighted to be speaking to Shelley rather than having to leave a message – it was nearly six o'clock, after all. 'I've just found your number on the internet. You make cakes for gypsy weddings, don't you?'

'Who's calling, please?' The woman on the phone had a slightly defensive tone in her voice now. Since her shop had been 'outed' by a local newspaper as a favourite of prospective gypsy brides in the county, she'd had some mixed responses – and a large chunk of unhealthy journalistic interest.

'I'm getting married,' explained Max. 'And I want a huge cake. I'm not a gypsy, but I'm having a gypsy wedding.'

'Ah,' said Shelley, warmth flowing back into her voice again. 'What sort of thing were you looking for?'

'A palace,' said Max. 'Like the one on the front page of your website. Only bigger and with more pink icing. I've got a scanned image with actual dimensions, so shall I mail it over to you?'

'Certainly,' said Shelley. 'Can you wait a minute, till I get to my desk?'

Max hit 'send' and waited until Shelley confirmed that she had received the design.

'My,' said Shelley, following it with a long whistle. 'That's a big palace. How many people are coming to your wedding?'

'Oh not that many,' said Max. 'But it doesn't matter if it gets eaten or not, I just want that cake. Can it be done? And how much will it cost – approximately?'

Max's eyes widened when Shelley gave her the figure, but never mind. It was what she wanted, what she had decided upon, what she could easily afford, and what she would have. Yes, most of it would be wasted, probably, but sod it – she only got married once and she was having the works.

'When's the wedding?'

Max winced and prepared to be disappointed. 'The second of July. Four and a half weeks.'

Shelley whistled again. 'It's tight,' she said.

'Tight but possible or tight and impossible?'

'Nothing's impossible for me,' said Shelley. She was used to working all hours because the gypsy community often wanted her massive creations quickly, and they were prepared to pay her handsomely for doing what she did better than anyone else. She metaphorically rubbed her hands at the prospect of such a lucrative job and quickly reached for a pen to take down Max's Visa number for the big fat gypsy cake deposit of fifty per cent.

Stuart opened the door and switched on the light, then he placed his hand on the radiator to check that the heating was on. It was, yet the house never felt warm. It wasn't cosy like his mum's terraced house. *Or Jenny's.*

He tapped his head with his fingertips, trying to break up yet another cluster of thoughts about Jenny Thompson. He wished he'd never set eyes on her again. It was as if some rogue part of his heart was desperately hungry and empty and looking to be filled, and finding that Jenny Thompson was exactly what would satiate its appetite.

He kicked off his shoes, padded across to the stark white kitchen and opened the fridge. He took out a beer and poked around for something to nibble on. The fridge was packed but there was little in there that appealed to him: yoghurts, a crustless quiche, anchovy paste, olives stuffed with garlic, a tub of salade niçoise, a crayfish-stuffed baguette, a bag of peppery rocket, a round of Brie. He hated poncy French cheeses; he liked Red Leicester, but it never arrived with the Tesco home-shopping consignment even though he kept asking Max to add some to the next load. No, it was always a garlicky Roule or Camembert or stinky stuff with blue veins running through it.

He bet Jenny's fridge had cider and an apple pie in it, beef spread, mini pork pies and Laughing Cow triangles. And a block of Red Leicester.

He flipped the top off the beer bottle and took a long swallow. The house was so quiet, still and chilly. Everything was neutral-coloured or black and he suddenly felt like going mad and throwing some red paint over everything. He was going loopy and he knew why he was so agitated. So he'd better make sure he didn't see Jenny Thompson again.

Chapter 55

Max finished work early on Friday and picked up Violet and Bel so they could all go to White Wedding together. She wanted to choose some bridesmaids' dresses.

'I don't want to pour any cold water on your plans but are you sure you're doing the right thing, Max?' Bel asked, when Max excitedly told them about the honeymoon she'd booked. And the cake. And the rest. 'Won't Stuart go mental?'

'No, I'm absolutely as sure as houses that he won't,' Max flapped a dismissive hand. 'Anyway, it'll be too late to do anything about it when I'm halfway down the aisle in my big frock. He'll just do his usual rolling of the eyes and go along with it. He's done that for seventeen years so one more afternoon won't kill him. He can't surely expect me – Maxine McBride – to get married in a church without a huge dress. He knows me too well.'

'Yeah, but how much further are you going with your plans, Max?' asked Violet, reaching out for the White Wedding door handle.

'How much further can she go?' Bel added. 'It'll end in tears if you aren't careful, Max – and I don't mean cake ones.'

Freya was unpacking tiaras from white tissue paper when the doorbell announced their arrival.

'Hello, there,' she greeted them. 'How are you all today?'

'Good,' smiled Max. She had hoped to have a word with Freya about some ideas she wanted incorporating into her dress design, but decided now to do that on a separate trip at the weekend. When Bel and Violet weren't around to spoil things with their 'be careful' caveats.

'And what can I do for you ladies this time?'

'Bridesmaids' dresses,' Max responded. 'Big ones.'

'Behave,' cautioned Violet, poking her in the arm.

'Colour?' asked Freya.

'What colour do you fancy, girls?' Max turned to her friends and spread her arms wide across the shop.

'It's your wedding, Max. What colour do you want us to be in?'

Max recalled gypsy Margaret's bridesmaids in that neon shade of sunburn.

'Pink,' she said. 'Very bright pink.'

Freya beckoned them to the middle of the long shop, where the bridesmaids' section was. She reached for a dress in a delicate blush.

'Don't even take it from the hanger,' said Max. '*That's* the sort of pink I'm talking about.' And she pointed to a dress so bright that they all needed sunglasses to view it. And intensive therapy afterwards.

Bel raised her eyebrows at Violet, but this was Max's wedding and they both knew that her dictionary did not carry the word 'understated'.

The dress was very plain in style, even if the perfect colour.

'I can adapt the design if you want something in the same style as the wedding dress,' Freya offered.

'Perfect,' Max decided. She knew that Freya would make a marvellous job of it too. There was something about Freya that elicited absolute faith in her.

'Have you got time to do that? The wedding is so close,' asked Bel, hoping Freya might say no.

'Yes, I have time,' said Freya. 'I'll just take your measurements, if I may,' she added, unlooping the tape measure from round her neck and addressing Bel. She already had Violet's, of course. 'It shouldn't take me too long to have them ready.'

'Lovely,' Max, Violet and Bel said in unison. One voice more enthusiastically than the other two.

Chapter 56

Stuart rolled over in bed and his arm fell on to the place where Max should be. He would have probably remained asleep if it had found her there, but instead he woke as his hand found only a fast-cooling quilt.

Max was buttoning her shirt.

She saw him open his eyes and quickly sit up, and immediately held out her flat palm to stop him asking questions.

'I'll be back as quickly as I can,' she said, her voice brimming with giddy excitement. 'I'm just going into the office to pick up some files. The American firm B.J. Brothers Industries rang me in the middle of the night and left a voicemail saying they want to talk to me urgently. They're massive, Stuart.'

'Bloody hell,' huffed Stuart. 'It's me that needs a massive BJ.'

'I'll give you the biggest birthday BJ I can when I come home. I shouldn't be more than an hour. If you'd stayed asleep, I bet I would have been back before you woke up.'

Stuart's head dropped onto the pillow.

'No point in asking you to turn your phone off at evenings and weekends, is there?' said Stuart tightly.

'How can I?' said Max. 'It's my company. I have to be available 24/7. I can't believe I bloody slept through the ringtone.'

Stuart kept conveniently quiet about the fact that he hadn't. It had woken him up at half-past one and he had leaned over Max and pressed the 'ignore' button on her phone.

She bent down and kissed his cheek, then asked, 'What time are you meeting Luke to go and look at wedding suits?'

'Half-past three,' replied Stuart with a low grumble. As if the day hadn't started off well enough, he had to spend part of his birthday trying on fecking wedding suits.

'Don't eat much. I have presents and cake and surprises and I'm going to whisk you out to lunch,' Max said breezily, hoping to cheer him up with that. 'Oh and the cleaner will be here – don't forget, will you? – although I'll be back by then. But if I'm not, will you ask her to give that downstairs toilet an extra good bleaching?'

'Yeah, bye,' said Stuart, turning his head sulkily into the pillow.

'Happy birthday, darling,' she said before closing the bedroom door quietly, as if he were asleep.

Stuart crossed his arms in bed and huffed. The annoying thing was that he knew Max would be buzzing as she drove to work. He wondered if she would ever leave that office if she didn't have to.

He didn't go back to sleep; he was too cross. Instead he got up and showered and shaved and was fully aware that instead of putting on sloppy weekend tracksuit bottoms, he hunted out his best Diesel jeans and splashed himself with aftershave – something he never did unless he and Max were going out, not that they'd done much of that recently. Jenny was coming this morning. And he couldn't help it: he was looking forward to seeing her again.

He collected the newspaper from the letter box and sat at the breakfast bar with a coffee. He should go out, really, before she arrived, then he wouldn't have to see her. He wouldn't fan any more flames that way. He was getting married in exactly four weeks and was obsessing about another woman. That wasn't good. Yes, he really should go out and avoid Jenny Thompson. So Stuart tipped his half-finished coffee down the sink, marched down the hallway and took his jacket from the peg. Then he drove off into town and mooched around aimlessly, trying not to wish he was back home instead.

Chapter 57

Bel sat bolt upright in bed. She had woken up crying after yet another awful dream. It was a recurring one, which varied a little each time, but it still left her reeling with guilt. She was back at her wedding reception and had just delivered her speech but hadn't marched off. Instead she was standing there waiting for rapturous applause to begin, but everyone was viewing her with their faces screwed up in disgust. Her father was shaking his head with shame and Dan Regent was there, his arm round a sobbing Shaden. Even Max and Violet couldn't meet her eyes. And Richard's heart was breaking. 'How could you do this?' he was imploring. 'I love you so much.'

Bel felt totally disorientated as the real world engulfed her conscious soul. She got up and made herself a coffee but it did nothing to quell the anxiety that was rattling her head. She hadn't heard any of Richard's side of the story yet. She needed to. When anyone had an affair it was never as clear-cut as 'all his fault and none of hers', or vice versa, so all the agony aunts said. There were always two sides to a story. Hadn't she said that to herself too, whenever she watched *Jeremy Kyle*?

She wished she was back in Charlotte, with no phone reception, and fighting with her ebony-eyed neighbour over a tin opener. She wondered what Dan Regent was doing now. If he was still there. And if he was there alone, or had twatty Cathy shown up and they were rolling around in bed sheets together under the white-painted eaves? She imagined that Dan Regent would be very nice to tumble around in bed with. He would be gentle and slow, not like Richard, who saw sex like an Olympic event. If it didn't involve a full *Kama Sutra* of positions, it wasn't proper sex to him.

Like Richard, Cathy must have been visited by the temporary-madness fairy and she had to have come back to her senses and thrown herself on Dan's mercy; and of course he would have taken her back. The Cathys of this world were irresistible creatures: evil witches armed with dangerous spikes that pierced hearts over and over again, yet still those hearts came back for more.

She tried to chase thoughts of Dr Dan out of her mind. She'd had to do that a lot since she left Haworth. So many things hijacked her thoughts, plucked her up by the collar and dropped her right back in Charlotte; any reference to barmy Dr Donald Reynolds in the news, any tin in her cupboard without a ring-pull top, even the cheese in her fridge. Plus, she had a heightened awareness of all things Bronte; there was a new adaptation of *The Tenant of Wildfell Hall* on the TV and as she passed the cinema she saw they were showing the old Orson Welles version – her favourite Rochester – of *Jane Eyre* at the Pensioners' Silver Screen morning.

She didn't feel strong enough to meet Richard yet, but she knew she had to soon. She was married to him, for God's sake, and her thoughts should be on him, not some doctor whose path she'd happened to cross when she was vulnerable and not thinking straight. She owed *her husband* the right to speak, to explain. Only then could she know if she had been truly justified in her behaviour. The more time went on, the more she doubted she had. She knew she had always been a stubborn cow, forming an opinion and then sticking to it despite whatever contradictory evidence might be thrown up. Her treatment of Faye was testament to that.

Bel reached into her jewellery box and lifted out the golden hoop. Then she tried it on the third finger of her left hand. It felt lovely. She had wanted to be married so much, to belong to a man who could find the soft, vulnerable part that existed inside her hard bolshie shell, and treasure it. A man who smiled when thoughts of her brushed past his brain.

She decided there and then that she would ring Richard and meet him within the week. Then she would give him every chance to make everything up to her.

Chapter 58

Max's car wasn't in the drive when Stuart returned over two hours later, having exhausted every shop in Barnsley's town centre. She was still at work, then, he thought with an inner sneer. So much for it being his birthday. He put his key in the door, but it was already unlocked. Jenny was in.

She jumped to attention when Stuart opened the kitchen door. She was standing there chewing a sandwich and drinking a coffee.

'I've finished,' she explained quickly. 'And I brought this sandwich with me.'

'Jenny, for God's sake, you don't need to tell me that,' said Stuart, smiling at her. She was so cute with her swingy ponytail and little pink apron.

'I didn't want you to think I was raiding your cupboards,' Jenny replied, wiping her mouth in case there were any crumbs round it.

'Don't be daft,' he said. His smile had extended to a grin now because she was there and he was happy to see her. More happy to see her than he would have been to see Max's car in the drive, if he were honest, even though he recognized how wrong such a thought was.

'Mum said it was okay to make myself a coffee here, you know, that you didn't mind that. But I wouldn't touch any of your food or anything.'

'Jen, give over, will you?'

Jen nodded. 'I do go on a bit, don't I? I've got to snatch a lunch today because I've got an extra cleaning job straight after this.'

'Where is it? I'll give you a lift.'

'No, you won't,' said Jenny forcibly. 'Especially not today.'

'Today?' said Stuart.

'You know, your birthday.'

'How do you know that?' said Stuart.

'Well,' Jenny coughed. 'I remember from school. It was the day after mine.'

'Oh—'

'You wouldn't have remembered,' Jenny jumped in quickly, flapping her hand dismissively. 'I'm not sure you even knew in the first place *to* remember. I happen to have the memory of an elephant, that's all.'

She had remembered it was his birthday from all those years ago. He suddenly felt his insides blush with warmth and grow ever so slightly mushy.

'Did you do anything nice for your birthday, Jenny?' he asked.

'Yeah, an intimate dinner for two at mine.'

'Oh.' A shadow of disappointment passed over Stuart's heart.

'Alan and me, I mean,' laughed Jenny. 'He had a stalk of broccoli and a banana, and I had a Chinese and too much Baileys.'

Stuart laughed and most of that laugh, he knew, was founded in relief.

'What are you doing for your birthday?' Jenny threw the remainder of her sandwich in the bin and reached for her coat.

'We're going out for lunch,' he looked at the clock. 'Supposedly,' he added, unable to keep the annoyance out of his voice.

'Has Maxine gone shopping?' Jenny asked, folding up her cloths and putting them in her bucket. 'I expect she's got a lot to do with your wedding being so close.'

'She's gone into work,' said Stuart. 'She's always at bloody work.' He looked up at Jenny and apologized for swearing. 'Sorry, Jen. Life with a workaholic, eh?'

'More to life than work, I always think,' said Jen, 'but it doesn't do for us all to be the same. The world would be very boring if we were.'

'Come on, I'll give you a lift.'

'No, you won't.'

'Yes, I will give you a lift.' He would have bet his life savings that he could drop Jen off, run a marathon and still Max wouldn't be at home by the time he got back. That said a lot, really, on his birthday. Too much.

Jenny gave a resigned sigh. 'All right. Thank you. If you can drop me outside Pogley Top post office that would be lovely.'

'Come on, then,' said Stuart.

As he followed Jenny out, his nose caught her trail of perfume: light and apple-scented. She was a foot smaller than he was and he imagined what she would feel like if he wrapped his arms round her and lifted her up. And then kissed her.

He drove the long way to Pogley. It gave him half a mile of extra time with her. Just sitting next to Jenny Thompson made his heart feel lighter by pounds.

When Stuart pulled up outside the post office, Jenny reached into her handbag and brought out a square parcel wrapped in jelly-bean paper. She held it out to him.

'It's just a little present I was going to leave on the work surface for you,' she said. 'Don't get excited. But I found it and copied it and I thought you'd like it.'

'Jenny, you shouldn't have.' He felt embarrassed now that he hadn't even remembered it was her birthday and here she was giving him a present for his.

'It didn't cost me anything,' she said.

Stuart opened the parcel and pulled out a framed photo of their old class dressed in costumes.

'Oh my God, the nativity we did for the old people's home. I'd forgotten all about that,' he beamed with sheer delight. 'Where did you get it?'

'The *Chronicle* came to take a picture of us but they never put it in the paper in the end. My mum went up to the office and asked them for a print, though.'

'Oh my God, look at me,' Stuart barked with laughter seeing himself as a grinning shepherd. He was standing between tiny Timmy Foster, the class softie, and Luke, who was playing a king and had an enormous black false beard that was bigger than his head. 'Where are you, Jen?'

'Top right, next to Gav,' said Jen, pointing to the place. 'We were donkeys.'

'Hey, nice ears,' said Stuart, his finger touching Jenny's hair on the photo. 'Ugh and Julie Armstrong. The Teacher's Pet.'

Stuart shuddered at the sight of the golden-haired angel with the butter-wouldn't-melt expression.

'Wasn't she just a horror?' nodded Jenny. 'She's got five kids to five different men now. Three of them have been taken off her. I see her sometimes in Asda. You wouldn't recognize her.'

'How we change,' sighed Stuart.

'You haven't changed a bit,' Jenny tutted. 'You still look the same.'

'You haven't changed either,' said Stuart.

'Oh I have,' argued Jenny. 'I was a right little fat thing back then.'

'No, you weren't,' said Stuart, unable to remember Jenny being anything other than as slender as she was now. 'Your smile is just the same. "Smiling Jenny" all the lads used to call you.'

Jen's mouth fell into a long O of surprise. 'Did they?' She was blushing now. Stuart had to stop himself from putting his arms round her and hugging her.

'Jen, this photo is lovely,' he said. 'It's just brought back so many nice memories for me.'

'Ah, I'm glad you like it.'

Stuart leaned over and kissed her cheek. His lips lingered on her skin as he breathed in her apple scent. 'Thank you.'

'Have a lovely birthday,' said Jen, completely flustered now.

She dropped her cleaning bucket as she got out of the car. She almost ran round the corner after picking it up.

Stuart was home an hour before Max returned from work. She was carrying a smile on her face so wide that the ends almost crossed over on the top of her head.

'Oh Stuart, I'm so sorry I'm late, but guess what? I emailed B.J. Brothers Industries and sent them all the info they asked for and they rang me. God knows what hours those people work. They want me to supply them with San Maurice products and they're going to market them all over the United States. I'm so excited, I can't breathe.'

Then Max noticed that Stuart wasn't sharing her enthusiasm and she remembered why that was. Mentally she sat on her inner bubbling self and turned her attentions to the birthday boy. 'Anyway, forget about all that, this is your day.'

Then Max made Stuart sit down at the kitchen table while she excitedly pulled presents out of their hiding places in cupboards and heaped them on him. Exquisitely wrapped parcels containing a cashmere sweater, a TAG Heuer watch, Adidas trainers, Godiva chocolates – it was all expensive and stuff he didn't really want or need, although he wouldn't have hurt Max's feelings by saying so. But still, there was nothing in the Santa-pile of presents that made him smile like Jenny Thompson's gift of the class nativity photo.

Chapter 59

'I don't like this at all,' said Stuart, looking at himself in the suit-shop mirror. 'I look like a twat.'

'No, you don't. But you're standing like a constipated duck,' said Luke. 'What's with the arms stuck out like that? Put them down by your side and straighten up your back.'

'Yes, Mum,' said Stuart, but doing as his friend said.

Stuart looked at the guy in the mirror in the tailed suit, snow-white winged-collar shirt and cravat foaming at his neck.

The shop assistant returned with a grey top hat.

'Not a chance,' said Stuart, holding up his hand to stop the assistant coming any closer. Stuart looked over his shoulder at Luke, whose eyebrows were raised. 'No. This is far enough. I'll do the penguin look if I have to but no way on this earth am I wearing a chuffing topper.' He pulled the collar away from his neck. 'How come you always look so bloody comfortable in a suit?'

'I'm just naturally stylish,' said Luke, lifting then dropping his broad shoulders like a cocksure Frenchman. Unlike his friend, Luke felt very at home in a suit. He enjoyed shopping for them, having them made to measure, looking good. At weekends he relaxed in Stone Island jeans but he had worked in suits for as long as he could remember. He bought expensive shoes and handmade shirts. 'Clothes maketh the man' was an adage his stylish dad had sworn by and passed on to his son.

Luke adjusted his friend's stance as if he were a tailor's dummy, pulling back his shoulders, pushing in his stomach. He looked much better then. Good, even.

'This wedding is getting bigger and bigger and I don't like it,' said Stuart, turning to the side to view his profile in the mirror. 'Church, suits. I've even ended up booking a small surprise reception and getting my mum to make a cake.'

'Have you changed your mind about taking a honeymoon?'

The look that Stuart gave him said that no, he had definitely not changed his mind about a honeymoon.

'We're going to have a quiet weekend at home,' said Stuart.

'You only get married once,' said Luke.

'So everyone keeps saying,' Stuart huffed. 'Do you know, I wish we hadn't started all this off. I don't know why we tried to fix something that wasn't broken. I'll never have any of my mother's cherry brandy again. God knows what I'd be letting myself in for next time.'

'You're a miserable bastard today,' laughed Luke, 'considering it's your birthday as well. Thirty-four? You old sod.'

'You're only a month behind, Appleby.'

'Don't you fancy going away for a weekend? I was thinking of giving you a honeymoon as a wedding present.'

Stuart rubbed his forehead wearily.

'Do you think I can't afford a honeymoon? Is that it?'

'Is it?'

'No, it bloody isn't it,' Stuart rounded on him, then held up his hands in apology. 'Actually, what I mean is that I can afford a honeymoon but not the sort that Max would be happy with.'

'What?'

Stuart tried, but failed, to keep the exasperation out of his voice. 'How overjoyed do you think Max would be if I said that I was taking her for a honeymoon to Blackpool?'

'I think she'd be very overjoyed,' said Luke.

'Yeah, right.'

'Max isn't a snob,' said Luke. 'She wouldn't care if you booked a weekend in the Bahamas or Blackpool. The only thing she would see is that *you* booked it.'

'What planet are you on, Luke? For my birthday Max bought me the equivalent of a Santa's grotto. Every year I have more of a mare trying to match what she spends.' Stuart felt like ripping his bloody collar off and throwing it to the other side of the room.

'I'm sure she doesn't want you to match it—'

'That's not the point,' snapped Stuart, interrupting him. 'Have you any idea how it makes me feel? Her giving me cashmere jumpers and TAG Heuer watches and buying me a house and a car? I feel like I've had my dick cut off.'

The shop assistant put one foot into the changing, room, then did an about-face and vanished.

Luke searched for some diplomatic words, but couldn't find any. How could he say that he understood Max far more than her partner of seventeen years obviously did? Luke knew that Max had a stupidly generous heart. She always had. Even at college Max was first in the queue at the coffee bar, buying everyone a round of milkshakes with her Saturday-job money. She was one of life's givers – it was as simple as that. Luke knew that it didn't matter to her if Stuart earned ten quid or ten thousand quid a week. The only person it mattered to was Stuart, and he was projecting his own hang-ups about it onto Max, which wasn't fair. Luke wondered how long all this resentment had been bubbling under Stuart's surface. A very long time, by the sounds of it. A very long silent time.

'What drives you at work, Luke?' said Stuart with a heavy sigh. 'What is it that makes people like you and Max love working so much?'

'Well,' began Luke, 'with me I suppose part of it is that I was brought up in a work-orientated household. I've been steeped in it from an early age. Dad always said that whatever I did, I should do it to the best that I could. He instilled that work ethic in me. I love it, Stuart. I love being good – the best – at what I do.'

'Max wasn't brought up by a high-powered family,' Stuart replied.

Luke trod carefully here. 'I expect,' – *I'd put my life savings on it* – 'that Max's dad had a lot to do with it. And what he put her through.'

'Graham?' Stuart knew that Luke was way off with that one. Graham McBride was a lovely bloke. Salt-of-the-earth family man.

'No, not Graham. Max's *dad*.'

'Oh him,' sniffed Stuart. 'How? He buggered off when Max was a bairn.'

'But she'll still remember bailiffs at the door and her mum crying and her parents arguing because he'd gambled all their money away. Didn't her mum end up in a refuge at one point?' It had always been obvious to Luke why Max was such a go-getter.

'And?' No. Stuart didn't get it. Luke despaired but answered patiently.

'Money is security to Max, Stuart. Money means she'll never be turfed out of her home again. It's her safety blanket. The more she earns, the more she can store and keep the wolves at bay, should they ever come calling again.'

'She doesn't store it, though,' said Stuart with a sarcastic laugh. 'She buys bloody his and hers cars and TAG Heuer watches.'

Luke stopped himself just in time from saying that what Max blew on extravagances was after her 'safe money' was taken care of. He was no master of psychology but he knew how Max ticked and he couldn't believe Stuart didn't. He also suspected that Max spoiled everyone because deep down she wanted someone to do the same to her, whisk her out for dinner, bring her flowers and chocolates. However much they cost. She would think more of a hand-picked bunch of bluebells than an expensive bouquet arranged to be sent by someone's PA. But he had preached enough to Stuart today and he let further comment die in his throat. He turned his attention back to the suit, nodding his approval at their reflections.

'We're looking good, mate,' he said. 'I think we should go with these ones.'

'Okay, if we must,' Stuart grumped. 'Oh bloody hell, I know what I've forgotten to bring.' He clicked his fingers in frustration. 'I was going to show you something. Jenny gave me a photo of all us lot doing that nativity for the old people's home when we were in Miss Shaw's class, do you remember it?'

'Jesus Christ, you're going back a bit.'

'Only twenty-five years. You've got the big beard covering your face and Jen was a donkey.'

Jen. Jen. Jen. Luke picked up how Stuart's mood had instantly lifted now they were speaking about Jenny Thompson. He didn't draw attention to it, though; instead he lifted the swatch of pink material that Max had given Stuart to match their ties to. Apparently her 'posy' was going to be in that colour.

'Funny,' said Stuart, 'but I don't think I ever really noticed Jenny that much at school. She was one of the background girls. Did you pay any attention to her?'

'Not really,' said Luke. 'Like every other lad I had eyes only for Julie Armstrong.' There were always some girls who stood out from the rest: Julie Armstrong with her early developed figure and long golden hair and big blue eyes. Then later, when he and Stuart had gone on to sixth-form college and encountered other girls, it had been the dark-red-haired, Bambi-eyed, curvy, scarlet-lipped Max McBride who was one of the top head-turners.

Stuart tried on a bowler hat, for a laugh.

'Max has been on the phone to America for most of the morning. Apparently B.J. Brothers Industries wants to deal with her. Heard of them?' he said.

Luke raised his eyebrows. 'Hasn't everyone?'

Obviously not, from the blank look Stuart was giving him.

'They are *big*. Very big,' Luke clarified. 'That's brilliant news.'

Stuart shrugged. 'Is it?'

'Well, yeah,' said Luke. 'Course it is. You must be so proud of her for brokering a deal with them.'

'I sometimes think Max should have gone out with you instead of me,' sighed Stuart, ripping off the hat and resisting the urge to frisbee it Oddjob-style at a mannequin to see if he could cut its head off.

'What, because we both get off on closing a deal?' laughed Luke, making light of the fact that he didn't like this turn in the conversation.

'Yes, that's exactly what I mean. And you like the same stuff,' said Stuart thoughtfully. 'Dressing up in pretty posh clothes for a start.' He unbuttoned the top button on the shirt and gave his neck a well-needed scratch. Do you ever wonder what would have happened if I hadn't nipped her bum and blamed you?'

'No, I don't,' laughed Luke. 'And, trust me, I've got more in common with Alan Sugar than I have with any woman I've ever been out with. Although that doesn't mean that I want him to turn up on my doorstep with flowers.'

'I wonder what happened to all the others in our class,' mused Stuart with a faraway look in his eyes. 'Ever heard the saying that, statistically, in a group of friends it's likely that one will become a millionaire and one a murderer?'

'I can't imagine anyone out of our class being a murderer,' said Luke.

'Well, would you ever have thought that Julie would turn out to be a darling of the Social Services? Who's to say that little mousy Timmy Foster wasn't the worm that turned and slit someone's throat? Are we really sure of anyone or anything in this world?' Stuart shook his head. He suddenly felt really low. He couldn't remember the last time in recent years when he could truly say that he had grinned and giggled like he had at school. 'I'll scan Jen's picture and send it to you. We all looked so happy in it.'

Jen again.

'Remember that you're talking about the days before life and all its complications hit us: mortgages, sex, jobs. We had more to smile about than we even realized,' said Luke. Then he dropped a big pebble in the water of their conversation and hoped Stuart felt its reverberations and took the hint. 'You see it all the time in the news these days, unhappy people hooking up with old schoolfriends and first loves on Facebook and hoping to climb back into the past again. Putting on rose-coloured specs can cause a lot of damage. We aren't those carefree kids any more and we never will be again.'

Stuart opened his mouth to blurt out to Luke that he was right, that his head was like a washing machine and he didn't know where he was, because he was trying on suits for a wedding to one woman and yet his head was full of another. He wanted to say to Luke, 'Help me,' but he shut his mouth before the first word came out. Luke would have just said that all the inner turmoil was down to infamous 'pre-wedding nerves'. It could only be a natural inner rebellion against the stigma of commitment and it would pass. He was infatuated with Jenny Thompson, it wasn't love – how could it be after such a short time? Love was what he felt for Max, the woman he had been with since they were sixteen, and it was Max he was marrying and would be happy with. He knew that, he did. Boy, Jenny Thompson really had stuck a big stick in his world and swirled up all the stinking mud from the bottom.

Stuart decided that he was going to make a booking at Curry Corner when he got home and take Max out for a late supper. They would toast his birthday again and her success in opening negotiations with the American B.J. Brothers and talk about their perfect little wedding and plans for the future. He had to pull himself back on track and forget all about Jenny Thompson. Luke was right; she was a small part of his past, not a big part of his future.

As they set off for Curry Corner, things were going well between Stuart and Max.

'No interruptions – leave your phone at home for once,' ordered Stuart at the door.

'Okay,' said Max, nipping back inside the house before they locked up and got into the newly arrived taxi.

They shared an Indian platter for starters, and Stuart made her laugh talking about the wedding suits and how Luke was like a mother hen, telling him to stand properly in front of the mirror. They giggled together and drank wine and Stuart felt himself relaxing about his forthcoming marriage. He was in such a good mood – plus a little bit pissed – that he even relented to Max's craftily timed request that they invite a few of their extended family to fill up the church. Just a few from each side, she promised. Honest.

He went to the loo after the waiter had collected the plates for the main course and happened to look back over his shoulder at Max. It was to see that she had whipped her phone out of her bag and was checking it. She hadn't left it at home as he had asked, after all. Not even on his birthday could she prioritize his feelings above hers. His anxieties had once again settled on his shoulders by the time he returned to the table.

Chapter 60

When Bel pulled up outside La Hacienda on Wednesday evening, Richard was waiting outside in the rain holding an enormous bunch of red roses in one hand and a golfing umbrella above his head in the other.

'Hi,' he said almost shyly when she emerged from the car. He kissed her awkwardly on the cheek and handed over the flowers.

'They're twee,' he said, 'but at least I know what red roses mean. I didn't want to be giving out any unintended messages by buying different flowers.'

'What, like pink roses mean "I hate you, you bitch"?' said Bel with a small smile.

'I hope they don't. I've just had some pink ones delivered to my mother.'

Bel bit her lip. If pink roses really did mean that, she would have had some sent every week to Madeleine Bishop, the miserable old witch. She couldn't wait for the first family meal with the Bishops senior after all this. She envisaged Madeleine hunched over her cauldron brewing up something poisonous to serve to her wild, gobby daughter-in-law.

Bel put the flowers in her car and turned back to find Richard holding out his arm for her to take. Blimey. That was a first, but very welcome nevertheless.

'Quite a while since we've been here,' he said, pushing open the door to *their* restaurant. In here Richard had proposed. An ancient violinist had appeared at their table and started grinning intensely at her with a selection of yellow and brown teeth as he drew the bow over his instrument. Bel had felt a bit of a prat, really, being the subject of such attention. She was just about to make an excuse to go to the loo when Richard dropped to his knee in front of her and held out a box with the name Tiffany on the lid. The rock within was a very impressive solitaire diamond.

Bel gulped at the strength of the memory and felt quite teary. She hoped she'd have more backbone than this for the rest of the night. The last thing she wanted to do was become a blubbering mess and forgive Richard everything in a mist of sentiment.

Richard had booked *their* table – a private corner niche. The waiter handed them menus and then lit the bright red candle that sat in the middle of the table. The light danced in Richard's very lovely blue eyes as he stared at Bel.

'I've missed you so much,' he said. 'It's just wonderful to see you again.'

Bel cleared her throat nervously and forced herself to concentrate on the menu. She wasn't even hungry. Or was she? She should be because she hadn't eaten all day. That was the trouble at the moment; she didn't know what she felt about anything. She might be back at work and in total control of her job, but she wasn't in a competent driving seat where her own emotions were concerned.

'How's life at the old chocolate firm?' asked Richard, after they had given the waitress their order.

'Busy,' Bel answered. 'But I like it that way. How's life in high finance?'

'Still boring as fuck,' replied Richard. 'But I'm in line for the CEO job. Naughty Francis will shortly be out on his flabby arse. He's been cooking the books.'

'That's brilliant news. For you,' said Bel, aware that she was talking to Richard politely, as if he were one of her new business contacts that she hadn't quite sussed out yet.

Her velouté soup arrived as Richard was talking about the company Bentley he would soon have the pleasure of being chauffeured around in. Bel looked down into the bowl and suddenly thought of a tin opener and had to suppress the smile. Funny, but this soup with all its fresh roasted ingredients and seasonings and its vastly inflated price and 'velouté' status didn't taste half as good as the mug of Heinz tomato with the cheese toastie dipped into it that she'd shared with Dan Regent in Emily. She wondered how far he'd got with his bride-slaughtering story. And if he and Cathy had had passionate make-up sex yet.

'What do you think, Bel?'

Bel snapped up her head. She realized she had slid into a simpler world devoid of samphire and beluga caviar and hadn't a clue what Richard had been talking about.

'I think it's great,' bluffed Bel, pulling herself fully back into the here and now.

'I thought you might,' winked Richard. 'The back seat of a Bentley is very spacious.'

Oh, thought Bel with a weary huff. Was he hinting that they christen the back of the Bentley when he got it? She thought of the coq au vin at her reception – and the text from Shaden that inspired that choice of dish. She remembered that Richard had told Shaden that the blow-job she had given him in the back of Trevor's work van had been the best one he had ever experienced in his life.

Now come on, said a warning voice in her head. *He can't turn the clock back. He's here to move forward and not rake up old ground and you shouldn't be doing that either. You can't build bridges carrying all that dynamite, can you, Belinda Candy . . . Bishop?*

She was married to this very handsome man who was buying her dinner; she had taken holy vows in church to seal their union.

Richard's spoon clattered down into his bowl.

'Bel, I'm sorry. I shouldn't be making smutty innuendo. The

thing is, I don't know how to behave.' His hands went up to his rakishly cut short dark hair and Bel saw that he was wearing his gold wedding band. 'I'm lost.'

Bel felt her heart ripple inside her. Richard looked more vulnerable than she had ever seen him. She breathed in deeply to brave the question. 'Is there any more I should know? Are there any more secrets, Richard?'

'Bel, if you read all the emails and the texts, you know everything.' He bowed his head and shook it shamefully.

'So this is definitely ground zero?'

'Ground zero, I swear.'

Bel believed him. They had a base now to work on, to build on. There were no more earthquakes lurking around to shake their foundations.

'I'm sure we'll muddle through,' she said. 'Somehow. If we take things really slowly.'

'I hope so,' he replied. 'I never thought we'd get this far, if I'm honest – talking again.'

'Well, we might not have if we weren't married,' said Bel. 'But we are.'

'Yes, we are, Mrs Bishop,' said Richard, and he reached for her hand across the table.

Back in her apartment, Bel snipped at the stems of the red roses and arranged them in a clear glass vase. Richard had been charm personified that evening. It brought back so many good memories of being in La Hacienda with him; but with every one recalled, a nasty weed of a darker memory suddenly rose up to twist around it. She wondered if he had ever taken Shaden to the restaurant. She wanted to know if he had ever bought red roses for her perfidious cousin – but then again she didn't. She wished she could reach into her own head and cut out the part of her brain that was labelled 'Richard's affair'.

She felt very alone that evening. She visualized Richard sitting at the dining table, working on his laptop as he sometimes did while she busied around throwing together a Greek salad. And their washing tumbling together in the machine

She thought of her dad and Faye. Her father was the one who mowed the lawn and climbed up on ladders and replaced dud light bulbs; Faye was the one who did the shopping and chose the furnishings. But they did the cooking together, they walked together, they talked together. Bel wanted the life that Faye shared with her dad. For all the strong, independent vibes that Bel gave out, she hated being alone.

That would have surprised all those who thought that Bel was an ardent feminist. Anyone who really 'got' Bel knew that deep down she was just a vulnerable girl with a huge heart, aching to love someone and needing a nice strong man to love her back.

The roses smelled beautiful, heady and perfumed. Bel wiped her leaking eyes with her fingertips. The roses were the colour of Shaden's bridesmaid's dress.

Chapter 61

The next evening after work saw the three friends eating take-away pizza in Postbox Cottage.

'How gorgeous is this cottage?' said Max, picking the chorizo from her pizza and putting it at the side of her plate. 'And how sweet was it of your nan to give it to you?'

Bel swiped the chorizo from Max and traded her some circles of pepperoni. 'So, Violet, when are you moving Glyn in?'

Violet gave only a shrug as an answer.

'He doesn't know that you own it yet, does he?' asked Max, reading into the jerk of Violet's shoulders.

Bel stopped chewing. 'Why wouldn't you tell him?'

'It's not that I'm "not telling him". I just haven't told him *yet*,' replied Violet, realizing immediately afterwards how rubbish and unconvincing that sounded.

'You don't talk about him much,' said Max after some more chewing of pizza. 'How is he? Any better?'

Violet groaned inwardly. There were twenty questions coming, she could feel it.

'It's a slow journey,' she replied.

'Is he on tablets? Having some therapy?' Bel joined in.

'Yes, he takes Prozac but he packed in the therapy. He said it wasn't doing him any good.' *He said I was all the therapy he needed.*

'What does he do all day, then?' Max observed how uncomfortable Violet was on the subject of her fiancé but still she carried on pushing questions at her. She wanted to know why Violet didn't gush about the man she was going to marry next month. Something wasn't quite right about it all.

'He cleans the flat, cooks, does some online food shopping ...' God, Violet was suddenly aware that she was making Glyn sound limper than a five-week-old stick of celery.

Max nodded and returned her attention to picking off the chorizo on her pizza. Glyn sounded limper than a five-week-old stick of celery, she thought. Not at all like the person she would have pictured for Violet. That man was a strong go-getter who would love to take care of such a delicate, lovely soul and provide for her and look after her. It didn't sound as if Glyn wanted to help himself recover very quickly. Either that or he was a lazy bastard who was pulling the lead.

Bel was thinking exactly the same. Violet was the sort of person who should be grinning and fizzing about her forthcoming marriage, so why wasn't she? It was obvious to anyone with a brain cell that all was not as it should be in sweet Violet's world. Why else would she keep from her man the news that she'd been given a house? No, something wasn't right.

Bel looked around her at the quaint interior. Postbox Cottage was like a smaller version of what Emily and Charlotte would be like if they were knocked into one. She had a sudden vision of herself stirring a big stewpot in the kitchen while Dan Regent sat on the large squashy sofa, scribbling notes on to a pad. My, oh my, did that man have his hooks in her head? He seemed to have squatter's rights and wouldn't leave.

'How's Carousel coming along?' asked Max, changing the subject. She didn't want to pull Violet's mood down any further. She knew that talking about the ice-cream parlour would bring the smile back to her face. The smile that she should also be wearing when she was talking about her soon-to-be husband, but there was time later to dig deeper into that one.

'Oh it's lovely. Pav's doing a really good job.'

'And what's *Pav* like? Are we talking totty?' Bel crooked her eyebrow.

'He's gorgeous and Polish but far too young to lust after. So put your tongue away.'

As if Glyn had heard her, her phone started vibrating again in her pocket.

'Is that yours again?' said Bel. 'You get a lot of calls, don't you?' She calculated that it must have gone off at least ten times in the last half-hour.

'Oh sorry, didn't realize you could hear it,' Violet said, visibly flustered and foraging in her pocket for it.

'I thought you must be enjoying it,' winked Bel.

'It'll be suppliers emailing costs and stuff,' said Violet, handling the phone with all thumbs. And there was a blush growing on her face as well, the others noticed. She was lying about it being suppliers. So why was that, then? Curiouser and curiouser, as Alice in Wonderland might have said.

The phone stopped vibrating and then immediately began again.

'Bloody thing, I'll turn it off when I can find the button.' As she was struggling with the minuscule 'off' switch, Max noticed that the screen showed it was an incoming call from Glyn. And said so.

'If it's from Glyn, just answer it,' she said. 'It might be important.'

'It won't be,' said Violet, at last powering it off. 'He gets fed up being in the flat by himself. I told him I wouldn't be late.'

'Late? It's only quarter to six,' said Max. She suspected that it had been Glyn who had been ringing Violet so persistently during their pizza-eating session. She was beginning to build up a picture of a man she didn't think she would like very much.

Violet flapped her hand as if waving the discussion away and then addressed Bel with a nudge.

'How did it go with Richard yesterday?'

'We went for dinner at La Hacienda. It's "our place", so if it was going to go well anywhere, it would be there.'

'Ooh very nice,' trilled Max. 'And expensive. I hope he paid and you picked the most expensive thing on the menu.'

'Of course he paid,' said Bel. 'And even the most expensive thing on the menu is well within his price range. I couldn't make him suffer that way. He's too loaded.'

'How was he?' asked Max, serious now.

'Contrite,' said Bel, nodding; the word that had just come to her fitted him very well. 'Neither of us really knew what to say.'

'Did he kiss you goodnight?' said Max.

'On the cheek.'

'Are you seeing him again?'

'We agreed that for the time being we'd see each other about once a week, work permitting, and see how we go,' sighed Bel. 'What a mess. I daren't tell my dad I've seen him.'

'So, where's your fucking bastard cousin?' said Max, with a sneery-Elvis lip.

'Richard hasn't seen her since the reception, so he says, and I believe him,' Bel replied. 'I don't think he dare stretch any truth at the moment. I got the feeling from Dad that my stepmum hasn't spoken to Shaden's mother since the wedding either. So I don't know where my dear cousin is, or what she's up to.' *Apart from selling her story to tabloids for plastic-surgery money.*

'Your family gatherings are going to be interesting from now on,' said Max with a naughty laugh.

'The Bosomworth clan can stay away for ever as far as I'm concerned. I shan't miss Vanoushka or creepy Martin, and Lydiana's once-yearly visits from her "house in Australia with both outdoor and indoor swimming pools" are more than enough. Anyway, they only come to the house to check out how they can attempt to better Faye. Or, in the case of "Uncle Martin", to grope my arse.'

'Your stepmother sounds very different to the rest of her family' Violet observed.

'Yeah, but she has Bosomworth blood running through her veins,' sneered Bel.

'Oh come on, she can't help which family she was born into,' said Max. 'She seemed lovely when we met her at the wedding.'

Bel didn't want to get on to the subject of Faye's virtues. She went into the kitchen for another bottle of Schloer and Violet asked her to fetch the large plate of assorted tiny cream buns that was stored in the fridge.

'I can't eat cream buns, Violet,' Max cried, as the cakes arrived. 'I've got a wedding dress to fit into. Oh sod it.' And with that she picked up a baby doughnut and popped it into her mouth whole. 'Oh you'll never guess. I got Stuart half-wankered and he agreed to invite a couple more people to the wedding.'

'Dear God,' said Violet. 'How many is "a couple"?'

'I reckon about fifteen each side. I've asked his mum for a list of addresses so I can invite them to the reception as well.'

'The reception that Stuart doesn't know anything about? How are you going to keep it secret now, Max?'

'I have thought of that,' Max replied with an indignant sniff. 'I'm going to put on the invitation that there will be "refreshments" after the ceremony, which is vague enough. I'm organizing a minibus to take people from the church to Higher Hoppleton Hall. I shall send a separate note to each guest to say that they've actually been invited to a full sit-down dinner reception but they must not tell Stuart as it's a wedding surprise for him.'

'How stupid of me not to think of that,' Bel smacked her forehead.

'He's stressed at the moment, I can tell,' said Max, reaching next for a mini cream slice. 'We went out for a curry on Saturday night and he was great company, then he went off to the toilet and came back with a cloud over his head. And he's totally gone off sex. That night it took me ages to—'

Violet screamed and held up her hand to stem Max's flow. 'Do you mind, I'm eating an eclair and you're putting me off.'

'We had a bit of a row in bed as well,' Max confessed, her eyebrows dipping into a frown. 'He has this really annoying habit of doing something nice and then totally ruining it.'

'What do you mean?' asked Bel.

'Well, on the rare occasion that he brings any flowers in he'll hand them over and then say something like, "They're not much, they were only cheap. Chuck them away if you don't like them." Once he bought me a surprise box of After Eights – which I love, incidentally – with the accompanying words, "I know you'd prefer posh ones but this is all I can afford right now, okay?" as if I'd actually asked him for a three-pound box of Patrick Roger Parisienne chocolates.'

'Sounds like he thinks you're worth more than he can afford,' suggested Violet.

'Why can't he just say that, then? "Max, I wish I could give you the moon, but here are some After Eights." I'd be so over-joyed I'd shag him on the spot.'

'God knows,' said Bel. 'If only they were from anywhere as near as Mars . . .'

'You should have heard him going on about Curry Corner when we were there. Anyone would have thought I was a queen that he'd dragged to a dump and force-fed chicken jalfrezi. I told him to stop it because he was spoiling the evening.'

'And he answered?' prodded Violet.

'He said that the evening had already been spoiled. I still don't know how. And he wouldn't tell me. Just told me to drop it.'

'Don't try to fathom them out,' harrumphed Bel. 'They're all fecking weird. I bet even Prince Charming turned into a bum-hole as soon as he got that ring on Cinderella's finger.'

That reminded Max of what she had to show them. She grabbed her handbag and started hunting in it. 'Look at this,' she said, pulling out a wad of paper and handing it over. Violet stared at it and her eyes grew as large as dinner plates.

'You. Are. Joking,' she said, passing it over to an impatient Bel.

'Oh. My. Good. God,' said Bel, looking at the pumpkin coach in pink, drawn by two white horses bearing pink plumage. 'You can't.'

'I'm not. I'm having six horses,' Max giggled.

'Stuart will hit the roof.'

'Tough. It's ordered. And it's his own fault. If he thinks I'm worth the best, then the best is what I shall have.'

Bel and Violet looked at each other and opened their mouths to say something – but there would have been no point. Stuart, it appeared, had played right into his gypsy bride's hands.

Chapter 62

Stu heard the downstairs door open. She was here. He hadn't been able to see her on her Tuesday cleaning visit because he had a boring meeting that he couldn't get out of, and he had been ticking off the days to today: Saturday.

He had tried not to think about her, forcing Max's face into his brain every time it wandered over to Jenny's, but he had failed more than he had succeeded. He ran down the stairs with a smile already beaming on his face to find Sheila hanging up her coat on the hook by the door. He couldn't stop his spirits sliding brutally into disappointment.

'Hello,' greeted Sheila. 'You've got me today.'

'Nice to see you again, Sheila,' said Stuart, sticking on a pretend smile of delight. 'Are you better?'

'Well, on the mend. Still a bit sore,' said Sheila. 'I hope our Jenny has been looking after you.'

'Jenny was doing a great job filling in. You shouldn't have come back until you were totally fit and well,' said Stuart, hoping Sheila would put on her coat and say that he was right and she'd send her daughter round immediately.

'Oh that's nice to know.' Sheila picked up her bag and for the first time Stuart noticed the resemblance between mother and daughter. How could he have missed that wide arc of a smile and the merry twinkle in her eyes?

'I would have had another week off, but she's busy today and I didn't want to let you down.'

Busy doing what? He wanted to ask. And with whom?

Max emerged from the study. She had been in there for three hours already that morning.

'Hi, Sheila, lovely to see you again. Are you better?'

'Aye, I'm not bad,' Sheila said, smiling Jenny's smile.

'Would you strip the sofa cushions and wash them, please?'

'Course I will,' replied Sheila, looking too chirpy for someone who was washing someone else's upholstery on a Saturday morning.

'Stuart, give me another half an hour and I'll have finished,' said Max, disappearing back to her desk. 'We'll go out for lunch.'

'Yeah, whatever,' said Stu to the closed door. He made himself a bacon butty and took the newspaper into the garden because he knew he was in for yet another lonely Saturday. Sure enough, an hour later and Max was still only halfway through all the emails she needed to answer before the weekend was out.

Chapter 63

Violet called in at Carousel before her wedding-dress fitting. She tried to fool herself by telling herself she wanted to see how the new flavour of ice cream she had made the previous day had fared in the freezer – but she knew in her heart of hearts that she was going there in the hope of finding Pav. She felt her spirits soar upwards as if they were perched on eagle's wings to find his battered red van parked outside the shop. *This is a dangerous portal you are opening, Violet Flockton,* said some sensible part of her head. She chose to ignore it as she locked her car and walked, with a quickened step, towards him.

The smile Pav gave her when she opened the door mirrored her own; deep and genuinely pleased to see the other.

'I didn't think you'd be here today,' fibbed Violet. 'I just popped by to check on something I made yesterday. Coffee?'

'Yes, please, that would be good.'

While the kettle was boiling, she pulled the large tub of pastel mauve ice cream out of the freezer and stuck a spoon in it. Clotted cream and flowers – she'd sourced some tiny edible petals and stirred them into the mix. It looked so pretty and she just hoped the taste matched.

'Don't suppose you fancy helping me out with something, Pav?' she called. Pav looked up and stopped painting.

'Yes, of course,' he said. 'Do you need me to lift something for you?'

'No, I want you to taste some ice cream.'

Pav grinned. 'This is a job I would very much like to help you with.'

'Lovely.' Violet brought out a large spoonful of ice cream. She intended to hand it over, but instead Pav opened his mouth. Violet carefully guided the spoon between his lips and tried not to notice that his summer-blue eyes were full on her. Her hand was ever so slightly shaking as his lips closed round the spoon and she saw how soft they looked.

'Mmm,' he said, as she took away the spoon, 'what flavour is it? No, let me guess. It's like – a little scented.'

'Flowers and clotted cream,' said Violet, willing her cheeks not to colour.

'It's very nice,' said Pav. 'Very nice. I like that you test out your flavour on me. The ice cream in Poland is very . . . like water ice, not creamy like yours.'

Pav downed tools while they drank coffee.

'Do you miss home, Pav?' asked Violet.

'No. I like it better here, in Yorkshire.'

'Do you have family over there?'

'I have only one brother and he is in Barnsley with his wife. I followed him over here. My father died when I was just a baby and my mother died last year.'

'That's really sad, Pav. I'm sorry.'

'It was sad,' replied Pav. 'She had a hard life and was only forty-six.'

It was no age at all, thought Violet. This she knew, because her dad was the same age when he passed away. And she still missed him every single day.

'Were any of your family painters like you, Pav?'

Violet looked at the horses on the wall. The detail was incredible – it was more than she could ever have asked for.

'No. No painters. Only me. I am the family freak,' he grinned.

Violet thought she could have listened to Pav's accent all day. Or all night.

'You're so talented,' she said. She almost believed that if she reached out to touch it, the pole in the dapple-grey horse's back would be cold, like metal.

'I work slow, though, ah? It's good that I can paint at night after I finish building,' said Pav.

'Aren't you tired by that time?'

'No, it's how I relax,' he said. 'It is nice to be here doing this than in my brother's house. His wife is ... er ...'

He struggled for a suitable word. He didn't find it and had to paraphrase. 'She would prefer it if I wasn't around and the house was just for her and him.'

'Oh that must be quite difficult,' Violet sympathized.

'Let's just say that I am at my happiest working here on your horses. I am saving for my own place. Things will be different then.'

Pav's lips curved into a smile as he put down his cup and moved back to the wall. The warmth of that smile soaked right through Violet to the core of her. Glyn had never made her feel as if her knees might knock together. Not even in the beginning when she thought she loved him. It had never been love; she had worked that one out since. It had been a mix of gratitude, need, pity, obligation – but not love. She was marrying a man she didn't love. It was no wonder that she wasn't excited one bit about the fact that she had a wedding-dress fitting in less than half an hour.

Violet stood in the dress, holding out her arms so that Freya could check the fit.

'It feels tight on me,' Violet said.

'It's not tight,' said Freya, pinching the spare material together so that Violet could see. It actually needed taking in because it was too loose, yet it felt tight. How weird.

Violet stared at her reflection in the mirror. She looked beautiful and delicate in the ivory dress with the peach rosebuds round her neck. With her pale perfect skin and slender frame, she resembled a china doll: a doll with a sad-painted face. And this doll was going to be taking vows to be married to Glyn in exactly seven weeks. She thought of Glyn's face, rapturous with joy, as the registrar said, 'You may now kiss the bride.' She thought of him leaning over, his lips covering hers, his tongue pushing into her mouth.

She staggered and Freya's arms came out to steady her.

'Are you all right?' she said.

'I think I need to sit down for a minute,' said Violet, her head as light as a helium balloon. Freya guided her onto a chair before going to get her a glass of water. She placed it in Violet's hand and closed her fingers round it.

'There, take some deep breaths then drink,' said Freya.

Violet held the glass in one hand and pressed the other against her forehead.

'Yes, sorry,' she said. 'There's so much to arrange. So much to think about.'

'Of course,' said Freya. Her hand rubbed Violet's arm, intending to soothe her. Oddly, it looked so much older than the rest of her. It was like Nan's hand, with its paper-thin skin.

Violet had the sudden impulse to throw her arms round Freya and sink her head into her neck and sob. She wanted to rip the dress off and run away. However much room there was in it, it felt constricting and uncomfortable and symbolic of her life.

'You know,' began Freya softly, 'if a wedding isn't a dream one, it can only be a nightmare.'

Violet flicked her eyes up at the older woman. Was it so apparent that she was unhappy? Was it so obvious that her head was full of alarm bells clanging inside her?

Freya's voice was as warm as a fireside and as Violet sat sipping her water, Freya remembered the young woman who had last worn the dress. She had the same frightened fawn-like eyes as Violet; the same vibes of panic were radiating from her; the same knowledge was sitting in her heart that she was marrying the wrong man. As with that bride, Freya wanted to close her arms round Violet and reassure her that everything was going to be all right. She wanted to tell her that if ever a dress would help her find her happy ending, it would be this one. But all she could do was let it happen.

Chapter 64

'Ta da – behold Sunday lunch.' Max announced, delivering two plates to the table with a smug flourish. Stuart smiled but it wasn't a real Sunday lunch in his book. A real Sunday lunch started with a raw chicken that was cooked slowly in an oven, pervading the house with roasting smells. It did not consist of a ready-cooked chicken from a supermarket, foil-packed potatoes dauphinoise, tinned carrots and peas, pre-made gravy bought from a chiller cabinet and Aunt Bessie's parsnips and Yorkshire puddings.

Still, it was better than the pasta or microwave meals that they used to have on Sundays because Max was invariably too busy catching up on paperwork to cobble up anything fancy. Stuart hated cooking and rather than try to throw something together himself he would suggest they nip up to the local carvery. More often than not Max would say she was too busy or not hungry and 'Why don't you just go to your mum's while I finish what I have to do.' So Stuart spent a lot of his Sundays enjoying his mum's home-cooked fare wishing that Max could metamorphose – just on one day of the week – into a woman who wanted to nourish him with Sunday roasts. A picture rose into his head of Jenny Thompson pulling a leg of lamb out of the oven, pans bubbling on the hob, while he set the table for the two of them. Or maybe three or four of them. Two little children helping to put the knives and forks out. He would have bet his

life savings that Jenny wouldn't have ever served tinned carrots –
not even to Alan the rabbit.

He lifted up the uncorked bottle of white wine and held it
over Max's glass.

'Ooh none for me,' she stopped him quickly.

'Why?' he said, eyebrows sinking crossly in the middle. He
knew what was coming.

'I might take a look at some figures later on so I want to keep
a clear head.'

Stuart banged the wine bottle down on the table.

'Oh for God's sake, Max. Can't you give it a rest for one day?'

That was the meal ruined.

'I'm talking about only half an hour. An hour – tops,' said
Max. 'I have a video conference with the Americans tomorrow
about—'

'Oh yes, "the Americans",' he sniped. 'I suppose you'll have to
go over there as well and so I'll see even less of you than I do
already, if that is possible.'

'Oh Stuart, don't be like that. It's a massive opportunity for
me. I have to be up to speed on everything.'

Stuart picked up his fork and stabbed it into a slice of potato.
He didn't like potatoes in sauce. What was wrong with simple
mash? 'I hate you working weekends.'

'The hours come with the job,' said Max.

'Then get another job.'

Max gave a gaspy laugh. 'Another job? I don't want another
job. I love what I do.'

'I hate your job,' grumbled Stuart.

'And I hate yours,' Max stabbed a carrot with venom.

Stuart's head jerked up.

'What's up with my job?'

Max dropped her head. 'Just leave it, Stuart. Let's not argue.'

'No, come on, I want to know what's so bad about my job.'

Max didn't reply. She chewed on the carrot and kept her
head down.

'Let me answer the question for you, then, shall I?' Stuart persisted. 'It's a shit job with a shit wage.'

Max shook her head and tried to remain calm so this didn't blow up. 'I never said that, Stuart.'

'But it's what you think. Go on, be honest.'

So Max was honest.

'If you must know, I think you're underestimating yourself.'

'No, I am NOT,' Stuart threw back. Max's eyebrows rose. She couldn't remember the last time she'd heard him raise his voice to her at this level. 'I like my job. At least I did before you pressured me into applying for a promotion. Now I don't like it as much, so I can guarantee you I won't be going any further up the bastard scale.'

'You've been there nearly eighteen years. You could have been running that place by now if you'd wanted to,' snapped Max.

'Precisely. "If I'd wanted to" – but I don't want to. I don't want to be stuck in an office from six in the morning until nine at night. I've got better things to do with my life than work myself into the ground. And what if we decide we want kids?'

Max looked at him, stunned.

'You are joking? I've never wanted kids. Neither have you.'

'What if you change your mind?'

'I won't,' said Max, definitely.

'What if I do?'

The question hung in the air like poison. Max gulped and said almost breathlessly, 'Have you?'

'No,' he replied. 'But I'm not as against the idea as I used to be.'

'Boy,' Max answered that breathlessly, as if winded.

'And I want a dog or a cat,' Stuart blurted out.

Max's eyes widened as if she was viewing an alien being rather than her very-long-term boyfriend. Where was he vomiting all this up from?

'I tell you, Max, if you're insistent on working all the frigging hours God sends, and then some more, I'm not rattling round in this dump by myself any longer.'

'Dump?' Max released a dry laugh. If there was one noun that didn't fit with the house they lived in, it was 'dump'.

'It is to me,' railed Stuart. 'I hate this bloody house. It's always freezing.'

'That's a lie,' parried Max. 'But if you're cold why don't you turn up the damned heating?'

'I have,' said Stuart. 'And it still doesn't alter anything.'

Max shook her head. She didn't know what he was talking about. But whatever it was, it ran deeper than a central-heating issue. It was as if he was a dormant volcano that had suddenly started to grumble after a hundred years.

'Stuart, what's up, love?' she asked softly.

Stuart stared across the table at the woman he had been in love with since he was sixteen. They'd had so much in common then. They spent their Sundays sitting on swings in the park talking for hours, or at her parents' house listening to music, playing Monopoly, watching TV. He'd had plans then too. To buy a little cosy terraced house near his parents and do it all up, spend week-ends by the seaside in a bed and breakfast and go for walks on the beach, get a dog. They weren't great big plans like Max's but they were *his* plans, and he hadn't realized any of them. Max's bigger wants had outshone his at every turn. And it was ultimately his fault because he had let that happen.

Stuart's head slumped into his hands. 'God, I'm sorry,' he said. He felt closer to tears than he could remember being for years.

'Forget it,' said Max with gentle firmness. She wanted to put her arms round him but she was scared, for the first time, that he might push her off. After all those years of togetherness, she wasn't a hundred per cent sure of how he would react any more. She felt as shaken as if she had been physically assaulted. Stuart really was stressed. 'Look, I will totally and utterly forget about work today, okay? See, I'm pouring myself a big glass of wine.'

Stuart resumed eating his lunch but he knew that Max not

working that afternoon wouldn't change anything now. He couldn't remember when the course of their lives had begun to split and started to take them in such different directions, but he faced the grim reality that travelling on those two roads would carry them further away from each other. And what was really freaking him out was that he feared his path had met up and joined with another that was heading to the same horizon as he was destined for.

Chapter 65

Once again Richard brought red roses to La Hacienda. Once again he was courtesy itself as he opened the door for Bel and complimented her on her outfit. It was a very simple black dress, boat neck, three-quarter sleeves, nipped in at the waist. She carried a mint-green bag, the same shade as her oval necklace, her earrings and her eyes.

'Good week?' asked Richard, smiling at her across the table.

'Not bad,' she replied. 'You?'

'Busy, busy,' he said, turning his attention to the menu. 'Easy choice: sea bass for me.'

'Did you ever bring Shaden here?' Bel blurted out. Not even she knew she was going to say that.

Richard looked at her as if she had just asked if his hobby was eating slugs.

'No, of course I didn't,' he replied calmly – but tightly. He was about to say more but the wine waiter arrived with two glasses of Pinot Grigio.

'You seem to be under the impression that it was a relationship,' said Richard when the waiter was at a safe distance away. 'It wasn't. It was primal and sex-fuelled and I'm disgusted with myself.' He shuddered. 'We didn't "date"; we didn't have cosy evenings in front of the fire. It was a few lust-driven shags, which resulted in something very unfortunate that I will bitterly regret to the end of my days. Now, please, let that be the end to it. It was sordid and I'm ashamed and I've truly learned the hardest lesson that life could possibly have to offer me.'

'Is that true, Richard?' asked Bel. 'I need to know the truth before I can truly move on. Why did you keep all her emails? As romantic souvenirs?'

'As if. I swear to you, Bel, there was no romance. There was only stupidity on my part that I didn't delete them. I filed the emails as a matter of convenience only. I had no intention of poring over them.' He looked intently at Bel and held out his hand across the table – the hand wearing his wedding band. She slipped hers into it and felt his fingers stroke her knuckles. 'You're the only woman I want to think about, Bel. You have to trust me.'

Bel could understand why Shaden fell under his spell. He had a way of looking at her that made her feel as if she was the only thing in the world that could ever matter to him. She wanted to believe the words he said to her so very much. She didn't want to be alone and unloved any more.

Chapter 66

The woman who waddled into White Wedding was as wide as a barrel and had hair of such a vibrant red dye that it could be seen from orbit. It managed to eclipse the brightness of her fire-engine shade of lipstick, which was a feat in itself. She was about seventy and the man whose arm she was linking was approximately the same age. He was dapper and considerably slimmer than she and kindly measured his pace to hers. In his free hand he carried a large pink-leather shopping bag initialled in huge diamanté lettering across the front: DDT.

'Vernon and Doreen Turbot. How d'you do?' said the elderly man, putting the bag down on the floor and holding out his hand for Freya to shake.

When the lady started to speak, the man tilted his head towards her and looked at her with such tenderness that Freya was reminded of someone whose attention she used to hold like that, once upon a time.

'I'm looking for a wedding dress,' said Doreen. 'White. Have you owt to fit me?'

'I have a dress for every shape in my shop,' said Freya softly, lifting a chair and bringing it over to allow the lady to sit down.

'Oh that's better,' said Doreen. 'We've shopped till we've dropped today. Holiday clothes. Vernon and I are renewing our vows on a cruise, you see.' She beamed to reveal red lipstick all over her teeth. Not that her husband seemed to notice. He couldn't have looked more love-struck if he'd tried.

'We're going on the *Mermaidia*,' added Vernon. 'We've got a room with a butler. We're making up for lost time, aren't we, cherub?' Vernon squeezed his wife's shoulder. 'We were reunited after forty years last year. We had a quickie wedding because we didn't want to wait. But now we're having the works.'

'Forty long years we were apart,' echoed Doreen. 'But we haven't half made up for lost time, haven't we?'

She nudged Vernon and they both broke into a cheeky secret grin. Freya remembered that look – the key to a lover's secret world.

'Quite right too,' said Freya. 'Let me find some things for you to try on.'

When she returned, Vernon strolled off, hands behind his back.

'He doesn't want to see them,' confided Doreen. 'Doesn't want to encourage bad luck by seeing me before the big day.'

Freya nodded. Tradition and romance were not confined to the young, she had been more than happy to discover over the many years in her profession.

Doreen was not interested in the plain soft satin gown that Freya suggested. She wanted forty missing years of drama embodied in one gown. She heaved herself from the chair to take a tour of the shop and her eyes lit up when she saw the dress that Freya was working on: Max's gypsy dress.

'Oh my life – that's what I've always wanted. I dreamed of a massive frock decades before those gypsies made them popular,' she gasped. 'We'll have to buy a special suitcase for it, but that's what I want. One of those big, big, big dresses.'

'I can vacuum-pack a dress for you,' said Freya. 'It would take up less room than you might imagine.'

'Can you put lights in it? In the shape of little fish ... and chips.'

Freya didn't even raise her eyebrows

'I can,' she nodded with confidence.

Freya pulled a dress from a rail, a voluminous one with lots of ruffles at the neck and a wide wide skirt. 'Try this for starters,' she said. 'I think it would look lovely on you.'

'Oh now, that's smashing,' Doreen's face melted into a besotted smile.

'Come with me and try it on,' said Freya, holding out her arm so the old lady had some support as she headed for the changing room.

Freya helped her first into three net petticoats, then into the enormous frock. The ruffles framed Doreen's formidable bosom perfectly and the puffed-out skirt gave her the illusion of a waist. Her figure in the gown was distinctly hourglass. Doreen looked in the mirror and saw Mae West staring back at her.

Freya chose a cathedral-length veil to go with it and a crown covered in hundreds of seed pearls. Everything the old lady wore should – by all the rules of fashion – have looked a bugger. But the dress wove its magic. In this white cloud, Doreen was a princess marrying the prince who had kissed her and woken up her heart again after forty years of a humdrum existence. Life without Vernon Turbot was all right but nothing special; life with him was full of fireworks and passion. In this dress, Doreen looked like the woman that she felt resided in her heart.

'I'll have it,' said Doreen breathlessly. 'Whatever it costs, I'll have it. I don't want to see any more. This is the one. But with those lights on, if you don't mind.'

'I'll make sure you have your lights.'

'And more underskirts.' She flashed the widest red-lipstick-toothed smile at Freya. 'It feels like it was made for me. You know when something's just right, don't you?'

'Oh yes, my dear,' Freya nodded slowly. 'Indeed you do.'

Chapter 67

Violet watched Pav filing down a hole he'd made through one of the tables so he could thread a long gold-painted twisting pole through it.

Glyn hadn't been very pleased when she said she had to meet with a builder on a Saturday, though he hadn't suspected she was lying about it. She hating lying, but Violet knew that if she had to spend all day sitting in the flat on the sofa with his arm round her, watching TV, she would scream.

'I love being here so much, working,' Pav said, now climbing up his ladder. 'Although this does not feel like work.'

His arms had dark hair on them and his biceps were pronounced, Violet noticed, as she brought over a bacon sandwich for him. She watched him drill into the ceiling joist and thought how incredibly manly he looked pushing down on a power tool. Then a contrasting vision of Glyn in an apron at home drifted into her head, bringing with it a hiccup of nausea.

'Violet, please can you hold the pole steady?' Pav asked.

Violet jumped to attention. She held it as he instructed, until he had fixed it firmly in place, then Pav climbed back down the ladder and they both stood back to view his handiwork.

'That looks amazing, Pav,' said Violet. Considering it was just a piece of painted wood, the impact was fantastic.

'Now it is beginning to look like a real carousel inside, don't you think?' said Pav, taking a bite out of his sandwich and nodding his proud approval. 'And once I put the other four poles in, you will really see the full effect.'

Violet smiled. She loved this shop so much and couldn't wait to open it. But then, it would only be ready to open when Pav had done his job and gone. And she so didn't want him to hurry. He would take all the light from her life when he eventually left. She felt unexpected tears rise up to her eyes and turned her head away, but it was too late, for Pav had seen them.

'Violet, are you all right?' His hand landed on her shoulder in a gesture of concern.

'Yes, yes, of course,' she said. 'Just a bit overcome with excitement about opening up Carousel.'

It sounded like the lie it was. Pav's hand lifted from her shoulder before she could press into its warmth.

Her phone rang in her back jeans pocket. For once it wasn't Glyn.

'Wotcher,' came Max's usual bellow. 'Did you get your invitation through the post this morning?'

'Yes, I most certainly did,' she replied.

'What did you think?'

'Beautiful,' said Violet smiling, recalling the heavy ivory card with the shocking-pink ribbon detail along the side. 'Has Stuart seen them?'

'Yep,' said Max. 'He quizzed me about the so-called refreshments I was putting on after the wedding.'

'And you said?'

'Well, I replied that a couple of our relatives are a bit old and doddery and will probably want a sandwich before they go home so I was arranging for a platter of light bites to be available after the service, seeing as we "aren't having a reception".'

'And he bought it? Bloody hell.' Violet was gobsmacked.

'Yes, funnily enough. In fact he did a weird smiling thing and said, "That's right, we're not having a reception".'

'Why did he say that, then?'

'Isn't it obvious?' laughed Max. 'He knows I've got something up my sleeve and he's okay about it. Anyway, why I'm ringing is that I'm popping up to White Wedding for a dress fitting in the next half an hour. Bel's coming too. Want to join us?'

Violet looked at Pav preparing his paints and knew she really should leave him to it. She didn't want to pester him, however much she wanted to stay near him for as long as she could.

'Yeah, I'll meet you up there,' she said. It would fill another hour of the weekend and postpone being cocooned in Glyn's flat watching comedies on Gold. And tomorrow there was another Joy and Norman lunch to look forward to and more wedding talk. Whoopee.

'Dear God, you are joking,' said Bel, drawing close to the dressed mannequin at the back of the shop. It was a gargantuan white explosion of net and ruffles and, rather bizarrely, sitting underneath the top layer of gauze it had flashing lights in the shape of little orange fish and yellow rectangular chips.

'That's not mine,' tutted Max. 'This is mine ...' She pulled back a curtain and they walked through to find another mannequin wearing another dress that made the fish-and-chip one look like a scrap of waste material. Max watched Bel's and Violet's mouths fall to their feet and their eyes round to the size of dustbin lids. 'Well, whaddya think, girls?'

Words failed her friends. The dress was as big as an igloo. What they didn't know was that twenty-five petticoats would be going on underneath it. Max weighed fifteen stone, her dress was going to weight twenty stone, so Stuart was going to turn round at the altar and see a thirty-five-stone tidal wave of white froth spilling towards him. He would think the River Dearne had broken its banks and come foaming into the church, and Bel wouldn't blame him. How the hell Max's dad was going to have room to walk at the side of her was anyone's guess.

'It's still not finished yet,' said Max, stripping off her skirt and shirt as Freya undressed the mannequin then pooled the dress on the carpet so that Max could step into it. 'You won't see the full effect until the actual day. I have to keep some surprises, even from you two.'

'There can't be any more surprises, surely?' Bel said.

Max said nothing. She merely climbed into the dress and Freya lifted it up so she could put her arms through the sleeves. At six foot, with gorgeous Amazonian shoulders, Max looked absolutely stunning in it, it had to be said.

'I've picked my tiara and my shoes and my veil, but I'm not letting you see them,' Max winked at her two totally flabbergasted friends, then she shivered with excited delight. 'I can't believe it's only a fortnight away, can you?'

'There are a lot of things I can't believe at the moment,' replied Bel, shaking her head. 'I can't believe you've totally reorganized your wedding in such a short time, for one thing. It's only just over a month since you had this brainwave. It would take a normal person at least a year to get all this together.'

'One: it's meant to be,' said Max. 'That's why everything has gone so smoothly. Two: I'm not normal. You should know that by now.'

'I have the bridesmaids' dresses almost finished, if you wish to try them on,' said Freya.

'Already?' marvelled Bel. Blimey, Freya was as mean a machine as Max was.

'Ooh yes, go and put them on and let's see what we'll look like in the photos,' Max clapped her hands together.

'So you've organized a photographer as well, then?' Bel said, although the answer was obvious and Max merely lifted up her eyebrows innocently.

Five minutes later they were all standing looking at themselves in the huge expanse of mirror in the dressing room: Max in her enormous eruption of white and her two shorter bridesmaids in shocking-pink crinolines.

'There's enough material in these frocks to make curtains for every house in Wales,' said Bel, twisting to the side to examine her profile.

'What are we wearing on our heads?' asked Violet. 'Those pink hula-hoop things?'

'Nope,' grinned Max. 'Show them, Freya.'

Freya reached for a box on a shelf behind them and pulled out two mantilla combs, pink and sparkling, with long bright-pink veils attached.

'Wa-hay – bring on the bullfighter,' laughed Bel, plunging the comb into her hair. 'Actually, I'm liking this very much.'

Violet giggled as Freya threaded the comb into her fine, silver-blonde hair. She looked so delicate in the headdress. Like the wispy ghost of a Flamenco dancer.

'The shoes will be ready next week when you pick up the dresses,' said Freya. 'I am dyeing them tomorrow.'

'Let's have a photo,' Max announced suddenly. 'Bel, have you got your phone on you? The camera on mine doesn't work properly. I need an upgrade.'

Before Bel could answer, Freya had taken an old Polaroid camera from the shelf.

'It's a little old-fashioned these days,' she said, lifting the camera to her eye, 'but it still works.'

She clicked, the photo protruded and they waited for the colours to develop.

'Oh my, we are fabulous,' laughed Max, looking at the image. 'Can I have it?'

'Of course,' said Freya. 'It's yours.'

'I'll send you both a copy when I get home,' Max promised.

'Marvellous,' said Bel, with a faux-deadpan expression. 'I honestly can't wait.'

Chapter 68

There were exactly three roast potatoes and two roasted parsnips on every plate, Violet noticed as Joy served out from the dishes on the table. Norman was carving the pork and would shortly distribute three slices to everyone. The Yorkshire puddings were even puffed up into clones of each other. Violet compared that to Sunday lunch at her mum's house, where chaos usually abounded as Susan rushed ladlefuls of food on to the plates so it wouldn't get cold and the Yorkshire puddings ranged from flat to enormously deformed. Not that they'd all had Sunday lunch in Spring Lane for ages; Glyn only felt comfortable eating at his mother's house.

'Forty-one days exactly,' said Joy excitedly, taking her seat at the table and pouring out four tumblers of cooled water from a glass jug. 'I can't imagine how thrilled you both must be.'

Violet didn't say anything. She was exhausted with the effort of talking weddings already and they'd only been there half an hour.

'We're having the caravan especially valeted for you,' said Norman, transferring three slices of meat onto Glyn's plate.

'Thanks, that's brilliant,' said Glyn. 'Isn't it, Violet?'

'Yes, lovely,' Violet said, wanting to drop the fake smile she was wearing and run off screaming out of the front door. She felt hot and was having palpitations, something that was affecting her more and more these days. She would wake up, her heart racing, her lungs clawing for breath, after dreams of being married. She had woken Glyn up last night and he had rushed to get her a glass of water and then tried to cuddle her when she wanted space. He was agoraphobic and she was getting claustrophobic. It didn't bode well.

'Very nice, Mother,' Norman judged his first mouthful of Sunday lunch. He always said that after eating the first roast potato, Violet noticed. She wondered if she were looking at a picture of what was to come for her and Glyn; matching home-knits, matching sprout-sizes and precision in all things.

'Daddy and I wondered if you would like to go out for a meal after the wedding service,' announced Joy. She held up her hand seeing Glyn open his mouth to speak. 'I know you aren't having a proper reception because of your health, but Daddy and I thought it might be nice for the four of us to have a little celebration.'

Violet shook her head. Was Joy on the same planet?

'What about my mum and Nan?' asked Violet.

Joy and Norman looked at each other.

'Well, we were thinking of Glyn's predicament, really. It's going to be quite hard on him being in an unfamiliar place for the wedding as it is. We thought it might be too much of a strain if he had to eat with str— I mean, with other people.'

Strangers. Joy was going to say 'strangers'.

'I don't think that would be very nice of me to leave out my family,' said Violet, as firmly as her voice could manage.

'Oh dear,' said Joy with a sad smile. 'I think we've put our well-meaning foot in it, Daddy.' She put her hand on Glyn's shoulder and squeezed it. 'Maybe we should pay for you two to have a quiet lunch somewhere and leave all the adults out.'

Adults? That summed up what Joy really thought of Glyn – that he was still a child at thirty-four – thought Violet.

'Thank you Mum, Dad, that is so nice of you but I think we'll just want to get home after the wedding and rest for a while before Violet drives us to our honeymoon destination,' said Glyn, making the decision for them.

'Don't I get a say in this?' said Violet crossly. She was as surprised as any of them that she dare say aloud what she was
thinking.

'Oh darling, I'm sorry,' said Glyn reaching over to touch her
arm. 'I just presumed . . .'

'It would be our wedding day,' said Violet. 'It might be nice to
have one day when I didn't have to sit and watch reruns of the
bloody *Vicar of Dibley*.'

'Dear me,' said Joy, as the profanity crossed Violet's lips. Violet
had never sworn in front of the Leachs before. From the effect of
that one word, Violet was only glad she hadn't used the F-word.
Joy was flustered and bordering on having 'the vapours'.
Norman, under his breath, said, 'I think we'll have less of that talk
at the table,' without breaking his eating stride.

'Sorry,' said Violet, feeling ridiculous and naughty-child-like
now. No one said another word through the roast lunch. The
only sound was the scrape of cutlery on plates. Violet felt as if her
nerves were a blackboard and someone was pulling their nails
down it.

Joy and Norman finished eating at exactly the same time.

'I think it's time for apple pie,' trilled Joy, rising from the table.
Normal service was once again resumed. Although Violet's grip
on 'normal' was becoming looser by the day.

Chapter 69

As Bel was driving from her third dinner date with Richard, she realized that her head was still as mixed up as ever. He'd asked her that evening when she was going to return the wedding ring to her finger. Soon, she had answered. She wanted to put it back on, but she owed it to herself not to rush things. In the back of her mind something was advising caution. A feeling, an intuition and the alert came from the same place that had told her to look at Richard's phone when it was charging in the kitchen that awful day – so she respected it and followed its lead.

The car was full of the scent of the red roses he had brought again. And tonight, when they were parting, she had let his lips graze against her own. And that was odd, because it had just felt like hers were being touched by a pair of lips belonging to anyone. She hadn't had zingy feelings zip around inside her as she used to have whenever he kissed her. *Or when you think of Dan Regent kissing you.* She kicked that thought right out of her head. Or at least attempted to, because the medical swine was still intent on invading her dreams at night, and at idle moments during the day. And because he was being so hard to shift, she had forbidden herself from looking him up on the internet. Even though she had been close to Googling him more times than she cared to admit.

Her heart was still in shock. That was the only possible explanation. Her head was still full of unanswered questions about

Shaden, which she shouldn't, couldn't and wouldn't ask – yet they kept torturing her. As she drove home, she had a mad thought about confronting her tart of a cousin and getting her side of things.

Sitting at the traffic lights, imagining what Shaden's reaction would be if she turned up at the Bosomworth-Proud family home, Bel happened to glance to her side and there in the adjacent sports car was Shaden herself. She was wearing dark glasses and a bandage across the bridge of her nose like a glamorous Adam Ant.

Bel's heart started to thump with adrenaline. She wondered if she had enough time to leap out of the car, dive through the blonde bitch's window and throttle her.

Shaden was looking intently straight ahead. She had spotted Bel and was desperately waiting for the lights to change, judging from the jerks her car was doing as Shaden's foot trembled on the accelerator. As soon as the amber light made an appearance, Shaden was off, squealing forward at warp speed.

Bel felt so shaky that she stalled the car and the impatient bloke behind started blasting his horn at her. He overtook her and threw her the Vs. When she did eventually set off, Bel was tempted to turn right at the roundabout instead of left and drive to the remote sanctuary on the moors that was Emily. But she didn't. Seeing Dan Regent again would have only further mushed up her brain, if there was any of it left to mush. And finding Emily empty and him gone back to the house he shared with Cathy would have been worse.

'Come in, darling,' said Trevor pulling her into the house. 'Are you all right?'

'It's not too late to call, is it?' asked Bel, noticing the antique grandfather clock with its big hand on the twelve and the little hand on the ten. Her dad had taught her to tell the time on that clock. Faye had bought her a lovely book with a big cardboard clock that had movable hands but Bel had shunned it. Another memory come to batter her when she was at a low ebb and show her what an awful unlovable person she must be.

'You're welcome any time, do I really need to say that?' said Trevor.

'Where's Faye?' asked Bel.

'She's gone to dinner with Vanoushka,' said Trevor, adding quickly: 'She hasn't spoken to her sister since the wedding. Vanoushka rang up in tears last night wanting to mend the bridge. Apparently she's broken her foot after falling from the cross trainer in her gym and is feeling a bit sorry for herself.'

Bel huffed.

'Faye's in a difficult position,' Trevor explained. 'Don't think she's on their side, Bel. She's been very worried about you. I wish . . . oh never mind.' He turned and went into the kitchen. 'I'll be back in a minute. You have a seat, love. I've just made a pot of coffee. I'll get you a cup.'

But Bel followed her dad instead. 'Wish what, Dad?'

Trevor turned slowly. 'I wish,' he began carefully, 'that you'd feel able to reach out to her occasionally. She's always seen you as her daughter and I know that she frets about you as if she were your mother.'

'But she isn't my mother, Dad,' said Bel. The words sounded so hard.

'I've never said this to you before, Bel,' said Trevor after pulling in a long breath, 'but it breaks my heart how you've always kept Faye at arm's length. She's never once said that it upsets her and I know that she would never dream of trying to come between you and me, but I've always felt very sad about it. If only you knew what a truly wonderful woman she is.'

Bel felt ashamed. She didn't realize that her dad was so aware of how she felt about Faye. And there was no reason for it because Faye had never put a foot wrong with her.

'I've just seen Shaden driving,' said Bel, moving the conversation on because it was becoming too uncomfortable. 'Has she been in an accident? She had a big bandage across her face.'

'I don't know,' said Trevor. 'The only contact we've had with the B-Ps was that quick phone call last night from Vanoushka, crying her eyes out. I must say, I haven't missed their visits.' Trevor smiled at his daughter. 'And I know Faye hasn't been overly distressed that Vanoushka hasn't bored her with tales of Martin's unsavoury habits.'

'I've been thinking about asking Shaden for her side of the story.'

'Which she would invariably twist until you felt savaged. It wouldn't be the best of ideas, darling. She's always been so incredibly jealous of you. She would relish the opportunity of hurting you with detail and you still would not be assured that she was telling you the truth.'

Bel nodded slowly. He was right of course. Bad idea, then. She was full of them.

She took the coffee which her dad handed over and launched straight in with the reason she was here.

'I've been seeing Richard again, Dad.'

Bel watched her father's spine stiffen. 'Oh,' he said, trying to keep the judgemental tone out of his voice. 'How did that come about?'

'I agreed to meet him to find out where we go from here. I couldn't just walk away entirely seeing as I went through with the marriage.'

'I see,' Trevor nodded. He didn't look very happy, but he wasn't the sort of man who imposed his own will on others.

'I've been out to dinner with him every Wednesday for three weeks, that's all. To talk.'

'And what have you decided?' asked Trevor.

'I don't know,' said Bel, feeling very close to tears. 'I don't know.'

'You're from Yorkshire. And you know what they say in Yorkshire: if you don't know what to do . . .'

He left the sentence hanging for Bel to finish. 'Do nowt,' she smiled.

Trevor extended his arm and Bel went to him. His big arm closed round her and she felt safe and warm and ever so young again.

'Promise me you'll take your time,' he said. 'Don't let anyone or anything rush you.'

'I promise, Dad.'

They moved into the lounge and Bel drank her coffee. She didn't come round to the house often enough. There was such a lovely calm atmosphere here. Faye really did know how to make a house a home.

'Remember that I'm always here for you,' said Trevor at the door when Bel was ready to go home to her empty, lonely apartment. He kissed her on the head, tenderly, a loving Dad kiss. 'And so is Faye. Let her in, love. It isn't too late.'

Chapter 70

Five days before his wedding, Stuart was on his way home after picking up the hired suits. He was wondering if it was normal for someone to feel so numb about his forthcoming nuptials. Luckily he had never been a whooping, excitable sort of guy, so Max was blissfully unaware that he felt the way he did. Anyway, she was whooping enough for both of them.

He called in at the Lamp to pay the balance for the reception. Even the landlady was more excited than he was, wittering on about getting some pink serviettes or something. He wasn't really listening. He hoped he was just suffering the pre-wedding nerves that everyone seemed to be going on about. His mum certainly cited them as the cause of him not jumping around the room with excitement on seeing the single-layer white wedding cake with the pink sugar-rose detail that she had made. And Luke was blaming pre-wedding nerves as the reason why Stuart looked so bloody miserable when they went for their final suit fitting last week.

Then he saw her. As he was about to drive past Pogley Top post office, he recognized the pony-tailed figure of Jenny Thompson in her beige coat, carrying her bucket of cleaning stuff. Suddenly his indifferent state was gone and his heart was in overdrive. He braked sharply, fiercely twisting the wheel, and took a left turn like Nigel Mansell so that he could pull up beside her.

He launched himself out of his seat.

'Jenny,' he said. God, it was so good to see her.

'Stuart, hello there. How are you?' Her smile spread across her lips and he felt its warm impact somewhere in his chest.

His legs were shaking as he walked round the front of the car. They seemed to be on automatic pilot; he didn't feel as if he was in control of himself.

'You look lovely,' he said.

Jenny laughed. 'Oh yeah, course I do. Old coat and—'

She was silenced by his kiss because his hands grabbed her arms and pulled her towards him and his mouth covered her own and it was wonderful. All the emotion that he didn't think he had rose up like a hot geyser inside him. Then he felt Jenny drop her bucket and shift position and her fingers thread themselves in his hair.

Their lips drew apart but their foreheads stayed touching.

'Oh God,' sighed Jenny. 'We shouldn't have done that.'

'No,' said Stuart softly. 'I don't know what I'm doing. But whatever it is, it feels so right. Oh Jenny, I can't get you out of my mind.'

'It'll be pre-wedding ner—'

'Don't say it,' said Stuart, pressing his finger against her soft pink mouth. 'It's not.'

Jenny moved gently but firmly away from him.

'Thank you for the kiss,' she smiled. 'I've wondered for years what it would be like to kiss you.'

'Have you?' said Stuart, as something akin to joy swished through him.

She touched his face with her small chilly hand.

'And now you have to go home and forget it happened.'

'Jen, I'm not sure I can.' He felt alive and empowered.

'Go home, Stuart,' Jenny bent to pick up her bucket. 'And be happy with Max. She seems really nice and I'm sure you'll have everything you want in life with her.'

And she smiled at him, her big Jenny smile, and her eyes were glistening with the first hint of tears. He watched her walk away and felt the first jab of a migraine in his head.

Chapter 71

Stuart's stag night was a conservative affair to say the least, much to Luke's disgust. The two of them in the Miners Arms drinking slow pints and eating cheese and onion crisps.

'I can't believe there are approximately forty hours to your big day and I'm not in the middle of some nightclub with a busload of mates who are planning which lamp post to strap you to,' humphed Luke.

'I told you I didn't want any fuss, and I meant it,' snapped Stuart. 'That includes the stag night.'

Luke held up his hands in surrender. 'Yep.'

'Soz,' said Stuart.

'Pre-wedding nerves,' diagnosed Luke.

'Oh don't you start,' said Stuart. 'It's not pre-wedding nerves. It's don't-want-to-get-fucking-married nerves.'

The words landed like a twenty-stone boulder in a sinkful of water.

'You'd better start talking,' said Luke, picking up their empty glasses. 'I'll get us another pint in.'

Max jumped down from the bar table to raucous applause. She was dressed in a white veil, L-plates and was wearing a T-shirt saying: 'On Saturday, I'm going to be a big fat gypsy bride'. The others were wearing 'We're with the gypsy bride' T-shirts.

'You're too pale for one of those gypsy brides, love,' said a man propping up the bar.

'Ah, but wait,' said a tipsy Max. 'The woman you will see tomorrow night will be a very different animal. I am being speyed to within an inch of my life.'

'She means sprayed,' corrected Violet, who was staying sober and on looking-after-Max duty. Max had given her strict instructions not to let her get too blasted as she had a lot to organize the next day. And Violet didn't trust herself to get drunk at the moment. She didn't know what alcohol might release in her, although what she most wanted in the world was to get horribly and totally smashed out of her skull and experience total oblivion.

'Here, have some lemonade.' Violet shoved a glass of pop into Max's hand.

'What the—'

'At your instructions,' Violet held up a warning finger. 'You have a lot of gypsy prep to do tomorrow.'

'I love Stuart so much,' said Max. 'I can't wait to see his face when I gush down the aisle.'

'Neither can I,' said Bel, reappearing from the toilet. 'I'm going to make sure my camcorder is fully trained on his face for the moment when you appear. It's got to be worth two hundred and fifty quid from *You've Been Framed*.'

'We haven't had sex for ages, though,' Max attempted to whisper and failed, causing a group of overhearing lads to break into a chorus of 'aws'.

Max's cousin Alison was now climbing on to the table. She was a huge girl with a bosom that made Max's look like a pair of goosebumps. Someone handed her a karaoke mike.

'I'm singing this for our Max, who I love,' slurred Alison, 'because she and her fella can't live without each other.'

The familiar introduction started and Violet shuddered as the haunting opening bars of 'Without You' by Harry Nilsson started up.

'Oh I love this,' said Max, slumping to a chair. 'One of the greatest love songs of all time. Dennis Nilsen.'

'Appropriate, as it's currently being murdered by your Alison,' added Bel, looking at Violet's face. 'What's up, V?'

'I hate this song,' Violet replied. *It reminds me of that night . . .*

'Is Alison coming to the wedding,' asked Bel.

'Yep. All my family are coming. And all Stuart's family. Not that he knows that yet.'

'Well, he soon will,' said Bel. She looked at her watch. 'You wanted to be home by midnight and it's five to. Say your good-byes, Cinderella. Before you turn into a pumpkin.'

'I kissed Jenny Thompson,' Stuart confessed after taking a long sip from his pint.

'You what?'

'You heard.'

'When?'

'Monday.'

'Monday just gone?'

'The very same.'

'What the fuck did you do that for?' Luke knocked on Stuart's head. 'Hello, hello, Luke calling brain.'

Stuart didn't even flinch. He carried on staring down into his beer. 'I think I'm in love with her, Luke.'

'You're getting married to Max this Saturday,' Luke said through gritted teeth.

'I know. It's a mess,' replied Stuart, lifting and dropping his shoulders. He felt the weight of the world on them. 'I don't know what to do.'

'Jesus Christ,' said Luke with a humourless laugh. 'I wait thirty-odd years for you to have a drama, but you don't half make up for lost time when you do eventually have one, mate.'

'Tell me about it.' He looked up at Luke and his friend saw the dull despair in his eyes. 'What do I do?'

'You can't hurt Max,' said Luke. 'You have to go ahead with the wedding. You just can't hurt her. She loves you.'

'I'm not sure I love her any more, though,' said Stuart, his voice barely above a whisper.

'Stay the night with us,' begged Max. She spread her arm across Bel's large apartment. 'It'll be like a girly sleepover and Bel's got loads of room here.'

'I can't,' said Violet. 'Glyn'll have a panic attack if he's left alone.'

'Do you know, I haven't said this to you before,' said Max, her tongue totally loosened by fizz now, 'but I am not liking the sound of your life to come.' She wagged her finger at Violet.

'Max, shut it,' said Bel, pushing her towards the sofa.

'I mean it,' said Max. 'You're like a caged animal, V. You go out to work all day and he dusts. I bet there's nothing up with him at all. How come he can't take you anywhere because he's scared of the outside and yet you're going off to a caravan for your honeymoon?'

'Ignore her,' said Bel. But, really, she didn't want Violet to ignore Max. Pissed as she was, Max was talking sense.

Right on cue, Violet's phone rang.

'See? How many times has he rung you tonight? Fourteen, I bet.'

'Don't be daft,' said Violet. Though he had. This, by coincidence, was his fourteenth call.

'Well, you're going to miss a great night with me and Bel in her lovely apartment,' said Max. 'Don't be late in the morning. I need you.'

Violet kissed her on the cheek and then she kissed Bel. Violet was crying by the time she reached her car.

Stuart pushed open the door to the empty house and saw his wedding suit hanging up. The hours were ticking down fast to his wedding – the wedding he had been looking forward to only five weeks ago – and now he didn't want it to happen. How could his whole life have been turned upside down so quickly and so chaotically? He wouldn't see Max now until they were at the church. She was staying at Bel's flat tonight and tomorrow he was staying at Luke's house. Tonight was the last night he would sleep in their bed as a single man. If the wedding went ahead.

Oh God.

He went to the fridge and took out a bottle of cider. They had a fancy bottle opener attached to the wall, which Stuart found awkward to use. It was as if the thing had a vendetta against him, refusing to work for him. True to form, it wouldn't prise off the lid and Stuart launched the bottle across the room, where it splattered against the white-tiled wall.

He stood, hands on his hips, and looked at the liquid trail down the wall then thought he'd better clear it up. He searched around for the long-handled brush and couldn't see it. It wasn't in the lounge either. Then he remembered Max taking it into the study to scoop up some pencil shavings. Sure enough, it was there, standing by her desk.

There was a framed picture of them both by her computer. Probably the first photo they had ever had taken together. He picked it up and looked closely at it. He was as skinny as a rake then with rocker-long blond hair. Max just looked the same as she did now, big red lips, big brown eyes, masses of hair. They enjoyed simple things like going for walks and buying a bag of chips en route, the cinema on Monday nights when it was cheap, swimming in the baths. They'd had the photo taken at a fair. He hadn't had a lot of money with him and it had soon run out, but Max had loads because she'd just been paid her Saturday-job money with some overtime. She'd treated him to rides and hot dogs and Coca-Cola. And so formed a pattern: Max, generous to a fault, taking the providing role; he pushed to be the one content with that. He propped the photo back on the desk and accidentally kicked over the dustpan in the process. As he bent to retrieve it, he noticed the pink box file stuffed under the desk.

Max's handwriting in a red Sharpie was across the front: My Big Fat Gypsy Wedding. He might have stolen a look inside had there not been a lock on it.

Stuart took the dustpan and brush into the kitchen and cleared up the mess. Then he went to bed and tried not to think about Jenny Thompson snuggling into his back.

Chapter 72

After a bacon and egg butty, Max was sufficiently revived enough to commence the final preparations for her wedding. Freya was bringing the dress over that afternoon, when Stuart had left to stay with Luke. The cake, however, was being assembled at ten o'clock at Higher Hoppleton Hall – their first port of call after the San Maurice tanning in Bel's bathroom.

'Are you having white bits?' asked Bel, shaking up the first can of the new medium/dark San Maurice spray tan. 'Or do I have to endure the sight of your bare arse?'

'I'm keeping my knickers on, yes,' said Max, taking her T-shirt nightie over her head. Her breasts had held up quite well considering they were so big. But she still lifted each one up so Bel could spray underneath The nice thing about this product was that only a twenty-minute wait was needed between coats. The first spraying gave Max a lovely subtle glow, but Max didn't want subtle today. She managed to pressurize Bel into giving her a second coat, but after that Bel put a stop to operations.

'Max, that's enough,' begged Bel. 'You'll look like a chuffing wotsit if I do any more.'

'Spoilsport,' said Max, pulling down the side of her knickers and seeing, from a white bit, that maybe Bel was right after all. The difference between the two skin tones was pronounced.

Max answered the door when Violet arrived, and Violet jumped back in shock.

'Blimey, I thought you were Sinitta,' she laughed.

'Ha, bloody, ha,' Max did a comic snarl. 'Right, now you're here, let's go and sort out my cake.'

When they arrived at Higher Hoppleton Hall, Shelley's Shellybrations van was already there. There was a Luton van as well, as Shelley couldn't fit it all in one vehicle.

'Who the frig is going to eat all this?' asked Bel, in a state of total disbelief as she watched a procession of people bringing in huge cake pieces and assembling them into one giant edible 3D jigsaw puzzle. The pink palace cake filled a seven-foot-long, five-foot-wide table. It had taken Shelley over an hour and a half already to assemble and deftly cover up cracks in the icing and disguise joins with yet more icing. Meanwhile one of her assistants was busy sticking flags in the turrets. Each one had a coat of arms on it and the initials M & S. (It was either that or S & M.) Then Shelley began to position the guests made out of icing. A dark-haired bride in a huge white dress carrying pink flowers stood with a brown-haired groom on the drawbridge. Behind her were two bridesmaids in frilly pink dresses.

'Who's this meant to be?' asked Violet, pointing to a very tall grey-haired icing figure in a pink suit.

'It's my mum,' said Max. 'I gave Shelley some photos so she could make as accurate a model as possible.'

'I'm surprised you haven't got Stuart throwing himself into the moat,' said Bel.

'Oh bugger off,' laughed Max.

'Was Glyn okay when you got in last night?' Bel asked Violet when the cake duty was over and they were driving off to Nail Diamond.

'Fine,' said Violet, excusing him. 'Well . . . he was having a bit of a bad night.'

'I'm sorry about slagging him off,' said Max, giving her a nudge. 'I was out of order.'

'Don't worry,' said Violet with a kind smile. *They know I'm not happy.*

An hour and a half later and Violet and Bel were reading magazines and flashing off their lovely silver-tipped pink-gel nails; Max was sitting in a chair having false lashes glued on to her eyelids while diamanté hearts and tiny pink roses were being applied to her new two-inch talons.

'They are so gorgeous,' said Violet, marvelling at Max's hands.

'Not exactly understated, are they?' chuckled Bel.

'Gypsy-chic,' said Max.

'Your mum and dad won't even recognize you,' said Violet.

Max laughed. 'Mum and Dad gave up on me being low key long, long ago.'

'Can't wait to see your eyelashes,' said Violet.

'Just on the last few,' said Jane, the eyelash-fitter. 'They're really something.'

'I'll bet,' nodded Bel. She was expecting to see someone resembling Danny La Rue any moment now.

'O-kay,' said Jane a few minutes later, reaching for a mirror and readjusting Max's chair to an upright position. 'What do you think?'

'Shift the mirror out of the way, Max, I can't see,' said Bel impatiently.

'Hang on,' said Max.

Then she moved the mirror and grinned at her friends. Two feathery bats appeared to be fluttering their wings on her eyelids.

'Christ on a bike,' said Bel. 'They are big.'

With her stained skin, big nails and flappy eyelashes, Max really was morphing into a gypsy bride. And what's more, she was loving every minute of it.

Stuart knocked back some extra-strength ibuprofen to counteract yet another migraine that was prodding at his temple. He looked at the clock in the kitchen as he lifted a glass under the cold tap. He had twenty-two hours of being a single man left. If Jenny Thompson hadn't blasted into his life he would be happy now, looking forward to a life with lovely Max. And she was lovely . . . fun, kind, big-hearted, sexy: the complete package. So what was his brain playing at? Maybe everyone was right and this was an extreme case of pre-wedding nerves. Oh God, he wished it was, but he knew deep down that it wasn't.

The house phone rang as he was scrubbing the kitchen wall again because it still had a distinct whiff of cider about it.

'Hello, love,' it was his mum. 'You all right today? Do you need anything?'

'No, I'm fine, ta.'

'Your dad has just taken the cake to the Lamp.'

'Cheers.'

'Do you want me to drop all your wedding presents off or will you collect them?'

Stuart laughed. '*All*. You make it sound like there are loads.'

'Well, there are quite a lot, yes.'

'Who from?'

'All the family. And quite a few neighbours.'

'Aw, why did they do that?' sighed Stuart. 'I thought people only bought presents when they were invited to the wedding.'

'Well, they are, aren't they?' said his mum, without thinking. Stuart heard her slight gasp of panic and picked up on it straight away.

'Who's invited?'

There was a suspicious silence on the end of the phone now. 'Mum?'

'Oh I wish I hadn't rung now,' his mum's voice was shaky.

'What's going on?' said Stuart. 'Mum?'

'I'm not supposed to say anything.' His mum sounded really flustered now.

'Mum, I've got too much on my mind for games so please just tell me, will you?' said Stuart, trying to keep calm. He heard his mum give a resigned sigh.

'Max invited a few extra people to the wedding, that's all. As a nice surprise for you.'

'For me?' Stuart laughed drily. 'No, Mum, she didn't do it for me. How many *extra* people did Max invite?'

'I don't know,' said his mum. 'Auntie Maggie and Bob are coming, Cyril, Phyllis, Kevin, our Sandra and Ken, the Robinsons, the Jacksons next door ...' The list went on and on and on.

And, knowing Max, she'd have balanced that out with numbers from her side of the family.

'Don't say I told you,' said his mum. 'Please. I feel awful. I only rang to ask you about what to do with the presents.'

Stuart injected as much calm into his voice as he could. 'It's fine. I shan't say anything.' But Stuart didn't feel calm at all. He felt cold rage shudder through him like an earthquake. He should have known.

He put down the phone and made for the study, where he dragged out that pink file from under Max's desk and snapped off the lock with his bare hands.

Chapter 73

Stuart lifted up the bill and tried to absorb the words he was reading.

Shelleybrations
One 7 x 5 foot pink Princess Palace cake
To be delivered to Higher Hoppleton Hall,
Friday 1 July

A seven by five FOOT cake? And why the fuck was it being delivered to Higher Hoppleton Hall? He found the answer to that in the thick pile of invoices – all paid in full. Higher Hoppleton Hall-headed notepaper: a reception for fifty people. And how many bottles of pink champagne? Then there was an invoice for flowers: displays to be delivered to Higher Hoppleton and the church; two trailing pink bouquets and one giant JEWEL-ENCRUSTED teardrop bouquet destined for their house on the morning of the wedding. An invoice for a spa-weekend honeymoon package, a receipt for a wig, a photographer, balloons – bloody balloons? Then an invoice for three dresses for *HOW MUCH*? He looked at the total on the White Wedding invoice and winced. But even that was aced by the next invoice in the pile: a Cinderella coach and six white horses. Then he saw the Polaroid of Max and Bel and Violet in their gigantic dresses and the long-dormant volcano inside him finally erupted.

That was it. The end for them. His anger left him in a flash and was replaced by a composure that was unreal. His migraine cleared up like magic. He could have laughed, really. She'd done his dirty work for him. Calmly Stuart went and packed a suitcase and waited for Max to come home.

Chapter 74

There were fifteen missed calls on Max's phone when she retrieved it from her bag after she'd paid the Nail Diamond bill. Violet had to access the voicemail for her as she couldn't press the small buttons with her new long nails.

'Ring me urgently,' said Jess's breathless voice. 'Whatever you do, don't use the medium/dark San Maurice spray.'

With the aid of Violet again, Max rang Jess.

'Jess, what's up?'

'Max, tell me you haven't used that spray yet,' Jess pleaded.

Max felt cold dread drench through to her bones. 'Why?'

'Oh God, you have, haven't you? Oh shit. Okay, okay, don't panic,' said Jess, panicking.

'Jess, what's wrong with it?'

'Okay, okay, keep calm, keep calm,' said Jess on the verge of hyperventilating. 'That box of sprays I brought up to your office has been flagged up as a faulty batch.'

'Faulty how?' Max was confused. She looked in the mirror and everything appeared fine. It hadn't streaked, it hadn't come off on her clothes . . .

'It'll get darker over the next forty-eight hours. Much darker.'

At her end of the line, Jess waited to hear Max explode. She didn't expect to hear her chuckle and say, 'Excellent.'

'Max, did you hear me? I said . . .'

'Cool your jets,' said Max. 'Obviously I'm glad it's been

spotted, and of course we'll have to recall any product that has left the warehouse—'

'None has yet,' Jess interrupted. 'We're safe.'

'But, as far as I'm concerned, that's fine,' said Max. She smiled at her reflection in the mirror. It looked as if she was going to get the third coat that Bel banned, after all.

Chapter 75

Max screamed when she walked into the kitchen and saw Stuart sitting at the breakfast bar. She ran to the other side of the door and talked to him through it.

'What are you still doing here? You aren't supposed to see me. Go away, Stuart.'

'Max, we need to talk,' he said, in a level, quiet tone. He didn't feel dread or fear or guilt. He felt relief, if he was honest. And free.

'You can talk to me without seeing me,' said Max, still through the door.

'Max.' He drew in the deepest breath his lungs would allow. 'I can't marry you.'

There was a long silence, then still through the door came the single word:

'Eh?'

'Come into the kitchen.' Even Stuart marvelled at how collected and in control he sounded.

When Max finally realized that this wasn't a joke and edged into the kitchen, Stuart saw a woman he didn't recognize: a dark-skinned woman with eyelashes the size of a flamenco dancer's fan. She looked like the stranger she was to him at that moment.

'Stuart, what's up with you?'

'This,' he said, and he picked up the stack of wedding invoices. 'This is what's up with me.'

'Oh bloody hell,' tutted Max. 'Why did you go snooping?'

'Why did you do it?' he said, his voice barely above a whisper. 'Why did you take over?'

'I didn't take over,' argued Max. 'I just added a few bits.'

'A Cinderella pumpkin carriage and six white horses? A dress that costs more than my wage for two years? Shall I go on?' He shook the invoices at her. 'I booked a reception as a surprise for you at the Lamp and my mother made us a cake.'

'The Lamp?'

He waited for her face to crease with displeasure. He imagined he saw that it had.

'Yes, the Lamp. I'm sorry it obviously isn't good enough for you, Max, but it was good enough for me and just for once we were going to have what I decided on our wedding day, weren't we?'

'I didn't say that it wasn't good enough,' said Max. 'You're doing that thing again that you always do: implying that I don't think anything you do is good enough when it is. It annoys the hell out of me, Stuart. Why shouldn't it be good enough for me? My name's Maxine McBride not Tamara bloody Ecclestone. Why didn't you tell me you'd booked a reception?'

'It was a surprise, Max.'

'So was Higher Hoppleton Hall.'

Stuart pressed at his temple.

'You rode roughshod over me, as you always do, Max.' His calm was slipping. His frustration was starting to ooze out from his pores. 'What I want and what I can afford isn't good enough for you, whatever you might fool yourself into believing. You whip out your Visa and have to alter things to what you want, and you do it every single time.' He swept his arm around the room. 'I didn't want this house. I wanted the smaller one in the town, but Max has to have her own way. I didn't want that bloody car, but we have to have his and hers matching shitting BMWs. And I didn't want a swanky wedding. I wanted you and me, our closest friends and family and some vows. And you knew that, which is why you arranged all this –' he slammed the invoices down on the work surface – 'behind my back. Because it's your way or the highway.'

Tears were now glistening on Max's enormous eyelashes.

'I'm sorry,' she said. 'I thought you'd do what you usually do and tut and just . . .'

'. . . Give in? Let you have your own way?' he butted in. 'Because that's what I always do. Good old soft-touch Stuart.' He shrugged off Max's hand when she reached out towards his shoulder.

'You might as well have cut off my cock.'

'Stuart!'

He laughed. And it was a hollow, bitter sound. 'You don't make me feel like a man. You make me feel like a ponce.'

'Please, Stuart. Is this pre-wedding ner—'

'Don't even think about saying it,' he covered his ears. 'Oh God, I wish it were. But it's not. It's the tip of a very big iceberg, Max. And it's sunk us.'

Max was frightened now. She and Stuart had never argued like this. There was a tone in his voice she hadn't heard before. 'Stuart, we've lasted seventeen years.'

'We've lasted because I've let it last,' said Stuart. 'I've put myself and my wants and my needs in second place every single time. And you've put my wants and my needs in second place every single time. I don't think I've been happy for a long time, Max.'

'You don't think?' Max snapped in confusion. 'What do you mean, "you don't think you've been happy"?'

Because I thought I was in love with you until I really was with someone else, said Stuart inside. But it would have been too cruel to say it aloud. Instead he looked around him at the swanky kitchen with the designer gadgets and uncomfortable chrome bar stools.

'All this stuff makes you happy, Max. But it doesn't make me. We want different things. We have for a long, long time, really, if we face it. I don't want to live here any more. I don't want to take second place to your work, I don't want to drive around in a car you've bought for me, I don't want to eat alone at night, I don't want to spend weekends by myself . . .'

He picked up the suitcase that was out of sight behind the breakfast bar. Max's hands flew up to her face.

'Stuart, don't be daft. You will be at the church tomorrow, won't you? You wouldn't let me down.'

'Max, you want the wedding, not the groom,' Stuart said, and he walked out and left her sobbing into her perfectly manicured hands.

Violet rang Max just before she went to bed.

'You all right?' she asked. 'Nervous?'

'I'm cool, calm and collected,' said Max, trying her damnedest to press down on the wobble in her voice. 'I can't wait for tomorrow.'

'Well, just thought I'd give you a quick ring before I turn in. Has Bel phoned you?'

'She texted.'

'So, see you bright and early at yours. Sleep well.'

'Mwah.'

Max put down the phone and switched off the light. She would be glad to see the back of that day. As far as tantrums go, that was Stuart's finest hour and he had worried her for a while. But she knew he was at Luke's because she had driven past and seen his car there. And his hired wedding suit had gone, so he had taken it with him. He would be there at the church tomorrow having slept on things, she was sure of it. He'd shake his head at her dress and the cake, but he'd pose for photographs and eat the lovely food and be happy because she had written an extra chunk of her vows that evening and she would promise never again to take over from him and alter his plans. She'd learned a big lesson today.

No way would he really walk out on her the night before their wedding, she was sure of that. After seventeen years, she knew him inside out.

Chapter 76

While the others were changing into their pink dresses upstairs, Freya was lacing Max into her dress from the back. Her hips were padded with special cushions that Freya had made for her because the weight of the dress would have scarred her otherwise. She had twenty-five petticoats on underneath her gypsy wedding gown and Max wished she'd asked Freya to make her a pair of wheels as well as she hadn't a clue how she was going to walk in it. Max's dad was waiting patiently in the kitchen with the shock-prescribed scotch that he needed when he saw the colour of his daughter's skin, which wasn't dissimilar to their walnut wardrobes at home. Not mentioning those eyelashes.

'Stuart stormed out on me yesterday after a row,' Max suddenly blurted out in a momentary lapse of self-control. 'I'm only ninety-nine per cent definite that he will be there today. Does that happen a lot?'

'The day before a wedding is often a very precarious time,' said Freya, pulling hard on the ribbon. 'People's fears about change are at a high. Even if they've lived together for years, the feeling of uncertainty is thick in the air.'

'Pre-wedding nerves?' asked Max, fishing for hope.

'Sometimes,' replied Freya.

'What if he jilts me?' said Max, forcing bravery into her voice.

'Then he's the wrong man for you. Now, try to sit down on

this chair, please, and check I haven't laced you in too tightly. You do still need to breathe.'

Freya picked up the operating box that switched on the lights under the dress and attached it with clips to Max's left fingerless lace glove. Then she put on Max's wedding boots for her and buttoned them up. They were four-inch-heeled, stiff white silk and embroidered with M & S in pink stitching. Then Freya took out the towering twinkling tiara and threaded it carefully into Max's Marge Simpson-high wig.

'I'm scared, Freya,' admitted Max, pushing down hard on the tears that threatened to dampen her enormous eyelashes.

Freya walked round to the front of Max and placed her warm hand on Max's cheek.

'This day, this wedding, will make you realize what is truly important in life, I promise you that. You must hold your head up high and own your wedding. Be that gypsy bride of your fantasies in this dress and see where it leads you.'

Max felt a surge of strength blast through her. Freya was right. The only way through today was to brazen out whatever came her way, like a strong gypsy woman. She'd have her big fat over-the-top day. She had wanted it for too long.

Chapter 77

For over two hours the previous evening, Luke had made Stuart sit on his huge leather sofa while he tried to drill some sense into him.

'It's not love, it's infatuation,' he said about Jenny.

'No, it isn't,' said Stuart adamantly. 'And, anyway, Jenny is just a part of it. Even if she doesn't want me, it's over between me and Max.'

'Because she invited a few of your relatives to watch you get wed?'

'You know it's more than that,' Stuart said. Luke had never seen his friend as calm nor as resolute. 'We're too different, Luke. You're more her type than I ever was. You both want the same things: big houses, fancy jobs.'

'She's a fantastic girl, Stuart. They don't come along like Max every day.'

'I know that,' said Stuart. 'But I can't help what is going on here,' and he banged his chest with a closed fist. 'Max doesn't make me feel like a man.'

'And Jenny does?' spat Luke.

'Yes, she does. She makes me feel protective and big. Max is too independent; she doesn't need me. She can provide everything she wants herself. And I need to feel needed.'

'Max loves you so much.'

'I think she will find that she doesn't. She'll miss me being around, being a presence in the house, but I don't think she will miss *me*.' He stood to leave.

'Where are you going?' asked Luke. And because Stuart didn't answer straight away, Luke knew where he was going. To Jenny.

Luke's heart felt like a heavy stone inside him because he knew without any doubt that Stuart had made up his mind. But Luke was so dreadfully fond of Max and he didn't want to see her humiliated and destroyed.

'Oh mate, I don't know what to say,' he sighed. 'Promise me you'll sleep on it. You may feel differently in the morning. I'll ring you at eight.'

Stuart laughed at his friend's attempt to try to the last. 'I promise you I'll sleep on it, but I won't feel any differently. And I'll tell you why. Because tomorrow morning Max will get dressed in her fancy frock and arrive in her Cinderella coach at the church because she will have no doubt in her head that I'll be there. She will always believe that she knows best and will get her own way. She won't cancel everything and arrive on my doorstep and ask me to run away to Gretna Green with her. Just her and me.'

Luke leaped on the note of hope. 'And if she did?'

'She won't.'

'But if she did?'

'It wouldn't make a difference. I would tell her she's too late. But she won't.'

Chapter 78

In the church there was a very strange atmosphere. Only a few of Stuart's relatives were there and they were looking around in confusion for the groom and his immediate family, who were a no-show. The best man was there in his suit, pink rose in his lapel, talking to the vicar and then dashing anxiously out of the church doors.

'Why is the best man hopping from foot to foot?' Bel asked Violet, recognizing him from photos Max had shown them. He was hard to mistake with his grey-white hair and incredibly tall physique. She climbed out of the Rolls-Royce that had picked them up from Max's house. 'Aw, aren't those bells lovely? Hi, there. It's Luke, isn't it? Everything okay?'

Luke came bounding over. At any other time he would have made polite introductions but he was in too much of a flap.

'He's not here,' he said. 'Stuart isn't here.'

'Where is he, then?' asked Bel with a lopsided grin. 'Stuck in the toilet getting rid of some brown nerves?'

'Ugh,' said Violet. 'How can you look all ladylike in that dress and have such a sewer-mouth?'

'When I say "he isn't here", I mean I don't think he's going to come.'

Bel and Violet looked at each other, then back at Luke.

'You aren't saying what I think you're saying, are you?' asked Bel.

'He came round to see me yesterday and told me that the wedding was off. But I asked him to sleep on it.'

'Wedding was ... Why?' Bel was clutching her bouquet so tightly that her knuckles were white.

'It's complicated,' said Luke.

'"Another woman complicated"? Please say no,' said Bel.

Luke didn't answer that question directly. 'Stuart found out about all Max's plans yesterday. He hit the roof and told her it was the last straw and that the wedding was off. He's not answering his phone and I don't know where he is.' Luke didn't think it wise to mention Jenny. He was still hoping that Stuart would realize he had been gripped by a temporary madness and arrive better late than never.

'What do you mean, "he told her the wedding was off"?' Now Bel and Violet really were confused. 'She *knows*? She can't know. She hasn't said a word to us.'

'He said this might happen,' said Luke, rubbing his forehead. 'He said she'd think he would give in and turn up. And if she did, that would say it all.'

'You're saying she should have cancelled the wedding?' said Bel, huffing. 'There was a fat chance of that happening, I can tell you.'

'I don't know what I'm saying,' said Luke. Even if Max had cancelled the wedding at the eleventh hour, there was still the subject of Jenny. Was it kinder to let Max think their ultimate differences had caused the split than to let her know that he had been spirited away by the cleaner's daughter?

'Oh shite.' This from Violet, who hadn't said 'shite' since 1985. Six white horses with pink plumes on their heads were rounding the corner. Bel's language was fruitier still. She ran to the coach, which was stuffed full with Max's dress and bouquet. She could just see the top of a male head in the sea of material and she presumed it was Max's dad drowning in a billowing ocean of white.

'Drive round the block again. Stuart's not arrived yet.'

'It's fine,' said Max with measured resignation, 'I know.'

'What?' said a male voice from the midst of the dress.

'Dad, trust me. Let's just walk down the aisle. Come on.'

'You can't have a wedding when the groom isn't here,' said her dad.

'Watch me,' said Max, sticking one silk-booted foot out of the coach.

In the fifteen-minute journey to the church Max had gone through every dark emotion it was possible for a human to go through; a veritable rainbow of uncertainty, guilt, anticipation, fear, shock, disbelief, pain, anger. By the time she arrived at the church a vortex of fury and self-preservation was spiralling through her core and it was this that kept her back as straight as a ramrod as she grabbed her dad's arm. Today she would show the world just what calibre of woman she was. Well, at least the Barnsley part of the world would be witness to it.

So, after an army of bridesmaids, ushers and church officials had managed to extricate Max from the fairy-tale coach, in a state of high confusion Graham McBride found himself about to walk down the aisle to an organist playing Mendelssohn and among a sea of bewildered faces, most topped off by very nice hats. He had adopted Max when she was seven years old and so he thought he knew her pretty well by now, but – as today was showing him – obviously not. For a start, he'd offered to pay for everything but she'd told him that their wedding was going to be so small that wouldn't be necessary. It didn't look small from where he was standing. It was out-blinging Elton John and Lady Gaga combined. And why wasn't the bloody groom here? The vicar started to pace towards them but when Max barked, 'Stay!' at him, he froze. The organist looked round, stopped playing and then started again. He presumed Luke was the groom.

'Max ...' began Luke.

'Luke,' she smiled. 'Thank you for being here. Now, let me drive this. Bel, Violet, prepare to follow. Dad, let's go.'

Max switched on her lights. The small butterflies stitched on to her shoulders began to waft their wings and the ones dotted around her voluminous skirt began to twinkle.

The poor photographer hadn't a clue what was going on but he had been paid to take pictures, so he started snapping.

'Maxine, what's happening?' asked a totally baffled Graham. 'Where's Stuart?' His traditional Yorkshire brain tried to make sense of it all and failed. The only conclusion it could come to was that it was some sort of modern wedding where tradition went to the wall. Stuart must be following the bride in. He was sure that Max wasn't that daft as to walk down the aisle if she wasn't going to meet her groom at the end of it. Knowing Max, her wedding wouldn't be a normal carry-on, but this was stretching it, even by her standards.

Max smiled beatifically as she drifted slowly down the aisle, taking pin steps and savouring every one. She and her dad had to walk sideways like well-dressed crabs because the aisle wasn't wide enough for them both. It was barely wide enough for her alone. Her bouquet was a weighty Niagara Falls spillage of bright pink roses and the dress weighed a ton and a half. Gypsy Margaret wasn't joking when she said that some brides were scarred for life wearing them. Max spotted her mum open-mouthed in the front pew. She was holding on to Auntie Sylvia's hand as if her life depended upon it.

As she reached the top of the aisle, where Stuart should be standing, Max turned round to the congregation and waited for the organist to finish the last bars.

'Ladies and gentlemen,' she began in a cool, clear, unwavering voice. There was a slight echo as her voice bounced off a nearby pillar. 'There has, alas, been a change of plan. There will be no wedding today, because there is no groom.'

'I knew it,' said Graham crossly. Although he really didn't know anything. Any minute now he was going to wake up and find out he was still in a nightmare after having too much Cathedral City last night.

'However, a great deal of preparation has gone into this day, so I ask you to please join me at the reception. A minibus has been provided for your comfort and will bring you back to the church afterwards if you so wish. Oh and wedding presents will not be accepted, obviously. I hope you've all kept your receipts. Thank you.'

Someone clapped and then shut up, embarrassed that they were the only one doing so. Everyone else started to gossip to a neighbour.

'Where's Stuart?' asked Kay McBride.

'Mum, just get in the minibus.'

'Bloody hell,' said Bel. 'I'm going to kill Stuart when I get my hands on him.'

'I feel like I'm in a bad dream,' said Violet, puffing out her cheeks. 'What do we do?'

'We get in the minibus,' said Bel, tugging her friend's arm. 'Trust me, when the bride is as determined as Max, it's best just to do what she says.'

Quite a few of the guests decided to not to join the wedding party for the reception, mainly Stuart's side, which came as no surprise. Most lined up in the queue for the minibus in shock; one or two old relations were convinced this was one of those bizarre weddings with a twist and the bridegroom was going to burst out of a cake. Max rode to the reception in her Cinderella coach alone when she should have been snuggled up in it with Stuart. She felt a prick of tears behind her eyes and stuck her glittery nails in her very brown arm to shock herself out of them.

'What the fucking hell . . .' said her dad when he saw the cake.

'Graham,' reprimanded her mum. In the twenty-six years they'd been married she had never heard him use that word before.

The photographer was having such an orgasm taking in the spectacle that he nearly forgot the fact that there was no groom. There were flowers everywhere, huge pink displays of them suffusing the air with their beautiful scent. Violet could have cried for her friend. So much effort, so much waste.

'Everyone, please enjoy the meal. Pretend you're here for an ordinary lunch. We can't let all this just get thrown away . . . it's all paid for.' Max announced. She knew that all the guests were from Yorkshire – they didn't do waste.

'Your bastard mate is dead when I get my hands on him for this,' growled Bel at Luke.

'Get in the queue, Bel,' said Luke. He looked over at Max standing by her cake, the huge bouquet of pink flowers in her hand. She must have been on the near side of seven foot tall with her heels and hair but she looked like he had never seen her before: fragile and vulnerable with a stoop to her shoulders. He wanted to put his arm round her and pull her away from all this; run a bath for her, make her tea and toast, sit with her and let her talk until she fell asleep. Luke and Stuart were too close to fall out for ever, but at the moment he hated him for what he had done to Max. He hoped she never found out about Jenny Thompson.

The staff were amazing. They quickly screwed up the place-name with 'Stuart' on it and moved everyone up a place so there was no empty seat next to Max.

'At least you won't have to do a speech, Dad,' said Max, as the main course arrived. Her mum said that he had been flapping about it.

'I'll do a speech when I get hold of Stuart,' seethed Graham, spearing some cauliflower cheese with a furious fork.

'I hope you're still going to that spa,' said Bel to Max. 'You'll need it.'

'No,' said Max. 'I don't want to go there and sleep in a big bed by myself.'

'Do you want me to come with you?'

'I'm sending Mum and Dad in my place,' said Max. 'My dad's going to have a coronary if he doesn't get some lavender oil slapped on him after all this.'

Coffee had just been served when Luke surprised them all by

standing up and clapping his hands for silence, which quickly ensued.

'Ladies and gentlemen,' he began. 'I think you'll agree with me that this has been a rather strange day. We're all in a bit of a daze but I'd like to take it upon myself – on behalf of Max and her family – to thank you for turning up today, for coming here to the reception to enjoy this wonderful food and for making this room not as empty and sad as maybe it could have been. As the best man, I should be talking about Stuart, but I'm obviously not going to do that. Instead I'm going to talk about Max.'

He looked over at Max with such warmth in his grey eyes that she had to gulp down a fat gypsy ball of emotion.

'I've known Max since we were sixteen because we went to sixth-form college together. And, really annoyingly, she hasn't aged as much as some of us.' There was a ripple of laughter as he gave his short white-grey hair a stroke from front to back. 'In fact, inside she hasn't aged at all. She's still the fun and fabulous, big-hearted beautiful person she always was. And she always will be. I have no doubt about that. She could have curled up in a ball and run away today, but she didn't. And that's because she's Maxine McBride. She doesn't run, she doesn't hide; she sticks out her chin and she rides whatever life throws at her. She survives and rises, and she will again. And that's why I'd like you to raise your glasses and toast the very wonderful Max. And wish her your support and all your best wishes – and your love.' He raised his glass and winked at her. 'To our Max.'

'To our Max,' said everyone in unison, except for Graham, who was too choked up to say the words, and Kay, who was sobbing into a hankie.

Then Auntie Sylvia broke into applause and the room was filled with clapping sounds, with warmth and affection. Max raised her glass and said in a very croaky voice, 'Thank you. Thank you, everyone. Thank you, dear Luke.'

Chapter 79

Max was still in her wedding dress at nine o'clock that night. She had stripped off the petticoats and kicked off her boots, but everything else remained. Her hips and waist were aching and rubbed raw and would have benefited from a warm bath and being massaged with Sudocrem, but she didn't want to take off her lovely dress. She looked in the mirror and a gypsy bride stared back at her – albeit one with skin the colour of a burned roast. Today she looked like the princess she had always wanted to be. But a princess with the haunted, sad eyes of Lady Diana when she found that she had a prince-shaped hole in her heart.

The door buzzer went and she looked at the CCTV screen on the wall to find that it was Luke. She padded down the hallway and unlocked the door. He was probably the only person she would have let in.

'Are you by yourself?' he said. 'Tonight?'

'Yes. That's the way I wanted it.'

'Tough,' said Luke, and he marched into the lounge, where he threw himself down on the sofa. Max sat down next to him.

'How long has it been going on?' she asked him softly.

'What?' he asked, with a stir of panic.

'Stuart's affair.'

There was a long telling pause before Luke scrambled together an answer. 'He's not having an affair.'

'Luke, you always were a crap liar,' Max smiled. 'I saw them.'

Luke opened his mouth to say 'Saw who?' but he didn't want to lie to Max and he didn't want to tell her the truth and so the words jammed in his throat.

'There I was in my Cinderella coach driving to the church this morning, sure that Stuart would be waiting at the altar for me. And because the driver thought he'd give me my money's worth and go down a few side streets so that I could have extra time to enjoy the ride and wave at the crowds, we passed the greasy spoon on Duke Street,' said Max, coughing a croak out of her voice. 'And there, framed in the window having breakfast together, were my fiancé and Jenny Thompson. As coincidences go, that was a belter.'

'Oh Jesus,' said Luke.

'Let me guess your next question: did they see me? Oh yes. The big loved-up smiles on their faces closed up like clam shells. And then I knew, you see, that he most definitely wouldn't be at the church. He told me that I might as well have cut off his willy for how I made him feel. It's a good job I didn't, isn't it? Seeing as he needed it to stick it in the cleaner's daughter.'

'He wasn't, Max,' Luke jumped in.

'Well, if he wasn't then, he will be now,' said Max with a brittle, bitter laugh. 'I haven't said anything to Bel or Violet. I will eventually, when I've got things straight in my head.'

'Have you got any brandy?' said Luke. 'I think we both need one.'

Max got up to pour out two glasses.

'I wish I knew what to say to make it all better, Max,' said Luke.

'There is nothing,' said Max. 'Do you know, I considered turning up at his door and saying, "Look, forget the dress, forget the reception, let's just tell everyone it's off and run away to Gretna Green." But in the end I wanted to wear my dress more than I wanted to do that. He said we'd grown apart and I didn't believe him, until he gave me the space to think about it. Jenny is only one of the reasons why we didn't get married today.'

'I think you should get that dress off and climb into a big bubble bath,' said Luke.

Max took a long slug of brandy. 'I'm never going to take this dress off,' she said. 'I'm going to turn into Miss Havisham. I'll get the rest of the cake brought over, put it on the table and wait for the cobwebs to grow over us.'

Luke put his arm round her and pulled her into his shoulder. As strong a woman as Max was, she felt small and soft and crushable at that moment.

'I won't let you shut yourself away. You weren't built for hiding and growing cobwebs,' he whispered.

'It'll save on the laundry if I never change clothes again or go out. I can do all my shopping online.' Max plucked at the skirt of her dress. 'How ridiculous everyone must think I am.'

Luke immediately pulled her round to face him.

'You're not ridiculous, Maxine McBride. You're beautiful.'

'Yeah, right,' said Max, not giving him eye contact.

'You are beautiful in this dress and you'd be beautiful in sack cloth and ashes. And anyone who loves you thinks the same.'

'You're a lovely man, Luke. But I want to be on my own,' said Max, feeling the tears rise inside her. His nice words were killing her.

'Okay.' He kissed her head and stood to go. 'Goodnight, Miss McBride. The very wonderful and brave and formidable Miss McBride.'

After Luke had gone, Max filled up her glass and sat back on the sofa. The house felt as chilly and spartan as Stuart always said it did. It was far too big for the two of them, and characterless. The sofa was stylish but so uncomfortable, the white walls hard on the eyes and unwelcoming.

Max was suddenly plunged into a cold pool of sadness that she and Stuart were over and there was no way back from that. She gulped down the brandy in one, then put the glass on the ugly designer coffee table in front of her and sobbed until she fell asleep on the hard leather sofa.

Violet's Wedding

Chapter 80

'So, between the three of us, we've had two shite weddings. You do realize the pressure that puts you under to give us a good one?' said Bel, slurping her tea in the Maltstone Garden Centre coffee shop. It was a week after Max's wedding debacle and three weeks before Violet's big day.

Max pushed the last mini cream cake in front of Violet. 'You have that. You need fattening up a bit. You're looking particularly scrawny today, if I might say so.'

'You're not looking exactly milkmaid-plump yourself,' said Violet. 'How are you doing?'

'I'm okay,' said Max with an unconvincing smile.

'Heard anything from Stuart?' Bel asked, spitting out his name like a snake that had just been given its VAT bill.

'Nope. I bagged up his stuff and Luke took it over to his parents' house. Except Luke brought back the watch and the sweater I bought him for his birthday. He hadn't even taken them out of the packaging.'

'Bumhole,' hissed Bel.

'And I found his BMW on the drive yesterday. He'd put the keys back through the letter box. He doesn't want that either.'

'Double-bumhole.'

'Hang on a minute, Bel,' Violet put in. 'Surely it would have been worse if he kept them. Do you want some help selling them on?'

'I can't be bothered,' said Max. 'I think I'll just stick them in a charity bag.'

'You can't stick a BMW in a charity bag!' cried Bel.

'Luke's a lovely caring fella, isn't he?' said Violet. 'You can tell he thinks an awful lot about you.'

Bel noticed that Max's eyes were starting to look a bit watery. She clapped her hands like a jolly Sunday school teacher.

'Right, enough of that. Shall we buy a dartboard and pin loads of photos to it?'

Max chuckled. 'Give us some hope. How are you getting on with Richard?'

'He's been in Ukraine for a fortnight on business. I'm seeing him again on Wednesday.'

She sounded very nonchalant about it, Max and Violet both simultaneously thought.

'Have you actually snogged him yet?' asked Max.

'No,' said Bel. The thought of being intimate again with Richard terrified her, if she was honest. She didn't so much have a wall round her heart as an armed watchtower and razor wire. 'If we got back together? Would you be really annoyed with me?'

Violet tutted. 'That's not how friendship works and you know it. It's your life. We'd be charm itself whenever we happened to be in his company and there for you if you needed us.'

'Although we'd be sticking pins in his wax image in the comfort of our own homes,' added Max. 'Why, is a reconciliation on the agenda?'

'Not yet, I just wondered what you'd say. If you'd think I was a disgrace to womankind for taking him back,' said Bel. Then she turned to Violet. 'Anyway, are you going to show us your swanky ice-cream parlour while we're in the vicinity? When are you planning to open it? Got a date yet?'

'The first week in August,' said Violet. 'When I get back from honeymoon.'

'In your in-laws' specially valeted caravan,' Bel teased. 'Smashing.'

To Violet's delight Pav's van was parked outside the parlour when they crossed the courtyard. She had been under the impression that he was away, working all week in Wakefield. A local firm had drafted in as many Poles as they could to avoid paying fines that a penalty clause on an unfinished job would incur.

'Ding dong,' said Bel in a lascivious 'whisper' when her eyes fell on the handsome dark-haired artist. Violet gave her a sharp nudge.

'Hi, Pav,' said Violet. 'I don't want to disturb you. I'm just showing off your work to my friends.'

Pav laughed rather bashfully.

'I like your pole,' Bel winked cheekily at Violet as she smoothed her hand over one of the gold-painted wooden poles that Pav had fixed through the tables.

'It's gorgeous,' said Max, turning a full circle. 'I can't wait to come here and eat all your profits.'

'How on earth can you draw all those horses free-hand?' Bel asked. They really were beautifully painted.

'I don't know. I just do them,' Pav shrugged his big shoulders. 'I can't remember a time before I was painting.'

'Well, thanks, Pav,' said Violet, feeling the urgency to shoo out the embarrassing Bel. 'I'll be here all day Monday. I'll see you then, probably.'

'Yeah, bye, Pav, see you soon.' Bel twinkled her fingers at him, parodying Violet, who pushed her out of the door.

'Bloody hell, he's gorgeous,' growled Bel when they were safely out of the door. '"I'll be here on Monday, Paaaav." Make sure you've got your tightest thong on,' she purred, in a breathlessly besotted voice.

'Do you mind?' said Violet, her face beginning to colour. 'I'm an engaged woman.'

'You've got three weeks to have a last fling,' Bel nudged her. It was only a part-joke, for she wished someone would whisk Violet away from the undynamic soggy dishcloth of a man that she imagined Glyn to be. Violet was such a sweetheart, she deserved a big hunky man who made her heart flutter. A man like the very lovely Pav. *Or Dan.* Jesus, was that man taking some shifting from her head.

Bel and Max waited outside White Wedding while Violet chatted to Glyn on her mobile behind them. They heard her saying in a very tight and impatient voice, 'About two hours, tops. We're just going to the wedding shop ... What do you mean, "What have I been doing up to now?" We've been chatting and having a coffee ... No, I haven't been to Carousel. I don't know if the painter is there.'

Bel whispered to Max, 'Why does she have to account for every breath she takes? Look at her face; she's stressed out.'

And why is she lying about not going to Carousel?

Max studied Violet's face while she was speaking on the mobile and noticed that Bel was right: Violet looked worn down.

'It's not normal ...' Bel went on, until Max tapped her.

'Shhh, she's coming.'

Violet strode to catch them up. 'Sorry about that. Glyn just wanted to know what to cook for tea.'

'Stuart couldn't tell a pan from a Golden Retriever. Still –' a bitter tone crept into the edge of Max's voice – 'he'll have more of a traditional relationship with Jenny. She'll do the ironing and he can hammer nails in walls.'

'Glyn must get fed up being in the house all the time,' said Bel kindly, although in reality she thought he needed a kick up the arse. She wouldn't have been surprised to hear that the big wet lettuce got period pains.

Violet huffed. 'I just wish ...' *He wouldn't make me the epicentre of his existence* ... 'Oh never mind what I wish.' Violet pushed open the shop door.

'Good morning, ladies,' said Freya, coming from the back of the shop to see who was entering. 'How are you today?'

'Fine,' they all said, sounding anything but.

'I've come in to pick some accessories,' said Violet.

'And to see if you have any idea what I could do with my gypsy dress now I'm finished with it,' Max added, getting ready to answer the question 'How did it go?' She was surprised when Freya didn't ask. It was almost as if she knew exactly how it had gone.

'I do know of a lady who is buying them and re-selling them. Let me give you her number,' said Freya, walking to her desk to hunt for a business card. Max thought she might have been a dancer when she was younger. She moved with such grace and poise.

'Thanks,' said Max, tucking the card into her purse.

'Should I have a veil or not?' asked Violet, picking up a pretty diamanté crown and putting it on her head.

'I always think your dress looks better with a veil,' said Freya, and she opened a drawer, took out a package and released a short ivory veil from it. There were tiny peach flowers stitched along the edge, the same flowers that appeared on her dress. Then Freya unlocked a cabinet in which there was a selection of tiaras and delicate coronets.

'Try this one,' Freya suggested, attaching the veil with a small clip to a delicate gold hoop that she placed on Violet's head.

'That's really nice,' said Max, standing with her arms folded and studying Violet. 'Try on another couple, though.'

She did, but none suited her as much as the simple hoop.

'You really know your wedding onions,' said Violet.

'I've been in the business a long, long time,' smiled Freya.

'Do you come from Barnsley?' asked Max.

'Yes, I was born here. But I've lived all over the world. London, Paris, Berlin . . .'

'Ooh I love Berlin,' Bel's hands crashed together with delight. Her dad had a lot of business interests out there and he and she and Faye used to go twice every year, at least, and stay in a beautiful hotel just outside the city. It was an old castle, with two great big stone swans standing guard at the door portal.

'I had many wonderful years living in Berlin,' smiled Freya with a happy look in her bright eyes. 'I'll need you for the final dress fitting in a week and a half, maybe Thursday the fourteenth if we can arrange a time,' said Freya to Violet, folding the veil and placing it with the hoop in one of her pretty White Wedding bags. Then she wrote an entry into her desk diary. 'You must be so excited.'

'Yes, of course,' said Violet with a big smile. A smile that was a brave facade because every day Violet was crumbling a little more inside. And there wasn't anything she could do about it but put on that beautiful dress and get married. Never did the expression 'ball and chain' ring so true.

Chapter 81

Glyn was holding a puppy by the back of the neck and the puppy was yowling. In his other hand he had a rope.

'If you leave me, I'll hang it,' Glyn was saying with a quiet smile.

And Violet was screaming as he wrapped the rope round the puppy's neck. She tried to run forward to help the puppy but she could only move in slow motion, her muscles aching from the battle with the thick, treacly air.

Then Glyn was screeching at her that she loved the puppy more than she loved him. And she was screaming back that she didn't and please could he let the puppy go. Then Glyn started crying and let the puppy fall from his grasp and it dangled by the rope, making the most awful sound, and when she snapped awake she realized that sound was coming from her own throat.

'Letty, love, are you all right?' Glyn's arms were round her and she momentarily struggled against him, disorientated, shaking and crying. 'Hey, come on,' he smoothed her hair back from her face and started to place small kisses on her cheeks.

'No,' she pushed him hard and he fell back on the quilt, a wounded expression on his face.

'I'm sorry,' Violet gasped. 'I was dreaming and I couldn't breathe.'

'It's all right,' Glyn's expression changed into one of

sympathetic understanding. 'I'm here. What were you dreaming about?'

'I can't really remember,' she lied.

'Poor darling, you're so stressed. Don't go to the shop today. You don't need to go.'

'I do. I have to, Glyn. I've got deliveries to take care of. I need some air, for a start,' she said, swinging her legs out of bed, but he surprised her by wrapping his arms round her waist and pulling her back on to the bed.

'Let's make love,' he said. 'We haven't done it for ages.'

'No, I can't. I'm having a period.'

'No, you aren't; you're not due,' Glyn said.

'Yes, I am,' said Violet. 'I've just come on.'

'I'm sure you used that excuse just over a fortnight ago. So you can't be.'

Violet's eyebrows knotted together in an impatient frown.

'What do you want me to do? Show you my tampon?'

'Yes,' replied Glyn with a petulant lip. 'Because if you aren't lying now, you lied then.'

'Oh for God's sake.' Violet marched over to the wardrobe.

'Okay, I'm sorry,' said Glyn. He started rubbing his stomach. Violet waited for him to say he wasn't feeling that well, hoping that it would entice her to stay. She was quite surprised when he didn't.

Violet chewed on her lip and wondered if she dare say what was on her mind. The tampon remark tipped the balance towards 'yes'.

'Glyn, I think you should consider getting another therapist,' said Violet. 'You haven't got a life.'

'I have,' he nodded. 'I've got all the life I need or want. With you. I thought we'd have griddled salmon for tea, what do you think?'

The look on Pav's face when Violet opened the door to Carousel brought a blush flooding to her cheeks.

'Good morning, Violet,' he said with a wide smile. The way he said it made her name sound like it belonged to an exotic French woman – *Vee-o-lett*. 'Here, let me help you.'

Violet let him take the two heavy bags of milk and cream that she had just bought from the local farm shop, and carry them into the kitchen.

'What flavours are you making today?' he called.

'Lemon, ginger and marscapone; black forest – when the cherries arrive this morning; and peanut-butter cheesecake.'

'Oh my, I am sticking around for those,' laughed Pav.

Violet felt her insides warming. How wonderful it would be to hear that voice every day of her life. He was always so cheerful; the smile rarely left his face. She imagined he would be a very passionate lover. How could anyone with a burning talent like he possessed be rubbish in bed? His brushstrokes on the wall were so gentle and yet he was strong and masterful when drilling the holes for the horse poles. She slapped her cheek discreetly to bring her back down to earth before he returned to the room.

'If you're very good, you can test out the blackberry I made yesterday and the summer-fruit pudding.' Violet tried to sound as if she hadn't just been fantasizing about them rolling around in bed.

'I will be a very good boy,' said Pav, walking out of the kitchen and saluting her. As they crossed by the till station, their arms brushed. Violet tingled all over from the contact. She knew that if he ever deliberately touched her she would melt as surely as her own ice cream.

Nan was huddled in a crocheted blanket on the sofa. With a heavy heart she watched Susan stuff the sheets into the washing machine.

'I'm so sorry,' the old lady said.

'Nan, it doesn't matter,' said Susan. 'They'll wash.'

Nan wiped at her eyes with the corner of the blanket. She had wet herself during the night. She had been trying to sponge down the bed without disturbing Susan, but her daughter-in-law was too light a sleeper.

'We'll have to start talking about homes,' said Nan.

'What?' Susan twisted her head round.

'I always said that if I ever started being a burden . . .'

'You've been a burden since the day you moved in,' said Susan drily. 'But I think I can just about manage to wash a few sheets without chucking you on a scrap heap.'

Nan was going downhill quicker with every month that passed and it broke Susan's heart. But she had to keep up her tough, no-nonsense act because it would disturb and upset Nan if she started acting right out of character and mollycoddling her.

'I wish you had someone nice to look after you,' said Nan, smiling at Susan, the woman who was like a daughter to her. If she was going to leave her soon, she wanted to see her happy and loved.

'Well,' Susan coughed. She was going to tell Nan so now seemed as good a time as any. 'I have met someone, actually.'

Nan leaned forward on the sofa. 'Have you, now?'

'I haven't been going to a book club. I've been dating a man called Patrick.'

If Nan's thin grey eyebrows could have risen any higher, they would have left her head.

'And where did you meet him, then?' asked Nan. Her blue eyes were twinkling with delight.

'He owns the butcher's shop round the corner.'

'The big grey-haired one with the smiley face?'

'Yes,' said Susan nervously. 'You don't mind, do you?'

'Mind?' Nan chuckled. 'That's the best news I've had in ages. Why would I mind? Of course I don't mind. I'm thrilled to bits.'

'I haven't told Violet. Not yet. I didn't know when I should tell either of you.'

'How long's this been going on?'

'Eight weeks. We didn't say anything until we were sure we wanted to be a couple. I was worried sick what you'd say.'

'Our Jeff's been gone a long time, lass. He wouldn't have wanted you to be alone when you could have someone in your life making you happy.'

Susan slumped down on the chair. 'We're silly sometimes, aren't we? Trying to keep secrets from those we should be confiding in most.'

'Yes, we are.' Nan's hand closed over Susan's and she squeezed it. So the angel was right about Susan. She smiled because it looked like the angel was real, then, and not conjured up from a batty part of her brain, after all.

Violet stood in the kitchen and let her voicemail take the call from Glyn, then she rang it to find out what message he had left.

'Hi, Letty,' he sounded weary. 'I'm just ringing to see if you're okay. I've come over a bit sick and wondered if it was something we ate or if I've got a bug. Can you let me know you're fine. Bye, love.'

Violet shook her head. She knew, of course, that he was building up to a bout of sickness so that she would come home early. Well, she wasn't going to fall for it this time. She didn't want to go home early. She didn't want to go home ever again, if the truth be told.

Oh Violet, what are you going to do? This wasn't supposed to happen, said that voice inside her again. She knew what was *supposed* to happen, but it hadn't and now she was trapped. Her feet were glued to an escalator and she was hurtling towards a place that terrified her and had her screaming herself awake in the middle of the night. Suddenly her chest was gripped with palpitations and she stood holding the side of the sink until they passed.

'Violet, is anything wrong?' Pav's voice came from behind.

'I'm fine,' she said breathlessly. 'I get skippy heart beats sometimes.'

'You should see a doctor,' he said. 'Sign of stress, or too much coffee, perhaps.'

Pav's gentle concern made her feel warm inside, quite different to how Glyn's persistent cossetting did.

'I can't stop drinking coffee, though,' said Violet. 'Do you want one?'

'I thought you would never ask me,' said Pav and he winked. And Violet's heart started to jump again, but in a very different way.

Did Pav think that Violet was the most beautiful woman he had ever seen? No. But did she make his heart smile? Did he think about her when she wasn't there? Would he have pushed his hand into her silver-blonde hair and edged his lips towards hers had she not been wearing an engagement ring? Oh yes.

He loved working on this mural, more so when she was near, whisking and mixing in the kitchen, humming, trilling to a low-volume radio. He loved that she brought out to him spoonfuls of her ice cream to taste. He could have sat all day drinking coffee with her, staring into those violet eyes, which carried a weight of sadness in them that he couldn't understand in someone about to be married.

Very soon now the horses would be finished and they would part company, and a sweet gentle part of his life would be over. He thought that her lovely face and those lavender eyes would stay in his mind for a long, long, long time.

Chapter 82

It had been three weeks since Bel had seen Richard as he had
been away on a business trip. Or so he said. As she was getting
ready to go to La Hacienda for dinner with him, it crossed her
mind that she had only his word that he was away on business.
For all she knew he could have been cavorting on a beach in
Nice with a blonde. Trust, it seemed, really was a long way off
yet.

'And how would you feel about that if he had been in Nice
with a blonde?' she asked herself *à la* television reporter. And the
honest answer was that she didn't know. How odd. The thought
of it didn't stir any jealousy in her at all. In truth, she wasn't even
champing at the bit to see him after a three-week break either.
She didn't know if that was a good or a bad thing.

She couldn't break out of that analytical mood all evening. It
was as if she had taken a backward step inside herself to observe
the date objectively. She thanked him for the roses but ques-
tioned if they made her feel warm and gushy inside and
discovered that they didn't, really. She asked herself if his beautifully cut Armani suit made her knees wobble, because she had
always thought men looked fabulous in suits – especially someone as groomed and handsome as Richard. It didn't. And at the
end of the evening, when he kissed her lightly on the mouth, did
she have any inclination to move towards him again and let his
lips linger longer on hers? No.

What she did notice was that when she went back to her car there was a tall man nearby with dark hair in longish soft curls and a thin line of beard on his jaw, and for a moment she thought it was Dan Regent. It wasn't, of course, but she climbed into the driving seat with a heart bumping around her chest like a giant Mexican jumping bean; she needed to sit for a few moments until it calmed down before she felt steady enough to drive.

Chapter 83

The next morning, Violet stood in the lovely silk wedding dress while Freya circled her, assessing the alterations she needed to make.

'You've lost weight again,' said Freya, pushing the white swoop of her hair out of her eyes.

'I can't have,' said Violet. 'The dress doesn't feel any less tight.' In fact it seemed to grow smaller every time Violet tried it on.

Freya remained silent but she knew why it felt wrong to the wearer.

'How are the wedding preparations going?' she went on, placing a marker pin in the dress.

'Everything's done,' said Violet, looking at her reflection and thinking how beautiful this dress was. She wondered how many brides had worn it before her. And if they had been happy.

'Are you having a big wedding?'

'Very quiet,' replied Violet. She didn't want to talk. It was an effort to converse. Even breathing was an effort at the moment. Her wedding was sixteen days away, her one and only chance to dress like a queen and say her vows. To love, to honour . . . *To stay in every night, to lie with you in bed and endure you pawing me, to answer your phone calls sixty times a day . . .*

Violet felt faint and had to take in some discreet long breaths to stop herself from keeling over. The tightness of the fabric wasn't allowing her to do that very successfully.

'The other women who wore this dress as well as you,' she asked. 'Were they happy? Do you know?'

Freya's lips stretched into a soft smile. 'I know that one of the women who wore this dress on her wedding day was very happy. And I know that another who chose this dress to wear is now very happy too.'

That was carefully worded, thought Violet. 'Did the one who chose it not wear it, then?' asked Violet, puzzled.

'I like to think that all my dresses bring happiness,' Freya answered her. 'But not always in the way you might expect. This dress especially.'

'What do you mean?' asked Violet, intrigued. Surely she wasn't going to try to say her dresses were magic or nonsense like that?

Freya pointed to the mirror. 'When you look at yourself in there, what do your eyes see? How can they see anything other than a pretty girl in a beautiful dress? But what does your heart see, Violet? Does it see the same?'

Violet's head and heart were totally out of sync and she knew it. In the mirror her eyes saw the pretty girl in a beautiful dress; her heart saw a trapped bird in a tiny cage with not even the room to sing for help. Violet tore her eyes away from her reflection and smoothed the few creases out of her dress at the front.

'I thought for a minute you were going to say that your dresses were magic,' said Violet, forcing some jollity into her voice. 'If only they were. Wouldn't that be lovely?'

Freya said nothing about that as she helped the ghost-pale bride out of the dress and took it to her sewing area at the back of the shop. She merely advised Violet that her gown would be ready to pick up and take home in seven days' time.

Pav noticed at once that Violet had been crying recently, even though she was smiling when she entered the shop. Her eyes were shiny and bloodshot and her mascara had run underneath her left lashes. He decided against pointing that out, not wanting to embarrass her, but he felt very keenly that all was not well in her world and that pained him.

The cheery opening bars of 'Mamma Mia' sounded on her phone as Susan rang when Violet was boiling the kettle.

'We've bought you a wedding cake. Now it's no good you protesting because I won't listen. You're not getting married without cutting a cake.'

'Oh Mum— '

'It's only a small one. It's breaking Nan's heart that she couldn't make you one. You know how she would have loved that. And I know Glyn doesn't want any fuss, but surely you can persuade him to go out for lunch afterwards. Or he and his family can come here and I'll make something.'

'I'll ask him again,' said Violet, but she knew that he wouldn't.

'You sound very down, love. Do you need help with anything?'

'No, I'm just a bit tired,' Violet affected a yawn.

'Well, you know where we are.'

'Thanks, Mum.'

Violet put down the phone and hoped that she wasn't going to get a call from Joy Leach saying she'd ordered three zillion flowers to tart up the caravan. She was so distracted that she poured the water from the kettle over her hand as she held the cup and her wounded yelp brought Pav running from the front of the shop. He grabbed her arm firmly and held it under cold running water.

'That's worse than the burn,' winced Violet, attempting to pull her hand away.

'You need to keep this under the tap for ten minutes,' he held on to her but twisted the hot tap to warm up the water slightly. As he did so, she noticed the black hairs on his arms, the white paint on his sleeve from the horse he was painting – the last one. 'If I let you go, do you promise to keep your hand there?'

'I promise,' she submitted grudgingly. Tears were swimming in her eyes and she stamped her foot in frustration at their appearance. They never seemed to be far away from the surface these days.

'I think,' said Pav, 'that you are depressed.'

'I've got absolutely nothing to be depressed about,' snapped Violet, wishing he would shut up, because she was inches away from breaking down and any hint of kindness was likely to make her totally shatter into a million pieces.

Pav went back to his paints while she stood by the sink with her hand in the stream of water. He had been gone only a few minutes when he returned.

'It's none of my business of course,' he said, 'but you don't seem like a very happy bride-to-be to me, Violet.' He came up to her. 'Look at me for a moment.'

'No, it isn't any of your business,' said Violet, shaking her hand and twisting the taps off. She couldn't look at him. She had to get away from him. From the way he said her name, from the way he made her heart bump around inside her chest. She grabbed her coat and her bag and pushed past him, hurrying out of Carousel, tears pouring from her eyes, ignoring that he was calling her name, asking her to please stay and talk to him.

When she got home, it was to find Joy and Norman there. They had brought their wedding present over: a hamper of his and hers towels, dressing gowns, mugs, cutlery . . . all sorts of things that must have taken her an age to collect. And she and Norman were apparently going to go down to the caravan at the weekend and decorate it for the newlyweds – she was tweeting like an excited bird about it. Outwardly Violet tried to appear pleased, but inwardly she felt as if another nail had just been hammered into her coffin.

Violet let her bride-happy facade drop when was in the bath. She prayed that Glyn would leave her alone and not come in offering to wash her back and, for once, he didn't.

He had been about to when Violet's mobile phone rang, but

it was in her coat pocket so she didn't hear it. Glyn did, though. It had clicked on to voicemail by the time he had found where it was. The screen said that it was P. Nowak – the painter. Why was he ringing her again? Why was he ringing her so late? Why was he ringing her at all?

Glyn replayed the message. P. Nowak's voice was chocolate-rich and deep.

'Hello, Violet, it's Pav. I hope you don't mind that I ring you at this time. I just wanted to make sure you are all right after what happened. Did I upset you? If I did, please accept my apologies. Okay, I will see you tomorrow. I hope. Goodnight.'

Glyn's scalp prickled with a sudden rush of anxiety. This Pav was a bit familiar for a bloody painter, wasn't he? He replayed the message, hunting for clues as to what his relationship was with Violet, then played it again and again. He foraged so deeply for evidence to substantiate his suspicion that something was going on between this Pav and Violet that he found it: the tenderness in his voice, the concern – and what did he mean by 'I hope'? How had he upset Violet? What had happened? Had they slept together? Was he ringing her to make sure that she didn't regret fucking him? He stabbed in the number 3, which deleted the message.

Glyn didn't have the best sleep in the world with that voice circling in his head, his mind warping it over the hours so that 'I hope' sounded as if was delivered on a kiss. He built up an image of the man behind the voice; tall, dark, handsome, straight off the cover of a women's magazine. Was he the reason why he and Violet didn't have much sex; why she seemed so unresponsive to his caresses; why she spent so much time at Carousel? The scenarios he wrapped around that voicemail extended it to a full-length film.

'Who's Pav?' he asked Violet, as he felt her throw off the quilt the next morning.

'He's the guy who's painting the horses in the shop. Why?'

'You were calling out his name in your sleep,' Glyn lied.

He noticed that she blinked nervously before responding.

'I don't know why that should be.' She might have shrugged, but he was in no doubt that he had shaken her with that fake revelation. And why was that exactly? He watched her take her clothes from the drawer and the wardrobe and walk off to the bathroom.

'Why do you go in there to take off your nightdress these days?' Glyn called, trying to suppress the rising anger and jealousy in his voice. 'I've seen your tits before, you know.'

In the bathroom Violet shuddered. She didn't think she'd ever heard him use the word 'tits' before. It stood out because he had never been a crude man or believed in swearing in front of women. He was too nice. He had always treated her like a princess, never abused her verbally or physically. God forgive her, but she wished he would slap her just once and give her a solid excuse for going. He was annoyed about something, most likely that she had been calling another man's name in her sleep. She couldn't blame him for being upset by that. She knew how his brain worked – he would obsess about that and store up a hundred questions for her about Pav. Pav who made her heart feel as light as a Chinese sky lantern, who filled her thoughts, whose touch made her skin sigh. She compared that with her feelings for Glyn. She had never loved him but she wasn't sure she even liked him any more. His hand just whispering against her flesh made it crawl.

This was a huge mess of her own making and all exits from it were blocked.

Chapter 84

Violet had said she would be at the wholesalers this morning, and so far it looked as if she might be telling the truth, thought Glyn, as the taxi pulled up in the Maltstone Garden Centre car park. There was no sign of her pink mini, just a beaten-up red van with a roof rack.

'Can you drop me here and wait a few minutes?' Glyn asked the driver, then he got out of the taxi and crossed to Carousel. He peered through the window and saw a man painting on the wall. A dark-haired man with broad shoulders and a trim waist.

Pav Nowak.

The name slid into his mind like a deadly silent snake and he felt momentarily weak with fear.

He wasn't as perfect as the image Glyn had formed of him, but he was still tall and young and *real* and thus even more dangerous. Glyn hated him. It was hard not to compare this painter man with his shorter, pudgier self.

He took a deep breath and knocked on the door. Through the glass he watched Pav stand up and saw how powerfully he was built. Glyn felt like a little fat old blob next to him.

'Hello,' said Glyn, hating himself for sounding so nervous, so unmanly. 'Sorry to bother you but is the owner in?'

'No, she is not,' said young, fit Pav, with the strong, rich voice. 'Can I pass on a message for you?'

'Oh no, I'll call back,' said Glyn with nod of gratitude. 'I'm a . . . a window cleaner. Like I say, I'll call back.'

'Okay,' said Pav, with his paint-splattered apron and his handsome youthful face.

Glyn walked back to the taxi with shaky legs. He knew without any doubt that Violet's head had been turned by him. He couldn't lose Violet to that man. She was his. His whole life.

Violet steeled herself before pushing open the door to the shop, her arms full of boxes. She owed Pav an apology for snapping at him the previous day. It was overdue. She should have turned her car round after driving off from him and done it straight away. It was a big relief when he bounded over and smiled at her with his soft lips and blue, forgiving eyes.

'I'm sorry,' she gabbled. 'I was so rude yesterday, Pav. I hope you'll accept my apology. I know you were just trying to be nice . . .'

'There is nothing to apologize for,' said Pav, relieving her of the weight of the boxes. 'I rang your mobile last night to make sure you were all right. I left a message.'

Violet pulled her phone out of her pocket. It didn't show any missed calls. She would have liked to have heard that message. 'Nothing here.'

'It was your voice, though, on the answering-machine message,' said Pav. 'I'd know it anywhere.'

Oh God, her cheeks were heating up. Again.

'It's obviously still in cyberspace somewhere, then,' said Violet, lowering her head and finding a nearby table top interesting.

'Oh a man called for you,' threw Pav over his shoulder as he walked into the kitchen. 'A window cleaner? He said he'd come back.'

'A window cleaner?' Violet shrugged. 'Don't know about that either.'

Then the phone rumbled in her pocket. Glyn.

'Where are you?' he said.

'I'm at the shop,' she replied.

'Can you come home?' Glyn sounded panicky, breathless. 'I can't explain over the phone. It's just important that you come home now.'

Max's PA, Jess, knocked on the door, opened it, popped her head round it and grinned. Then she produced a pretty bouquet of flowers from behind her back.

'Present for you,' she said. 'Secret admirer, I reckon.'

'Yeah, right,' said Max. It had to be a supplier because no one she knew would send her flowers. For a split second she entertained the idea they might be from Stuart, but that was dismissed immediately. She was out of his life, she knew that. She jerked out the card from the holder.

> To cheer you up.
> Luke X

'Luke – Best-man Luke?' asked Jess with round eyes.

'Yes, Luke my old friend. One that's like a brother to me. So take that salacious tone out of your voice,' smiled Max, picking up her mobile phone.

'I'm in receipt of a lovely bunch of flowers from you,' said Max when Luke picked up.

'Bunch?' he bellowed. 'Bouquet, surely?'

'Bouquet, then,' Max tutted. 'There was no need to—'

'I know there wasn't,' Luke butted in. 'And I'm not hitting on you either. It was an impulse buy. To do exactly what it said on the tin and cheer you up. How are you?'

'Very cheery,' replied Max.

'Liar,' said Luke.

'Okay,' Max nodded. 'I'm better than I was. I've sold the dress on, am very grateful that the *Chronicle* didn't hear about it and have me plastered all over the front page, and I've had the big eyelashes pulled off at the salon.'

'Ouch!' Max could almost hear Luke wincing. 'And what's the tan like?'

'I'm fully restored to my usual Caucasian,' said Max.

'Shit, Max, I've got to shoot off to a meeting,' said Luke, catching sight of the time. 'You know where I am if you want anything.'

'I do,' said Max. 'And thank you.'

'Pleasure. Now bugger off.'

She put down the phone and wondered, not for the first time, why lovely Luke Appleby hadn't been snapped up.

Violet charged into the flat expecting a medical Armageddon. What she didn't expect was the table set for lunch for two with a bottle of wine in the middle of it.

'I thought ... what ... Glyn ...' There were so many words trying to come out of Violet's mouth they all glutted together in the crush.

'Ah there you are,' said Glyn, grinning. 'Take a seat, why don't you?'

Violet's jaw locked open in disbelief as Glyn's back disappeared into the kitchen. She stood there stunned into silence. What the hell was he playing at? A question she voiced to him, when he returned to the table ferrying a giant dish of lasagne.

'If I'd said to you, "Come home for lunch" what would you have replied? "I can't, I'm busy."' He affected a whiney voice in imitating her. 'It says a lot about our relationship when I have to reduce myself to these tactics to share a meal with you.'

'I nearly crashed the bloody car,' growled Violet. 'I thought you were ill or Mum had rung you about Nan or your dad had had another heart scare ...'

'Well, I didn't mean for you to think that,' said Glyn, spooning a huge slab of lasagne on her plate. 'I just wanted to surprise you. No need to swear at me, Violet.'

Violet dropped her head into her hands in an effort to calm her nerves and her temper.

'Pour yourself a glass of wine and chill. Okay, I was probably a bit out of order and I'm really sorry if you thought that someone was poorly, but you're here now, so let's enjoy it.' He had a smile on his face the size of a new moon. He looked so calm and ordered that for a moment Violet wondered if she were the mad one here.

'I can't drink wine; I need to go back to work.' The words came out through clenched teeth, which needed to be close together to stop a mother lode of fury being released.

Glyn sat down and his shoulders slumped.

'Letty, I am really sorry if I worried you.' He said with a contrite sigh. 'Please, sit down and have lunch with me. I wanted to rescue you from working too hard. That shop seems to be taking up all of your time. And headspace.' He rapped on his skull. 'I could kick myself now. You're right: you could have crashed because of me. Letty, I am so sorry.'

He had gone to a lot of trouble. There were flower petals sprinkled on the table, a bowl of salad with warm bacon and avocado, fresh warm bread. She found herself pulling out the chair and sitting. She knew she had been manipulated. Again. It would have been so much easier to fight a mean man than a kind one.

'What exactly do you do in the shop at the moment?' asked Glyn after a few silent forkfuls of food.

'There's loads to do. Making ice cream, inventing menus, the books . . .'

'Couldn't you do all that here?' Glyn asked. The question sounded casual enough but Violet suspected it was the first of many which had been brewing in his head since she allegedly said Pav's name in her sleep last night. She was ready for him.

'How could I? All my cooking equipment is at Carousel—'

He interrupted her. 'I know that, but you could do your books at home, and all the other stuff.'

'I could, but I like to keep work separate. I can concentrate more when I'm by myself in a working space.'

'You're not by yourself, though, are you? You've got workmen in, haven't you?'

He watched her closely to see what her reaction to that was. He was almost disappointed that there was none. That was because she was one step ahead of him.

'One workman and he's in a different room. I'm either in the kitchen or in the office.'

'And what's *he* like?'

Glyn's eyes were trained on her face like those of a hawk hovering over a field mouse.

'He's just a painter.'

Glyn noted that she was finding her lasagne suddenly interesting.

'What does he look like?' said Glyn.

'Tallish, dark hair,' she shrugged her shoulders in a disinterested way.

'Handsome?' Glyn supplied and waited.

'He's okay, if you like that sort of thing.' Violet reached for some bread.

'And do you?'

Violet snapped her head up now. 'What sort of question is that?'

'Well, if you're shouting out his name in your sleep you must like him.'

'It was a dream. I don't have any control over what I dream about. I certainly have no recollection of dreaming about anything last night. Least of all about a man who's painting horses on my walls.'

'You seem to be spending more time with him than me, that's all,' Glyn sniffed.

'He's not there that often when I am,' Violet said sternly. 'He works a lot in the evenings when I'm here with you.'

'Or at your mother's or out with your friends,' Glyn said under his breath, but deliberately loud enough to be heard.

Violet felt her temper rumble awake again. 'Am I not allowed to see my family or my friends these days?'

'Well, how do I know that you're there when you say you are? You never answer your damned phone. I could be dying here while you're chatting and having nice cups of tea and slices of cake.'

Violet looked up at him then with his tear-filled eyes and she knew that she was viewing her whole future. Glyn would never change because he didn't want to. He would try to track her constantly with phone calls and push her guilt button continuously to make her bow to order.

She stood and let loose a groan of frustration. 'I'm not having this argument,' she said, picking up her coat from the sofa arm. 'Not again.'

'Don't go, Letty,' Glyn sighed heavily. 'I just adore you and I'm feeling really alone. We don't make love any—'

'I'm going to my mother's to see how Nan is,' Violet said, her words loaded with a tired sigh. 'You can ring her if you want to check up on me.'

When she looked at Glyn his eyes were full of watery pleas. *Look at what you're doing to me, Letty. You're breaking my heart.* It was all wrong, so wrong. This was doing neither of them any good. God, she needed oxygen before she drowned in the stale recirculated air of the flat. His love felt like a tourniquet round her chest and she couldn't breathe.

She walked outside leaving him pushing his lasagne around on his plate like a child, tears dripping down his nose, and she had to fight against the weight of guilt pulling her back. She had made herself his rock and then tried to cut him adrift from it. She really was the biggest cow in the world.

Chapter 85

'Do you want one of my little beers or shall I put the kettle on?' Nan said, putting her arms round her granddaughter's shoulders and rubbing her back. She could tell straight away that something was wrong.

'I'll have one of your little beers. I'll get it.'

'No, *I'll* get it. I'm not that infirm yet,' Nan snapped, which was becoming more and more the norm these days, according to Susan. Nan was rebelling fiercely against the progression of her illness, denying that she was forgetting and misplacing things. 'You go and sit down and then you can tell me why you're the colour of Irene's cat.'

Violet smiled a little. Irene was the woman next door whose cat was pure white and deaf. She called it Ludwig.

Nan busied around making coffee for two and tipping out her favourite Jaffa Cakes on to a plate. She'd forgotten that Violet had asked for a beer, not that Violet mentioned it.

She watched Nan, who used to be so straight and now her shoulders were crouching over. Her hands were shaking slightly as she carried the cups over, before going back for the plate of biscuits. Violet stamped down on the urge to help her.

'Come on, then, what's up?' said Nan.

'Nothing's up. I just came round to see you. Where's Mum?'

'She's nipped into Morrisons. You've just missed her.'

Violet knew her mother wouldn't be very long. She didn't like to leave Nan these days at all. She had even asked if Violet would teach her how to use a computer so she could do her shopping online.

'She's going to make herself a prisoner in this house, if she doesn't watch out,' said Nan quite crossly. 'Do you think I want to be responsible for that?'

'She only wants to know you're safe.'

'Of course I'm safe,' barked Nan. 'She's being stupid. I've done nothing for her to be on my back twenty-four hours a day checking up on me.' Her voice sounded alien. But doctors had told both Violet and Susan what stages Nan was likely to go through so Violet knew that Alzheimer sufferers often refused to believe they were anything but competent. Nan now categorically denied ever wetting the bed or talking in the middle of the night to the 'red-haired angel'.

'I've got a dress for your wedding. I bought it from Susan's catalogue,' said Nan, after a slurp of coffee. 'It cost me nearly two hundred pounds.'

Tears sprang to Violet's eyes. More expense. Every penny spent, every effort expended made it one degree harder to stop the process.

'Eeh love, what's up?' Nan reached over and stroked Violet's cheek, and that one action almost tipped Violet over the edge.

'Oh nothing, just wedding nerves, I think,' said Violet, pulling herself together. How could she burden Nan with anything? Although once upon a time it would have been Nan to whom she would have poured out her heart.

'Nerves? What are you nervous about, love?' said Nan. Her hand dropped to rest on Violet's knee. The skin was as thin as rolled-out filo pastry, and spotted, the tips of her fingers warped and knotted by arthritis.

'Were you nervous, marrying Grandad, Nan?'

Nan tilted her head back and conjured up a host of warm old memories, and they, at least, were still as sharp as the day they were made.

'Nice nervous,' she responded with a nostalgic grin. 'I was so in love. It couldn't come fast enough for me. I took that aisle in leaps and bounds. I shall look forward to seeing him again. I bet he says, "Nanette Flockton, where have you been till this bloody time?"' and she laughed. 'Eternity with your grandad still wouldn't be long enough. I miss that man every day of my life.'

An eternity with Glyn. Violet felt as if her head was a cake mix in a blender.

'You know it means a lot for me to see you settled before I go,' said Nan, as Violet drank the coffee and hoped it would push down the rising emotion in her throat. 'He is good to you – Glyn – isn't he? He looks after you, doesn't he?'

'Oh yes, he looks after me,' said Violet, with no warmth in her voice.

'I wish he had a bit more spark to him but I know he loves you a lot.'

'Yes,' said Violet.

'I'm so looking forward to the wedding,' said Nan with a chuckle. 'So is your mum. Oh I must tell you. I've got an outfit for the wedding. It cost me nearly two hundred pounds.'

'Oh Nan,' said Violet, not sure she could hold herself back from crying any longer. She felt as if her body was cracking and her tears were going to spurt through the faults at any moment.

'Will you make me another coffee, love? The one you've just made was far too strong for my tastes,' said Nan.

And Violet knew that her nan was slipping away from her fast. Violet's constants were changing. She was losing hope of ever escaping the quicksand that her life had become. *And life without hope is a living death.*

Glyn snatched up the plates of half-eaten lasagne and scraped them roughly into the bin. Then he up-ended the almost full salad bowl on top of it instead of putting it in the fridge.

Of course he knew that Violet didn't want to marry him. He knew that he had railroaded her into it, but he had done that because he also knew that she would grow to love him again. No one would ever care for or cherish her like he would.

He could tell straight away when he saw Pav that he would use women and leave them heartbroken. Most men did, especially the good-looking ones. He remembered how fragile Violet was when he first met her, crushed by the ex who had left for her someone else. In fact his last five girlfriends had all been mashed by men and he had loved them and given them back their faith before they, in their turn, dumped him so cruelly. He had been determined from the first that Violet wouldn't do that to him. So when he felt the pattern begin to repeat, he made sure that it would not end the same way as the others. What was wrong with women? They wanted someone who wouldn't hit them, would love them, put them on a pedestal, cuddle them in bed, and then when they found someone like that they ended up dumping him for another man. For someone like fucking *Pav*.

Chapter 86

Richard had a meeting on the Wednesday evening, so suggested that he and Bel have lunch in Leeds instead. He knew of a very swish new restaurant he was keen to try out, and there was no one he would rather try it out with – so he said.

The last time they had been to Leeds together was when they picked their wedding rings, Bel recalled. They'd had dinner at the Hilton and energetic sex afterwards in a suite upstairs.

Lunch was very swish, even if the salmon portion was the size of a tadpole, served with a single asparagus spear. Maybe the restaurant owners didn't think anyone would notice the ridiculously small – but ludicrously expensive – portions if they dressed the walls in sumptuous red silk and concentrated all their efforts on the wine list. Bel felt as hungry when she left it as when she'd entered.

They strolled around the arcades like they did on the wedding-ring-buying day. There was a large knot of people gathered outside Quillers, a small independent bookshop.

'They must be doing a signing,' sniffed Richard, turning the other way. He had no interest in books or authors.

'Ooh let's see who it is,' said Bel, tugging at his sleeve.

She couldn't see at first because there were too many people. Then she spotted the poster.

**JOHN NORTH will be here signing his first three
books on Wednesday, 20 July, 2 p.m.
Pre-orders will be taken for his new book**
Who Kissed the Bride?

Bel felt her hands prickle. Dan Regent was in there, behind
that glass window. Then a couple in front of his signing desk
moved and she saw him. He was talking to a quivery woman
who was holding out her book for him to enscribe. Bel's whole
body started to vibrate from a chemical rush. He's had a haircut,
she thought. It wasn't as wild as it was when she had encountered him in Emily. *Emily, where they had laughed at Ricky Gervais
and dipped cheese toasties into soup, where they had waged war over a
tin opener – and where he had once nearly kissed her after a cushion
fight.* She watched as he held his head at an angle, listening
patiently to the twittering fan, and felt herself smiling – inside
and out.

She tapped lightly on the window and he turned towards her.
She saw his eyes widen, a grin appear, watched him spring from
behind the table, manoeuvre himself through the crowd and
throw apologies behind him as he did so, and then he was there
outside on the pavement, in front of her, his hands on her
shoulders.

'Well, well, well, if it isn't Jane Eyre herself.'

'Strangled any brides recently?' she smiled up at him, sounding more composed than she felt. Her heart appeared to have
traded places with her cochlea and was booming in her ears.

'It's so good to see you,' he said, his eyes grinning as much as
the lovely curve of his mouth was.

'You too,' she said, thinking, how could I ever have imagined
you were a loony psychopath? His eyes were gentle and shining
and looking at her with sheer undisguised delight.

'Are you—' he began, then his eyes shifted focus to the man
who had just appeared behind Bel and who didn't look that
happy to see another man's hands on his wife's shoulders.

Dan's arms dropped to his side. Bel thought she saw the light fade in his eyes, as if a dimmer switch in them had just been turned down.

'Dan, this is Richard,' she felt obliged to add, 'my husband.'

Oh God, she hoped Dan didn't hit him.

'Richard, this is Dan. He's an . . . author friend of Dad's.'

'Hi,' said Dan, making no attempt to hold out his hand. There was a stiffness to his jaw that hadn't been there seconds ago.

'Hello,' returned Richard, politely but cool. Then he swivelled his head round imperiously and looked bored.

'Well, I'd better get back inside,' said Dan, taking a step backwards. 'To my adoring fans.'

'Yes, yes, of course,' said Bel, not wanting him to go.

'It's been really great seeing you again,' he said, flicking his eyes towards Richard. 'I'm happy for you.'

No, I haven't decided what I'm going to do yet, she wanted to shout, not that she could really do that with Richard at the side of her, his hand now possessively on her arm.

'Take care,' said Dan – and he was gone, swallowed up in the crowds inside the book shop. Bel felt as if the temperature around her had dropped by twenty degrees.

'Who's that, did you say?' said Richard.

'He's an author called John North,' said Bel, drifting reluctantly away from the bookshop behind Richard. She tried to catch another glimpse of Dan through the window but there were too many people standing round the desk.

'Never heard of him,' Richard sniffed.

'Let's go for a coffee,' said Bel, hoping to divert her chaotic thoughts with cake.

'Okay, where?'

'There's a lovely little shop down by the old post office,' said Bel, steering Richard in that direction.

'What, here?' he said, when they arrived at it. His nose wrinkled at the shabby facade and the blackboard menu swinging at the side of the door.

'I know it doesn't look much from the outside but the cakes are delicious. I always come here when I'm in the centre.'

'There's the Queens Hotel nearby. If you must insist on having afternoon tea that would be a better place, surely?'

'I'm not bothered about a posh afternoon tea,' Bel pushed open the door to the café. 'You'll love it. They do the best coffee and walnut cake in the world.'

'Coffee and walnut cake? Are you sure you've got the right person, Bel?' Richard snickered. 'Come on, let's go to the Queens. It's just over there.'

Bel let the door close and allowed Richard steer her to the Queens. But she had no appetite for the tiny macaroons and minuscule scone rounds that came with the tea. Because it wasn't just about the cake.

Chapter 87

Violet had not managed to visit Carousel at the weekend because Nan had fallen, sprained her wrist and shaken herself up and Violet had spent a large chunk of Saturday sitting in the hospital with her, and then keeping her company at home on Sunday. Nan appeared to be fading before her eyes. She looked as tiny and frail as a spring chick.

When Violet returned to her ice-cream parlour on Monday, she'd found that Pav must have been working solidly over the weekend. The mural was almost complete; it was almost time for him to go. He had not turned up that day, or for the two days after. As Violet made test batches of ice cream she keenly felt his absence, though she knew it was going to be something that she would have to get used to.

The shop was beautiful but Violet had little energy to appreciate it at the moment. All she could think was that she felt as trapped as one of the horses that Pav had drawn on her wall – destined to go round in circles in one direction only, operated by someone else's will, never riding free.

Violet locked up shop and wondered what she had to go home to because she'd had a very strange call from Glyn at eleven that morning. Did she have a favourite font, he'd asked. She didn't but answered 'French Script' to satisfy him because she'd just used that for her menus and it was the first one that came to mind.

Whatever Violet imagined would be waiting for her fell short by a golden mile. She parked the car and got out. When she looked up it was to see Glyn's face at the window. He was grinning and waving at her to hurry up.

'I've got a surprise for you,' he said, trotting so close behind her as she walked into the kitchen that he trod on her heels.

'Oh have you?' she tried to inject some enthusiasm into her voice. 'What is it?'

He waggled his finger at her. 'Ah-ha. Can't tell you. You have to spot it.'

Violet looked around the room. 'Is it in here?' she asked, bored already by this game.

'Yes,' he said, grinning. It wasn't a nice grin. It was almost manic. The sort of grin that Jack Nicholson did a lot in *The Shining*. He was practically tittering with childish excitement as Violet pretended to be interested in searching the room. She hoped he didn't expect her to open every drawer.

'Am I getting warm?' she asked.

'Nope,' he grinned.

She shrugged her shoulders impatiently.

'Come on, guess,' Glyn urged. 'What do people in love do?'

He'd bought her some jewellery and had it engraved, it was obvious.

'Oh Glyn, I hope you haven't spent a lot of money on me.'

He grinned even more widely. 'Not *on* you. But *for* you.'

He was making *The Times* crossword look like a two-piece jigsaw.

Violet pretended to think, but everything she guessed at resulted in a 'Nope'.

'Give up? Okay, then, I'll tell you,' he said. 'Ta da.'

He presented her with his arm and started rolling up his sleeve. Violet's first thought was that he had a new watch, but it was just his old one that his parents had bought for his twenty-first and that he always wore. Violet noticed the skin on his arm was getting redder as more of it was revealed. Then she saw the black writing, a tattoo in French Script: Glyn & Letty. The words were bordered with a long twisted stem of tiny roses and thorns. Violet's eyes focused on it all but seemed reluctant to pass the information to her brain for then it would be real, not a mirage. A swell of claustrophobia overcame her, as if it was she and Glyn themselves who were bound together in a tight and inescapable rope of thorns and not just their names.

'Don't you like it?' he said, puppy eyes pleading for approval.

'What have you done?' said Violet, her voice a horrified whisper.

'I've done it for us.'

'You've scarred yourself for life,' said Violet.

'Oh the redness will die down and it doesn't hurt that much,' he chuckled. 'I thought you'd like it. I know you are partial to a tattoo or two.'

'I said Johnny Depp had a nice painted tattoo in a film, I didn't mean for you to go out and copy him.'

'Well, I know I'm not exactly Johnny Depp,' said Glyn, his spirits nose-diving before her eyes, 'but I thought you'd be a little bit pleased at least.'

He had rolled his sleeve down but the sight of that tattoo was ingrained on her retinas.

Glyn & Letty, Glyn & Letty. He was the only one who ever called her that and she didn't like the version of her name, never had. She'd thought it churlish to say, 'Don't call me that,' so she had left it, but it grated on her. She should have spoken up. About that and everything else. She was a fool, an idiot. How had things got this far?

She was picking up her wedding dress tomorrow. Then, the next day they were having a birthday tea with the Leachs Senior as it was Joy's birthday. There would be more wedding talk about caravans and babies. It was just a non-stop thrill fest.

Violet feigned a headache and went to bed early without having a bath. She didn't want to feel Glyn's hands massaging her shoulders, neither did she want to see his curled and sulky hurt lip if she shrugged him off. When she eventually got to sleep, it was to dream that Glyn had tattooed their names all over her body in all sorts of different colours and fonts. *Glyn & Letty, Glyn & Letty, Glyn & Letty.*

Richard had kissed Bel properly on the mouth when they parted. His lips had been soft and insistent, his tongue entered her mouth and his arms crushed her to him. Bel had let him because she wanted to be sure, and experiencing his kiss she was now as sure as she could be.

Once at home, she took her wedding ring out of her jewellery box and studied it. She had wanted to show off that ring so much when they bought it. It was a symbol of their union. The next time she saw Richard she would, once again, be wearing it.

Chapter 88

'When do you want it back?' Violet asked Freya as she picked up the dress, protected in its plastic cover.

'Within a calendar month of the wedding, please,' said Freya, wrapping ribbon around the box that contained Violet's veil and tiara. 'You can leave the dry-cleaning to me.'

Then she surprised Violet by taking her chin in her hand and tilting up her face. 'You are a very lovely girl,' said Freya in her soft voice. 'I wish you all the best that life can give you.'

'Thank you,' said Violet, pushing down the rising tide of emotion. 'It's a beautiful dress and I'll take good care of it.'

'The dress is a good fit on a happy bride,' smiled Freya, 'but wild horses shouldn't be able to drag down an aisle anyone that doesn't want to be there.'

Violet bravely attempted a joke. 'Thank goodness there're no aisles in the registry office, then.'

Freya looked into Violet's large sad eyes, which were the colour of spring bluebells. She saw all the thoughts, the frustration, the panic, the guilt in them before Violet dropped her head, picked up her gown and the box and turned to go.

'Be happy,' called Freya, as Violet closed the door behind her. 'Be as happy as I was.'

Chapter 89

Violet hung the gown on one of the hooks at the side of the door in the shop and put the box of bridal accessories on the floor underneath it. Then she went into the kitchen, washed her hands and started to weigh out ingredients to make some strawberry and white-chocolate ice cream.

The mixer was on full blast so she didn't hear Pav enter. She wasn't aware of his presence until she felt his hand upon her shoulder.

She cried out in momentary shock, whirled round, saw it was him and then felt his hands upon her arms, steadying her – his beautiful big hands that she would soon never see – or feel – again. She couldn't have stopped the tears with the Hoover Dam. Down her cheeks they poured while she stood there in embarrassment, trying to escape his hold.

'My God, Violet, Violet, whatever is the matter?' For a few moments he was unsure whether to let her go or hold her closer to comfort her. Then he pulled her against his chest and Violet abandoned herself to his force, breathing in the smell of his leather jacket and the fresh-scented cologne that he wore. His arms were a sweet cage around her, then, suspecting that he might not know how to let go, she stiffened and removed herself from his embrace.

'I'm sorry. I'm sorry.'

'Come sit down,' he said, draping his hand over her shoulder and leading her into the front of the shop and over to one of the tables. He stripped off his jacket and sat down opposite her, a golden horse pole between them.

'I am a very good listener,' he said in his deep rich voice. 'Last night I had to listen to my brother telling me that he is going back to Poland and leaving his wife. Again. It's not a good place to be, in that house. I come here for smiles and find you crying.'

Violet shrugged and dabbed at her eyes, hoping that she didn't look like Chi-Chi the panda.

'We are friends, I would like to think,' said Pav. 'So you can tell me what is making your big violet eyes so red.'

Violet swallowed hard at the intensity of his attention. She could feel that his sea-blue eyes with the thick dark lashes were locked on to her face and when she raised her head it was to see that the stubble on his chin was longer in some places than in others as if he had been using a rubbish razor.

'It's nothi—'

'Ah.' Pav raised an admonishing finger. 'Don't say nothing. This is not nothing.' He lifted a tear from her cheek with that same finger only for another to take its place immediately.

'I can't say it,' said Violet. Her head fell down again.

'Try,' said Pav.

'Really, Pav, I can't.'

She made to stand, muttering that she should carry on mixing, and Pav and his big artist hands reached over and pushed her down into her seat again, and the walls holding everything back inside her began to crumble.

'You aren't leaving this table until you talk,' he said.

Violet's eyes were in full betrayal mode now, pumping out tears faster than she could wipe them away. 'I . . .' she began.

She was shaking, as if things inside her were physically breaking down, shifting, rushing to freedom. *Oh God, dare she say it?* She sensed the words rise within her, rumble past her voice box; she felt her mouth form itself for their exit.

'I don't want to get married,' she said on a frightened low

breath. She felt engulfed by a crashing weight of guilt for releasing the sound to the air.

'Then don't,' said Pav gently. 'Tell him.'

'I can't,' sighed Violet. 'I'm everything to him. Really. Everything he does is for me. When I met him, sixteen months ago, he was like a kicked puppy. He was so gentle and caring and desperate to love and be loved.'

She didn't think he'd understand.

'Let me guess,' Pav mused. 'Maybe you had not been treated so well in the past and this attention was . . . nice for you.'

'Yes, it was,' Violet nodded, and she felt encouraged to go on. 'It was so flattering to be cared for the way he cared for me. Nothing was too much trouble; he sought my approval for everything he did. It felt lovely to be so . . . so revered. I moved in with him too quickly, I know that now, but he was so kind and I wanted to return the favour by helping him through his breakdown.'

'Do you love him?' asked Pav, taking a serviette from one of the opened boxes on the floor and handing it to her.

'No.' Violet took it, shook it open and buried her head in it.

Even talking like this was making her feel as if the air had been removed from the room and replaced with something difficult to pull into her lungs.

'You need to calm down and breathe deeply,' said Pav slowly, breathing with her, inviting her to join the rhythm until she felt able to carry on talking.

'I began to feel trapped, stifled, buried. More and more I started to do all the trademark things like tell him he was silly when he tried to kiss me, say I was tired when we went to bed. I never liked it that I couldn't have any privacy in the bathroom.'

'Why didn't you just lock the door?'

'He had the lock taken off. He was scared that I might have an accident in the bath, he said.'

She saw Pav's expression darken.

'Violet, you must not marry this man.'

'I know, but I can't get out of it.' There was real rising panic in Violet's voice now, bordering on hysteria. 'I want to stop it but everyone has bought outfits and is looking forward to it and my nan wants to see me married and she's ill. And his parents have bought us presents and they've had their caravan cleaned especially . . .'

Pav's hands came out and grabbed her wrists and it shocked her into silence.

'These are not reasons for getting married, Violet. This is why you get married.' He dragged her hands on to his chest where his heart was. She felt the slow, steady thump underneath his shirt, the rise and fall of his ribcage. 'Because you feel a person in here.'

'You aren't telling me anything I don't know, Pav,' Violet cried. 'But if I don't go through with it . . .' Her voice folded again.

'What?' Pav was still holding her hands on his chest. 'What will happen if you don't get married?'

'He'll kill himself,' wept Violet, totally breaking down. 'That's what he tried to do the last time I left him. He won't fail again and it will all be my fault.'

Chapter 90

'Where've you been, Susan? You were hours,' said Nan impatiently, as Susan appeared in the doorway with a cheese sandwich.

'I've been in the kitchen getting this for your lunch,' said Susan, quelling the urge to snap. Not because she was angry at the old lady, but because she was dog-tired. Nan had wet the bed again during the night and she'd had to get up and strip and change the sheets. And Susan was worried. Nan was going downhill too fast. And it was killing them both that such a proud woman was wetting her bed.

'I don't like cheese. I never have,' said Nan, wrinkling up her nose as Susan put the sandwich plate down on the table in front of her.

'You do,' said Susan. 'You love cheese.'

'Don't tell me what I like and what I don't like,' Nan said crossly, as if Susan were a naughty child.

Susan sighed and tried not to look as sad as she felt. 'Shall I get you something else?'

'I'll have tinned salmon,' said Nan, aggressively pushing the plate across the coffee table as if the sight of it offended her.

'I haven't got any salmon but I've got tuna,' said Susan. 'Will that do?'

Nan folded her arms across her thin chest. 'I suppose it'll have to.'

So Susan went into the kitchen and buttered some more bread. She could hear Nan in the next room singing to herself. It was one of those songs that she had taught Violet when she was a child sitting on her knee at bedtime. It was a song about a fairground horse.

Horsey turning circles
On my carousel
Listen very closely
I've a secret I must tell
If you hop upon my back
Of gold and dapple-grey
I will leave my carousel
And take us far away.

When Susan went back into the lounge, Nan was singing it to the chair opposite, as surely as if she had a real audience. Susan felt her heart snap like a biscuit inside her.

Chapter 91

'A year ago I realized that I had to leave Glyn,' Violet went on, as Pav took her hands from his chest, put them down on the table and covered them with his own. 'I began to find all the attention too much. On the evening when I decided I was going to tell him I was moving out, I went home from work to find the flat covered in rose petals and champagne on ice waiting for me. He had cooked lobster, oysters, caviar, you name every romantic gesture and it was there. He dropped to his knees and produced a ring and I had to say no. He was heartbroken, panicky, kept questioning me on and on about what was wrong, what he could do to make me change my mind. I tried to talk to him but he wouldn't listen. He refused to accept it was over. It was awful. He was distraught.' Violet puffed out her cheeks. Telling Pav about that horrible evening was making it feel very close again.

'There was a big room above the old shop I used to rent and I intended to stay there for a few days until I'd sorted out my head. I'd been there for only four hours when Joy – Glyn's mum – rang me on my mobile to tell me that he'd taken an overdose and was in hospital. A massive one. It wasn't a piddly little cry-for-help overdose; he'd really intended to kill himself. He left me a note saying that he loved me so much that he couldn't live without me, and a note to his parents to say thank you and that he loved them. But in his drugged state he rang them to say goodbye. Afterwards he said he couldn't remember doing it and was angry at himself because he really did want to die. He said that everyone had wasted their time saving him because as soon as he was out of hospital he was going to do exactly the same again. Joy and Norman were in a real state when I got to the hospital. They're in their seventies. They had to hook Norman up to an ECG because the shock of it was affecting his heart rhythm and they thought he might be having a cardiac arrest. Glyn's their only child, you see. The lucky thing was that Glyn'd taken so many tablets his stomach had thrown most of them back up.'

'And you agreed to marry him?' put in Pav. 'To stop him killing himself.'

'In a nutshell,' nodded Violet. 'I moved back in with him hoping that I could help him shift his depression so that he didn't rely on me so much for approval. Then I'd be able to leave him without him feeling that his life was over. The wedding was booked a year in advance. I thought that would give me plenty of time to get him well.' Violet groaned like an animal in pain. 'It sounds mad, I know – why in this day and age am I marrying someone when I don't want to? I didn't think it would get this far. There seemed to be lots of time, but Glyn was getting worse not better. He was relying on me more not less and it got even harder to get out of it. The wedding date was getting nearer and nearer and Joy was asking me when I was going to get a dress and so I had to start looking for one to stop them realizing what I was really meaning to do. Then they started talking detail and Mum bought an outfit and ... I've made everything worse by letting things get this far. The rejection would be far worse now. He will succeed in killing himself if I leave him and his parents will never recover ... All I can do is go through with everything and keep trying to make him independent and then divorce him ... but he's talking about us having children ...'

Violet's head fell forward as if she were totally spent. There, it was done, admitted, and it changed nothing.

'Oh Violet, this is not good,' Pav's voice was patient and understanding. 'You cannot marry this man.'

'I can't find a way to leave him without killing him. He loves me so much.'

Pav squeezed her hands. 'Listen to me, Violet. This is control, this is obsession, this is not love. You have to stop his game. He will not kill himself.'

'Pav, he will.'

'No, it's twisted. He rang his parents last time to rescue him. He wants to control you and he can't do that when he is dead.'

Violet lifted up her head knowing that she must look a total wreck, not that she cared any more.

'If you stay, it is you who will die,' said Pav.

She thought that could very possibly be true. She was slipping more and more into a dark, cold world of depression and panic attacks.

'Oh Violet,' he said, and he left his seat to go and sit next to her. His arms came round her and she surrendered against him. She felt his lips on her hair and his finger on her chin lifting it up. Then his face came closer still and his lips touched hers. They barely butterflied past but something blissful tore through her and sped to every nerve ending. He pulled away gently to see if he had offended her but saw instead that her lips were flushed, soft, and his met with hers again. Then he pressed her head into his shoulder and sighed in the manner of one who had just found home.

'I'm sorry, Violet. This is unforgivable of me,' he said, his hold unrelenting. 'I don't want to let you go.'

'You're caught up in my confusion,' said Violet, afraid to let herself believe that this beautiful man holding her could really be offering her anything but comfort.

'My timing is not good, but my feelings are not confused,' said Pav firmly and she knew without any doubt that she could not live a life without ever being kissed like that again. Pav's kiss had sealed the fate on the charade of a wedding. Whatever the fallout of that decision would be.

'I'm scared, Pav. I'm scared of the power I have over his life,' said Violet, savouring the warmth of him.

'Don't you see,' Pav replied, 'it is he who has more power over you? And he wields it like a stick to beat you with. You have to leave him. Today. He will cry and he will plead and he will threaten and manipulate but you must be strong and go.'

He was right. All this time Violet felt weighed down by responsibility for Glyn, and it was an illusion: he called the real shots.

'Do you want me to come with you?' asked Pav, locking the shop. No painting had been done that day, but more important things had been achieved. 'I want to know that you are safe.'

'Glyn wouldn't harm me,' said Violet.

'Yes, he would,' said Pav. 'By hurting himself, he knows he hurts you. This is the way he affects you. It has to stop.' His hand came out and cupped her cheek. 'I am here for you.'

Violet pushed her face against the roughness of his palm and drew a badly needed strength from it. She was shaking with fear as she got into her car, knowing that what she was about to do was probably going to be the hardest thing of her life.

Chapter 92

As Violet locked her car door, she resolved that in half an hour – max – she would be back inside it, driving away from Glyn's flat for the last time. Well, maybe not the last time because she doubted she would be able to gather all her stuff together tonight, but certainly the last time as his fiancée. She felt her resolve slipping with every step she took towards him. Visions fired at her of Glyn wired up to machines in the hospital, Joy crying, Norman clutching his chest, a coffin, a grave, guilt, blame. Then she thought of that gold and dapple-grey horse on the wall breaking away from Carousel, like the horse in that old song her nan used to sing, his heart free.

'Please, God, keep me strong,' said Violet as she walked up the staircase. The sound of each step she took felt amplified as if she were watching herself in a slow-motion film. Then she was at the door. She opened it. Glyn was setting the table.

'Hello, lovely Letty. Tea's nearly ready, darling. Lemon sole tonight.'

'Glyn . . .'

'Come on, Letty. Sit yourself down.'

'Glyn, I'm leaving you.'

The words slipped out so easily that she wondered why they had been so difficult for so long.

'Don't be daft,' he turned and went into the kitchen. She heard him open the oven door. She heard a tray clatter to the floor and him grumble.

'Glyn. Please come and sit down. Leave that.'

'Leave it? Give over, Letty. I've been cooking for ages. I'm not just going to leave it,' and he laughed – a horrible, forced noise. He knew she wasn't joking. He was refusing to hear the words. It was all happening again, but this time she had to stick to her guns. This time she had to go and he had to know that she would not be back. Whatever he did to himself.

'I'm sorry,' she said gently, but firmly, to his back as he wiped at the mess of fish with a dishcloth. She took in a big breath to deliver the death knell: 'There's no good way to say this but I'm not in love with you.'

'I know,' he said, rinsing the cloth. 'But you were once and you can be again.'

'No, I can't,' she said. 'It's over.'

She twisted the engagement ring from her finger and placed it on the coffee table for him to find later. Then she went into the bedroom and pulled her suitcase from the top of the wardrobe. Next stop was the bathroom, where she put her dirty clothes that were in the wash basket into a carrier bag and then threw in her make-up. By the time she returned to the bedroom, Glyn was lifting the case back up on to the wardrobe again. This time she knew, though, that nothing was going to stop her leaving – suitcase or no suitcase, she was going. Just as Freya had picked up her bag one day and walked out on her abusive husband.

He expected her to try to wrestle it from him, but she didn't. She grabbed a handful of carrier bags from the kitchen drawer and proceeded to fill them with her underwear, skirts, jeans, phone charger, jewellery.

He stood with his back pressed against the second wardrobe so she couldn't get to her clothes in there. She had to remember to stay firm and focused. Making her battle with him gave him the opportunity to manipulate her, physically and mentally. Indifference was a stronger tool. She could live without a few blouses and skirts.

She took the four filled carrier bags and strode out of the room.

'Letty, what's happened? What is it? Is it *him*? Is that what this is all about?'

'Him? Who?'

Glyn spat out the name. 'That Pav bloke. You know I can't live without you, don't you? I can't spend every day thinking about you together with him. I just couldn't go on.' He was crying now. Heavy tears were rolling down his face and yet Violet forced herself to stay impervious. *Don't fall for it*, said a voice inside her. *He is using all the ammunition he can.*

'Glyn, I stayed with you because I couldn't bear to think you'd harm yourself again. But what basis for a relationship is that? Fear and blackmail?'

'Well, at least you won't have to worry about me getting in the way of you and *Pav* if I'm dead,' he yelled.

Violet's resolve wobbled, then she heard Pav's words so clearly in her head it was as if he were at her side, whispering them into her ear: *This is control, this is not love.*

'You'll hurt your parents far more than you can ever hurt yourself, Glyn. They went through hell last time.'

'I don't care,' he screamed at her. And she saw that he didn't. His wants came first. All this time she had thought he was the most generous person she had ever met, and in truth he was the most selfish. She feared for Joy and Norman. But she couldn't stay with Glyn just to protect them.

She took a deep breath and said something that felt cruel and alien to her.

'I won't grieve if you injure yourself, Glyn. You can't hurt me by hurting yourself any more.'

'We'll see, shall we?' he said, in the manner of a petulant child intent on pulling out all the stops to punish when he couldn't have his own way.

'I'll be staying at a hotel,' she said flatly, without any emotion. 'Mum and Nan have enough to deal with at the moment and I won't be telling them where I am so there's absolutely no point in ringing them unless you want to get yourself a police harassment order.'

'God, you've changed,' he spat bitterly.

'I hope so,' she replied.

'I won't be here after tonight, if you change your mind, you do know that,' he said, in a voice so quiet and calm that it chilled Violet to the bone. She pulled all her reserves of strength to the front line and stared him straight in the eye.

'Goodbye, Glyn.'

Then she took a step towards the outside door and he sprang in front of her, barring her way. He was using his full toolbox of tricks.

'Please,' he sank to his knees. 'I'm begging you not to leave me. I'll change. I'll do anything.'

'No, Glyn.'

'I love you so much.' His hands were clenched as if he were praying to her. 'Look after my mum and dad for me.' Her pity for him segued into revulsion at that.

'This isn't love, Glyn. And you know it isn't.'

'You did this to me,' he yelled. 'You came into my life and you made me love you and now you're ripping out my heart.'

She opened the door, determined to do whatever was necessary to get out, but, to her surprise, he didn't stop her. Instead he collapsed to the floor, prostrate, sobbing. Violet walked out and shut the door behind her, half expecting it to open again and for an arm to drag her inside with brute force, just like in an old horror movie after the tension had been released, only for it to crank straight back up again.

Once she had left the building, she gulped at the outside air as if her lungs were starved of it, just as she had been in her own dreams. She felt as if a thick rope that had tethered her to something heavy and rotten had been severed. She dared to glance upwards hoping that she wouldn't see him at the window, ready to jump out. But all was still. She opened her car door, climbed inside and, with a severely trembling hand, slotted the key into the ignition.

She drove straight to her mum and Nan's house. By the time she got there, there were fourteen missed calls from Glyn on her phone. She would have to change her number in the morning. Another job to add to the list.

She breezed in with a lightness of step she hadn't felt in a long time.

Susan was ironing in the lounge watching a *Come Dine with Me* rerun. Nan was in her dressing gown, asleep in the big chair. She looked tiny, bony and suddenly very old.

'Hello, love, this is a nice surprise,' said Susan, folding up one of Nan's nighties. She studied her daughter's face. 'Are you all right? You look—' she hunted for the right words – 'bloody awful.'

'Mum.' Violet swallowed. 'I've left Glyn.'

'Oh,' said Susan, and she switched off the iron. 'Come into the kitchen and we'll talk.'

Violet followed her mum out of the lounge. 'How's Nan?'

'Not brilliant,' said Susan. 'I could weep at some of the things she comes out with: talking to angels and singing that song about the carousel horse all the time. I made her a cheese sandwich and she swore blind that she'd never liked the stuff.'

'Nan? Not like cheese?' said Violet with a nasty feeling of dread. She remembered having her tea every Sunday at Postbox Cottage. Lots of cheese and crackers and celery and pâté, and Nan and Grandad would have a glass of port with it and pour her a glass of Ribena so she didn't feel too left out.

'Lately she hasn't been able to manage a dry night,' said Susan.

'You must be so tired, Mum.'

'I'm her carer so it comes with the job,' said Susan. 'I don't care how hard it gets; she's not going in a home.' She took a bottle of white wine out of the fridge and screwed off the top. 'I think I need one of these before you start, and I'm sure you do. So come on, out with it.'

And so Violet told her. Everything. And at the end of it Susan felt the drag of sadness in her heart.

'You silly lass,' she said. 'I'm your mother. It doesn't matter whatever else is going on in my life, you should always be able to talk to me. What if you'd got a daughter and she were sitting where you are now and you were sitting here? How hurt would you be that she didn't come to you for help?'

Violet nodded. 'I've made a right mess of everything.'

'No, you would have made a right mess if you'd married him. I'm glad you've had the sense to pull out if you feel like you do. I mean, I know he thought the world revolved around you but ...' Susan stopped, afraid she was saying too much.

Violet urged her on. 'But what, Mum? Go on, say it.'

'I'd always wanted you to have someone with a bit more fire in them. Life with Jeff might have been cut short but, my God, we had some fun. I never saw much light in your eyes when you talked about Glyn.'

Susan reached over and hugged her daughter. 'Life's too short to be a martyr, Violet. Promise me that your life starts again right now, right here.'

'I promise,' said Violet. But she had a dreadful feeling of foreboding that she wasn't quite out of the dark woods yet.

Chapter 93

'Christ on a bike,' Max exclaimed, as she sat in Postbox Cottage about to dig into a fish-bit and chip supper.

Listening to Violet's story both her mouth and Bel's had dropped open so much that they looked like two copies of Munch's *Scream*.

'How many times has he rung you now?' asked Bel, hearing the phone vibrate yet again on the table.

'One hundred and two,' replied Violet.

'Well, at least he's still alive, then,' said Max, crunching down on a chip.

'That was a bit harsh,' winced Bel.

'True, though,' sniffed Max. 'You can do better. Next time—'

Violet held up her palm towards Max to halt her and chuckled. 'I think I'll have a rest from men for a while.'

'That's three cock-up weddings now.' Then Bel made chimp noises as the chip she had just put into her mouth was too hot.

'If Roy Castle were still alive, I'd be writing to *Record Breakers*,' said Max. 'Pass me that vinegar, V. My fish bits are crying out for it.'

'That sounds so wrong,' winced Violet. The phone vibrated again.

'I'm going to pick up that thing in a minute and tell him to piss off,' hissed Max. 'You need to change your number.'

'I know. I'll do it tomorrow,' said Violet. She still couldn't believe that she had broken free of Glyn. After all this time of being totally and utterly miserable, she had just walked out of his life today. Euphoria didn't even touch it. But she needed company tonight. She wasn't so sure any more that Glyn wouldn't try to hurt her. Max and Bel had been only too happy to come over when she rang them and told them the news. Max had picked up fish and chips on the way; Bel had picked up a bottle of chilled Sauvignon Blanc from Rhythm and Booze.

'Heard anything from "you know who"?' Bel asked Max.

'Only that he's moved in with Jenny. Luke thought I ought to know. Poor bloke was in a state whether to tell me or not.'

'I'm sorry,' said Violet, giving her an affectionate nudge.

Max shrugged her shoulders. 'I can't say I wasn't expecting it. It didn't actually hurt as much as I thought it would. Funny that. You can be with someone for so long and then overnight you become strangers.'

The phone began to vibrate yet again.

'Answer it or I will,' commanded Bel.

Violet picked it up and put it on speakerphone.

'Glyn,' she said calmly into the mouthpiece. 'You have to leave me alone.'

'I just want to talk to you.' He was crying hard and the words came out in stuttering chunks. 'P-p-please come h-home.'

'No, Glyn. It's over. I won't be answering the phone again.'

'C-can we talk when you come to get your things? I'll m-make us a meal and—'

'I think it's best if someone else comes and gets them,' Violet interrupted him. Max pointed to herself and Bel.

'Please, p-please—'

'Don't ring again, Glyn. It won't do you any good.'

'But what d-did I do?' he pleaded.

'Goodbye, Glyn.'

His tone hardened. 'I will kill m-myself, Violet. You'll be s-sorry. I'll haunt you—'

Violet pressed the 'disconnect' button and shivered. She hadn't even taken a breath before it rang again.

'Well, that worked well,' said Bel. 'Bumhole.' She picked up Violet's phone and switched it to silent. Violet wouldn't have turned it off just in case her mum needed her.

'Anyway, for anyone who is interested,' Bel announced, 'Richard and I went to Leeds for lunch yesterday. We even walked around the shops like a married couple.'

'You are a married couple,' said Max. 'At least one of us got to sign the register.'

'I win,' laughed Bel. She seemed in amazingly good spirits. Just like the days when they had all first met.

'That's it? That's all you're going to say about him?' asked Max. 'Come on, one of us surely will have some sort of success story to inspire the other two.'

'That's all the news I have for now,' said Bel.

'I think we are all due a bit of a quiet period,' Max said and the humour had slipped from her voice. The others knew that whatever brave front she was putting on, she was still very raw inside. The fact that Stuart had moved on so quickly to another relationship had really twisted the knife into her side.

'Yeah, here's wishing us a quiet spell,' Bel raised her glass of wine and chinked it against the drinks of her friends. It was, however, a wish that was to be far from granted.

Pav arrived at Carousel at ten p.m. that night. He knew he wouldn't sleep. His brother and sister-in-law weren't speaking and the atmosphere in the house was horrible.

Violet had been on his mind all evening. He had hoped she would ring him to tell him she was all right, but he knew tonight would be hard for her and he did not want to pester her.

At least he could finish off the wall for her and make her smile that way. Then she could open her ice-cream parlour and have something to take her mind off things. He'd had a brainwave to touch up the dapple-grey horse with gold paint. Then, when he was too tired, he could nap on the couch in the room upstairs and finish it before she came to the shop in the morning.

Chapter 94

It was three o'clock in the morning when Glyn arrived at Carousel. It had taken him over two hours to walk there but there was no need to keep up the pretence of agoraphobia. He was convinced she would be staying here. He knew that she was telling the truth that she wouldn't be at her mother's house, but he didn't buy the hotel story, not when she had a room in the shop she could stay in.

When he saw the red van parked there, a hit of rage blasted through him because he recognized it as the painter's vehicle. He had been right, then. She had left him for another man. And they were both here, together.

Glyn took out the spare shop key that he'd had cut ages ago and slid it into the keyhole. He entered stealthily and then closed the door carefully behind him. Everything was still and silent. The light from the full moon was silver-bright and highlighted the gold paint on the grey horse's back. Glyn looked around. *They* must be upstairs. She must have put a bed up there for them to fuck in.

He was about to look in the kitchen when he noticed the wedding dress hanging up at the side of the door in the protective plastic coat. Why was that there? *Because she's going to wear it for him, for Pav,* came the answer from a warped, irrational part of his brain. And he couldn't let that happen, could he?

He went into the kitchen. There was a lighter and a packet of foreign cigarettes on the work surface. *His.* Glyn quietly searched the drawers and found a huge pair of scissors among the cutlery. He opened the scissors and slashed at the dress with the blade. He wanted to scream with anger as he was doing it, but he wanted to surprise *them* in bed more, so instead all the fury that would have been vented verbally channelled down the arm and into the hand holding the scissors. Peach roses fell to the floor, the silk cutting easily as the blade plunged into it and ripped down. He was so caught up in the frenzy that he didn't hear Pav pad down the stairs.

'Who's there? What are you doing?' *That voice, that dark, rich Pav voice.*

Pav rounded the corner then saw the dress on the floor and the man standing above it. Pav lunged at him, grabbed his shoulder and Glyn gasped as he felt his arm twist behind him. The younger man was fit and toned whereas he was soft and flabby.

'Get off,' he yelped, as Pav propelled him forward, to pin him against the wall.

'You're the one who came the other day and said you wanted to clean the windows, aren't you?' asked Pav. He nodded to himself. 'So you were really staking out the building.' Glyn was no match for him strength-wise but Pav did not realize what he was holding in his left hand. Pav crushed Glyn against the wall and reached in his jeans pocket for his telephone.

'I'm going to ring the police,' he said. 'You have been stupid. There is nothing here to steal.'

He thinks I'm a burglar, thought Glyn. He has no idea who I am.

Pav punched in the first 9 and, as he did so, Glyn pushed all of his weight against Pav and freed his arm. He lifted it high in the air then watched the scissors swoop down in a smooth arc towards the young man's chest. Glyn heard Pav's groan of pain as he crumpled to the floor. He saw the scissors sticking between his ribs.

Adrenaline coursed through Glyn's panicking body. He hadn't

meant to stab him, merely to escape. His first thought was to help, and he grabbed the savaged silk from the floor to staunch the wound. Then his brain pulled rank on his instincts. He couldn't be seen here. He would be arrested and lose Violet for ever.

'Help me,' Pav pleaded. His hands were pressed against the wound, uselessly trying to stem the flow of blood, which was pulsing out between his fingers.

Glyn looked around and saw a bottle of the turpentine that Pav used to thin his paint. Quickly Glyn screwed off the top and soaked the material. He stepped over Pav to retrieve the lighter he had seen in the kitchen. The fire would destroy the evidence that he had been here.

'Please,' said Pav again.

'I can't,' said Glyn. 'I'm sorry.'

He clicked the lighter and the material bloomed into flame. Then Glyn threw the lit rag down on to the box of paper serviettes and left Pav to die.

Chapter 95

Violet was a little girl again on Nan's knee. And Nan was singing that old song about the carousel horse.

Horsey turning circles
On my carousel
Listen very closely
I've a secret I must tell
If you hop upon my back
Of gold and dapple-grey
I will leave my carousel
And take us far away.

Then the room went dark and smoke started to billow through the windows and she and Nan were coughing. And Nan was saying, 'The horses, Violet. Rescue the horses.' Violet could hear their terrified whinnying. And she could still hear them when she woke up.

Something was very wrong. Violet's heart was galloping with anxiety as she grabbed her jeans and stuck her bare feet into her boots before pulling a jumper over her pyjama top. She opened the bedroom door cautiously, expecting to see smoke rushing up the staircase, but there was none.

The cottage was clear of any danger when she went downstairs and she wondered if she had just had a bad dream about

Glyn. She knew she was too shaken up to sleep so grabbed her car keys from the coffee table. Maybe she needed to drive past Glyn's flat, just to be on the safe side. That dream was too real.

Nan's song was reverberating in her head. *Horses. Carousel.* She did a three-point turn on the road and set off towards Maltstone first instead. She knew she was being ridiculous going over to Carousel at this time in the morning, but at least if she could prove to herself that she was being stupid, she might get back to sleep.

As she turned into the garden-centre car park, she saw a light in the shop window. Then she saw that light flicker. Flames. And Pav's car was there. *Dear Jesus.* She pulled her mobile phone out of her jeans pocket. She had never rung an emergency number from it before – was it 999 from a mobile as well? She couldn't remember afterwards what service she had requested. She was talking at the same time as smashing the shop windows with pieces ripped from a nearby dry stone wall. She burned her hand when she grasped the door handle. Then she heard the blessed sound of sirens in the distance getting louder and louder.

Chapter 96

People appeared from nowhere, some in clothes, some in dressing gowns. Arms were holding Violet back as masked firemen fell into a long-practised routine. The ambulance men were waiting for clearance to go in and attend to the wounded man. Police were talking into radios and muffled scratchy voices were answering back.

'Okay,' a fireman signalled to the ambulance crew, who strode in purposefully with their equipment.

'Please let me in,' sobbed Violet. 'He's my friend.'

And one of the firemen must have nodded because Violet was suddenly free and she flew into the building and saw Pav lying in a huge pool of blood, an oxygen mask on his face, her kitchen scissors protruding from his chest.

'What's his name, love?' one of the ambulance men was asking her.

'Pavel Nowak. Pav,' she answered, her throat full of smoke.

'Pav, hello, Pav, we're going to need you to stay with us, mate,' the ambulance man said to him, while the other injected him and spoke into his radio.

'Come and talk to him, keep him with us,' said the ambulance man, beckoning Violet over. She dropped to her knees and pulled Pav's big hand between her own. It felt so cold, so heavy, so lifeless.

'Pav, it's Violet. Don't leave me. Please don't leave me.'

The sight of him lying there, still and bloody, was tearing her apart and yet she couldn't cry. The feeling inside her was too big for tears. It was as if the whole of the inside of her had collapsed; it was a sensation of utter devastation. He couldn't die. All that talent, that beauty, his youth – it couldn't just be extinguished as easily as the firemen had snuffed out the flames.

Violet lost all concept of time. On the one hand it seemed ages before Pav was wheeled out on the trolley towards the ambulance; on the other it flashed past as if whole frames of action were missing.

'You'll need to get to the hospital yourself, pet,' said the ambulance man. 'There will be no room in this ambulance, shall I send for another?'

'I'll take her,' said a man she didn't recognize, one of the people from the nearby houses.

'Please look after him. Don't let him die,' Violet pleaded with the ambulance man as he shut the back door.

'We'll be doing all we can,' he said. 'I promise you that, lass.'

While the ambulance tore away at break-neck speed, the siren cutting the air with its augmented shrill, the kind stranger put his arm round Violet and gently guided her to where his wife was standing. 'You just stay here, love, and I'll go and get my car.'

The police were questioning a man from round the corner, who had seen a man with a grazed face run past him when he let his dog out for a wee. The dog had nearly tripped him up. The man was able to supply a description of someone about five foot seven with mid-brown hair, stocky, wearing a dark-blue padded jacket. When they asked Violet if she knew who that could be, she answered yes. Nothing felt real. Surely Glyn wouldn't have done this?

As she sat in the stranger's car, sad silent tears eventually began to leak out and slide down her face, making white tracks on her soot-painted skin. If only she'd had hindsight, then she would never have gone back to Glyn a year ago. If she hadn't gone back,

Pav wouldn't be on the critical list now. There was no way Pav would survive, she knew. There was too much blood. The fire had raged in the corner by the window and not spread to him, but she knew that the smoke was as dangerous as the flames and the shop had been full of it. The flames had licked away the beautiful horses. Only one dapple-grey head remained with its flecks of gold.

When they reached the hospital, she let the nurses put her in a wheelchair and take her inside. Violet didn't even feel the pain in her hand or on her arms where glass had sprayed and cut her. And inside she was numb. She wasn't sure that she would ever be capable of feeling anything again.

They cleaned her up, tended her cuts and burns and stuck a giant plaster on her cheek, which made it nigh-on impossible to see out of her left eye. She didn't want to go home so she sat waiting for news, but all they could tell her was that Pav was in the operating theatre and could be for hours. Every time a doctor rounded the corner her heart seemed to freeze. When that doctor passed without stopping to face her and tell her that he was sorry but there was nothing they could do, it began to beat again. 'No news is good news,' she repeated to herself like a mantra. Nan always said that where there was life there was hope. She prayed to any god who would listen; she asked her grandad to help Pav; she imagined her affection for him as a big white ball and rolled it towards the operating theatre. Then, in the distance, she heard her name being called and turned to find her mother walking towards her.

'How did you know I was here, Mum?'

'I didn't know. Violet, what's happened to you?' Susan burst into tears.

'I'm fine, Mum, really. Don't cry. Why are you here?'

'I came with Nan. I've been trying to get hold of you.' Susan bent and put her arms round her daughter. 'She's gone, love. She had a massive stroke during the night and she's gone.'

Chapter 97

Nan was cremated five days later. The dear vicar of St Jude's told some lovely and funny stories about her, including the one about the phallic bottle opener. After they had said their good-byes, thirty of them went for a four-course sit-down meal at Arden Country Hotel. Susan was determined that her last duty for the mother-in-law she adored would be to give her the best send-off she could. They toasted Nan with port after the cheese course. Violet had managed to hold off the tears until they did that.

Max gave her a big hug. 'I think we should all go on a bloody cruise after this week.'

'Knowing our luck it would sink,' said Bel, from Violet's other side. 'Are you eating that Stilton?'

'Help yourself,' chuckled Violet, drying her eyes. 'I see your appetite's back in town.'

'Can I have your crackers as well?'

'They say you are what you eat,' winked Max. 'How's Pav doing?'

'I'm going up to the hospital after I drop Mum off,' said Violet. 'This is the first day he's been allowed visitors. The doctor said he must have had a guardian angel. The scissors missed his vital organs by that much –' she held up a finger and thumb barely apart. 'He's very sore, though, and his lungs are a bit smoke-damaged, but, boy, has he been lucky. He'll need lots of peace and quiet.'

'You're going to move him into Postbox Cottage, aren't you?' Max accurately prophesied. She could see where this was going.

'Until he's well, yes. If he wants to come,' Violet replied.

'How can he not want to be nursed by you?' said Bel through a mouthful of Jacobs cream cracker. 'He'll be after your bedbaths.'

'What's happened to *him*?' shivered Max. 'I can't even say his name.'

'Glyn? Not sure if he's been charged yet. He admitted what he'd done straight away when the police went round to question him. I feel so sorry for Joy and—'

Max gently grabbed Violet's bandaged arms and pulled her round to face her. 'None of this is any of your fault. It's his and only his. Remember: he is the one to blame.'

'So many bumholes, so little time,' sighed Bel. 'I wonder if there's a bumhole dot com where you could meet people like that and cut to the chase without having to spend years with them before you discover the truth.'

'Someone's in a sceptical mood today,' Max raised her eyebrows. 'Seeing Richard tonight?'

'Yep,' replied Bel, wriggling quickly away from the question. 'Who's the fellow who looks like a big butcher sitting next to your mum, V?'

'He's a big butcher. Mum's secret boyfriend,' giggled Violet. 'Patrick. He has the shop round the corner, and he seems really sweet. Mum had to fess up about him when he came over to see how she was after Nan died.'

'That's nice and handy, him living there, then,' said Max.

'The shop is there but he lives out in Hoodley. Mum says that he has quite an impressive semi.'

'I'll bet he has, the dirty sod,' crooned Bel. 'Mummy's going to be okay for fresh sausage, then?'

'Oh behave,' snorted Violet, then she reached for their hands.

'Thanks for coming. It means a lot to me. I wish you'd met Nan, though; she was just brilliant. You've really cheered me up. I don't actually know how I've ever coped without you both.'

Neither Bel nor Max said a word. They didn't have to. The warm friendly feeling that sat between them said it all.

When Violet approached the hospital bed she could see instantly that Pav had lost weight. His cheeks were hollow and his eye sockets dark. He looked asleep and so Violet thought she might just leave the parcel of goodies she had brought for him and slip away.

But as she put it down on the cabinet at his bedside he opened his eyes and what he saw made him smile.

'Lovely Violet, how are you?'

'Never mind how I am, how are you?' said Violet, holding back the urge to throw her arms round him and kiss him. She sat down in the chair at the side of his bed.

'Your face is cut,' he said.

'Just scratches,' said Violet.

'And your poor hands.' He indicated the bandages on them both.

'I think you win on the injury score,' said Violet.

'It's so good to see you.' She could see that he meant it. His hand came up to her face and stroked her hair.

'Has your brother been to visit you?' asked Violet, her insides sighing as he carried on stroking her.

'Yes, he has been. Alone, of course. He is going back to Poland. He and his wife have had their last argument, I think.'

'Pav, I want you to come to my cottage and stay with me until you get better.'

'Because you feel guilty about me? No, Violet. I will not have you feeling guilty about me.'

'No, because I like you and I want you to get better,' said Violet.

'You are another guardian angel,' said Pav.

'Another?'

'Yes, the nurses say I must have had a guardian angel to look after me in the fire.'

'You must have had, Pav,' smiled Violet. 'And I wish I could meet her to thank her.'

Pav joined in the joke about the guardian angel because he didn't want to be ridiculed. But it was no joke. When he felt his life slipping away, a light enveloped him and he found himself being pulled towards it. But in the near distance was an old lady and a tall angel with red hair and they were laughing and chatting with each other.

They both turned to him as he approached them and the old lady said, 'Oh no, you mustn't come with us. It's not your turn. She needs you.' And she flapped her hands at him to shoo him away from them.

'Go back,' said the red-haired angel. 'We will keep you safe.'

Pav would never tell this story, though. He didn't want anyone to think he was a crazy man.

Chapter 98

Vanuoshka's foot injury still prevented her from driving, so it was down to Shaden to act as chauffeur for the present time. She had enough brass neck to walk into Aunt Faibiana's and Uncle Trevor's house, especially as her mother was desperately pushing for a full family reconciliation. Step one had been achieved – a meeting between Faye and Vanoushka at the Bosomworth-Proud residence; step two – here and now – was a visit by Shaden to her aunt's house. Step three would be meeting Bel again. That would be interesting. And she was ready to bring it on.

There was no customary kiss from her aunt Faye as Shaden walked into the house following her limping mother. Faye merely nodded her head at her and said, 'Hello, Shaden' in a tight but dignified tone. She noticed immediately that her niece's face was very different from the last time she had seen it. Her nose had been chiselled and straightened and tipped up at the end. A Barbie nose. And were those cheek implants?

Trevor had gone to the golf course to get out of the way. He could understand why Faye felt obliged to listen to Vanoushka's efforts to smooth things over – they were sisters, after all. But he wasn't sure he could ever forgive Shaden. In truth he had never liked the girl. She was spoiled and selfish, jealous and destructive. Shaden might be driving her temporarily crippled mother to his house, but he wouldn't be there to receive them.

Vanoushka was at her most contrite and polite, enquiring after Trevor – and Bel. And if she was in touch with Richard.

'They're talking things through and seeing if they can go forward,' replied Faye, not wanting to divulge Bel's business, but at the same time wishing she could wipe that smug look off her niece's face.

'That's good,' said Vanoushka meekly.

'He's making an effort. He's taken her to their restaurant again tonight. La Hacienda. But Bel has a lot to forgive him for. She must take her time.'

Their restaurant? How sweet, having their own romantic restaurant, thought Shaden.

'Bel should go back to him,' said Vanoushka. 'His family are very well connected. His grandfather is a life peer.'

Typical Vanoushka, thought Faye. Thinking of the money. No wonder Shaden grew up to be so shallow.

'That's up to Bel. We will support her, whatever she decides,' returned Faye firmly, casting a sideways glance at the bleach-blonde elephant in the room. 'I certainly get the impression that he regrets his mistake and wants to heal his marriage.'

Mistake? Marriage? Oh how Shaden wanted to laugh.

Chapter 99

They were indeed meeting again for an early supper at La Hacienda and again Richard greeted her with red roses. Bel noticed the bouquet was smaller this time by four main flowers but padded up in volume with gypsophila. The greeting kiss was longer and more intense, but not necessarily as tender as of late.

She had known since they returned from Leeds how tonight would play out. That day trip had told her everything she needed to know. But after making her decision she let it lie in her head, waiting for doubts to attack it and try to change her mind. They didn't even get close.

'You look lovely,' said Richard, gently guiding her by the arm into the restaurant.

And she knew that she did because a woman empowered exuded a certain beauty that transcended any physical imperfections. Bel had always been fascinated by how Mae West, quite plain and thick-waisted, could be such a sex siren. That inner va-va-voom was a magical tool with a direct hit on male pheromones.

Bel studied Richard as he read the menu. He was such an attractive man, and she knew that he would become even more so as he got older. The few white hairs at his temples would spread and give him a commanding air that would make him irresistible to women even half his age. He had impeccable dress sense and style; tonight he was wearing a Tom English charcoal suit that looked as if it had been designed especially for him. And Bel knew he would have Calvin Klein boxers under the trousers because he never wore anything else.

'I've been thinking about whisking you off to Paris,' he said, without his eyes leaving the menu.

'Have you?' replied Bel. At this point her heart should have started break-dancing but the rhythm remained steady and calm.

'I want to consummate our marriage.' Now he looked up and his eyes were full of suggestive promise. And Bel knew that any honeymoon in Paris would be full of sex. Going to bed with Richard was often like a Guinness World Records attempt to achieve the most positions in one session. It always felt more about having sex, and very little about making love.

'I think I'll have the prawn-stuffed cod,' Bel decided, dropping her eyes back to the menu. 'With the menagerie of vegetables.'

'Ménage à trois,' he corrected.

'I know,' said Bel. 'I was joking.'

'Ah.' Then, 'Oh my, you're wearing your wedding ring,' Richard exclaimed in a delighted voice.

'Yes,' said Bel. 'Richard, I've made my decision . . .'

'Excuse me,' said a waiter, zooming to their side and addressing Bel. 'There's just been a call to say would you please check your mobile phone for messages. Your father needs you urgently and can't get through to you.'

Max opened the door and there stood Luke holding a bottle of wine and a box of chocolates. Expensive chocolates.

'For after dinner,' he said, proffering them to her.

'It's only chicken chasseur,' said Max. 'The sauce came out of a packet.'

'I'll take them back, then,' he grinned.

'Will you hell as like,' she said, snatching them from him. 'Come in. It's cold.'

'No, it isn't,' said Luke, 'it's a lovely evening. Why do you think I'm not wearing a jacket? It's colder in here than it is out there.'

'Oh don't you start. Stuart always said it was freezing in—'
Max stopped herself. Luke gave her a playful nudge then leaned
over and kissed her cheek.

'Early days, Max. Don't beat yourself up for saying his name.'

'I know,' Max nodded and injected some extra cheeriness into
her voice. 'Haven't you brought any files with you?'

'It's all on my faithful memory stick,' said Luke, taking it out
of his pocket and waving it at her. He pulled a lungful of
chicken-scented air into his lungs.

'Smells good, even if it is out of a packet.'

'The vegetables aren't out of a packet,' said Max. 'I thought I'd
better make an effort if I'm going to pick your brains.'

'Nick all my marketing ideas, you mean,' chuckled Luke,
going into the kitchen for a bottle opener. Then he rolled up his
white shirt sleeves. 'Come on, then, how can I help? I'm starving.'

'I haven't finished my prep – you came early.'

'Well, show me the way to a knife and a chopping board, Max.
Come on, what are you waiting for?'

Together they made dinner, ate dinner, talked shop, cleared the
plates, scoffed banoffee cheesecake, talked more shop and drank
Rioja. As he was bending over to fill up the dishwasher, Max
looked at him and saw what a very nice bum he had. It was a bit
odd thinking that and she averted her gaze very quickly. She
hadn't looked at him like that since they were sixteen. Max filled
up her glass and took a very big gulp.

'Thanks for filling my glass up as well,' huffed Luke sarcasti-
cally, making her laugh. Again. He had always made her laugh. 'I
don't know. You give someone all your expertise and in return
they give you a packet-mix chicken dish and swipe all the booze.'
He picked up the bottle and took it into the lounge and Max
followed. They both sank on to opposite ends of the sofa and
silence reigned for a short – and entirely comfortable – few minutes until Max broke it.

'Any more news about Stuart?'

'None,' replied Luke. 'He's absorbed in his new life at the moment. I'm way down on the list of priorities.'

'Well, you shouldn't be,' Max twisted to face him.

'It's okay,' said Luke. 'It's awkward, anyway. He thinks I've taken sides.'

'I wouldn't blame you if you did take sides, Luke. You've been friends since you were babies.'

'Your side, not his,' said Luke.

'Oh Luke,' smiled Max. 'You're too nice. Why aren't you married to someone gorgeous with loads of kids?'

'Never got over my first love,' Luke grinned while bashfully scratching his head. 'I fell for her at college, she wasn't interested and I never met anyone who could best her.'

Max's lips spread out into a long gossipy smile. 'Who was that, then? No – wait – it's obvious: Julie Armstrong. All the boys used to salivate over her.'

'No,' said Luke, locking his kind grey eyes on to Max's. 'No, you numpty, it was you.'

Chapter 100

Bel drove far too fast over to her dad's house. After checking her phone – which she had switched to silent during the meal because she wanted no distractions – there were four texts from him, all saying the same.

PLEASE COME NOW. I NEED YOU. DAD

That wasn't like him. For a start, Bel couldn't ever remember him texting her in his life. Trevor was notorious for never having his phone with him. It was nearly always on charge in the kitchen. She had tried to ring him back but it went straight on to voicemail. And Faye wasn't answering her mobile either. Or the house phone. Something was wrong. She pressed her foot on the accelerator and wondered what it could be.

Richard was tailing her in his Porsche; she could see him in her rear-view mirror as her car turned into the Nookery's private drive. Her father's car wasn't in its usual parking space, but there was a taxi with its engine running and the driver reading the newspaper. And, to her annoyance, Shaden's cocky little sports car was there as well.

Bel threw on the brake and crunched over to the taxi driver. Her first thought was that her father was ill and the taxi was here to take him to hospital.

'Hi,' she said, knocking on the window. The taxi driver wound it down. 'Who are you waiting for?'

'Didn't get her name, love. I'm just sitting her biding my time like she paid me for.'

'This is odd,' said Bel, turning to address Richard, newly arrived. 'What's going on and why is Shaden here?'

Though Bel always rang the doorbell to gain admittance to her father's house, this time she went straight to open it, but it was locked. She pressed her thumb into the doorbell impatiently, over and over again, until she saw Faye through the glass in the door. Faye unlocked it but opened it only a few inches. She looked horrified to see Bel.

'Faye, let me in, please,' said Bel.

'I'm sorry, Bel, not tonight. I'm busy,' said Faye, attempting to shut the door in her face.

'Oh no, you don't,' said Bel. 'Where's Dad?'

'He's not here,' said Faye firmly. 'Just go, will you, Bel?'

Bel threw her weight at the door. 'He's just texted me to tell me to come here. He rang me at the restaurant.'

'He can't have,' said Faye, pushing back. 'Please, Bel, don't come in.'

Bel had never seen Faye like that before. She was cross and cold: proper fairy-tale stepmother mode. Well, something strange was going on, and if her dad was in trouble, *she* wasn't going to keep Bel from him.

Bel gave an adrenaline-fuelled charge at the door and knocked it fully open, flattening Faye against the wall. As Bel marched into the house Faye was at her heels, reaching for and finding Bel's arm and attempting to pull her backwards.

'You get out of my house, Belinda. Now.'

'I bloody well won't. Not until I find out what's wrong with Dad,' said Bel, attempting to shrug off her strangely behaving stepmother.

'Please, Bel,' pleaded Faye, making one last tug. 'I'm begging you, please go home.'

But it was in vain. Bel was now wondering if her dad was lying with an axe in his head on the carpet and the mystery woman whom the taxi driver was waiting for was some sort of backstreet medic.

Bel pushed open the lounge door to find Shaden sitting on the sofa, Vanoushka pacing up and down on a rug with a fat bandage on her leg, and a rough-looking woman in red standing by the fireplace with her arms folded. Bel tried to make sense of what was going on in front of her, while behind her she heard a car squeal up on the drive and Faye's voice say, 'She arrived with no warning, Trevor. Thank God you're here.'

'Jesus Christ,' said Trevor, entering the room. *This is what hell must look like*, he added to himself: Vanoushka, Shaden, Richard – and *her*.

'Hello, Trevor,' said the woman in red, smiling widely, switching her attention from Bel to Trevor. She sounded like she had just climbed out of the television when they were showing *Home and Away*.

'Dad, what's going on? Who's this?' said Bel.

Shaden took in a deep delicious breath to deliver the news. 'I think she's called your mother, Bel,' she smirked.

'Me?' said Max with a gasp. Then she realized he was joking and broke into amused laughter. 'You had me there for a minute, you daft sod.'

'I'm serious,' said Luke, his eyes unblinking. 'I think I've loved you since the first time you spoke to me. I even remember your exact words.'

Max was gobsmacked. 'What were they?'

'"Fuck off." I was behind you in the dinner queue and you thought I'd nipped your bum.'

Max was still in a state of shock. 'You did nip my bum.'

'No, I didn't. It was Stuart. He knew I fancied you, but you presumed it was me who'd done it and stormed off in a huff and he jumped in like a bloody white knight. Two minutes later you were a couple.'

'I can't stand anyone pinching my bum,' Max shuddered. 'If only I'd known it was him. I wouldn't have looked at him twice.'

'If only I'd dobbed him in,' said Luke. They looked at each other and then laughed.

'All these years and I never knew,' said Max, shaking her head.

'I know it might be a bit weird if I asked you to dinner,' said Luke, after clearing a nervous cough out of his throat, 'but would you suck it and see?'

'Bit forward,' tutted Max.

'Oh God,' said Luke, dropping his head into his hands. 'How long have we known each other and now I'm nervous. I was scared to ask you out in case I ruined our friendship, or I upset Stuart, but sod it – I don't care any more. I want to risk giving it a try because I really like you, Max. I think you're fabulous. I want to take you out on a date. I know it's early days but sod it, I'm asking anyway. Do you think you could ever see me as anything other than a mate? Oh God, I just wish we were sixteen again because I'd have told you it was Stuart who nipped your bum and claimed you for myself. What do you think? Help me, Max. I'm out of my depth here.'

Max looked at him, this dear sweet man who had stood in the background and loved her for all this time. The person she probably had most in common with in all the world. They had always laughed at the same things, had the same work ethic, the same ambitions. And he still had a bloody gorgeous bum.

'Okay,' she said, feeling herself grow a bit quivery because it was early days but yes, she was already seeing Luke Appleby in a different light. 'We'll suck it and see, shall we?'

Bel stood rigid in the middle of a vortex of confusion. How could this be her mother? Her graceful, statuesque mother was dead. This woman before her was blousy and broad, with shoulders that would have made her a cracking tight-head prop for a rugby union side, and a hard, hard face.

'Helen, what on earth can you possibly want after all these years?' asked Trevor breathlessly as he rushed to his daughter's side and put his arm round her, as if the woman was going to suddenly snatch her away.

'I think you might know,' said this so-called Helen in a voice that sounded as if it was full of barbed wire.

'Dad?' said Bel. Her arms were prickling with anxiety. She could feel her heartbeat thumping madly in her eardrums. Trevor tightened his arm round her.

'Oh God,' said Faye, wringing her hands together. 'Why did you have to come over today of all days, Bel?'

'Dad texted me,' replied Bel.

'I don't know how to text,' said Trevor. 'I didn't even take my phone out with me.'

Ah. I bet the phone is in the kitchen, where it usually is, thought Bel. She narrowed her eyes at Shaden. It didn't take a genius to work out what had happened. The shit-stirring cow.

'Second wife, I presume?' Helen thumbed at Faye. 'Well, thanks for bringing up my daughter. Looks like you did a bonza job.'

'*My* daughter,' said Faye, her voice suddenly full of strength. 'And I won't let you upset her.' She came to the other side of Bel, her chin jutting out as if she meant business.

'I don't want to upset anyone,' said Helen, as unruffled as could be as she inspected her long red nails. 'I just want what is rightfully mine.'

'Which is what, precisely?' asked Trevor.

'I heard about the wedding. It made the papers in Oz. I saw how much your company is worth. Treffé Chocolates? The same company that used to be Trevelen Chocolates once upon a time?'

'That company sank, as you well know,' Trevor ground his

words out. 'You bled it dry. Thirty-three years ago. Treffé was a brand-new company I formed with Faye. You've had all you're getting out of me.'

Bel felt Faye and Trevor close into her side even further.

Helen looked at the touching family scene, then she swept her eyes round to the subsidiary characters. They settled on Shaden, sitting forward on the couch and enjoying the floorshow.

'So you're the "blonde beauty" who slept with the fiancé?' She threw back her head and laughed as if the newspaper's description was the biggest joke ever. 'Oh and that must be the "man in the middle".' She pointed over at Richard who was lurking by the doorway, not sure where to put himself.

'Never mind who is who,' said Trevor. 'I think you should leave. Get out, Helen. You've caused enough damage. You were always very good at that.'

'No, don't go,' cried Bel, rushing forward. She threw her arms round Helen, but the woman stood unyielding and straight, her hands remaining by her sides.

'Look, love, it's all a bit late for the grand reconciliation,' Helen stepped back out of her daughter's embrace. 'I didn't come here for this.'

'So it's true, you really are my mother?' said Bel, sobbing now. She whirled round to Trevor and Faye, but she directed the question more at her stepmother. 'Why did you tell me she was dead? Why did you lie?'

Trevor stepped forward. 'That's the way she wanted it.' He addressed Helen. 'Tell her the truth at least, for God's sake, Helen. I'm begging you.'

Helen was born a hard nut and the years in Australia being married to a man whose fortunes were up and down as much as his trousers in other women's bedrooms had made her harder still. She needed her own independent means and seeing as her ex-husband was so incredibly wealthy these days, and no doubt would pay anything to keep her away from screwing up his daughter, it was more than worth attempting a little extortion.

Unfortunately that stupid newspaper and even stupider Lydiana Bosomworth-Greaves had grossly overstated the fortunes of the Treffé Chocolate company, it seemed. And then, as if that knowledge wasn't bad enough, in walks her daughter – tipped off by someone in this very room. *Bye, bye, blackmail.*

'Ten thousand pounds and I'll tell her the truth,' said Helen. At least she wouldn't walk away empty-handed then.

'Give it to her,' said Faye. 'Trevor, the cheque book is there in the drawer.'

Shaden wished she had brought popcorn. This was better than a movie. It had everything in it – drama, pathos – just a shame there was no violence.

Trevor scrabbled in the drawer, hurriedly wrote out a cheque and then ripped it out of the book. 'I've left it blank. I don't know what your name is these days.'

'Eleanor Swindell,' she said, holding up her hand to stem any comment. 'Please, save your breath.' She examined the cheque. 'I should have asked for twenty, shouldn't I? That was too easy.'

'It's not easy,' snapped Faye. 'We're having to batten down the hatches like everyone else in this economic climate.'

'Helen, please,' said Trevor.

'Okay,' Helen turned to a totally and utterly numb Bel. 'I didn't want kids. You were an accident. We'd filed for divorce and then I found out I was pregnant. Trevor begged me not to have an abortion. We struck a deal that he would take the baby and I'd go home to Australia. It was my idea that he told you I was dead. I didn't want anyone coming searching for me hoping for the big family reunion.'

'Don't forget the bit about taking every single penny Trevor had as well,' snapped Faye. 'He had to buy the life of his own daughter.'

'What about the wedding dress?' gulped Bel. It was all she could think of.

'What wedding dress?' said Helen. 'I got married in a trouser suit.'

The tears sliding down Bel's cheeks increased in volume. She felt warm arms round her. Faye's. And heard her gentle voice trying to soothe.

'So our business is really concluded, then,' shrugged Helen. 'Still, interesting to see what the kid turned out like. I think we did a good mix, Trev.'

'You didn't just do "good",' said Faye with iron in her voice, 'you did brilliantly and you've missed out on some very precious years. She's a wonderful daughter.'

'Sorry, love,' said Helen to Bel. 'I didn't plan on you being here.'

Vanoushka tried to get to her feet and called for Shaden to help her. She saw an opportunity to ingratiate herself with Trevor and get back in his good books.

'Get out,' she said. 'Get out of my sister's house, you cruel bitch.' She hobbled towards Helen, using Shaden's arm as support.

The silly woman with the paralysed forehead didn't even show up on Helen's radar. She ignored her and turned to face the daughter that she had never thought of in all these years. Bel noticed they had identical moles on the side of their jaws.

'I tell you what,' Helen said, leaning close and whispering as if imparting a great secret, 'there is a gift I can give you that you will always remember.'

Bel waited for her real mother to kiss her cheek. She didn't bargain on Helen twisting on her heel, pulling back her head and nutting Shaden in the nose – a direct hit on the bridge. Shaden screamed and blood oozed through the fingers clamped over her face. Vanoushka threw herself at Helen, missed and fell over, then all attention shifted to Richard, who was bent double in the doorway, holding his nuts and uttering a string of profanities in the direction of the retreating iron-kneed Helen.

Bel ran down the hallway in pursuit, just in time to see her mother climb into the taxi.

'Mum,' she yelled, springing over to it, her fingers just managing to touch the glass of the window before the car pulled away from her and was gone. Helen didn't even wave goodbye.

Bel hadn't a clue what she felt as her mother disappeared from her life a second time. Her head was thrown into momentary panic and distress, mixed in with confusion, grief and a childlike desire to sink to the ground and howl, yet she remained standing and silent. The long-held image of her perfect mother had gone for ever and never again would Bel think of her without also remembering how Faye had moved in to protect her, like a caramel-haired lioness squaring up against a bulky, nasty rhino.

Bel walked back inside the house to find it in a state of pandemonium.

'My nose, my lovely nose,' Shaden was screaming. 'It's broken.'

Vanoushka was trying to apply the tea towel that Faye had just run under the tap to Shaden's nose, but she was pushing her mother away, shrieking in pain and anger.

'Shouldn't someone ring for an ambulance?' said Vanoushka.

'Richard can drive me. It'll be quicker,' said Shaden.

'Oh no, he can't,' snapped Faye. 'I'll take you, if I have to, you little bitch.'

Vanoushka gasped. She had never heard her sister talk with such venom.

'Oh yes, because it was ALL my fault, wasn't it?' snarled Shaden. 'He was the one getting married. I was single.'

Richard suddenly straightened up.

'Okay, let's bring this down,' he said, attempting a peace mission.

'I'm ashamed that I'm related to you, Shaden,' Faye went on. 'You'd better stay right away from other people's husbands from now on.'

Despite her pain, Shaden appeared to be smiling. Dangerously, like Caligula. 'Are you going to tell them, or shall I?' she said to Richard.

'Shaden, I'll get you another nose,' he said, his voice full of desperation. 'Just don't. Please, I'm begging you.'

'Don't what?' said Faye, her eyes slits of suspicion. 'What is this?'

She grabbed her niece and shook her hard by the shoulders and Shaden shrieked. 'What's all the secret code going on between you and Bel's husband?'

Shaden shook herself free. 'Bel's husband? Precious Belinda's husband? He's not *her* husband,' she said, loading the 'her' with enough poison to bring down a blue whale.

'Shaden, noooo . . .' yelped Richard.

'He's my husband,' said Shaden, so slowly and deliberately that each word seemed to last for minutes.

Behind them Richard groaned so low and long that he sounded like an inflatable airbed with a slow puncture. Everyone else could have been musical-statue champions.

'I think you'd better explain yourselves,' said Vanoushka eventually, her eyes flicking repeatedly between Richard and Shaden as if she were watching a tennis match.

'He took me to Vegas for the weekend,' said Shaden imperiously.

'I know,' replied Bel with the hint of a yawn. That would take the wind out of her sails.

'Do you know that we also both got pissed and married? No, I bet you didn't. Ha.'

A nuclear silence landed on the room. It was so intense that it set Shaden off giggling, happier than ever that she had made such an impact.

'Yeah, it seemed a good idea at the time,' she added casually.

'It seemed like a good idea?' said Trevor, unable to keep the furious incredulity out of his voice. 'It seemed like a good idea?'

'We didn't know it was legally binding,' said Richard with a desperate tremble in his voice. 'It was just a drunken prank.'

'Elvis married us,' said Shaden, thoroughly enjoying the destruction she was causing, which offset the pain of her pretty new nose being smashed all over her face.

Bel threw her hands up in the air. As if today wasn't bizarre enough already with a dead mother coming back into her life and nutting the cousin who had bonked her husband, she now discovered that the husband in question, currently fondling the blood circulation back into his nuts, wasn't her husband after all.

'When exactly were you going to tell me?' Bel asked Richard, hearing her own voice slow and calm despite the turmoil going on inside her head.

'He wasn't,' smiled Shaden smugly. 'We were going to have a quiet divorce, then he was going to set you up to renew your vows and hoped that would be enough.'

'And he paid you enough money for a new nose to keep quiet?' It was a question, but Faye already knew the answer.

'Oh Bel,' Richard limped forward with one hand cupping his groin. 'Don't let this spoil things between us.' He threw a pointed finger at Shaden. 'You evil bloody cow. You've ruined everything. Bel put her wedding ring back on tonight. It was all okay again and if you—'

'Actually,' Bel butted in, 'it wasn't okay again. I only wore the ring because that way I'd remember to give it back to you.' Bel twisted the ring from her finger and popped it into the breast pocket of Richard's suit.

'It wouldn't have worked,' she said. 'I thought it might have, but then you didn't do it.'

'What?' squeaked Richard. 'What didn't I do?'

'You didn't have cake,' said Bel. And she turned and walked out of the door.

Chapter 101

When Bel went back to her father's house later that night, she didn't ring the bell, she walked straight in and found Faye putting newly washed covers on the sofa and her dad helping. She'd always resented them being so 'together' and yet now the sight of them made her fill up with nice tears. They both looked shocked, but delighted to see her.

'Hello, love,' said Trevor, straightening up to give her a hug. 'We've been worried where you got to. Again.'

'Oh Dad, you know I have to go and hole myself up and think things through.'

'You've had such a rough time. I'm so sorry.'

Bel gave her dad a quick kiss then turned to Faye.

'You're a peach, Faye,' she said. 'And I've never said.'

She closed her arms round her stunned stepmother and when she pulled away it was to find that Faye's eyes were dripping with tears. Faye's hand came out to rest on her cheek.

'You've always been so precious to me,' she said. 'We never wanted you to find out the truth about your mother.' Bel fell back against her. She was wearing another one of her soft fluffy jumpers and smelled of her familiar Guerlain perfume. Faye Candy was a gentle constant presence with a hidden backbone of steel. Bel hoped she could make it up to her for all the years of not appreciating that.

'What about the wedding dress, Faye?' Bel asked, as Trevor poured them all a reconstituting brandy.

'Well, all little girls want their mother's wedding dress, don't they? We were in Berlin and I saw this tiny wedding-dress shop – *Hochzeit in Weiss* – it was called. I've never forgotten it. The woman who owned it was just putting the most beautiful dress in the window and I suddenly had the idea of buying it for you and pretending—'

Bel had heard enough. She could guess the rest.

'Oh Faye, it's such a shame you never had kids of your own. You'd have made such a lovely mum,' smiled Bel, hugging her again. 'You *are* a lovely mum.'

And that was the last remaining secret, but this one would stay a secret. Faye wasn't infertile, but when she and Trevor married she convinced Trevor that they shouldn't try for a child. She knew that the strange little girl she had taken on needed to be the sole focus of their attention. Underneath her feistiness, Faye recognized a child who needed a hell of a lot of love and reassurance. And now, with the daughter she had always wanted clasped in her arms, Faye knew that her decision had been the right one.

Chapter 102

The next morning, Violet double-checked that she had her Maestro card in her handbag before she set off for the White Wedding shop. She would have to pay for the dress that was destroyed – she knew that and it was only fair, especially after all the kindness that Freya had shown her.

When she pulled up in front of the shop it was to find the usually decorated bay window empty and a man about to nail a wooden board in front of the glass.

'Excuse me,' said Violet, getting out of the car. 'Isn't it open?'

'No, love,' said the man. 'It's for lease. I'm going to put up the sign after I've boarded it up.'

'Where's the woman who ran it, do you know?' asked Violet.

'Dunno, pet. I just go round doing this.'

Violet peered through the glass in the door. Sure enough, except for the built-in rails and the central counter, there was nothing but bare walls, floor and ceiling.

Chapter 103

Bel took the next day off work and drove up to the moors. She had owed it to herself to try to mend her marriage but she knew, when Richard refused to go into the cake shop, that she might as well try to knit smoke. There was no fun in him, no little boy who occasionally made a giggly appearance. He was all grown-up – inside and out. They never laughed in or out of bed, he never giggled, he never bashed her with a cushion or had tickling fights. All those revelations came to her in a rush when he said that he didn't want to go in for cake; it just took her brain a little time to work that out.

She had loved Richard, but she had loved the idea of marriage and of belonging to someone and living with them more. But she knew now that she couldn't be truly happy with a man who would never know the joy of the odd Pot Noodle or giggle about a Bronte-based menu.

Bel wanted to take a last trip up here and remember the mad few days she had spent with a doctor/author who fought with her over a tin opener and showed her what she was missing. Then she would go back and begin single life again. It was better to have no man than the wrong man.

Richard had tried to call many times but even he knew it had to be over. He didn't want Shaden, although Shaden was gearing herself up to be evil in the divorce settlement. Faye had made it quite plain that she would have a relationship with her sister but never with her niece. Even the Bosomworth sisters' relationship was on a different footing now, with Faye no longer the underdog.

Bel drove up the lane that would take her to the cottages. It was no longer quiet and deserted up there; she found vans and a cement mixer churning and stacks of bricks and towers of wooden planks. Bronte Cottages were no longer owned by the Candy family.

They looked so different already. Charlotte's door had been sealed up and she could see through the window that the walls between her and Emily had been taken down. The noise of hammering was coming from inside Anne at the end.

'Hi,' said Bel, approaching a stodgy little man with a hard hat and an air of authority. 'My dad used to own this and I just wonder if I could take a last look at the inside. For old time's sake, please?'

'I'll find you the owner, love,' he said in a West Country accent. 'He's round the back somewhere.'

Bel waited by the car, watching a man bring the old sink out of Anne and dump it in a huge skip.

'Hi, can I help you? I'm the owner,' said a voice at her side. A big, gruff, deep Yorkshire voice. The one that he had used to demand back the tin opener.

'You?' said Bel with amazed delight. 'You're the new owner?'

'Yep,' said Dan Regent. 'That's me. And this is my writer's retreat.'

She saw him glance down at her fingers. Then he lifted the left hand and examined it.

'Didn't work out, then?' he said, tapping the third finger.

'It was never going to work out. He didn't like cake,' said Bel, her face beaming as if there was a midday sun trapped behind her teeth. 'You and Cathy?'

'It was never going to work out. She didn't like chocolate,' said Dan. 'Or tinned soup. Come in, I've got something to show you.'

He pulled her into Emily and foraged in a pile of papers, eventually retrieving an envelope.

'You've saved me a stamp,' he said, urging her to open it.

Puzzled, Bel pulled out the folded sheet of paper inside. It was a typeset dedication page.

To the crazy tin-opening bride who set me back on the road –
and to whom I wish all the happiness in the world.

Bel swallowed down a huge lump of rising emotion. Maybe there was a reason why it had been so hard to shift Dr Dan from her heart since she left him: because it was his rightful place and he was staying put.

'Wow,' she said, trying to keep the nervously thrilled vibrato out of her voice. 'I've never been mentioned in a book before.'

'Care for some Branwell coffee and a Villette Jaffa Cake?' asked Dan.

'How about a Rochester soup?' asked Bel, hardly able to see him now for the water in her eyes.

'I think I can do better than that, Miss Eyre. How about a Rochester snog?' he said, picking her up, whirling her round and kissing her until she was breathless.

Epilogue

Nine months later

'You don't half scrub up well,' said Max, grinning at Bel, who was wearing her mother's wedding dress. At least the dress that her lovely stepmother had chosen so many years ago from a little shop in Berlin. A dress that fitted her so beautifully it was as if it had been made for her.

'Ta, that's good of you,' tutted Bel, pretending to be insulted.

Violet adjusted the simple lace veil on Bel's hair. 'You aren't going to bugger off at the reception again, are you?' she said. 'I'd like one of us to have a wedding where it all goes perfectly.'

'Trust me, I won't be leaving this one,' Bel said, and she sighed because thinking of becoming Mrs Regent left her weak with delight. She wouldn't have admitted this to the others, but she had actually been practising writing 'Mrs Belinda Regent' for nearly eight months now. Two months before Dan proposed to her. He left the ring looped on the tin opener on the first night they spent in the fully renovated cottage.

'You next,' said Bel, nudging Violet.

'We're happy as we are,' laughed Violet. It had taken Pav nearly three months after the fire to heal. Then he announced that he was leaving the cottage because he was well enough and he didn't want Violet to think he was taking advantage of her kindness. He packed his bags and said he would see her soon, but she didn't believe him.

Then she walked into the newly white-painted Carousel the next morning to find him there, painting the first horse again – a dappled-grey and gold one.

'How could you think I would leave you, Violet?' he said, running to her when she burst into tears. And when the ice-cream parlour finally opened, three months later, he moved back into Postbox Cottage. And this time, he wasn't in the spare bedroom.

'Actually, you're wrong,' said Max. 'I'm next. I didn't want to steal your thunder, but seeing as we're on the subject, Luke asked me to marry him last night and I said yes. I've been dying to tell you all morning.'

'Oh Max, I'm so happy for you.' Bel ran to hug her but Max held her off. 'Give up – you'll spoil your make-up. Don't you dare start blubbing. Oh all right, then.' She chuckled and let Bel give her a big squashy hug and then felt Violet's arms close round them both.

There was a car beep outside.

'Sounds like we're off,' said Violet, adjusting the flower in her hair. It was lavender blue, the same colour as her and Max's dresses, the same colour as her eyes that Pav loved so much.

Bel picked up her skirt and walked outside to where Trevor was having a nervous fag.

'So this time you're going to run off to Gretna Green, are you, Max?' asked Violet, as the chauffeur opened the door for them and they climbed inside. They were all travelling together today.

'You are joking,' said Max. 'Do you think I'm going to marry a bloke called Appleby and not have the full shebang? I tell you, this wedding will make the last one look like an Amish funeral. I've had the practice run and know what works and what doesn't work – i.e. that it might be a good idea to have a groom next time. I'll throttle back on the tan but up the bling factor.'

'Up the bling? How on earth could you up the bling factor?'

'I know –' Max raised a delighted finger in the air – 'I'LL

HAVE A VAJAZZLE.' Then she remembered that Bel's dad was in the car. 'Oops, sorry, Trevor.'

'Oh don't you worry, love,' said Trevor, turning round from the front passenger seat. 'I know what you girls and your hand-bags are like.'

Bel, Max and Violet all collapsed forward into giggles.

'I'm thinking gypsy caravan, I'm thinking Rapunzel wig, I'm thinking a thirty-foot train on my dress. Princess Diana's was only twenty-five foot, you know,' Max went on.

'Oh God, here we go again,' sighed Bel.

'I'm thinking a cake you can actually walk inside . . .'

'Max. Does Luke know about all this?'

'Of course. He said I should "go for it". Because he's just wonderful like that. As daft as me. I'm thinking pink horses . . .'

Trevor turned round again and winked at his daughter. And Bel linked her arms into those of her two lovely friends, who turned to her together and grinned as a quote from her school-days flashed through her head. Strangely enough, it was a Charlotte Bronte one.

There is no happiness like that of being loved by your fellow crea-tures, and feeling that your presence is an addition to their comfort.

Bel couldn't have put it better herself.

Acknowledgements

Well, Billy Idol might have said that nothing was a sure thing in the world – but I'm pretty sure of these marvellous folks to whom I owe a load of thanks.

My absolutely fabulous publishing gang: Suzanne Baboneau, Maxine Hitchcock, Nigel Stoneman, Libby Yevtushenko, Clare Hey, S-J, Georgie, Ali, Alice and everyone at Simon & Schuster. I couldn't wish for a more supportive and friendlier bunch fighting my corner in the marketplace.

My wonderful agent – and my friend – Lizzy Kremer and the David Higham Agency gang.

Herr Mike Bowkett at Reedmoor Distribution for his help with German wedding dress shops . . . ho ho.

My lovely lovely author friends who are a constant support both professionally and personally – especially Tara Hyland, Sue Welfare, Kate Hardy, Carole Matthews, Jill Mansell, Victoria Howard, Jane Costello, Katie Fforde, Louise Douglas and Sue Diamond.

The gorgeous Mel and Dawn at Hothouse – www.hoth.co.uk – for supplying me with their silky super St. Moritz tanning products for research purposes. And with bubble bath to get it off with.

Yummy Yorkshire – www.yummyyorkshire.co.uk – where I have to go lots to sample their amazingly wicked ice creams so my writing is credible (!).

My private army of financial wizards – Alex Bianchi at www.alexbianchi.co.uk, John Philbin at www.john-philbin.com and the divine Phil Lofthouse at Stead Robinson – the man whom I can't live without – my accountant, because he knows I'm total pants with numbers.

And lastly but by no means least – Traz, Kath, Cath, Tracey, Rae, Judy and Chris and all my smashing old faithful Barnsley mates. And my beloved family – who give me so much material, I can't write it down fast enough.

If you loved

White Wedding

read on
for more brilliant novels
from

milly
johnson

**SIMON &
SCHUSTER**

Milly Johnson

The Yorkshire Pudding Club

Three South Yorkshire friends, all on the cusp of 40,
fall pregnant at the same time following a
visit to an ancient fertility symbol.

For Helen, it's a dream come true, although her husband
is not as thrilled about it as she had hoped. Not only
wrestling with painful ghosts of the past, Helen has to
deal with the fact that her outwardly perfect marriage
is crumbling before her eyes.

For Janey, it is an unmitigated disaster as she has just been
offered the career break of a life-time. And she has no idea
either how it could possibly have happened, seeing as she
and her ecstatic husband George were always
so careful over contraception.

For Elizabeth, it is mind-numbing, because she knows
people like her shouldn't have children. Damaged by her
dysfunctional childhood and emotionally lost, she not only
has to contend with carrying a child she doubts she can
ever love, but she also has to deal with the return to her
life of a man whose love she must deny herself.

**Paperback ISBN 978-1-84983-410-0
Ebook ISBN 978-1-84739-483-5**

**SIMON &
SCHUSTER**

Milly Johnson

The Birds and the Bees

Romance writer and single mum Stevie Honeywell has
only weeks to go to her wedding, when her fiancé Matthew
runs off with her glamorous friend Jo MacLean. But Stevie
knows exactly how to win back her man. By undergoing a
mad course of dieting and exercise, she is sure things will
be as sweet as nectar again before very long.

Likewise, Adam MacLean is determined to win back his
lady. All he needs to do is convince Stevie to join him in
his own cunning plan – a prospect that neither of them find
attractive, seeing as each blames the other for the mess
they now find themselves in.

But when her strategy of self-improvement fails dismally,
Stevie finds that desperate times call for desperate
measures. She has no option but to join forces with the big
Scot in a scheme that soon reaches lengths neither of them
could ever have imagined. So, like a Scottish country jig,
the two couples change partners but continue to weave
closely around each other. And Adam and Stevie find they
have to deal with the heartbreaks of the past before they
can deal with those of the present. When Adam's crazy
plan actually starts to work, the question is: just who will
he and Stevie be dancing with when the music stops?

Paperback ISBN 978-1-84983-409-4
Ebook ISBN 978-1-84739-482-8

**SIMON &
SCHUSTER**

Milly Johnson
Here Come the Girls

Shirley Valentine, eat your heart out . . .

Ven, Roz, Olive and Frankie have been friends since school.
They day-dreamed of glorious futures, full of riches, romance
and fabulous jobs. The world would be their oyster.

Twenty-five years later, Olive cleans other people's houses
to support her lazy, out-of-work husband and his ailing
mother. Roz cannot show her kind, caring husband Manus
any love because her philandering ex has left her trust in
shreds. And she and Frankie have fallen out big time.

But Ven is determined to reunite her friends and realise
the dream they had of taking a cruise before they hit forty.
Before they know it, the four of them are far from home,
on the high seas. But can blue skies, hot sun and sixteen
days of luxury and indulgence distract from the tension
and loneliness that await their return?

Paperback ISBN 978-1-84983-205-2
Ebook ISBN 978-1-84983-206-9

**SIMON &
SCHUSTER**

Milly Johnson
A Spring Affair

When Lou Winter picks up a dog-eared magazine in the
dentist's waiting room and spots an article about clearing
clutter, she little realises how it will change her life. What
begins as an earnest spring clean soon spirals out of
control. Before long Lou is hiring skips in which to dump
the copious amounts of junk she never knew she had.

Lou's loved ones grow disgruntled. Why is clearing out
cupboards suddenly more important than making his
breakfast, her husband Phil wonders? The truth is, the
more rubbish Lou lets go of, the more light and air can get
to those painful, closed-up places at the centre of her heart:
the love waiting for a baby she would never have, the
empty space her best friend Deb once occupied, and
the gaping wound left by her husband's affair.

Even lovely Tom Broom, the man who delivers Lou's
skips, starts to grow concerned about his sweetest
customer. But Lou is a woman on a mission, and
not even she knows where it will end . . .

**Paperback ISBN 978-1-84739-282-4
Ebook ISBN 978-1-84739-866-6**

**SIMON &
SCHUSTER**

Milly Johnson
A Summer Fling

When dynamic Christie blows in like a warm wind to take
over their department, five very different women find
themselves thrown together.

Anna, 39, is reeling from the loss of her fiancé, who ran off with
a much younger woman. Her pride in tatters, these days Anna
finds it difficult to leave the house. So when a handsome,
mysterious stranger takes an interest in her, she's
not sure whether she can learn to trust again.

Then there's Grace, in her fifties, trapped in a loveless marriage
with a man she married because, unable to have children of her own,
she fell in love with his motherless brood. Grace worries that Dawn
is about to make the same mistake: orphaned as a child, engaged
to love-rat Calum, is Dawn more interested in the security
that comes with his tight-knit, boisterous family?

At 28, Raychel is the youngest member of their little gang. And with
a loving husband, Ben, and a cosy little nest for two, she would seem
to be the happiest. But what dark secrets are lurking behind this
perfect facade, that make sweet, pretty Raychel so guarded and
unwilling to open up? Under Christie's warm hand, the girls
soon realise they have some difficult choices to make.

Indeed, none of them quite realised how much they needed the
sense of fun, laughter, and loyalty that abounds when five women
become friends. It's one for all, and all for one!

Paperback ISBN 978-1-84739-283-1
Ebook ISBN 978-1-84983-102-4

**SIMON &
SCHUSTER**

Milly Johnson
An Autumn Crush

*In the heart of the windy season, four friends are about
to get swept off their feet . . .*

Newly single after a bruising divorce, Juliet Miller moves into
a place of her own and advertises for a flatmate, little believing
that, in her mid-thirties, she'll find anyone suitable. Then, just
as she's about to give up hope, along comes self-employed
copywriter Floz, and the two women hit it off straight away.

When Juliet's gentle giant of a twin brother, Guy, meets Floz,
he falls head over heels. But, as hard as he tries to charm her,
his foot seems to be permanently in his mouth. Meanwhile,
Guy's best friend Steve has always had a secret crush on
Juliet – one which could not be more unrequited if it tried . . .

As Floz and Juliet's friendship deepens, and Floz becomes
a part of the Miller family, can Guy turn her affection for them
into something more – into love for him? And what will happen
to Steve's heart when Juliet eventually catches the
eye of Piers – the man of her dreams?

As autumn falls, will love eventually bloom for them all?
Or will the secrets of the past turn the season's gold
to the chill of winter?

**Paperback ISBN 978-1-84983-203-8
Ebook ISBN 978-1-84983-204-5**

**SIMON &
SCHUSTER**

Coming in winter 2012 . . .

Milly Johnson
A Winter Flame

The final part of the brilliant seasonal quartet . . .

Eve Beresford never liked Christmas, but now she hates it
with a passion after her soldier fiancé was killed in action on
Christmas Day five years ago. And since then she has closed
herself off, concentrated on her career and become
a successful businesswoman.

Then she is left a plot of land by a distant old aunt with
the express instructions that it must function
as a winter theme park.

The trouble is, the land is jointly owned with a tall,
playful and ridiculously cheerful stranger – Jacques Glace.
And he has every intention of having as much
of an input into Winterworld as Eve.

So how will Eve put up with jolly Jacques and his
crazy ideas to make Winterworld more Christmassy than
Lapland? And can he and his reindeers and his big mulled-
wine laugh melt Eve's frozen heart at last . . . ?

Paperback ISBN 978-0-85720-898-9
Ebook ISBN 978-0-85720-899-6

BOOKS AND THE CITY

Home of the sassiest fiction in town!

If you enjoyed this book, you'll love...

978-1-84983-203-8	An Autumn Crush	Milly Johnson	£6.99
978-1-84983-205-2	Here Come the Girls	Milly Johnson	£6.99
978-1-84983-409-4	The Birds and the Bees	Milly Johnson	£6.99
978-1-84983-410-0	The Yorkshire Pudding Club	Milly Johnson	£6.99
978-1-84739-283-1	A Summer Fling	Milly Johnson	£6.99
978-1-84739-282-4	A Spring Affair	Milly Johnson	£6.99

For exclusive author interviews, features and competitions log onto
www.booksandthecity.co.uk

Credit and debit cards
Telephone Simon & Schuster Cash Sales at
Bookpost on 01624 677237

Cheque
Send a cheque payable to Bookpost Ltd to
PO Box 29, Douglas Isle of Man IM99 1BQ

Email: bookshop@enterprise.net
Website: www.bookpost.co.uk

Free post and packing within the UK.

Overseas customers please add £2
per paperback.

Please allow 14 days for delivery.

Prices and availability are subject
to change without notice.